ACCLAIM FOR
JOHN HERRICK'S NOVEL
FROM THE DEAD

"Eloquence with an edge. In a single chapter, John Herrick can break your heart, rouse your soul, and hold you in suspense. Be prepared to stay up late."
— Doug Wead, New York Times bestselling author and advisor to two presidents

"A solid debut novel."
— Akron Beacon Journal

"Evocative ... I felt breathless ... You'll want to get this book."
— Michelle Sutton, author of Danger at the Door

"A solid read with a powerful spiritual message."
— The Midwest Book Review

"A well written and engaging story. It moves, and moves quickly.... I don't think I've read anything in popular novel form as good as this in describing a journey of faith."
— Faith, Fiction, Friends

"An inspiring story about second chances, faith and the power of family."

D0912333

ALSO BY JOHN HERRICK

Fiction

The Landing
From The Dead

Nonfiction

8 Reasons Your Life Matters

BETWEEN THESE WALLS

A NOVEL

JOHN HERRICK

SegueBlue

PUBLISHED BY SEGUE BLUE

Copyright © 2015 by John Herrick

All Rights Reserved

Published in the United States by Segue Blue, St. Louis, MO.

Layout by The Scarlett Rugers Book Design Agency

www.scarlettrugers.com

Library of Congress Control Number: 2014948188

ISBN-13: 978-0-9915309-1-5

ISBN-10: 0-9915309-1-8

Publisher's Cataloging-in-Publication Data

Herrick, John, 1975-

Between these walls / John Herrick.

pages cm

ISBN: 978-0-9915309-1-5 (pbk.)

1. Homosexuality—Fiction. 2. Interpersonal relations—Fiction. 3.
Self-perception—Fiction. 4. Redemption—Fiction. 5. Ohio—Fiction.
I. Title.

PS3608.E7746 B48 2015

813`6—dc23

2014948188

Scripture taken from the NEW AMERICAN STANDARD BIBLE®, Copyright © 1960, 1962, 1963, 1968, 1971, 1972, 1973, 1975, 1977, 1995 by
The Lockman Foundation.

Used by permission. www.Lockman.org

To Pam Rempe.

You've encouraged me through every book.
This one's for you, friend.

ACKNOWLEDGMENTS

At the risk of overlooking anyone, thanks to the individuals who helped make this novel happen …

To my family. In the years since my first novel hit the shelves, God has expanded us. By the time the next book is published, someone marries or a new baby is born. Therefore, I've decided to keep this generic so nobody will find themselves excluded down the road.

Healing Touch Massage in Agoura Hills, California, introduced me to the world of massage therapy.

By God-coincidence, Michelle Sutton was the first to know what this novel was about, and for several years, she was the only one who knew. She encouraged me that this story was needed and had faith that I might communicate the story in an effective way. A fearless writer, she has urged me to be fearless with the written word. I appreciate her prayers and words at the right time.

Kelly Corday had no idea of the subject matter of this book, but she knew I had a story burning in my heart. When I shared one of the trigger events that pulled me toward the development of this book, she encouraged me to follow my heart and flat-out said, *You need to do this*. Kelly, your friendship is a gift from God. You're one of the most genuine Christians I know. Thank you.

Maryglenn McCombs is a talented publicist but, more importantly, a kind and generous soul. She believed in this story, believed in me as a writer, and provided vital input without knowing whether she would be hired to promote the book. When I was tempted to ditch the Prologue altogether, she convinced me to keep it as part of Hunter's story. She was a Godsend.

To Pam Rempe, Marnie McDole, and Christen Santoscoy.

To all the friends who have provided moral support and listened to my ugly vents of frustration.

To the reviewers and bloggers who have helped increase awareness of my work, starting with *From The Dead* in 2010.

To those I have forgotten or who have lent their support without my awareness.

To my readers. Thank you for investing a portion of your life with this novel. You are appreciated and loved.

Finally, to God. Thanks for not giving up on me. I would've given up on myself long ago.

BETWEEN THESE WALLS

AUTHOR'S NOTE

Readers ask why I choose particular storylines for my novels. Many stories are worth telling, but I've discovered the best stories result from characters who come to me when I'm not looking for them.

Such was the case with Hunter Carlisle and *Between These Walls*.

Early in 2011, I had almost wrapped up the first draft of my third novel. One afternoon, when I went for a walk, a character arose within me: a middle-school kid who was a Christian but harbored an attraction to the same gender. I pondered facets of this character's circumstances as I walked. His fears, his feelings of guilt, the hits to his self-esteem—everything about his struggle grabbed my heart.

At that point, I wouldn't have had the courage to write a book about him. But when characters arise from within, I believe it is God's way of telling me individuals share the character's struggle and need a book written for them *right now*. A novel about homosexuality, however, would test the boundaries of my comfort zone. Though I hate to admit it, I worried about what others might think. So I tucked the idea, safe and silent, in the back of my brain.

But as the ancient prophet Jonah discovered, you can't hide from God. He'll find you.

One year later, the concept remained unexplored—until a feature story caught my attention on the television news. The nationally syndicated story revolved around the plight of a high school student on the verge of suicide. This student, about fifteen years old, had endured a continual onslaught of bullying.

The bullying occurred for one reason: The kid was gay.

After enduring all the emotional damage he could handle, this kid reached his breaking point. Desperate and exhausted, wrought with pain, he posted a video online. Too hurt to speak—I imagine the bullying included poking fun at the way he spoke—the kid had written his words in black marker on sheets of paper. So here sat a blond-haired kid who looked like an average high school freshman, wiping tears from his eyes, making a desperate plea for somebody to hear him, for someone to care … for someone to offer him hope.

My heart broke for him. I know nothing about that student. The reporter didn't mention the his name. She didn't mention his city or state. I don't even know if he's still alive. But I couldn't erase the sight from my memory.

Anger arose in me. My immediate gut response was, *Never again. Not on my watch. Not if I can help it.*

Allow me to explain: A close family member of mine ended his life at sixteen years old. I was thirteen at the time. If you've never experienced such an event, trust me when I say it changes you forever. It changes your perception of life and people. From that point on, you view life with the awareness that many people appear happy but live in pain. You look into some people's eyes and wonder if their happiness is a charade. You wonder which individuals feel they don't matter. While others might assume few individuals consider suicide, you know better.

As I pondered the news story about that high school student, I thought, *Nobody that age should know what it's like to feel that kind of pain.*

Never again. Not on my watch.

At that point, I knew I needed to pursue the book topic and pursue it immediately. So my third novel, still in its first draft, returned to the back burner, where it has resided off and on for eight years. I began work on my fourth novel, *Between These Walls*, which you now hold in your hands.

My novels aren't geared toward the Young Adult genre, and I wanted to make the book accessible to as many individuals as possible. So I took my initial character idea—the middle-school kid—and doubled his age, which brought him into early adulthood. To capture the struggles and vulnerability of his teenage years, I could weave some of his memories into the fabric of the story.

I don't have quantitative data to back up my hunch, but I've long believed more people deal with same-sex attraction than we assume. I believe many simply hide it well or have a simultaneous attraction to the opposite gender, which enables them to live a "typical" life without raising suspicions. Therefore, I constructed Hunter as a character who finds himself attracted to both genders—technically, a bisexual male—with a stronger attraction toward males. This characteristic would allow him to remain in hiding for years. In fact, I chose the name *Hunter* to call to mind a hunter-gatherer image, the classic male stereotype—and the last place we might expect to find a gay male. His name symbolizes his attributes and interests, yet belies his deepest secret.

Regardless of whether the reader has experienced Hunter's battles, I attempted to tell his story in such a manner that the reader can find points of commonality with him. So, as a reader, you might not have experienced homosexual feelings, but you might hold another secret that torments you. A dark secret you never want revealed. You might relate to Hunter's fears or guilt. In that respect, perhaps Hunter's story is your story, too.

Between These Walls is not a political statement or a judgment of church bodies. It is not an attempt to interpret Scripture or resolve an argument. My purpose was to put the reader into the shoes of one character, to experience his emotions and inner fire—a story *behind* the story.

As you read this novel, I hope you know you are loved.

John Herrick
June 30, 2014

PROLOGUE
JULY 1995

If six-year-old Hunter Carlisle had secrets to hide, he would have kept them in this room.

Deep underground, the room had no windows along its walls. Were it not for the overhead lights he knew must exist or the handful of nightlights he spotted throughout this finished lower level, Hunter could imagine himself descending into cryptic, furry blackness. But surrounded by his brother Bryce and three other teenagers, Hunter felt safe.

Fourteen years old and too young to drive, Bryce and his friends found themselves stranded, limited by how far they could walk or ride their bicycles. Football practice had not yet begun. By this afternoon in early July, boredom had set in.

Today marked the first time Hunter had entered this house. Bryce's friend Pete, who flipped on a light switch, had lived here for as long as Hunter could remember—a time period which didn't stretch back far, but to Hunter, it seemed an eternity.

Hunter found the silence strange. He couldn't recall walking into someone else's house without finding an adult inside. For young Hunter, the rare occasions in which he couldn't locate an adult nearby were when Bryce babysat him for a few hours.

Hunter could trust his big brother Bryce and felt secure in his company. Bryce was almost as tall as an adult and had muscles that peeked out beneath the sleeves of his T-shirt.

With Bryce around, no harm would come to Hunter.

Upon entering the house, the first thing Hunter had noticed upstairs was how sunlight gleamed through windows and cast shapes upon the carpet. He'd never given much thought to the noise that home appliances made, but in the stillness of Pete's empty house, Hunter heard the low murmur of a refrigerator and the hum of an air conditioner. But he had seen neither en route to the basement.

Now, as Hunter reached the bottom of the stairs and peered around the basement, the room looked like a fancy cave. Its brightest feature, besides the lights, were its tan walls. The carpet was the color of the chocolate candy bars Bryce often bought with his allowance.

Drake and Ethan, Bryce's other two friends, made a beeline for the air hockey table in the corner of the room and plugged it in. Hunter wandered over to watch, though the tip of his nose brushed against the upper edge of the table. Within seconds, he watched a plastic red puck dart back and forth across the slick surface. Puffs of air tickled Hunter's nostrils as they blew through tiny holes that pockmarked the playing field.

With a tad too much aggression in his block, Ethan sent the puck airborne. When it made contact with Hunter's forehead,

Hunter giggled. No pain, not even a sting. In a way, it made Hunter feel part of the game, accepted by the older boys.

Ethan grunted. Hunter smelled bologna on his breath.

"Bryce, why don't you grab your little brother?" Ethan shouted. "He just fucked up my shot over here!"

Hunter cringed. If Hunter said a bad word and his parents heard about it, he knew punishment would be imminent.

Drake snorted. "Whatever, man! Blame it on the kid because you can't score a goal without a gallon of sweat dripping off your forehead. And that's a foul. My move now."

Bryce jogged over and put his fingers on the top of Hunter's head like a suction cup on a science-fiction gadget. He turned Hunter around and guided him to the sofa, which sat in front of a big-screen television.

"Why'd you bring your brother along, anyway?" Ethan asked, waving off a cheer from Drake, who had scored a goal.

"My mom's at the grocery store. I can't leave him home alone." Bryce turned toward Pete, who was on his hands and knees at the side of the sofa. "Pete, are we watching your Jim Carrey movie or not?"

Pete swiped his hand back and forth beneath the sofa. Hunter wondered why he would look so hard for a lost popcorn kernel.

"Not if I can help it," Pete said, a strain in his voice as he thrust his arm behind Bryce's legs. "Change of plans. My mom isn't home. I've got something better for us." At that, Pete grinned and let out a sigh of relief. "Whew! Thought they might've found it."

"Found what?" asked Drake as he yanked the hockey table's cord from the electrical socket. He wandered over and sat against the edge of the sofa, next to Bryce's feet. Hunter bounced on the middle cushion beside his big brother. Ethan leaned on the back of the sofa.

Pete stuck a video cassette into the VCR, flipped off the lights in the room, raced over to the sofa, and plopped onto the remaining empty cushion. Though Hunter tried to hide it, he felt a bit scared in the pitch blackness. He wished the nightlights were brighter, but the older boys would laugh at him if he asked them to turn the lights back on.

"Check this out." Pete aimed the remote control, turned on the television, and hit Play. The television emitted an initial gray glow, a comfort to Hunter. "My parents have no idea; I've been putting it together at night after they go to bed. They think I'm down here watching *Beavis and Butt-Head* till all hours."

The first thing Hunter noticed about the program before his eyes was that it wasn't *Beavis and Butt-Head*. It wasn't even a cartoon. Squinting, Hunter leaned forward and tried to decipher the scene on the screen. In the background he saw an abundance of white and silver: a small white sink; a narrow, silver shelf with jars of cotton balls and cotton swabs; a white floor. He heard a high-pitched sigh, the sound of a woman, but she didn't sound like she was in trouble. The camera panned left, where he noticed the edge of a vinyl cushion and—now he recognized it. It looked like a doctor's office. The sighs continued and, once the camera finished panning left, he discovered the source.

The woman had blond hair that fell to her waist. Her fingernails, which she dug into the examination table, were a fiery red. Eyes shut, she tilted her head back, whimpered again, and smiled with a wide, open mouth.

She wore nothing. A fully dressed man pressed against her and smothered any view below her waist. But from under the man's hands, Hunter caught a glimpse of the woman's full breasts.

The woman tugged at the man's tie. He loosened it, then tore it off over his head while the woman ripped open his shirt, button by button.

Hunter fixated on the images before him as the camera angle shifted to a side view. At this point, as far as he could tell, the man would take whatever action occurred next. So enthralled with the video, Hunter forgot about the other people in the room. Drake's voice startled him.

"How'd you get this channel on cable? Did a storm knock it in?"

"My dad subscribes to this," Pete said. "The channel has a parental control on it, but I figured out the code to unlock it. It's the same damn code he uses for the garage door opener!"

Riveted, Hunter returned his attention to the screen, where the man had undressed almost all the way. Would he? Hunter couldn't imagine himself getting undressed with someone else present in a doctor's office. Curious to see what would happen next, he leaned forward. From the corner of his eye, Hunter noticed Bryce, who looked uncomfortable as he shifted in his seat. Bryce caught a quick glance at Hunter, then turned his attention back to the screen. Bryce's foot tapped in furious rhythm on the carpet.

When the man on the screen took a half-step back, Hunter caught his first glimpse of the woman's loins. Hunter's blinked once and opened his eyes wider. His mouth opened into a round *O*. At the age of six, he'd couldn't remember seeing a woman naked, except his mother once. But this woman looked different—fuller, perfect, with a different color of hair, even down there.

Sure enough, the man slipped out of his navy-blue briefs and—Hunter was shocked. The man looked different from Hunter. This man had hair down there and his—whatever had happened to him, Hunter could recall it happening to himself but he didn't understand why. But this man's was much, much larger than Hunter's.

Bryce, Pete and Drake had leaned forward. Drake burst out laughing, pointed at the screen, and made a joke Hunter didn't understand. Whatever it meant, the other two guys cackled, hurling comments at the woman as if she might hear them.

Before long, the man had begun to thrust himself against the woman. She still didn't seem in trouble. She continued to make noise, but her noises had grown louder, closer and closer to a shout. And before Hunter knew it, it looked like part of the man, the stiff part, went missing. The man and woman moved together.

Pete glanced over the back of the sofa. When Hunter noticed Pete turning around, he broke eye contact with the television and followed Pete's line of sight, in case Pete had decided to look for something else.

Pete looked confused. "Where the hell's Ethan?"

"Shut up, man."

"I don't believe this!" Pete threw his head back and laughed, then returned his attention to the rear corner of the room. "Dude, are you seriously jerking off right now? Right here in my basement?"

"Shut the fuck up, man! You turned this shit on!"

Though that corner of the room was dark, Hunter caught sight of a figure with its back turned toward them. It looked like Ethan's shape with one arm in vigorous motion.

Hunter returned his attention to the television screen.

Bryce peered down at his little brother and nudged him. When Hunter looked up, Bryce shook his head in a firm *No* gesture, but Hunter shook his head in response and looked back at the television to see what would happen next.

"Hey guys, maybe we should turn this shit off," Bryce blurted out. "My little brother's here. He's only six." With another nudge to Hunter, he whispered, "Hunter, are you okay?"

Pete rolled his eyes. "He's okay. Look at him, he's learning something. His eyes are glued to the TV. Hunter's probably amazed at the *dude.* Tell the truth, Hunter. Your eyes are fixated on the guy's pecker, am I right?"

Another round of cackles.

At that, the man on the TV separated from the woman and turned her around so she faced the table.

Bryce looked down at Hunter once more and shot to his feet. He lunged for the television and pressed his chest against it, blocking their view, stretching one arm across part of the screen as though to block more of the view. With his free hand, he started pushing buttons on the television until the screen went dark.

"What the fuck, man?! Turn it back on!"

Ignoring the remark, Bryce grabbed Hunter by the arm. "Listen guys, I'd better get him out of here. He's too young to see this."

"Hell, man, *we're* too young to see this! Look at her—"

Bryce didn't wait for a round of agreement. In an instant, Hunter felt Bryce's hand under his armpit, hoisting him from the sofa and dragging him toward the stairs.

Bryce didn't say a word for most of their four-block trek home.

The neighborhood remained the same, yet Hunter sensed from his older brother that something had changed. He sensed discomfort. Bryce's strides seemed a tad longer than usual, judging from the way Hunter needed to take an extra step every few seconds to keep up with him.

Bryce towered over Hunter in height. Along the way home, Hunter peered up at his brother's face and tried to decode what he saw. With a sober expression, Bryce fixed his eyes straight ahead. Was he worried? Fearful? Hunter couldn't put a finger on it, but yes, something seemed wrong.

They passed house after house along the suburban street. After countless bike rides through this neighborhood, Hunter knew each house. He found comfort in the familiarity of its order: The two-story house with the maroon shutters sat beside the ranch home with the little pear tree in the front yard. Next came the two-story house with the rock garden on either side of the front door.

As he nodded at the pattern of homes, Hunter's mind returned to Pete's video. He'd never seen anything like it. What were they doing on that television screen? Why had Bryce gotten furious? Maybe it was Hunter's fault. As Hunter thought back to the images on the television, his stomach grew sour, the way it had one summer afternoon when he'd swallowed two heaping tablespoons of butter.

Hunter didn't know what was wrong, but judging from Bryce's reaction, he had watched something bad.

As they passed beneath a tree, Bryce's shoulder brushed against one of its branches, which sent the tree in a shudder. Its motion startled a bird, which darted out of the tree and escaped into the sky. Hunter listened to the frantic sound of wings flapping as it escaped from view.

At last, when they were yet a block away from home, Hunter felt his brother patting his shoulder. Though a gentle pat, the size of his brother's large hand jostled Hunter's tiny shoulder with as little effort as it had required to set the tree branch in motion.

Bryce broke the silence, his voice subdued, as if someone could overhear him through an open window.

"Look, Hunter, I didn't know Pete was gonna put that stuff on TV. Mom and Dad would kill me if they knew about this, so you can't say a word to them, okay?"

Hunter gazed up at his brother. He bit his lower lip in a childlike manner and nodded—anything to please his big brother. The broken silence brought comfort to his young soul, a return to normalcy. A barrier broken, Hunter hoped. The freedom brought a hop to his next step. He harbored so many questions about what he had seen minutes earlier and hoped Bryce would ask him if he had any questions. The awkwardness of the journey home had left Hunter afraid to ask on his own initiative.

"It'll make sense when you're older," Bryce continued. "Just forget you ever saw that video, okay?"

And with that, the conversation ended.

Hunter never forgot the images on that television screen.

No matter how hard he tried.

PART ONE

SILENCE

CHAPTER 1

Had Hunter seen what he thought he'd seen? Had he given Hunter a second glance?

At twenty-six years old, after so many years, Hunter wished the temptation would release its grip on him.

Hunter's heartbeat increased at the possibility of mutual attraction, but he steadied himself.

Surrounded on three sides by frosted glass walls, the conference room sat in an interior section on the fourth floor of a suburban professional building. Pipeline Insurance Corporation offered extensive packages for life, home and automobile coverage. Its customers ranged from individuals to small businesses to large corporations.

Hunter had pursued this potential client by phone for three months, trying to get one foot in the door to explain the benefits of his own company's products.

Two weeks ago, he had secured an appointment for ten o'clock this morning with Jake Geyer, a manager in the technology services department.

Hunter had expected a few Pipeline staff members to attend the demo session, but at the last minute, the others had canceled. This occurred often with Hunter's cold-call appointments and, after four years in sales, Hunter had learned not to take offense when it happened.

Side by side, Hunter and Jake sat at a large, mahogany table, facing the frosted glass walls. The polished surface of the table cast a reflection of Hunter's laptop computer.

"So the program offers dynamic address formatting to satisfy postal standards," Hunter explained. "The program is Internet-based and interacts live with our central server. As you know, to obtain discounted rates for bulk mail, the postal service has strict requirements that vendors must meet. Our program ensures compliance at the point of entry."

Jake stroked the stubble beneath his chin as he examined the sample data-entry program on Hunter's laptop screen. With one arm bent at the elbow, the sleeve of his polo shirt wrapped taut around his bicep, revealing enough shape to suggest Jake worked out. Jake wore stylish, olive-green glasses, which blended well with his dirty-blond hair and enhanced the color of his green eyes. Hunter estimated Jake was only a few years older than he. Thirty years old at best.

"I understand how meeting those standards benefits us," Jake said, "but our data entry staff keeps a printed document of postal standards on hand. One question my director would ask is, 'What does your product accomplish that we can't accomplish ourselves?'"

Hunter had anticipated that question. Every prospective client asked the same question during their first meeting. But Hunter, who worked with the software every day and understood its benefits, had learned to respect his prospective clients and allow them to grasp the concept at their own paces. Moreover, Hunter had discovered that he could read between the lines. Individuals would express their own needs and desires through their comments and questions, which, in turn, helped Hunter customize a case for how his own company's product offered a solution. For Hunter, the sales pitch focused less on convincing a client of their need than presenting his product as a hero that would save the day. Hunter *believed* in the product he sold. He viewed his visits as opportunities to enhance the work of others.

"That's a good question," Hunter said. "You mentioned on the phone that you enter a large collection of records to your database throughout each day, plus a load of address changes when people move to new apartments or buy new homes. I assume you run quality-assurance reports on those entries?"

"Yes, we deliver the reports to our data entry staff each morning."

"Do you ever find errors in those updates?"

"Nothing major. The data entry clerk might enter a wrong digit in the street address. They might spell out 'Street' or 'Post Office' instead of using the postal abbreviations. Things like that."

"That's typical for my prospective clients. The benefit our program would bring is to eliminate that second step from your business process. By formatting your addresses automatically upon entry, we eliminate user errors, which increases your efficiency rate and allows your data entry staff to start its day entering new data instead of revisiting the prior day's work."

Hunter glanced over at Jake, who nodded. Hunter sensed Jake had absorbed and understood the details.

Shifting in his seat, Hunter scooted so his back settled flush against the back of his chair. For the last few months, he'd felt recurring soreness in his lower back. Though frequent and lasting several hours at a time, the aches didn't occur daily. The pain level ranged from minor discomfort to occasional bursts that would stab his lower back like a knife. He could sense it wasn't a medical issue, though, and attributed it to stress on the job.

Hunter continued his pitch to Jake Geyer.

"Plus," Hunter added, "we receive regular updates to verify the physical existence of homes and buildings, which helps prevent a wrong digit or character in your address. Our data ensures that, yes indeed, a building actually sits at 1234 Main Street and hasn't been torn down. That would increase your deliverability rates and eliminate the cost of mailing material to addresses that don't exist. You can take the money that used to go down the drain in returned mail and reinvest it to increase your profit margin."

Jake glanced over at Hunter, held his gaze for a few seconds, the way he had several minutes ago, then examined the laptop screen again. Though Hunter wasn't sure, he thought he caught a change in Jake's eyes during contact. Jake's pupils had dilated a trace.

Why did he glance at me?

Sure, it's a normal human response in a business scenario. Yet Hunter couldn't help but wonder if Jake was focused on Hunter's explanation of the program, or if he'd used the glance as an excuse to take a quick inventory of Hunter's eyes.

Jake tapped the edge of the laptop. "So this is the program here?"

"Sure is. I can walk you through a demo if you want."

Jake slid his chair toward the laptop, leaned in closer to the screen. And closer to Hunter.

Jake set his glasses aside to view the screen, so perhaps he was nearsighted. Hunter noticed Jake's eyes were closer to olive than standard green.

Hunter picked up the scent of a fresh shower. The scent was pleasant but possessed a sharp tang. Men's shower gel.

Hunter's heart rate began to roll with the steady pace of a treadmill. A quiver ran up his thighs. His right arm rested on the mahogany table an inch from Jake's.

Hunter wished he didn't enjoy the proximity. Such simplicity would come to his life if he could free himself from the appeal he found in other men.

When in the company of others, often he wondered if he was the only one who struggled like this.

He forced himself to refocus on the screen ahead.

"Here's a sample program for a magazine subscription company." Hunter waved his finger over the program window. "The company isn't real."

"How about the colors and layout? Our software application is branded with our logos and a couple of company Intranet links. Is this what the program would look like if we purchased it?"

If we purchased it? When a client started talking about purchase scenarios, Hunter considered it a positive indicator. Hunter smiled with fresh vigor. He stretched his lower back to the left, then to the right.

"We integrate our software into yours. We've done it that way with all our clients. Our product is compatible across any format you throw our way." He pointed to a small icon of a company logo beside the address line. "We incorporate that little icon into your screen in case you'd want to visit our website to research a particular address further. Other than that, you won't notice a difference onscreen. It's seamless; everything else gets woven in behind the scenes. We store our data on our own server, so you maintain full privacy of your data."

Hunter paused to allow the logistics to soak in, swiped his finger along the laptop's touchpad, then tapped it. "We'll create a new record for Hunter Carlisle."

As he hit the keys on the keyboard, Hunter kept his eyes glued to the screen. But in his peripheral vision, he saw Jake tilt his head and run his fingers through his hair, the way you do to make yourself appear casual. But then, as Hunter continued speaking, he noticed Jake had broken his gaze from the computer. Jake's irises moved toward Hunter's face and lingered there, assuming Hunter didn't notice. Hunter felt a flutter in his chest. He could hear the soft sound of Jake's breathing.

If Hunter could create a product, he would invent a method to read another person's mind. In times like these, a mind-reading tool would allow him to decipher why Jake studied him with such intentness. For all Hunter knew, Jake could be trying to figure out whether Hunter was an honest sales person who believed in his own product. Yet Hunter couldn't help but wish for a kindred spirit, someone who struggled with the same attractions he did.

For someone to find him attractive—a *mutual* attraction.

He wanted to ask but knew he couldn't mix personal affairs with professional business. Not that he would dare to out himself anyway.

Hunter cleared his throat. Jake's eyes darted back to the screen.

Okay, he didn't want Hunter to know he'd sneaked that glance. The question for Hunter was, *Why?*

Statistics would render chances slim that Jake held any attraction toward Hunter. Hunter knew the percentage of those who concealed homosexual urges was small. But he also knew that percentage wasn't zero. Hunter remained aware that, with all the people who crossed his path in a year, *someone* out there harbored the same secret he did.

The question was, who are those *someones?* For Hunter, attempting to find the answer carried, at minimum, a heavy risk. And Hunter hadn't sharpened his senses enough to detect those *someones* on his own.

The what-if scenarios, like the one in which he found himself right now, felt like mental torture: a continual flow of questions never asked and never answered. After all these years, it exhausted him.

"In my mailing address, I typed the full words 'Street' and 'Suite.' Also, I typed '4738' as our street number—but our address is 4739. There's no building at 4738," Hunter said. "Now, keep an eye on that address line when I move to the next field."

When Hunter moved his arm, he brushed Jake's arm by accident.

But Jake didn't move his arm right away. Usually others did. It took Jake an extra second before he even blinked.

With a hit of the Tab key, the cursor moved to the next data field. In the address line, as Hunter had predicted, the street number changed to 4739 and abbreviations replaced the full words Hunter had mentioned.

"And that's how it works, in real time," Hunter said. "Without those abbreviations, a piece of mail to that address would not have qualified for a discounted mailing rate. And with a nonexistent street number, unless your postal worker delivered it on his own initiative, the piece of mail would have returned to you, with the cost of postage wasted. And with our program, your data entry staff wouldn't have needed to correct the address in the morning, despite the address errors typed into the record. Multiply that by the thousands of addresses you enter and use per year, and it can add up to a lot of savings."

With that, Hunter allowed his words to settle. He would let the prospective client have the next word, to which Hunter would respond.

Jake leaned back in his chair. He crossed his leg, stroked his chin.

"I can see the benefit behind it," Jake said. "The question for us would be, 'Does the benefit outweigh the cost?' That's the first thing my director would ask. Our data entry people enter 95 percent of the data in its correct format. So for those remaining cases, are we spending more money on data entry hours than we would spend on the cost of the product? Looking at the cost structure you emailed me yesterday—well, I hate to say it, but I just don't see how we'd end up ahead."

Hunter dreaded that response. As good as his company's product was, and as much money as it could save a client, their current efficiency rate proved a wild card every time. Hunter had no way of knowing those efficiency rates when he entered into these initial meetings, and clients tended to avoid answering that question if he asked too early.

Jake's reply wasn't good. Demonstration meetings like these were uphill battles from the onset, so Hunter entered them prepared to counter a variety of possible scenarios. In each case, he would help the potential client see the long-term value his product offered. But in one sentence, perhaps without realizing it, Jake had all but shut down Hunter's case. In one sentence, Jake had addressed not only their present situation, but also applied high-level analysis and reached a conclusion. And he also served as gatekeeper to everyone else at Pipeline Insurance Corporation.

Hunter decided to go for the next-best scenario. If he couldn't sell the full product, he would try to sell one of his company's smaller products.

"I understand what you're saying," Hunter said. "Although the solution I demonstrated for you is our top-notch, flagship product, we also offer a range of other services to help improve efficiency."

In a halfhearted manner, Jake thumbed through a brochure Hunter had laid on the table earlier. "Do all of your services require integration into the software? Do you offer a standalone product we could use on an as-needed basis? That would reduce our cost of implementation."

Hunter winced inside. He saw where this conversation was headed, and it wasn't headed toward a sale. He knew he couldn't offer a viable alternative to meet their needs. The discomfort in Hunter's back inflamed further.

"The software-integration aspect is a foundational piece of all our products. In fact, it's one quality that sets us apart from other data providers because it provides a seamless user experience."

Jake shifted in his seat. "I'm afraid you'd have a tough time selling that to my director. With the upfront costs that would come with integrating the software, and the work involved by the tech staff on our end … I can tell you right now, he won't go for it. I can pass along to him anything you'd like me to pass along, but I've walked through enough projects with him to tell you there won't be a sale." He drummed his fingers once upon the table. "To be honest, I could tell from the literature you emailed yesterday that the software wouldn't be a good match for us, but I wanted to give you a chance to stop by anyway, in case I'd misunderstood some of the details."

Jake glanced at Hunter. Hunter caught a twinge of disappointment in his eyes.

"Man, I'm sorry," said Jake, one young adult to another. "Working together would've been good."

Hunter appreciated the remark. He also wondered if Jake had meant his comment about working together at face value, or if he'd referred to getting to see *Hunter* more often, had the deal worked out. Hunter couldn't decipher the answer. Though he would never admit it to a soul, the latter notion incited a longing inside him.

"Hey, I understand." Hunter bit his lower lip, started shutting down his laptop, and retrieved a flash drive from his saddle bag. "I'll leave this flash drive with you. It contains a demo of our product for you to pass along to your director. If he expresses interest, feel free to contact me, okay?"

Jake reached out to receive the flash drive. Their fingertips brushed. Jake's eyes caught Hunter's again, as if searching for a potential next move. Hunter wanted more time to see what, if anything, hid behind the signals—or non-signals—he'd detected from Jake.

In the end, however, professionalism disallowed either man from asking questions or taking another step. In a social context, or if they knew each other better, perhaps they would have had more flexibility.

But today they didn't.

Hunter hoped the forlorn expression in Jake's eyes meant what he wished it did.

Chances were, it didn't. But the fact that someone like Jake—a peer, an equal, and a handsome one at that—might have looked at Hunter and considered something more …

It left Hunter with a surge of warmth combined with the ache of another letdown.

Whether out of courtesy or a desire to savor the final moments their paths would cross, Hunter didn't know, but Jake walked him down to the lobby.

They shook hands. They exchanged formal smiles. And Hunter walked out the door as Jake turned back toward the elevator.

Five steps out the door, with more than enough time for Jake to have reached the elevator, Hunter glanced back.

Through the glass walls of the lobby, he noticed Jake lingering at the elevator, glancing back at him.

The elevator door opened. Jake seemed to hesitate for a split second, as if caught between options of what to do next, then turned and entered the elevator.

Hunter nodded.

Another opportunity … vanished.

CHAPTER 2

Heading west on Interstate 480 after work, Hunter's mind drifted back to that morning's unsuccessful meeting. Another potential sale lost.

His third major turndown this month.

He hadn't seen this one coming, though. In fact, he had considered Pipeline Insurance Corporation a hot prospect, with high likelihood of becoming a long-term client. In his phone conversations with Jake Geyer, he had perceived genuine interest in hearing more about the software product. Jake had acknowledged how the product could help, but hadn't mentioned his employer's limited scope of need.

Hunter's manager, Wayne, held a one-on-one status meeting each week. When he'd mentioned Pipeline to Wayne during one recent meeting, Wayne had inquired about Hunter's ability to secure the client. Though he'd prefaced his response with caution, noting it was too early to know for sure, Hunter had estimated his chances as high.

Wayne latched onto that estimation and forgot the preface.

Today's development couldn't help Hunter's employment status. He hadn't just underperformed this month. His dry streak had lasted six months and counting.

Once the top-performing member of his team's sales force, Hunter hadn't worried about losing his job. Nowadays, however, he'd grown concerned.

His back ache persisted. Hunter scratched his head. The bristles of his brown hair, which he kept short and styled with a touch of gel, tickled his fingers. He rubbed his neck, a nervous habit, and tried to ignore the sickening feeling in his stomach.

"Lord, please help me," he murmured.

After the meeting with Jake, Hunter had stopped by a current client's office to ask how well the software continued to work for them and to let them know if they ever needed anything, they could give him a call. An unnecessary visit, but it would only strengthen their business relationship.

More than that, Hunter had needed to revisit a past success. It provided a visual reminder that the dry streak could end and his fortunes could turn around.

He heard a single buzz from his cell phone as he veered toward Cleveland Hopkins International Airport. Grabbing the phone from the empty passenger seat, he checked its display and found a text message from his girlfriend, Kara.

Her flight had arrived. To avoid wasting time waiting in the baggage-claim area, Kara always brought a piece of luggage small enough to fit into a plane's overhead bin. That meant she was now on her way through the airport concourse, heading for the pickup area.

Perfect timing. Hunter wouldn't need to pay to park.

Standing at the curb, Kara looked diminutive compared to most passersby. At five foot four, the top of her head could rest comfortably beneath Hunter's chin when he tilted his head at the proper angle. He found it cute.

When she saw his car approach, she gave a feverish wave, as though her trip had lasted weeks rather than a few days. By the time Hunter reached the curb, Kara had already begun dragging her luggage toward his car. Hunter chuckled at the sight. She looked adorable: a diminutive elf lugging a sled through the snow. Throwing the car into park, he popped the trunk and climbed out.

"I'll take care of your luggage," he said, jogging toward the rear of the car.

"Don't you worry, Carlisle," she said with a glint in her eye. "I've got your back."

Despite the honking of car horns behind them, Hunter allowed himself the luxury of ignoring them for a few seconds. Pulling Kara into his arms, he lifted her a few inches from the ground and held her. She loved when he did that. Petite and slender, she felt like a feather to anyone who tried to lift her. But Hunter visited the gym often, so Kara presented even less of a challenge for his athletic build and toned arms. Hearing her giggle made him grin.

She ran her finger once along his upper lip before he planted a kiss on hers.

"It's good to be home," she said.

Another horn shrieked behind them. The sound echoed amid the concrete surroundings and brought Hunter back to the moment.

"Door's unlocked." He shoved her luggage into his trunk and made his way back to the driver's side. "We don't want to keep Jerky waiting behind us."

When he climbed in, he found her buckling her seat belt. Strands of her blond hair had gone astray in all the right places. She couldn't look a mess if she tried.

Pulling out of the parking area, Hunter tapped his finger on the dashboard clock, which approached 6:30 in the evening.

"Are you hungry?" he asked.

She shook her head. "I grabbed some sushi during my layover in Denver," she said, then leaned toward him with a genuine, vulnerable longing in her eyes. "I missed you."

Hunter's mind raced back to his encounter with Jake earlier that morning. He caught himself bouncing his left heel at a nervous pace and brought it to a halt before Kara noticed. He gave her a quick glance, then returned his eyes to the road.

"Missed you, too."

———————

Hunter lived toward the eastern edge of Hudson, a suburban community situated between Cleveland and Akron in northern Ohio. He had grown up in this community, where he'd played on the high school baseball team and had run cross-country. Hunter's career in sales left him with constant pressure and challenging goals. Living in Hudson lent a sense of familiarity and balance, the luxury of coming home to something he knew he could count on.

He rented a small home from a white-collar family that had relocated to London for two years as part of the husband's career. Though the kids were several years younger than Hunter, he had known the family since his early teens.

Hunter followed Kara into his kitchen by way of an entry door from the garage. Kara set her purse on the kitchen table, removed her shoes, and wandered into the living room.

"You're sure you don't want me to order Chinese? We can have it delivered," he called out.

"Thanks, I'm in good shape," came her voice from the other room. "Just ready to relax."

From a miniature wine rack he kept at the corner of his kitchen counter, Hunter grabbed an open bottle of cabernet sauvignon—Kara's favorite wine to help her relax. He poured two glasses and carried them to the living room, where Kara had settled onto the sofa with her head tilted back and her eyes shut. Her hair splayed across the back of the sofa.

When she heard him approach, she opened her eyes and accepted her glass, raising it in toast-like fashion in appreciation for his gesture.

"You're such a sweetie." She patted the cushion beside her.

Hunter took a seat, settling into the sofa and closer to Kara.

The discomfort in his back had eased a bit. Hunter had played sports since childhood and had suffered a wide variety of sprains, pulled muscles, headaches and anything else imaginable. *Pain is part of life,* his father had always said. *Walk through the pain. Let others complain, but you be the strong one.* Hunter seldom talked about discomfort—external *or* internal—and, over the years, had developed a high tolerance for pain.

Aware his back issue wasn't severe, Hunter had never gotten around to mentioning it to Kara. It hadn't seemed worthy of a special remark and hadn't made its way into the course of everyday conversation.

Just another secret, thought Hunter.

Hunter always held back little secrets in his romantic relationships.

He couldn't put his finger on why he held himself back from someone else. Maybe it was his way of marking his territory or preventing anyone from venturing too deep into his psyche. Whatever the reason, he treasured his guarded space.

Within time, he suspected, women sensed he held something back. They seemed to have radar for that sort of knowledge. They could tell something was wrong but didn't know why they sensed it. They would ask if he was okay, and he would tell them he was preoccupied with work. Women seemed to accept his response and regard him as a complex individual—still waters run deep, as the adage goes. They resigned themselves to the fact that they had entered a relationship with yet another male who seldom showed his emotions.

Hunter could see the trace of hurt in a woman's eyes when she knew he only trusted her 99 percent.

But it wasn't the woman's fault Hunter didn't trust anyone more than 99 percent.

Within that remaining one percent, Hunter guarded his personal torment, his darkest secret.

And he couldn't confide in anyone about that secret. Certainly not with a woman with whom he was involved in a romantic relationship. Not as long as he made an honest effort to stifle his temptations and walk through the hidden pain.

Taking a sip of wine, Hunter reached for Kara's hand and massaged her fingers with his free hand.

"How was New York?" he asked.

"I found a new line of purses I'd like to take a closer look at. I didn't catch them until the end of my trip, but I'll be back there for a few days next week and can follow up at that point. We've never carried this particular line in our stores. In the meantime, I'll get some more demographic information from our marketing people to help me determine if the line is a good fit."

Kara worked as a buyer for a national retail chain. With a focus on purses and jewelry, she traveled often, visiting major cities throughout the world, on a mission for the products her stores should carry. As a result of her travels, she and Hunter spent much time apart. Large blocks of time—a few days here, a week or two there. Hunter, by comparison, covered a large region of northern Ohio in his sales position and traveled by car. Kara's frequent flyer miles were the envy of anyone who took the time to perform a few mental calculations. Most people dreamed of traveling to an exotic city as a capstone event, the vacation of a lifetime. Not Kara. At twenty-six, the same age as Hunter, Kara dreamed of seeing few cities. She had already visited them. While Hunter dreamed of discovering new places, Kara savored their familiarity while passing through. She spoke of Tokyo the way most Americans spoke of a local pub.

"How was work?" Kara asked. "Didn't you say you had a big sales opportunity with an insurance company this week? How'd that go?"

Yes, he'd said that.

"It doesn't look promising." Hunter fixated on the television in front of them, which they hadn't turned on. "In the lead-up to the demo meeting, their interest looked high, but they re-evaluated their situation by the time I got there."

Kara leaned her head toward him, searching his eyes. "So where do you go from there?"

Though disappointed, Hunter pushed his frustration into hibernation. He refused to pull Kara into his pity. He resolved to let it go.

"I'll find another prospect to replace them."

"I know you've had a dry spell for a while."

He rubbed her fingers again, then moved his hand over her shoulder blade and massaged her back with his thumb. He smiled. "No big deal. It's part of the game."

In truth, he wondered whether the floor was about to collapse beneath him.

Kara squinted a moment, as though to evaluate him in her pixie manner, then grinned at him. She set her wineglass on the coffee table, then lifted Hunter's glass from his hand and set it beside hers. She peered into his eyes and held his gaze. For a split second, her pupils dilated, inviting Hunter into her world.

He wanted to feel drawn into her world. He really did. And he'd tried so hard.

Over and over, he'd tried to will it to happen; nevertheless, he couldn't take that final step across the broad gulch he knew existed between Kara and him. Between *any* woman and him.

With a tender expression on her face, she ran the tops of her fingers along his cheek and leaned in for a kiss. Hunter closed his eyes and responded, but sensed an absence of involvement from his heart. In a flash, his mind flitted back to an image from that morning, the way Jake had studied him when it didn't look like Hunter had noticed.

And in another flash, the memory vanished. Hunter smothered it, forcing it into hiding the way he would fold a sweater and shove it into a dresser drawer. He closed the drawer tight. Concealing such memories and feelings from others had served as his protocol for the last 14 years, since he was twelve years old.

Two light kisses before Kara hesitated. "Are you sure you're okay?"

Hunter hoped her question referred to his day's professional loss and that she hadn't picked up on his lack of romantic response. "Yeah, I've got plenty of other possibilities. Pipeline was my biggest and best, but I'll find another one. In the meantime, I'll start the day tomorrow by following up with other irons I have in the fire."

Kara squinted again, then shook her head. "No, it's not today. You've seemed, I don't know, distanced lately. Everything's okay?"

Despite his inner conflict, Hunter hadn't faked his fondness for Kara. He harbored deep feelings toward her and felt comfortable around her. Without exaggeration, he loved Kara, in the sense that he cherished and cared for her in a profound way. He just couldn't find a way to give his whole heart to her.

One piece short of a puzzle. The most critical piece, unfortunately.

Without a cornerstone, a building would end up lopsided or angled wrong, perhaps even implode.

A tiny rudder can guide an enormous ship. The flicker of a flame can set an entire forest on fire.

Sometimes little things matter. A lot.

But Hunter had had years of practice. He'd learned when he needed a surge of passion, he could incite it within himself, like drawing on a car's reserve tank for fuel. The key, he'd discovered, was to relax and melt into the moment.

Hunter focused on Kara's face. He felt intensity begin to rise and willed it into his stare. The moment the doubt in her eyes broke, Hunter discerned it. He laid his lips upon hers and kissed her deeply, as though to draw air from her lungs into his own.

With his hand on her arm, he felt her muscles relax as she closed her eyes and dissolved into their kiss.

Hunter brushed his lips against hers. He moved his mouth along her cheek, laid a kiss behind her earlobe, which he knew she enjoyed, then swept down to her neck. He slid his hand down to her waist, where he placed his other hand on the opposite side.

They shared one more kiss.

"Stop," Kara gasped, then kissed him again.

"Stop what?" he whispered. Another kiss.

Kara pulled back and grinned. "We'd better stop while we're ahead. The no-sex-before-marriage policy, remember?"

Hunter was a Christian and believed in saving sex for marriage. He held to the concept as a core component of his faith. And it wasn't pious showmanship; he believed positive results would follow if he saved himself for another, giving himself to another as a gift. The concept served as an anchor for his heart.

But in light of his personal struggle with attraction—or lack thereof—to women, the concept of saving sex for marriage had also proven convenient. Not that Hunter had planned it as such; it had merely worked out that way. But it had brought him refuge over the years. By its nature, waiting revolved around time, and this particular wait afforded him an abundance of time to find his way out of his struggle.

Kara glanced at her watch. "I should head home anyway. I started typing up a summary on the plane and want to have it ready for tomorrow morning."

"What about your need to relax after the flight?"

"I wish I could."

She gave his arm a squeeze, got up from the sofa, and flicked her hair behind her shoulders. Hunter followed her into the kitchen, where she rummaged through her purse and retrieved her keys. As with all of her business trips, she had left her car in the second spot in Hunter's garage. Airport parking lots made her nervous, the way people in a hurry tended to bang against car doors, and she preferred not to leave her car at her apartment parking lot around the clock.

"You could stay in the guest bedroom and save yourself time," he suggested.

"I'm eager to get my bag unpacked and climb into my own bed. Thanks anyway, though." She jingled her keys and shot him a wink. "I'll lock the door behind me."

Hunter had known Kara for years through a friend from church. A few weeks ago, when their relationship hit the five-month mark, Hunter had gone ahead and given her a key to his house. That way, if a coworker picked her up from the airport instead of Hunter, she could get her car. In the years Kara and Hunter had known each other, he'd learned that she wasn't psychotic and he could trust her with a key.

Hunter kissed her good-bye. She walked out the door and, sure enough, locked it behind her. That made Hunter snicker. Yeah, she was cute, indeed.

CHAPTER 3

A roar erupted as the Cleveland Indians scored their first run at the bottom of the third inning.

Hunter kept his eye on the television as the batter crossed first base and continued around the diamond until the third-base coach signaled for him to stop running at second.

Ten high-definition televisions hung throughout the bar and grill. On Sunday afternoons, they displayed different football games. But tonight, all eyes focused on the Indians.

Kara reached for Hunter's hand beneath the table. She intertwined her fingers with his and gave them a quick squeeze. He responded in kind. While he enjoyed giving affection to women and receiving it in return, the women in his life initiated contact more often.

"I can appreciate a run as much as the next guy." With a swish of her head, Ellen Krieger sent her brunette hair behind her shoulders. "But you'd think word hadn't gotten around that the Indians' post-season hopes have vanished. Why didn't they try this hard in July?"

"You don't just give up, Ellen." Hunter winked, his voice raised so she could hear him over the voices from surrounding tables. "If you're gonna go down, you go down fighting. That's what guys do. We never go down without a fight."

"That was a surprising remark of resignation from you, Ellen," her fiancé, thirty-year-old Brendan Pieper, chimed in. "Do *you* go down without a fight when you want me to put glasses in their proper row in your dishwasher?"

A broad smile swept across Ellen's face as she gave Brendan a playful slug to the arm. "Proper row in the dishwasher, my ass! If I could get you not to leave them in the *sink,* I'd call it a miracle."

With a snicker to reveal he understood Ellen's comment but would admit nothing, he pulled her into him with one arm and kissed her forehead. When they parted, he straightened his eyeglasses.

Ellen and Brendan's relationship struck Hunter as natural, as if they fused together without effort. Hunter knew they'd had their share of arguments—with her blunt personality, Ellen had a way of locating people's farthest boundaries. But as far as Hunter could tell, neither Ellen nor Brendan doubted the strength of their relationship.

How satisfying to find love and not be looking around, Hunter mused, not fearful you're missing out on something better, not wishing for something different.

Hunter picked up a trace of cigarette smoke from a table across the room. Between the Saturday-night crowd and the televisions, the restaurant was loud, but the noise didn't prevent Hunter and his companions from hearing each other if they leaned into the square table to talk.

"I always liked the Indians' mascot as a kid, even before I lived here," Kara said, her eyes on the game. "Didn't he look like a Saturday-morning cartoon to you?"

"I think that's the biggest reason Hunter wore his Cleveland baseball cap every day as a kid," Ellen jibed. "For the picture."

How does she know these things? Hunter wouldn't give Ellen any satisfaction, though. His competitive spirit wouldn't allow it. "Yeah, right. And I suppose your avoidance of Phillies gear has nothing to do with the fact it's not your home team. You just don't like that cursive *P* on the front."

"Touché." Ellen clinked beer bottles with Hunter, who sat toward her left. She followed up with a long pull from the bottle.

The server arrived with two dozen chicken wings in two round baskets. From one basket, Hunter could smell the sweet, sticky tang of Jamaican jerk sauce that covered the wings, but he reached for the basket that contained the crispy buffalo wings instead. He whispered a quick prayer to thank God for the meal, then took a bite. As he breathed in, spices from the buffalo sauce sent a tingle through his nasal passage. He stifled a cough and took his first bite.

Before starting her dinner, Kara excused herself and headed to the ladies' room.

Hunter looked over at Ellen, who grabbed Brendan's napkin from his lap and applied a playful dab to the jerk sauce at the corner of her fiancé's mouth.

"Now that you're engaged, I can tell you this," Hunter said to Ellen. "As independent as you always were, I never thought I'd see the day you'd settle down and get married." He shot a conspiratorial look toward Brendan. "You must see something in her nobody else can see."

"Digging for it tends to wear me out, but there's a price to everything," Brendan replied.

Ellen rolled her eyes. "I never realized it before, but if you crack the same jokes over and over, they *do* sound more clever with time."

Hunter had known Ellen for as long as he could remember. Ellen was the type of girl you'd hear about on the national news from time to time, the feature story of the middle-school girl in a small community who wanted to join the boys' football team. Ellen had several female friends and maintained a feminine side that rendered no doubt about her sexual orientation. That said, while coming of age, she had related to guys as buddies more than flirts. Nonetheless, the guys had managed to view her as nothing less than female. Ellen had never lacked a date in high school. She'd proven a popular female with effortless appeal and brass balls, the Lisa Marie Presley of Hudson High School. The cheerleaders had hated her for it.

Ellen nudged Hunter, a knowing look in her eye. "Now that your significant other has left the room, why don't you tell us how your relationship is *really* going."

"We're fine." Hunter wiped buffalo sauce from his hands and reached for a wing from the jerk basket.

"Uh-uh!" Ellen shook her head. "I'm not buying that."

"What do you mean? Where's that coming from?"

Now Brendan rolled his eyes. "Ellen, let it go. He doesn't want you putting him on the spot."

Hunter gave him a quizzical look. "You're in on this too, whatever it is?"

"She has this idea …"

"It's not an *idea*. It's nothing much," Ellen said, "it's just—"

"She thinks something's *askew*," Brendan added, wrapping the final word in finger quotes and drawing out its last syllable in a hinting, teasing manner.

"I can see it in your eyes, that's all," Ellen said, ignoring her fiancé's jest, a look in her eye that said, *Come on, don't try to hide.* "I know you, and I know when something's off."

Hunter took a pull from his beer. A long one to buy himself a few seconds to think.

"I guess you could say it's maybe gotten a little, well, distant." Hunter said.

"Distant? For her or for you?"

"For me. As far as I can tell, she's content. Maybe distant is the wrong word."

"It's lasted six months. That's a new record for you." Ellen smirked. "Maybe you're not used to settling down."

Brendan leaned his forehead against his fiancée's. "Give him a break, Ellen. Considering how long it took *you* to settle down…"

"Fine," she said. "Point taken."

Hunter finished off another chicken wing. He grabbed another napkin from a small pile the server had left on the table and wiped his fingers. He shot Ellen a wry look. "You've never been Kara's biggest fan to begin with."

"Speaking of her, did she fall into the toilet bowl? Where is she?"

Hunter scanned the room and caught sight of her standing at a table near the restrooms, chatting with another couple. "Looks like she ran into someone she knows."

Ellen finished a wing and washed it down with a drink. "I like her. I'm not the biggest fan of *you and her.*"

"Babe, don't say that. And by the way, Kara's adorable." Brendan grinned. "Not as adorable as *you*, of course. You're adorable when you play mother hen. I'm sure Hunter will thank you for it when he grows older."

"Whatever. He knows I mean well." She turned back to Hunter. "It means I respect your relationship. As well as I know you, she seemed like a—let's say an outside-the-box fit. And you try so hard to make sure everyone else is happy, so I'm being your friend, making sure you're happy because you *deserve* to be happy."

If anyone could tell Hunter how to reach happiness, he would have loved to know. Given his struggle inside, he'd given up on the concept of full contentment long ago. Nowadays, when it came to romance and relationships, he wondered if the next-best thing was the best he could hope for. But he couldn't tell *that* to Ellen.

"I'm happy."

Ellen studied his eyes. Hunter felt his heart pound as he tried to maintain composure in his face. When it came to conversations, his biggest challenge in keeping his secret was to avoid appearing off guard. That might trigger suspicion: Ordinary remarks and observations seem random to other people until a change in the eyes or facial expression occurs. Then they wonder why the sudden change happened. When you harbor a secret in your soul, you notice double entendres that people never intended amid innocent comments.

Comments like, *One day, you'll find the perfect woman.*

At that, Ellen shrugged with an air of calm resignation. "Good. How's your back feeling these days?"

Relieved that Ellen had changed topics, Hunter eased back in his chair.

"Still sore, depending on the day. Feels fine now. I think it's stress."

An *A-ha!* expression filled Ellen's face. She splayed her hands in his direction. "I know what you need! You should try my massage therapist!"

Hunter choked on the beer he had just swallowed. With a few coughs, he managed to recover, yet couldn't help but laugh at the notion. "Yeah, right."

"I'm serious, Hunter. It's done wonders for me." She pulled her cell phone from her purse and started scrolling through her address book.

"*Women* go to massage therapists!"

"Not only women. You'd be surprised."

"How can you suggest that with a straight face?" Brendan teased.

"You're too chicken shit to go. Hunter isn't."

"I wouldn't be so quick to say that," Hunter joshed.

"When you got injured playing ball in school, didn't it feel better when I rubbed the spot for you?" Ellen asked Hunter.

"Yeah ..."

"So there you go. It's the same thing, only you make an appointment and my massage therapist is far better at it. Therapists have these awesome techniques."

"So I'm supposed to pay some beautiful woman to give me a back rub?"

"Yeah, a beautiful woman," Ellen chuckled. "I'd recommend the full body massage."

"Thanks, but I think I'll be fine without the magic fingers."

"Trust me. Here's the number for the clinic." She reached for a cocktail napkin, wrote down a phone number, and slid the napkin against Hunter's hand. When Hunter shot her a wary glare, Ellen held her arms out sideways. "Keep the number with you. If you change your mind, call the clinic and tell them you want an appointment."

Without a second look at the napkin, Hunter folded it and shoved it into his wallet as far back as possible, behind a twenty-dollar bill.

"And tell them I referred you," Ellen said. "I'll get a discount on my next visit."

Hunter shook his head at the whole idea, as did Brendan.

Kara returned and eyed the baskets of wings, which now sat half full. "Sorry, I saw someone I knew. Did I miss anything?"

"Not much," Ellen said. "Hunter's about to experience a personal renaissance."

Hunter rolled his eyes.

CHAPTER 4

On Monday morning, Hunter engaged in his normal routine at the office to start the workweek. He perused his calendar for upcoming appointments, then opened his email and deleted the junk items. Without fail, first thing on Monday mornings, a client would send an urgent question, which he would answer. When you face a problem, it feels as though that problem is unique to you. You don't realize how many others have faced the identical challenge. And in this case, Hunter offered a boilerplate answer.

To help keep his skills sharp, he spent time each Monday reading a sales-oriented newsletter or two in his email, searching for a tip that might help him seal his next deal. Especially in his current dry season.

This morning, Hunter decided to drink his coffee black. He poured himself a cup in the kitchenette down the hall, then settled back at his desk. He had an appointment after lunch, which left him a few hours that morning to conduct research online. Company websites, news stories, marketing software—

he tended to find his golden nuggets when and where he least expected them.

He sure needed one.

"Where are you?" Hunter murmured as he browsed news stories looking for any small, local companies that had announced plans to expand their operations or develop a new product.

"Please help me find it, God," he added. Throughout his days, Hunter tended to maintain recurring prayers to God. More like conversations with a friend than prayers.

Hunter sensed his job was in danger. How much longer could his drought last before the ceiling crashed?

His father had worried about his own job for as far back as Hunter could remember. The man, like Kara, had traveled on a constant basis all through Hunter's childhood. Most often, Hunter saw his father on weekends, and by that point, his father had grown exhausted and wanted to relax.

As a child, Hunter, on a constant search for connection with his father, found it difficult to develop the father-son bond he had seen among his friends' families. Even as a youngster, when he spent the night at a friend's house or joined them for dinner, he watched the interaction his friends' fathers initiated with their kids. It looked so effortless to Hunter, as if neither party tried, yet an unspoken bond existed between them. Pats on the back; words of encouragement; those final, extra seconds of rough-and-tumble play before dinner. The kids seldom requested those things. And when those incidents occurred, they just happened. None of his friends entered into verbal agreements to engage in that behavior with their dads.

Not a word spoken. Yet it spoke volumes to young Hunter.

Here at his desk, Hunter craned his neck around the entrance of his cubicle and caught a glimpse of sunshine through a nearby window.

Hunter recalled one Friday afternoon when he was seven years old. He had gotten home from school and had holed himself up in his bedroom. Sitting on the floor, thumbing through his collection of baseball cards, he separated his Cleveland Indians cards from the rest of the pack. He picked up his new Orel Hershiser card and admired its crispness, ran his finger along its firm edges. Its sharp corners took him by surprise as he tapped his finger upon them. His friend's father had said the team was on the road to improvement and might even make it to the World Series in a year or two. Hunter's eyes gleamed at the thought of going to a World Series game with his dad, though even at his young age, he knew his father wouldn't be able to go.

He'd heard a shout outside the house. Then laughter. The voice of someone several years older than Hunter. A voice, Hunter had noticed of late, that had developed a deeper timbre. Then he heard the voice of an adult who had joined in the fun.

Hunter made his way to the bedroom window. From his vantage point on the second floor, he looked down upon his backyard and saw Bryce, his fifteen-year-old brother, throwing a baseball to their father. From the sight of Dad's dark suit coat and blue, striped tie resting at the edge of the patio, Hunter figured his father must have just arrived home for the weekend a few minutes earlier. Bryce had caught him before he'd had a chance to walk into the house.

Donned in baseball gloves, father and son tossed the baseball to each other, back and forth. A rare sight, given Dad's constant travel.

Bryce's face beamed. He shouted something at their father, then planted his feet on the ground to ready another pitch. A sophomore in high school and a gifted pitcher, Bryce had qualified for the varsity team since his freshman year. He was *that* good. And Dad mentioned it often.

When he'd wound up for the pitch, he released the ball. A breaking ball! But Bryce hadn't given Dad advance warning. By the time it reached their father on the other side of the lawn, it had caught Dad by surprise. He reached to grab the ball—and took hold of it at the last possible second.

"Ooh!" Bryce's voice boomed. "You got it, old man!"

Dad laughed. "Almost threw my back out doing it! Great pitch. I used to pitch those back in school. Seems like a lifetime ago …"

Looking down from the window, Hunter wished he could be his big brother.

With a surge of energy coursing through him, Hunter raced to reassemble his baseball cards and return them to the shoebox he kept under his bed. If he hurried, he might get downstairs in time to get some tosses in. The sun would set before they'd finished with—

"Dinner time!" He heard his mother's voice bellow from the open window in the kitchen. A moment later, he heard her voice from the stairwell. "Hunter! Time for dinner!"

His heart sank.

He couldn't believe he'd missed the rare chance to play catch.

Hunter had never shared that memory with another soul. It struck him as random. Meaningless.

So why did he ache each time he recalled it?

Staring at his computer monitor, Hunter shook himself out of his stream of consciousness.

Doesn't matter, Hunter thought to himself. If he didn't focus on finding new clients, he might end up with a lot of time to play catch. And that would make the bills difficult to pay.

As he browsed through a list of results on a search engine, he dug the knuckles of one hand into his back, just above his waist, and moved them around in tiny circles. When he'd awakened that morning, his back had already felt sore. Now it really hurt. The discomfort ran from his lower back to his below his waistline. It would feel better if he got out of his chair and walked around the office, giving his muscles a chance to stretch, but he couldn't spend his whole day doing that.

Hunter thought back to Ellen's suggestion at the restaurant on Saturday night.

Maybe a massage was worth a try. It couldn't make matters worse.

Embarrassed at the notion, he started to think it through anyway. He could keep it discreet. He didn't need to tell anyone, did he? It wouldn't be the first secret he had kept in his life.

Did he still have the phone number Ellen had given him? He forgot where he had placed it, but his best guess would be his wallet.

Retrieving his wallet from his back pocket, he rifled through it, checking behind his credit cards, frequent-customer reward cards, business cards. He didn't find it. Then he remembered: Ellen hadn't given him a business card. She had written it on a cocktail napkin.

He fingered through the section in the back of his wallet, where he kept his cash, and—there! Stuck between a twenty-dollar bill and a five, he found a thin napkin folded in quarters. With one final glance around him, as if an informant had sneaked into his cubicle, he picked up his phone and dialed the number. A receptionist answered and asked if she could help him.

Hunter kept his voice low. He hoped the person in the next cubicle wouldn't hear him. He'd never hear the end of it.

"Hi, I'd like to, uh, make an appointment, please."

"I'm sorry, sir, could you please repeat that? I couldn't quite hear you."

Oh brother. Hunter sealed his lips tight. *No, I don't want to say it louder!*

"I'd like to make an appointment, please," he said, his voice a tad louder. "A massage one."

"We can do that. Have you visited us before?"

"No. Never," he replied, making sure she heard the second word.

"So you probably don't have a particular massage therapist you'd like to see. I can schedule you with—"

"Actually, a friend of mine goes there. Her name is Ellen Krieger. She told me to let you know she referred me. Whoever she sees is fine with me."

"Oh sure, I love Ellen! She always makes us laugh."

"Do you have an opening this evening? I'd like to stop by on my way home from work, if possible."

CHAPTER 5

The small lobby reminded Hunter of a sunrise.

From the framed prints on the wall to the color of the chairs, the room featured early-morning pastels in blues and pinks and sherbet oranges. On any other day, Hunter wouldn't let anyone catch him dead in a place like this.

Ellen better be right, he thought. At the sound of spa music coming from speakers overhead, he sighed to himself. Then the discomfort in his back caused him to shift at his waist toward his left, and he remembered why he'd come in the first place. He took a quick look around the room and breathed a sigh of relief to find it empty. No one would see him here.

He made his way to a receptionist's glass-topped desk. At the corner sat a glass globe filled with sand and seashells. A starfish sat atop the contents, as though a perfectionist had left it behind in her haste. Kara would have loved it here.

"May I help you?" asked the receptionist, who had wispy, sandy-brown hair and a winning smile. From a few feet away, Hunter could detect the scent of bath oils on her skin.

"My name is Hunter Carlisle. I spoke to someone on the phone this morning about a massage thing."

"Ellen's referral?" she said as she slid a sheet of paper into a clipboard. She grabbed a pen from a cup on her desk and handed both items to Hunter. "This is a client intake form. We'll need your name and address. Please also note any past injuries, health problems, or if you have a specific area of discomfort you'd like us to focus on."

Hunter filled out the form, noting the discomfort in his back as the reason he had made his appointment. He picked up a chill in the room but attributed it to self-consciousness about showing up in such a place at all. He returned the form to the receptionist, who started typing its details into a computer, and he took a seat on a plush chair.

A minute later, the receptionist waved him over to follow her.

"You caught us at a good time, between the afternoon appointments and before a lot of people show up after work," she said. She opened a door and allowed Hunter to lead the way inside.

Hunter swept the quaint little room with his eyes. "Do many guys show up here?"

"You're not the first," she replied with a smirk that implied she understood the self-conscious origin of his question.

Hunter's eyes went straight to a massage table in the middle of the room. Covered by a striped bed sheet, the table appeared a few inches longer than his height. One end had what looked like a cushioned doughnut, which Hunter assumed was for his head, with a hole for him to look through.

"Would you like the table warmed up?"

He had to grin at the thought. No one had ever pre-warmed a bed for him.

"I guess that's fine. Does it come with the package? I've never been to one of these places before." *As if she couldn't tell by now.*

She flipped a switch beside the table, took a final perusal of the intake form on the clipboard before leaving it on a small desk. As she did this, Hunter turned around and noticed a small bookshelf behind him. He examined its shelves and found books on various topics, from massage techniques and anatomy to healthy-living cookbooks and inspirational literature. A small boom box sat on top of the bookshelf.

On the other side of the room, certificates hung above a small desk. Hunter noticed two taller bookshelves accented with candles, lotions and oils. The room had a lightness to it. Tinted windows lined one wall, the kind where you could see outside but outsiders couldn't see you watching them. The receptionist adjusted the blinds that covered the window before getting ready to leave.

Hunter returned his attention to the massage table. How was he supposed to ask the most obvious question without appearing insecure or flat-out ridiculous? He decided to go the laid-back route.

"So how, uh, how much do I take off? You know, for the …" He nodded toward the table.

"Oh, that?" she said, her voice nonchalant, as though she answered that question more than any other. "Whatever you prefer. Half the clients stay in their undershorts, the other half gets fully undressed." With another perusal of the clipboard, she said, "Lower-back pain? How far down can you feel it reach?"

"Down to my waist." Then he clarified, "Farther below my waist."

With a nod of understanding, she replied, "It's up to you. It's easier to address the pain if you're fully undressed. It allows the therapist to make direct contact with the flesh. If you've ever tried to give your girlfriend a back rub, you might have noticed how the fabric, to an extent, blunts what you're doing."

She was right about that.

She pointed to the corner of the massage table, where a folded, pastel-green towel sat.

"You can cover up with a towel." She took a final glance at Hunter and winked. "It's not as awkward as you're thinking. When you're ready, go ahead and lie down on the table and make yourself comfortable. It'll be just a few minutes."

And with that, she walked out the door, closing it behind her.

Hunter took another look around the room, then closed the blinds a little more. He examined the tinted windows closer and tried to recall an instance where he *could* see in from the outside of one of these buildings, but nothing came to mind. His heart thumped. Why was he nervous? It was an appointment, that was all—albeit an appointment far outside his comfort zone.

With an exhale, he began undressing, tossing his clothes onto a chair in the corner of the room. As the layers came off, he was thankful he'd agreed to the table warmer. And the feeling of his bare feet on a carpeted floor that wasn't his home struck him as odd.

He put his fingers to the waistline of his boxer shorts, then second-guessed whether he wanted to take the plunge. But if Ellen was right and this would relieve his discomfort, then in the end, awkwardness wouldn't matter.

Plus he thought about the massage therapist. Despite the receptionist's claim, he still didn't believe she had many male clients. Would it be as awkward for *her* as it was for Hunter? In that case, the scenario gave them a level playing field. It would be no different if Kara had decided to become a massage therapist and started practicing on him.

He stepped out of his boxer shorts and tossed them on top of his other clothes. The chill of the air against his skin seemed strange. Then again, how many times had he changed clothes in a locker room? Same thing, he figured.

He climbed onto the table, face down, and managed to drape the towel over the area his boxer shorts had covered. He crossed his arms and buried his face in them, ready for a nap. He melted into the table's heat.

A minute later, when Hunter had all but dozed off, he heard a quick, quiet knock, followed by the click of the door as it opened. The massage therapist walked in and closed the door, back turned toward Hunter.

Hunter hadn't expected the therapist to be another guy.

Okay. Hunter braced himself mentally. He couldn't exactly race out the door. How stupid would that look? His mind raced in a matter of two seconds.

Hunter looked up again to take in the sight of the person as he turned around. Dressed in short-sleeved, navy-blue scrubs, the guy was a slender six feet tall. His short, blond hair carried a hint of red. Combined with his fair skin, it suggested a Scandinavian background. Hunter was a sucker for light complexions and that hair color.

"Hello, I'm Gabe Hellman." The therapist extended his hand for a handshake.

Hunter wriggled his arm from under his chin.

"Hunter ... Carlisle."

As they shook hands, Hunter noticed Gabe's forearms boasted a solid bulge, the type that develops when you spend a lot of time lifting heavy materials. He attributed this toned feature to the result of applying massage pressure day in and day out.

Gabe smiled and headed to the desk. In a split second, on his way there, his eyes flicked back to Hunter a second time. Something in that glance hooked into Hunter, caught him somewhere within. In that moment, Hunter wondered why the second glance had occurred, then assumed it was because Gabe didn't receive many male clients. Maybe the sight of a male client had taken him off guard. That made sense. After all, hadn't Hunter felt awkward coming here in the first place? And seeing another male enter the room for the appointment had brought Hunter himself to a halt. Maybe it had had the same effect on Gabe Hellman.

No, on second thought, Hunter was positive he'd seen something else in Gabe's glance. But he also knew how these situations went, how mixed signals occurred. It always turned out that way, as far as he could tell. So, in line with how he approached this type of scenario, he resigned himself to not read anything into what he thought he'd seen.

Reading between the lines left him disappointed every time, as it had with Jake Geyer a few days ago. And it reminded him of how alone he felt.

Immediately Hunter felt guilty for thinking such a thought about another man in the first place. He shook the notion from his mind. Hunter willed himself to appear indifferent, to hide any clues about what had tiptoed through his thoughts.

"So, Ellen referred you?" Gabe dragged a stool toward the massage table and sat down. "I love her. Any friend of Ellen's is a friend of mine." Gabe struck him as a guy-next-door type, but of a creative variety. He appeared confident, comfortable in his own skin. His voice carried a lilt, a subtle one, not overbearing. His enunciation contained precision beyond the norm, each word a dainty morsel.

"Yeah, she's … This was her idea. This massage."

Gabe gestured toward the clipboard with his thumb. "You're having back discomfort?"

"It comes and goes. Intensity changes by the day."

"And you mentioned on the intake form that it occurs in your lower back?"

"It starts a few inches above my waist and stretches south from there."

"Many people make appointments for that type of issue. For the vast majority who come here, massages help relieve the pain. Oftentimes, it's nothing medical, just stress-related."

"I figured the same thing." Hunter relaxed. He realized Gabe's conversation had eased him into comfort, though Hunter hadn't noticed it happening step by step. "I was an athlete back in my teens. Lots of pulled muscles, never a medical emergency."

If ice caught fire, it would take on the color of Gabe's blue eyes. A trace of bashfulness ignited inside Hunter. It melted the courage to look directly into Gabe's eyes, which left Hunter frustrated as he slipped further into the attraction zone.

But those eyes also communicated compassion, like Gabe understood—or, at least, *wanted* to understand—what Hunter told him. That alone caused Hunter to relax further. Hunter didn't experience that comfort often, especially among friends. Men didn't seem wired that way. Although Hunter didn't consider himself to need it often, he had wished for that connection every once in a while. And that subtle yearning had grown in the four years since he'd graduated college.

More than that, Gabe struck Hunter as familiar. Had Hunter met him before?

"What's your idea of heaven on earth?"

"Huh?"

"Heaven on earth," Gabe said. "If you could escape today, leave your life behind and go anywhere, where would that place be? What would it sound like?"

Was this his attempt at conversation? Nonetheless, Hunter contemplated his answer. He drew his arms tighter together beneath his chin, and his biceps flexed before returning to their mode of rest. "I'd drink a Red Stripe on the beaches of Jamaica. Or any island down there. Hot sun, hot sand, ocean."

Gabe shut the blinds completely, then dimmed the lights to a snug glow. He walked to a bookshelf and thumbed through a row of compact discs. "And the ladies, right?"

"The ladies?"

Gabe inserted the disc into the boom box and hit Play. The sound of steel drums coasted through the speakers at low volume. His hand lingered midair for a moment as he turned. "Sure. There's always a beautiful woman that ends up sitting beside you at the little grass-hut bar in the tropics, right?"

"Oh, right," Hunter said, humming to the drums before he could stop himself. He gave a halfhearted nod toward the boom box. "I like the music."

Gabe rubbed his hands together. To warm them up, Hunter assumed.

"I'll start at the top near the shoulders and work my way down," said Gabe. "When I reach your back, I'll focus more time there. Does that work for you?"

"Sure." Might as well. Hunter wouldn't know what to suggest as an alternate plan. He removed his arms from beneath his chin and settled them flat upon the table, one arm parallel to each side of his body. Then he shut his eyes, focused on the music, and anticipated the relief he hoped would come.

Gabe began at the lower edge of Hunter's neck, rubbing in concentric circles. His slender figure belied the strength in his fingers, which felt determined and firm. As Gabe progressed, he incorporated his fingers, forearms and elbows along surfaces and crevices in creative ways. Hunter picked up the faint aroma of unlit candles from the nearby shelf. Though he couldn't identify the scent, it contained a pointed, woodsy tone that kindled vibrancy in his senses.

As Gabe's arms brushed past Hunter's face, once again Hunter picked up traces of his masculine, invigorating scent. The hair on Gabe's arms possessed a wintry color tone, so fair that it glowed in the room's dim light.

Hunter sensed his physical tension heading for unseen exits. Muscles shuddered and settled inside him. He hadn't realized how much tension he'd stored until now, as his body melted into relaxation.

Though he kept his eyes shut, Hunter analyzed this massage scenario in the recesses of his mind. He probed the sensations and his responses to them.

He'd never had another man's hands or fingers on him like this. Well, that wasn't accurate. Back in school, he'd experienced it from team staff members after extreme muscle pulls. But today marked the first time a man his own age had touched him for an extended period of time.

This also marked the first time a man he'd found *attractive* had touched him like this. His belly quivered in a combination of sweet and sour. Hunter stifled it. What would Gabe Hellman think if he knew Hunter had enjoyed this moment for a reason that didn't involve tension or discomfort? Though he'd admit it to no one, Hunter found himself searching for an innocent way to savor the moment. He had a rare occasion to dip his toe into this experience, a simulation of physical affection from another man, without anyone knowing it. Just one more secret to hide within the walls of his heart.

After lying still and enjoying the contact for a few minutes, nervousness crept in—the sense he had treaded into territory he shouldn't have entered. With a mental sword, he attempted to slice away the attraction he felt. He constructed a wall to guard his heart from further exposure.

The salesman in Hunter couldn't help but break the silence in the room. It would also distract his own attention and help prevent his mind from wandering again.

"How did you get into this line of work?" Hunter asked.

"Not what you'd expected, huh?" Gabe's tone indicated he knew what Hunter had *really* wanted to ask—why a guy would become a massage therapist—and could appreciate the humor in it.

"I guess you could say it goes against the stereotype I had."

Gabe chuckled. "Stereotypes aren't always accurate, but they sure are convenient, aren't they?"

Hunter shrugged his shoulders but said nothing. His conscience reminded him of how much protection he'd found in the masculine, athletic stereotype over the years. It made for the perfect hiding place. Yet his greatest fear was that, one day, he would make a small—yet critical—error, and his house of refuge would come crumbling down on him.

Once, in a college psychology class, the teacher had remarked that, according to statistics, those dealing with homosexuality are more likely to be individuals we would *least* suspect. For men, we build an image of limp wrists, curves around a voice, and flamboyant or feminine qualities. But oftentimes, the instructor claimed, a homosexual is a man's man. Your favorite coach or star player. To this day, Hunter could remember his posture growing rigid in his chair at that remark. It had struck the fear of God into him. In that moment, the class of forty students felt much, much smaller. And in Hunter's mind, all eyes had turned toward him, waiting for him to blink first and thereby shoot his whole masquerade to hell. Hunter didn't know if the teacher's claim was true, but it had affected him more than he wanted to admit.

"Believe it or not," Gabe continued, "my career started with a summer job. The summer after my junior year in college, a friend of mine got me a job working in a hotel in Akron—you know, to earn cash. She worked as a massage therapist at the hotel and made decent money with it. They had me doing laundry at the hotel, so I delivered towels and sheets to her office. One day, as we talked, I took a look around her office, and she convinced me to let her give me a demonstration. It felt amazing." Gabe shrugged, working his way farther down Hunter's back. "It seemed like I could get the hang of it if I tried, so she started showing me techniques. After graduating college, I needed an actual job. So she convinced the hotel to hire me as an assistant while I earned a certificate in massage therapy."

"So what's your college degree in?"

"Fine arts. My emphasis was on performance art—acting, stage production." With a smirk, he added, "Not a lot of demand for actors in this area, and I needed to pay the bills. So years later, here I am, relieving the Hunter Carlisles of the greater Cleveland-Akron area."

Hunter sniggered. "And you couldn't ask for a better client, right?"

Gabe's eyes darted to a clock on the wall.

"For the remaining 37 minutes, you're my *favorite* client." Gabe continued with deeper, more prolonged motions in Hunter's lower-back region. "What's your field of work?"

"I'm in sales. Computer software."

"Sales? No wonder you're stressed."

"It's been a tough few months," Hunter said. Preferring not to delve into the details, he decided to tie up the loose end of the conversation. "But that's part of the sales industry. You have ups and downs."

As little as Hunter had said about the pressure he felt on his job, it had felt so good to get it off his chest. The way Gabe nodded, the compassion in his eyes, calmed Hunter. He realized he was in the company of someone to whom he could talk, one with whom he could open up, if he wanted to. Hunter didn't have friends who relished substance-based conversations. On the contrary, their conversations gravitated toward professional sports—which teams were in the lead in a division, which teams traded which players, the amazing play they'd seen in a game on television the prior night.

Hunter suppressed a smile. He hadn't realized how much he needed someone to talk to. He tucked away the notion for future reference.

Hunter drew his arms toward his head again, crossed them, and rested his head sideways upon his forearms as Gabe continued the massage. By this point, Hunter's bones had morphed into rubber and he'd started to breathe deeper. He kept his eyes open but retreated into his thoughts. He turned a candle into a focal point and examined its shade of anemic green. Without intending to do so, he found himself yielding to the massage and wading into its waters of vulnerability.

The slide of his towel jolted Hunter back into the moment. Though the movement was slight and the towel had shifted less than an inch, the contact of Gabe's fingertips on the flesh just below his waistline caught him off guard. Hunter jerked in reflex, which sent his body into one quick, full-scale flinch, the type of reaction that occurs when you catch yourself off balance.

Hunter had forgotten he wore nothing under the towel. He'd expected a female massage therapist and had given it no further thought. Until now.

Gabe halted at the abrupt motion.

"You okay?" Gabe asked.

"Oh, sure. I …" Embarrassed at having drawn attention to himself, Hunter tried to appear calm as he recovered from his own awkwardness. "I'd forgotten about the … never been to one of these massage things before, so I just … reacted."

Gabe nodded like he understood. He changed the subject as if he suspected nothing. "The discomfort in your back might relate to your sciatic nerve, which is why it would extend below your waistline. For that matter, it might have *originated* below the waistline and worked its way up."

Come to think of it, that was, indeed, how the pain traveled.

"When I address this area where the towel is," Gabe continued, "I try to uncover only a small area at a time and focus on that area so my clients have privacy. Maybe I should've mentioned that in advance. Does that work for you?"

More than you know. Relieved, Hunter replied, "Yeah, that'll work."

It still felt strange. Then Hunter reminded himself that people came to this place every day to have this work done on them. Gabe was a professional. And there was nothing exposed that people in locker rooms hadn't already seen. It went with the territory here, much as it had there. It just seemed more sensitive in this context.

For Gabe, this was part of the massage technique for lower-back pain, a matter of going through the motions. But Hunter knew he had given Gabe a second glance earlier, which altered the scenario and rendered conflict within Hunter's conscience.

He decided to endure it, though. If Gabe didn't have an issue with it, why should Hunter? And the whole point was to resolve the physical pain.

So Gabe continued, one bit at a time, exposing a small patch of flesh, working a massage into it, then covering it up again before moving on to the next patch. He progressed along the left side, then moved toward the right.

Hunter closed his eyes before he embarrassed himself again or caused suspicion. One side of him wanted to escape the moment. Another male's hands on a sensitive area reminded Hunter that he lacked answers and didn't have a clue how to *begin* to find them. At the same time, however, curiosity crept in. And so, while he used his closed eyes and deep breathing to signal neutrality toward Gabe's touch, the opposite rippled beneath the surface. Hunter remained fully aware of each movement. He examined every detail as it occurred.

Hunter had experienced a female's touch many times in the past, especially before he'd become a Christian. The sensation of someone touching him, with his full approval, where no one else was allowed, sent his hormones into a rush. Especially as a young teenager and the groping involved during those years of discovery.

But today? This was different.

It wasn't that Hunter didn't enjoy those touches from women. He did.

He just enjoyed this current physical contact more.

The roots of his attraction to women rested not in their sexuality, but in their beauty and tenderness. Affection rather than physical urge.

If the salesman in him were to convert his gender attraction into a percentage split, he would split it 60 percent to 40 percent. The needle hovered in both directions, but it tipped toward that 60 percent and toward the same gender. Such a close call. Unfortunately, those extra points caused him shame beyond words, and if it ever became public—well, Hunter didn't want to think about what the backlash would be among his peers. If that needle could just tip toward the lower percentage, life would become easier overnight.

Gabe had long hands, and the contact of his fingers sent solar warmth through Hunter's arteries. As Gabe progressed around the towel-covered area, Hunter tracked each section like the hour markings on a clock. When Gabe reached the fleshy surface of the four o'clock mark, Hunter felt himself stir, relieved he was lying on his stomach and wouldn't need to get up in the next few minutes.

Hunter knew he wouldn't forget any of today's details. He had carved them into his memory, where they would resurface later, as had countless other innocent scenarios that had morphed into a form both confusing and complex.

Hunter didn't want to enjoy the moment. But in truth, he *did* enjoy it. He wondered how disappointed God might feel about him right now. That concerned him most.

But in a short while, the moment ended with Hunter wishing it had lasted longer. With Hunter covered in full by the towel, Gabe moved south to the back of Hunter's left thigh and began working the firm muscles in his legs.

Hunter's mind veered back to when Gabe had first entered the room. Now he looked behind himself at Gabe, whose eyes remained glued to Hunter's leg, his jaw line firm as he worked, his face a portrait of concentration. Once again, Gabe looked familiar. Some people have one of those common faces, but that wasn't the case with Gabe. Not only did Gabe *not* have one of those familiar faces, his was unique and memorable. Few individuals possessed strong Scandinavian features.

"I can't help but think I recognize you," Hunter said, taking care to remain nonchalant. Granted, the question was genuine, but he didn't want to give Gabe any clues of interest beyond the platonic. When Hunter found himself attracted to another man, he overcompensated to conceal his interest. While growing up, when he was unsure the sentiment was mutual, he had disguised his attraction toward girls in a similar manner. "Have we met before?"

"The classic conversation piece." Gabe grinned. "The you-look-familiar starter."

"Seriously, I think I recognize you. I didn't try to sell you software, did I?"

"Not to my knowledge. But that doesn't mean we haven't run into each other at some point."

"Did you grow up around here?" Hunter asked.

"Yeah, down in Tallmadge." An area not far from Hudson.

"Did you play baseball? Maybe we played each other."

"I wasn't exactly the jock type, and it doesn't sound like you were involved in drama productions." Gabe stopped the massage for a moment. "Besides drama, I kept involved in the youth group at my church down there."

Gabe was a Christian, too?

A wave of shame hit Hunter. Christians consider themselves a family, showing brotherly and sisterly love toward one another. Hunter should have considered Gabe his brother in the Lord, yet he knew in his heart he'd lusted after him. Or had, at least, checked him out.

"I suppose you could've seen me perform in a play." Gabe continued with the massage. "Do you watch any of the community theater productions around here?"

"Can't say that I do …"

"Then you couldn't have seen me there." Gabe shrugged. "The only other drama I've done was downtown in Cleveland at a big youth event, one of those regional events where youth groups from a ton of churches in Ohio come together. But that was so long ago."

Hunter went rigid with shock and looked over his shoulder at Gabe. "Was the event called Youth Vision?"

Gabe halted, his face beaming with surprise. "Yes, that was the name of it! Ten years ago?"

"Yeah! I was sixteen back then."

"I was fifteen, so we're a year apart." Gabe resumed his work, making his way toward the bottom of Hunter's right calf muscle. "Wow, great memory! No wonder you're in sales." Then, in the subdued tone of an afterthought, he added, "Of all the people you could've noticed on that stage …"

For a moment after that comment, Hunter's guard shot up. He prayed Gabe didn't interpret it as more than a random memory, but Gabe didn't appear to have noticed. So Hunter relaxed again, resting his head on his arms to relish the final minutes of the massage.

For Hunter, the coincidence regarding their past left him with a feeling of satisfaction and ease regarding his massage. He couldn't recall the last time he'd felt so relaxed.

Gabe wrapped up the session by working his thumbs into the balls of Hunter's feet. Hunter glanced up at the clock on the wall and marveled at how fast an hour had passed. Gabe had the routine down to perfect timing.

"You mentioned you're not the type who makes massage appointments," Gabe said when he'd finished, "but I hope you'll consider coming back."

In that moment, Hunter could have sworn time slowed. Sincerity returned to Gabe's eyes, and his gaze seemed to linger for a split second—or maybe Hunter's wishful thinking had conjured an image all its own.

Gabe thumped his fingers on the massage table, which barely made a sound on the padded, sheet-covered surface. "I'll head out and let you get dressed."

With that, the men shook hands. Gabe headed for the door. As he took hold of the door handle, he peered back at Hunter. "Thanks for coming in. If you see Ellen before I do, tell her I said hello."

A final glance, a click of the door handle, and out walked Gabe. A pang hit Hunter's gut.

His skin prickled in the cool air as he removed his towel, slid down from the table's heated surface, and got dressed.

CHAPTER 6

"*An excellent wife, who can find? For her worth is far above jewels,*" the group leader read from chapter 31 of Proverbs. "*The heart of her husband trusts in her, And he will have no lack of gain.*"

Every Thursday evening for an hour, Hunter and fifteen other men met at one member's house for this weekly men's Bible study. The men ranged in age from early twenties to late fifties. Although they focused on specific books or topics, discussions tended to ebb and flow. Oftentimes, the group strayed off on a tangent, which led to spontaneous conversation in which members would ask questions or share their thoughts. By the end of each meeting, however, their focus came full circle and the group ended with prayer.

The group leader, Dan, wore a wedding ring which gleamed beneath the table lamp in his living room. "The writer is talking about the value of a wife," the man replied. "I think he's saying when you find a good wife, it's a gift from God. She completes you by filling an empty hole, the way Christ completes you when you give your life to Him. Maybe it addresses temptation, too: It can help keep our eyes from wandering. When it comes to romance, you find everything you need in her."

Some group members were married, others were single. Hunter had known a couple of them since his youth. Though he wasn't friends with them back then, they had become friends through these Bible study meetings.

Hunter joined this group upon graduating college and returning to town, and noticed his faith had grown stronger as a result. He learned from the experiences the older men shared. He'd also discovered he could bounce questions about life and faith against other members to gain insight or help him sort through scenarios. The group considered itself open to any discussion. At these Bible study meetings, Hunter had encouraged members through tough seasons, and he had confided about his recent challenges on the job. He felt he could share anything in his life and find support from the other guys.

Well, almost anything.

"Did you guys hear about the big event coming up next month?" asked Joe Garza, who sat at Hunter's left. Hunter foresaw a conversational digression on the horizon. "It's one of those extreme competitions where they incorporate army-training exercises and an obstacle course. Are you in, Hunter Man?"

Hunter cringed with regret. That sort of competition piqued his interest. Given his back discomfort, though, such physical exertion at this juncture didn't strike him as a wise endeavor.

"Normally I would," Hunter replied, "but my back's been giving me trouble lately. Extreme anything wouldn't be the best idea."

"I've had back problems ever since an injury in college," a thirty-something man chimed in. "I feel your pain, man."

"Catch me next time you hear of another competition like that, okay?" Hunter added.

"Will do." replied Joe, a guy around Hunter's age with dark, shaggy hair. So dark, in fact, he'd developed a five o'clock shadow by the time he'd turned fourteen. He'd played on the football team in high school, a mid-range talent who'd also acquired an unfortunate reputation for his hairy backside, a quality impossible to hide in the locker room.

Hunter shifted in his seat as he turned his attention to his own back, which, to his continued surprise, felt much better. Three days since his appointment with Gabe, and he continued to feel at ease. Gabe had proven Ellen correct. Hunter considered setting up another appointment next week to see if his progress would continue.

Dan brought the meeting to order once again, returning the group's focus to the topic of marriage and the verses he'd read in Proverbs.

Hunter's mind drifted to Gabe. He recounted random details about their encounter: the scent he'd picked up from Gabe's body wash, the confident touch of Gabe's fingers as they worked their way along his back and legs. As Hunter recalled the moment Gabe entered the room and the final moment before his departure, he tried, once again, to decipher whether Gabe's lingering glances had been real or imaginary. And if they were real, did they possess meaning beyond face value, or was that wishful thinking on Hunter's part?

Hunter felt a shudder of guilt at the thoughts that coursed through his mind regarding Gabe.

Shut it down.

Those verses in Proverbs had left Hunter frustrated. Bible verses regarding marriage and sexual relationships often did. Especially while he sat in the midst of a Bible study meeting or church service, where he might let loose a signal that he struggled with attractions they considered taboo.

Verses like the ones Dan had read in Proverbs also reminded Hunter of how *effortless* others found attraction to the opposite sex. It seemed to come to them naturally; meanwhile, he floundered alone, left to tussle and hide. It didn't strike him as fair.

Why did *he* need to be the one to struggle in an off-limits area, the one area he felt he couldn't discuss with anyone else?

Sometimes, when Hunter sat in the midst of a group of people, he wondered if he was the only person who struggled that way. Surely someone else understood. Surely he'd crossed paths with another individual who wrestled the same way and Hunter hadn't known it about him. Or, at least, Hunter *hoped* so.

Not that he wished his inner torment on anybody else. He just craved someone who could understand.

As the group continued its discussion, Hunter looked around and wondered if anyone else *in this room* faced what he did. Oh, what he would give to find out, but he wouldn't dare ask! Even if they dealt with the same thing, he knew they would deny it rather than face public embarrassment. That would leave Hunter humiliated with nothing gained. If anything, other guys went overboard in their efforts to quash mere *speculation* about their sexuality. Hunter could play that masculine game with the best of them, yet he wondered why they played the game in the first place. It made everything harder for the people who faked it.

He had considered mentioning the topic of homosexuality in the group, perhaps find a way to weave it into the tapestry of a related conversation, to gauge his peers' reaction to the topic without the distraction of jokes about it. But that idea led to apprehension. Hunter envisioned the suspicions that might arise from the fact he'd asked the question in the first place. And once those suspicions arose, then what? Even if the other guys engaged in an honest discussion and downplayed their suspicions, what would happen after the meeting ended? What if one member confided Hunter's question to his wife or friend, and *that* individual mentioned it to someone else during casual conversation? What if it ignited a rumor about Hunter Carlisle? Christians aren't perfect. They have weaknesses. Some give in to the temptation to gossip. If that happened, the chatter would spread like wildfire—and Hunter would lose control of his own destiny.

Any time he considered allowing someone to walk beside him through this inner hell, fear shut him down.

Fear of becoming the focus of gossip among people he knew. Fear of becoming the butt of jokes among people he'd never met.

Fear of disappointing his family, his pastor, other Christians he'd encouraged over the years.

Hunter's peers had remarked on the value he placed on his relationship with Christ. And Hunter knew that relationship—his faith—was genuine. But they didn't know the hurts that lurked deep inside. Those hidden facets made him feel like a hypocrite, even though he'd give anything to open up and confess what he'd suppressed since childhood.

He wanted help but didn't know to whom he could turn.

Back and forth. Back and forth. Back and forth.

That tug-of-war, which others might consider their exception, was Hunter's norm.

No way. He could never confide in anyone.

In the end, he told himself, despite the challenge of stifling a secret for years on end, at least he still controlled his own destiny. Nothing had erupted. He'd managed to keep it all contained within the dresser drawers of his soul.

"Okay, I'm just gonna say this," said a young guy named Ross, who sat across from Hunter. A student at nearby Kent State University, he'd started attending the group a few weeks earlier. "The whole lust thing—I don't know, it's a major challenge for guys."

Hunter's ears perked up.

"I guess it's okay to admit that here," continued the college student. "I've done okay so far, but a lot of the girls out there— well, they're just as bad about it as the guys are, you know?"

Lust for women. On one hand, Hunter admired the guy's honesty. On the other hand, Hunter *wished* that were his own admission. The guys could relate to it and provide encouragement. Hunter watched it unfold: the caring words, the you-can-do-it pats on the back.

"I struggled the same way," said a middle-aged man with short, graying hair. "My wife and I were college sweethearts, and waiting until marriage for sex—it was difficult to resist the temptation, but in the end, we both found it worth fighting for."

"It could be worse," Joe chimed in with a chuckle. "I mean, at least you're not gay, right?"

Hunter seized control of his facial muscles before his eyes could react. He felt his arm and leg muscles tighten as he fought to maintain his composure, the way he did any time a conversation in his vicinity turned to homosexuality, jokes or otherwise.

And like always, Hunter waited as each second doubled in length and time ticked slower. In a silent, desperate prayer, he begged God to cause the discussion to wrap up before anyone noticed how uncomfortable he must have appeared. Frustration simmered within.

Ross's face warmed to a shade of pink as he emitted a nervous laugh. "Yeah, you're right about that. No worries there."

Joe wouldn't say those things if he knew what it's like to deal with it, thought Hunter.

Focusing on his knees, a self-conscious Hunter didn't risk eye contact, convinced one glance or blink would betray him. Eyes are the window to the soul, according to what he'd read in the Bible. From his peripheral vision, he tried to glimpse the reactions from other group members, but he couldn't capture much while keeping his eyes down.

Though Hunter couldn't catch his facial expression, he could tell that Jesse Barlow, the preacher's son who sat beside Hunter at most Bible study meetings, had leaned back in the sofa with his arms crossed. Jesse, who was several years older than Hunter, observed the conversation but didn't say a word. Jesse had returned to town a few years earlier and Hunter had gotten to know him. Hunter pegged him as a reserved sort who said little but processed much.

Bible in his lap, Hunter kept his feet planted on the floor, pointed straight ahead. His heart pattered. He crossed his arms, the way he did when he relaxed. As Joe talked, he leaned slightly in Hunter's direction. Hunter's back muscles stiffened.

He responded to Joe's physical shift by leaning slightly away to maintain safe distance. He didn't want to attract Joe's attention—or anyone else's—and stumble into this conversation. Especially not because Joe happened to brush against his shoulder at random.

"What do you think, Hunter?"

In running through his checklist of damage control and face-saving options, Hunter now realized he had tuned out the whole conversation.

The question had come from Ross, the college student. From the first time they'd met, Hunter could see the guy looked up to him as a role model, an individual close in age yet established on a career path. Hunter had given him a tip for an intramural softball game and, by that simple gesture, had won the heart of a new buddy.

Ross's expression spoke of innocence, of someone caught in the canyon between adolescence and adulthood. Searching for answers, trying to identify the balance between enjoying life and walking in faith.

"What do I think about …" Hunter tried to buy himself a few extra seconds to think.

"I mean, you're single. Not to put you on the spot, but how do you handle it, the no-sex-before-marriage thing?"

Hunter exhaled, clucked his tongue, tried to remain calm.

Ross had intended the question as harmless. Sometimes you needed to know somebody else understood, even if it meant dropping your guard and exiting your comfort zone. Hunter met his eyes. The kid truly sought companionship through his struggle. Of all people, Hunter understood that need and found it difficult to turn his back on those who desired his support. Yet while Hunter wasn't ashamed of his no-sex decision, that didn't mean he felt comfortable talking about it in public. And now, of course, all eyes were on him. He saw the relief among a couple of the other young guys in the group. No doubt they'd thanked God that Ross hadn't asked *them.*

Hunter pursed his lips as he sought how to phrase an honest answer in a way that would help the kid.

"I wish I could say it's easy, but it's not," Hunter replied. "I've always looked at it as a decision that you stick with. Self-discipline, where you've drawn a line for yourself and, in any given moment, you choose not to allow yourself to cross it. That's how I try to handle it, anyway."

Hunter knew the answer was forthright. Granted, his private inclinations made his decision easier to honor, but his response was honest nonetheless. Silently he asked God if He was pleased with the answer he'd given Ross, and Hunter felt at peace that God was indeed fine with it.

"So when did you become a Christian, Hunter?" asked Ross.

That question brought Hunter back to life. Of all the milestones he cherished in his life, the day he had become a Christian continued to flood his heart with gratitude. If anybody wanted to know, he was eager to tell them about it. Its simplicity required no secrets, no filter on the words he chose or how he looked.

"I was sixteen years old," Hunter replied. "My sophomore year in high school. I didn't grow up in church, and my family wasn't religious. We weren't *against* religion; it was more like we didn't give it much thought. Over the years, my friends had invited me to come to church with them here and there. A lot of them were Catholic, so I'd visit Mass, where I'd watch the priest say one thing and the people respond. It was fascinating to see. But more than that, I'd look around and notice some of the older people, the ones you could tell had been around a while. The look in their eyes, the hope they held—as a little kid, I couldn't identify the why or what behind it, but it made an impression on me. That was all the church exposure I had as a kid, though: visiting church with buddies."

"So how'd you end up a Christian?"

"When I was a freshman in high school, a friend invited me to a Youth Vision meeting. It's one of those national organizations where they have chapters in all the schools. Our chapter met on Monday nights. You'd start off singing—not just church songs, but also Beach Boys oldies, oddball stuff like that, for fun. Then they'd have a Bible lesson with a lot of humor in it, the kind teenagers didn't find cheesy, with a message you could relate to. Then they'd have a fun activity afterward.

"I'd heard about Youth Vision at school—you'd hear people mention it here and there, like 'I was at Youth Vision last night.' A friend invited me for months before I decided to come. I had underestimated how popular the program was at my school. There had to be two hundred kids at the meeting when I showed up one Monday night! I ran into people I didn't even know were involved in it. I knew some of those people were Christians; I had no idea about others since I'd never interacted with them. The kids had a good time, and for an hour or two each week, the boundary lines dropped: the cliques, the popular kids, the artsy kids, the super-smart kids—everyone was along for the same ride. It intrigued me, so week after week, I kept going. Toward the end of each meeting, they asked if anybody wanted to become a Christian. One night, after attending for several months, I raised my hand to respond. I'd seen happiness, a contentment, in those other kids. They had peace, and it struck a chord in me. Wherever it came from, however they'd gotten it, I wanted it. If it was Jesus, then that was what I wanted. So I gave my life to Christ that evening."

Ross nodded. Maybe he'd had a similar experience in his life. No one in the group commented on what Hunter had said so far, so Hunter continued.

"Some people talk about an emotional experience when they give their life to Christ. I can't say it was that way for me. I simply reached out for what God made available to me. Afterward, step by step, growth took place. That's the way I'd describe how my faith has played out: a daily walk, step by step. But that first night, I found peace I'd never experienced, the peace you feel when you know any mistakes you've made in your life, or ever *will* make, are covered. I didn't have all the answers in life—I still don't—but I know my *biggest* question is answered."

For all the secrets he held, Hunter clung to the knowledge that God loved him in spite of them. His actions might not always please God, but he didn't believe it peeled away God's love from his life.

For all Hunter's faults, his faith was the one thing he'd never doubted.

CHAPTER 7

Hunter felt a bittersweet pang in his gut as he climbed out of his car and sauntered across the parking lot late Monday afternoon.

Though some discomfort had returned to his back by the weekend, he had noticed a significant reduction in its intensity since his massage appointment with Gabe a week ago. And although their conversation hadn't delved into great depths, it was the deepest conversation Hunter could recall in months. He felt as though a door had opened, like he had someone anonymous he could talk to, an individual who didn't know him outside of that context. Someone with whom he needn't worry about how his words would reflect upon himself. Although it was a massage therapy session, it had felt like the precursor to a "talk therapy" session, too. He appreciated the acceptance he found in Gabe's compassionate eyes.

Hunter enumerated those reasons to himself when he made another appointment for today.

While all of those details were true, another simple truth loomed larger: He looked forward to seeing Gabe again.

If asked, he wouldn't admit it to anyone. He refused to admit it to *himself,* at least verbally. His rationale, all those enumerations, provided the excuse he needed to see Gabe once more.

Curiosity lured him closer and closer to the building—to Gabe's clinic—before him. And Hunter yielded to that curiosity.

He didn't know why he yielded to it. He questioned whether he should. Perhaps he wanted to see what might unfold—an ulterior motive which triggered the nervousness he felt now. This was his final chance to resist his urge, climb back into his car, and drive away. He could pretend this moment of decision never happened.

As he walked into the clinic, Hunter determined not to let the somersaults in his stomach betray him. So he constructed another guard around himself, a nonchalant exterior, and prayed that God would prevent Hunter's tongue from getting tied up during conversation, the way it did when nervousness hit him.

He noticed the same receptionist who'd greeted him on his previous visit. Would she remember him from last time? He'd told her he wasn't accustomed to these appointments. Would she wonder why he'd shown up a second time?

She greeted him in the same manner as before, with the same effervescent smile. Hunter gave her eyes a quick perusal but couldn't read whether she suspected anything. If she did, he hoped she wouldn't make an offhand remark to Gabe before the appointment. But Hunter couldn't control that.

"You're Hunter, right?"

"Yeah, it's—I—yeah, I'm Hunter." *No, keep your words steady!* He took a deep breath to calm himself. Had she given his response a second thought? For extra coverage, he added, "I had my doubts, but the last massage helped ease my back. I decided to give it a second shot."

"Gabe works wonders," the receptionist said, "so he gets a lot of referrals and repeat visits. Clients also tell me he's easy to talk to."

Hunter gave a shrug of indifferent agreement, cautious not to reveal too much, and paid in advance. Several minutes later, he headed into the same small room as last time and closed the door behind him. He'd done everything according to the rules. He was confident the receptionist believed the only reason he'd returned was for the massage itself. A pure, platonic appointment.

Yet Hunter knew the truth. Part of him felt like a trespasser who had wandered into territory where he didn't belong. If he knew Gabe wouldn't mind, or that Gabe had the smallest degree of interest in him, he wouldn't have felt as edgy. But the mystery remained. Besides, the chances of Gabe's interest in him were slim to nonexistent. Hunter was positive he'd misread any signals he thought he might have seen last week. Well, almost positive.

Hunter prayed for God to settle the jumble in his belly. He wondered if God felt disappointed in him today. After all, Hunter could hide his motives from people, but God knew his every thought and action—and the intentions behind them. Nonetheless, whether right or wrong, Hunter waded into this scenario and trusted God for mercy.

Despite his questions about God's approval, Hunter sought temporary relief to his relentless battle. It's not like he sought a relationship or to *act* on any attraction he felt. He just sought a taste of companionship, the sensation of touch from someone he found attractive rather than someone he *should* find attractive. For once, Hunter wanted to be happy, even if it lasted one brief hour.

He undressed and laid down on the massage table. Hunter had decided to keep his undershorts on for this appointment. His decision rested less in personal preference than in the desire not to give away any clues about why he had returned. He could concoct an explanation if Gabe mentioned it.

Hunter heard the door click. A grinning Gabe walked into the room.

"So you decided to return, huh?"

Immediately Hunter felt at ease. "Yeah. I had my doubts, but you were right. It helped so much."

"Glad to hear it," Gabe chuckled. "You probably still have minor discomfort, but that can dissipate with time. Same music? Anything different?"

"Heaven-on-earth works for me, same as last time."

Gabe hit the Play button on the boom box and began working his fingers and thumbs into Hunter's shoulders. "Should I give your back extra focus again?"

"I'd appreciate it."

Hunter shut his eyes and listened to the steel drums. The rolling motion of Gabe's fingers summoned images of Caribbean ocean breakers.

A minute later, he heard Gabe's voice. "How's your job going? Last time, you mentioned you were under pressure. You figured it might have caused some of the stress in your back."

"Not much improvement there." Hunter weighed whether to open up further, then decided to step forward. "The truth is, I'm scared my job is in danger. Really scared. But I don't have actual evidence of it, and I'm not one to sound an alarm for no reason." Hunter opened his eyes and recounted his last few months. "I haven't changed any of my methods, so that didn't cause it. Do you ever feel like you're doing everything you can do, but nothing seems to work?"

"I can relate to what you're saying," Gabe said. "I have my ups and downs too. I have two business partners here, and all three of us go through our feasts and famines. People consider massages a luxury, which I can understand. People will put their kids, their food, their prescriptions ahead of a massage, and they should. When the economy hits a tough curve, our appointment schedules take a dive. That's when it gets scary."

"It's like you're falling, but you don't have a trampoline beneath you to break your fall."

"Trampoline?" Gabe said with a twist at the corner of his mouth. "The athlete in you has made its appearance for the day."

"I didn't say I was a gymnast," Hunter joked in return.

As each offered a halfhearted chuckle, Hunter peered behind him and caught a glimpse of that compassion he remembered in Gabe's eyes. Gabe's glance seemed to last a fraction too long, but Hunter figured that might be wishful thinking yet again.

"I've got a solution for you," said Gabe as he worked his way toward the middle of Hunter's back. "You should quit your job and move to the Cayman Islands. Just you and a hearty bank account. Hang out on the beach and catch your own dinner at night. No luxuries, no bills. Sound good?"

"I'm on board!" Hunter replied, playing along. "I doubt that would go over well with my girlfriend, though," he added out of habit, before he'd given it thought.

Hunter noticed a subtle shift in Gabe's conduct. Gabe's fingers didn't stop moving, but Hunter detected a drag in their motion, a split-second difference. Gabe gave him a quick glance, then returned his eyes to his work. Something in Gabe's countenance fell. It all unfolded in a few seconds at most, brief enough for Hunter to doubt the meaning behind it, but he was sure something had changed. Nonetheless, a grin returned to Gabe's face.

"Duty calls," Gabe responded at last, his tone good-natured. "What does your girlfriend do for a living?"

"Kara?" Hunter said, now regretting he'd mentioned her. "She's a buyer for a chain of retail stores. She decides what merchandise people will see on the shelves."

"Does she enjoy it?"

"Loves it. It comes naturally to her."

"I've always wondered how that works. Where does she find merchandise?"

"By traveling. Name a major city in the world and it's a safe bet she's seen it. For the most part, she focuses on New York, Hong Kong, Tokyo, the usual suspects."

"She must rack up frequent flyer miles."

"She's gone all the time."

"That can't be good. For a relationship, that is."

"It becomes routine. I go into pseudo-bachelor mode. It's convenient, if you think about it: You're in a relationship, yet you never lose your freedom. Then again, how close can you grow to someone who's seldom around?" Hunter shrugged. "In any case, it gives me time to think."

"About what?"

"The relationship itself. A distance exists to it, but it has nothing to do with physical distance. It's like my heart's not fully hooked up to it."

"Like the two of you want different things?"

Hunter considered that notion for a beat, but it lacked precision. "More like it's a ... I don't know ... a mismatch, maybe? The kind where a fraction of it is missing, or was never there to begin with."

That remark seemed to catch Gabe's attention. With a quick look, Hunter noticed a slight edge to Gabe's eyes, reminiscent of guilt or shame.

Hunter realized he had confided in Gabe more than he'd confided in anyone—especially another guy—about his relationship with Kara. He had intended to release a sliver of the burden, not open up to the fullest extent.

"Have you shared your job concerns with her?" Gabe asked.

"No," Hunter replied. "She's not around long enough to have that sort of conversation. By the time she returns to town and we get together, she's in a great mood. She wants to clear her head, have fun, no worries. If you knew Kara, how vivacious she is—she's the kind of girl where you don't want to pop her bubble."

Gabe's strokes slowed. "Wouldn't she want to know about your concerns, though? Just to be there for you?"

"Sure, she cares enough to want to know. But I play a role in that, too. The way I'm talking right now—I don't normally do this. It's not my nature to open up, wear my heart on my sleeve, pour out my problems to anybody who'll listen. I don't know why I opened up about all this to you."

"I'll take that as a compliment," Gabe smirked. "Besides, it happens all the time: People open up during these appointments. I guess they get relaxed enough to tell their life stories."

"Maybe you should've gotten your degree in psychology."

"No kidding. You're getting a great rate for psychotherapy, huh?"

Gabe resumed his normal work speed. He used his forearms to apply pressure to an area on Hunter's back, followed by broad sweeps of his thumbs, his palms flat against Hunter's flesh.

Hunter savored the touch. But Gabe's touch didn't ignite excitement in him today. Instead, his contact brought comfort to Hunter's heart. This was how it felt to be touched by someone who cared. Someone who wanted to know you for who you are, where the sentiment was mutual.

"I wouldn't be much help in the relationship department," Gabe said. "As far as your job goes, I don't have answers. We never have all the answers, but we trust God to show up and cover our bases. He's come through for me on my job more times than I could count. And suddenly, when things look darkest, you find yourself face to face with one of life's surprises, one you never would've imagined. *Better* than you would've imagined. One you never would've considered if you hadn't reached the low point."

Hunter allowed Gabe's words to hang in the air as he considered them. He wondered how low his own situation could go. Then he shifted his thoughts to what Gabe had said, that an unexpected development could arrive around the corner when he least expected it. A surprise sounded nice.

Then he remembered Gabe's mention of God covering their bases, and he grew curious about Gabe's faith.

"I still can't believe our paths crossed at the Youth Vision conference years ago."

Gabe looked up, his face beaming. "Small world!"

"The drama you were in: Didn't you play the part of a teenager who'd gotten hurt or caught in the middle of rough circumstances?"

"A teen whose parents had told him they were getting a divorce."

"Yeah, now I remember it," Hunter said. "That was an emotional scene. You must've practiced it a ton before the event started."

"We did. The role was natural for me, though. I grew up in a single-parent home."

"Your parents got divorced?"

"My dad was in the military. He fought in the Middle East during the war with Iraq in the early 1990s, the one where we defended Kuwait. It lasted less than a year, but he died in the combat zone when I was a baby," Gabe said. "I have no memories of him."

Hunter froze. So few military members had died in that war, you never ran into a family who had lost a loved one. "I'm sorry to hear that, man."

"No worries. Like I said, I don't remember him. And now that I'm in my twenties, I've moved forward. The downside, besides the obvious one of losing your dad, is that you don't have a male role model while you're growing up. That makes it tough."

"What about an older brother?"

"I'm an only child. And Mom never remarried. She remained committed to Dad after he died, even though she didn't need to." Gabe paused as if in reflection, then added, "My mom's faith pulled her through."

"So she's a strong Christian?"

"Yeah. I owe my faith roots to her. I grew up in church. In fact, I don't think we ever missed a Sunday service."

"Growing up without your dad must've made your faith that much more important to you."

"Let's say God became my best friend. Where my dad couldn't be present, God showed up and filled the void. It's not quite the same, since God is invisible. You can't feel Him wrap His arms around you—that's the one thing I always wished for as a kid, the feeling of having my dad's arms wrapped around me to bring me comfort. Even as an adult, it would be nice to have my dad's arm wrapped around me. But you don't always get what you want in life, right?" Gabe shook his head. He shaded his eyes with two fingers in an effort to hide embarrassment. "Whose therapy session did you say this is?"

"I don't mind." Hunter sensed his heart draw closer to Gabe's. "When you're in a struggle, it's good to know you're not alone. That's the worst feeling, when you feel like you're on your own, with nobody to talk to—*really* talk to, even if you don't know how."

Gabe said nothing in response. He offered a simple nod.

Hunter perceived a bond had formed between them and didn't want the chat to end.

Yet, before he knew it, the appointment had wound down. Gabe had already worked past Hunter's calves, down to his feet. And a few minutes later, Gabe finished.

Hunter got up from the massage table. They said good-bye and shook hands. Gabe's palm felt warm against Hunter's.

Standing still, Hunter studied Gabe as he headed toward the door.

When Gabe looked over his shoulder with a lingering gaze, Hunter thought he saw a trace of disappointment in his eyes.

Perhaps Gabe, too, thought the appointment had ended too soon.

Maybe he felt the way Hunter did about him.

CHAPTER 8

Hunter inhaled the scent of coffee beans fresh from the grinder. The kind that permeates your clothes and leaves you with a memento from a carefree portion of your day.

After meeting with a client in town, Hunter had decided to stop by his favorite deli for lunch. Regardless of what unfolded during his workday, an hour here felt like a miniature vacation. Even amid the bustle of the lunch hour, Hunter found this place conducive to leaning back and pondering. He often stopped here for a latte after work.

Located in a small strip mall in Solon, the deli was a local, mom-and-pop variety that specialized in creating its own unique coffee blends. Unlike many coffeehouses, the ambience here emphasized light, from the bright florescent lighting to colors of spring that washed over its walls. The grill ignited an aroma of charred meats and bread that traveled throughout the dining area.

Upon placing his order and paying the cashier, Hunter moved past the refrigerated display case of cream-cheese spreads, fruits and packages of lox. He eyed the baskets of bagels that hung behind the display case as he made his way to the pickup counter. The flavored brew of the day, pumpkin spice, gave him such a boost, he felt ridiculous for getting excited about a simple cup of coffee. The owner once told him they blended their coffee beans with real pumpkin seeds to capture their rich flavor and fragrance. By the time Hunter filled his cup, he found his order ready for pickup.

When he made his way to the dining area to search for an unoccupied table, he looked toward his right and noticed Ellen sitting in a booth against a window. Focused on the open laptop computer before her, she poked at a salad with her fork and took a bite. She didn't notice his approach.

"Hey gorgeous! Looking fine," he teased.

He hadn't expected Ellen to find humor in such a comment from a random passerby. And she didn't.

"Look, man, why don't you kiss my—" She raised her eyes and caught sight of Hunter, who couldn't hold back his laughter. "That never gets old for you, does it?"

"I'm batting 249-0 with it. A perfect record, and an impressive one."

"Are you gonna sit down, or just stand there and volunteer your services as eye candy?"

Hunter took a seat across from her and bit into his toasted Reuben sandwich. Its hot sauerkraut and corned beef exploded with flavor. Swiss cheese, which had bubbled beneath the rye bread, melted in his mouth.

"How long can you hang out?" Ellen asked.

"A half hour or so. I'm headed to the office after this."

Ellen had a stack of paperwork beside her, printouts of recipes for dishes Hunter wouldn't attempt to cook for himself.

Ellen's typical recipe contained an ingredient or requirement foreign to him. An odd spice or vegetable. A specific method of chopping, smashing or heating. Once, Hunter had watched a weekly cooking competition on television with her. The home cooks received an assignment to prepare a dish using a technique Hunter had never heard of. Yet the amateurs went right to work, as if everyone knew what the host's rambling had meant.

"Preparing a menu?" Hunter asked.

"A company dinner at a winery. It takes place in early October, so considering the environment and season, I'll propose a harvest theme. Maybe a special take on a baked ham, maybe a pumpkin bisque. I haven't figured out how I want to tie it all together."

Hunter admired Ellen's tenacity. After several years working in the kitchen at a four-star restaurant and observing chefs at work, she decided to branch out and pursue her dream of owning her own business. She started a small catering outfit in her home with a focus on local social gatherings and company dinners. Her first jobs were for friends and family members. As visitors passed along referrals, however, her customer base expanded.

"Have you opened your office suite at the pinnacle of downtown Cleveland yet?" Hunter quipped.

"Don't I wish," Ellen replied. "I've got a long way to go before I can rent my own office space. But I'll get there one day. Slowly but surely."

"You seem to have a steady job flow. You must be earning a decent living from it."

"It's enough to pay my half of the rent." Ellen paused, then added, "My roommate isn't thrilled when she discovers food and baking dishes spread all over the kitchen counter and dining room table every week, then opens the refrigerator door to find it packed with groceries we don't get to eat. But at this point, it's only a short-term situation for her."

"That's right, less than a year away! A perfect June wedding for a delicate princess." Hunter shot her a wink.

"The stuff dreams are made of."

Hunter sipped his coffee, which went down smooth. Liquid velvet, as he described it.

As Ellen talked further about her roommate and an argument she'd had with the landlord, Hunter got distracted by a sudden brush against his shoulder as two individuals made their way in opposite directions beside his booth. Hunter looked up.

"Sorry about that," said a guy around Hunter's age as he steadied a tray in his hands. Dressed in jeans and a short-sleeved polo shirt, he looked like the type of person who would wear short sleeves in the middle of winter. Judging from the jeans, Hunter guessed the guy had taken a vacation day.

"Oh, you're fine," Hunter said, waving it off with his hand.

As the guy walked past, Hunter noticed the flex of his biceps as he carried the tray topped with a sandwich and a heavy bowl of soup. The guy had added a dab of gel to his hair. His dark hair and deep skin tone suggested Mediterranean genes. Italian, probably.

Hunter returned his attention to Ellen and tried to focus on her face. Yet, at frequent intervals, Hunter flicked his eyes to the guy who had brushed his shoulder, who had settled into the booth behind Ellen, facing Hunter and in his direct line of vision. Unaware of Hunter's glances, the young guy started his lunch and paid Hunter no further attention.

"Anyway," Ellen continued, "when Brendan and I build our new home, I'll have plenty of room to cook."

"Wouldn't it be easier to buy an existing home?"

"Are you kidding? This new home is *Brendan's* dream. After all these years he's spent working for the construction company, managing projects and walking people through the options for their homes, he gets to build one for himself."

Another quick glance toward the guy in the next booth, then back to Ellen.

"In that case, it sounds ready-made for him," Hunter said. "Brendan probably has all the research and connections in place."

"Connections, skills, plus we get to buy all the materials at cost, which is a huge savings," Ellen said. "And since we're designing the house ourselves, we can plan the kitchen with my business in mind. I'd *love* to have a nice, big kitchen to work in. It's every professional cook's dream."

"A new home for a new marriage."

Ellen ran her fingernail along the edge of the table, peered at a distant point past Hunter's shoulder. "Everything changes from there, doesn't it …"

To Hunter, Ellen appeared absentminded. Perhaps she thought she recognized another customer standing in line. He tried to decipher what had captured her attention, but he wound up short and figured he had read too much into it. While Ellen tended not to hide her opinions, Hunter could tell she stifled her share of personal thoughts.

"How long before you build?" he asked. "Do you have an area picked out?"

"Oh, I didn't tell you! Over the weekend, we checked out a plot of land we love! I'll show it to you some time. If Brendan can negotiate the price and the sale goes through, we can break ground and get the walls built this spring."

Hunter sneaked another glance at the guy in the next booth, who thumbed through his phone as he ate. Studying the man's face closer, Hunter found it handsome. Not the chiseled features of a model or someone who would render Hunter too bashful to look him directly in the eyes, but everyday, all-American good looks. Hunter also had no doubt the man was straight.

At that point, the man gave a final tap to his phone and looked up. At random, his eyes landed on Hunter. Before Hunter had a chance to think, he cut his glance away from the guy.

Gritting his teeth, Hunter prayed the guy hadn't noticed. For Hunter, these frequent glances were akin to habit. He did it as second nature, without thinking about it first, the way other guys—and even Hunter himself, when his interests tugged him in the opposite direction—checked out females.

But there was a difference: If a female caught a guy checking her out, the guy could wave it off. She might even consider it a compliment. When Hunter checked out another man, however, the thought of getting caught left him anxious—as anxious as he felt right now. But the man, who returned his attention to his phone, didn't appear to give Hunter's actions another thought. Hunter whispered thanks to God, who had rescued him from another close call.

"You've got a big life change coming up, getting married. Are you looking forward to it?" Hunter asked. Then, reconsidering what he'd asked, he snorted and took a sip of coffee. "What am I saying? Of course you're excited."

Ellen reached over and gave his elbow a playful jab. "Way to go, Hunter Carlisle, ruining a bride's ride upon her fluffy cloud of bliss."

"You're right." He gave Ellen his most wicked grin. "Maybe you should give me another look at your engagement ring so we can giggle together over the size of the diamond."

"Great comeback. So you're saying women are pathetic?"

"Just trying to dig myself out of this hole I've stumbled into. My chances don't look promising, though."

"Don't worry, you're not the first to ask about the wife thing," Ellen said with a wink. "Why do you think everyone's shocked that I'm getting married?"

"I don't think *shocked* is the best word. I'd say it takes a lot of us by surprise because you've always been the independent type. You've had relationships, but you've never *needed* them."

"I do take care of myself, huh?"

"That, plus you're a ball-buster."

"Whatever. Be glad you're not on my enemy list, Carlisle." Ellen took a final bite of her salad before shoving the bowl aside. "In all honesty, I surprised myself by getting engaged—for the same reasons. It happened so fast. When Brendan popped the question, it threw me off balance. That doesn't happen much. Immediately, I said yes—just blurted it out before I had a chance to consider what was coming out of my mouth. But as the weeks passed, it started to make sense: Brendan and I love each other. Why not dive in? I mean, if you're gonna do something, why do it half-assed?"

"You have a way with words. You should include that in your wedding vows."

Ellen laughed as she sipped her iced tea. Hunter finished off his Reuben sandwich and picked at the remaining homemade potato chips. He felt the warmth of sunlight as it emanated through the window and settled on the back of his neck.

"Marriage changes everything. But it's a *good* change, right?" Ellen said. "It's not the kind of disruption that causes the roof of your life to come crashing down while you're still surrounded by walls."

Ellen seemed to step deep into thought for a moment, then shook herself out of it.

"Wedding plans are keeping me busy. Then again, there's never a convenient time to become extra busy," she said. "That's one difference between other women and me: They shriek over their weddings, making sure they fulfill every detail of an elaborate dream they've constructed for themselves since childhood. But for me, the wedding's functional. I love Brendan, and that's all that matters to me."

"It's your wedding. You should do whatever makes you happy. If simple makes you happy, more power to you."

"Brendan's parents have a different perspective on that. They want a big wedding and are paying for it themselves. I don't even know how it happened. It's like I woke up one morning, got into my car, and drove right into the middle of a fairy tale. Which reminds me, have you seen my magic wand? I seem to have left it behind somewhere."

Hunter leaned over and feigned a quick search. "I don't see it under the table …"

"Where, oh where, is my magic wand? Don't worry, it'll show up." She patted her seat. "I'll get comfortable, sit down on a comfy booth like this one, and then—*Ping!*—that magic wand will poke me in the ass when I least expect it. Watch it happen."

They chuckled together. Hunter took their trays to the trash receptacle, got drink refills for Ellen and him, and returned to the table.

"How's your back?" Ellen asked. "How long did it take for my little napkin with the massage clinic's phone number to hit the trash can?"

Hunter debated whether to keep his visits a secret, but decided he had no need to do so. Ellen didn't suspect anything beyond functionality.

"As a matter of fact, I took your advice for once."

Ellen plopped back in her seat with such force, her brunette hair bounced against her shoulders. "You actually showed up for an appointment?"

"Twice."

"And?"

"And …" Hunter sighed. "Okay, fine. It helped. You were right."

"I knew it!" Ellen beamed. "Gabe is a miracle worker, isn't he?"

"I feel much better. So I owe you my thanks."

"Are we talking eternal gratitude here?"

"Don't push your luck." Hunter focused on his coffee cup. He jiggled it in his hand and felt the liquid slosh around inside. "I couldn't believe what a difference the first appointment made, so I went again yesterday." He sipped his coffee and avoided eye contact. No telling what Ellen might decipher from it. "We got to talking, and as it turns out, our paths crossed at a church youth event, way back when we were teenagers."

"No kidding?" Ellen crossed her arms as a smirk formed. "It sounds like you got along well with him."

"We had a good time. We talked and joked around, shooting the breeze while he did his job. We're as different as night and day but got along real well. Great sense of humor. It made the whole massage concept … bearable."

"That Gabe is such a sweet guy. And you know I don't say that about many people." She shook her head in disappointment. "I wish I could find him the perfect girl. He's not seeing anyone."

At that, Hunter's ears perked up, but he allowed no outward signs of reaction. Feigning nonchalance, he said, "He's not?"

"Nope," she said, then snickered, "I must admit, I've wondered at times if Gabe is secretly gay."

Hunter almost choked as he swallowed his coffee. "Why would you wonder that?"

"I can't put my finger on it." Ellen squinted in thought. "A couple of his mannerisms, maybe an inflection in his voice. I don't know." She leaned forward. "What do you think, Hunter? You've met him. Did you notice what I'm talking about?"

Hunter gave a halfhearted shrug to indicate he didn't care one way or the other. His heartbeat jack-hammered.

"But then I give it more thought and realize I'm flat-out wrong," Ellen added. "He can't be gay."

"Why not?"

"What do you mean, 'Why not?' He's a Christian. You can't be a Christian and be gay, right?" Ellen said. "You all seem immune to it."

Hunter took a long draw on his coffee.

CHAPTER 9

When Hunter asked how Kara wanted to spend her Friday night, she said she wanted nothing but to curl up on her sofa with a movie. So Hunter left work an hour early, picked her up from the airport, and took her to her apartment, where they ordered from a Chinese restaurant around the corner. Now, with nothing but two glasses of wine before them on her coffee table, Kara nestled against him.

At first, she suggested they pick a movie from their streaming rental queue online, a film on which they could agree. But Hunter insisted she pick a movie she wanted to see—her perfect moment to relax after returning from two weeks in Paris.

Kara loved romantic dramas. The more tears, the better. And this film contained plenty of them. Hunter often teased her about her taste in movies because their plots always anchored on a death or illness of some variety. In Hunter's words, *I can tell you what will happen in this movie: Either someone dies in the beginning, or someone has an illness and dies a slow death through the film, or someone has a sudden death at the end.* And he was seldom wrong.

True to form, he found this particular film a tad too melodramatic for his taste. But what intrigued him was the fact that Kara, effervescent as she was—the young woman who kept Michael Bublé on constant rotation in her car—had such dark taste when it came to the films she watched. Yet when he looked around her apartment and noticed things like decorative flowers and scented candles, jars of bath salts and beads of oil or whatever they were in her bathroom, the fresh vegetables she picked up from a farmer's market when she stayed in town long enough to shop there, he saw signs of a woman who could probe the simplicity of life and uncover treasures the rest of mankind would overlook.

Hunter wrapped his arm around her and she nuzzled against him further. He listened to her breathing as it slowed. She reached such a point of relaxation, he couldn't help but check to see if she still had her eyes open.

On the screen before them, a married woman had wound up in an affair with a chef. It had started with an exchange of glances on a subway in New York. Before she knew it, she had created excuse after excuse to stop by his restaurant. In fact, she took many people in her life along with her. They knew she had met the chef. They themselves had met the chef, partaken of his cuisine, recommended his restaurant to their friends and family. Whenever the woman visited the restaurant, the chef would stop by the table to greet her fellow patrons, charming them with his wit and anecdotes of training in Paris. Upon closer examination, they might have noticed the chef had stopped by their table while ignoring all others in the dining room. They might have observed how close the chef stood to the woman.

The indicators were obvious. Yet no one suspected the woman and the chef had succumbed to their desires. Least of all, the woman's husband.

Now, as her husband searched for a specific necktie in their walk-in closet, the woman listened to his voice as he spoke from the other side of the closet wall. Torn between the shame she felt and the hefty price honesty would require, she vacillated on how to approach the subject with her husband. Hunter could see the angst in her eyes, in the way she pursed her lips, in the way she rubbed her temples. Despite his disinterest in the film, Hunter noticed he had clung to every detail in the scene before him.

Hunter sipped his wine. For the sake of his male ego, he decided to give Kara a little tease about her movie. He gestured toward the actress. "That woman's tormenting herself night after night. Why doesn't she get it over with and tell him the truth?"

"It's not that simple, Hunter," Kara replied in innocence. "She's conflicted. Her secret has spun out of her control."

"I don't know what she sees in the chef anyway. The two of them are polar opposites."

"It's not a matter of similarity. She has emotional needs that are rooted from when her twin brother ran a red light and got killed in an intersection on Prom Night. Remember that from the opening scene?"

"Yeah, but that was thirty years ago."

"It still scarred her. It was her *twin*, Hunter. A piece of her went missing after that night. She didn't simply lose her brother; she lost her best friend, her closest confidante."

"He was her brother, not her lover."

Kara released a playful sigh. "I *know* that, but it left her with unresolved issues and feelings of abandonment. So when she perceives that her husband loves his career more than he loves her, she feels like her closest confidante has started to abandon her all over again. So, now, she has these emotional needs that she wishes her husband could fulfill, but the chef has fulfilled instead. She's in a worse pickle than when she started, but she can't find her way out. All because of one critical mistake."

"Which was?"

"She thought she could solve her issue with sex. One night of intimacy. Forbidden fruit. But it solved nothing and created a slew of new problems for her."

Hunter hadn't read into the character's motivations the way Kara had. Then again, she was used to these films. His preferences veered toward movies that involved explosions in cars or skyscrapers. Now that he thought about it, Kara's and his preferences both involved people clinging for their lives. In Hunter's case, however, the characters clung in a literal sense— from a building hundreds of feet above rush-hour traffic in Manhattan.

As Kara grew absorbed in the film again, Hunter ran his fingers through her blond hair. He nuzzled his nose and mouth in her hair for a moment, inhaled the scent of jasmine. Kara didn't seem to notice, other than the absentminded response of running her thumb along the palm of his hand as she kept her eyes glued to the television, listening to every word.

Moving his head lower, Hunter twice brushed the nape of her neck with the tip of his nose, then planted a kiss on that spot. Closing his eyes, he tried to imagine himself in love with her. And although, considering his faith, he wasn't sure whether he should do this, he pictured her without clothes on. He had seen her in a bathing suit but had never caught a glimpse of what hid underneath. He relaxed, envisioned himself exploring the shapes and textures of what might exist beneath her layers of clothing.

Hunter wished he could arouse a sexual attraction toward her. Though he found women attractive, its foundation rested in outward appearance—the pretty factor—rather than a sexual desire.

Despite his attractions to the same gender, however, Hunter found peace in the fact that he hadn't *deceived* Kara. He had focused on her the way an attentive boyfriend should and had made an honest investment in their relationship. His distractions came by way of little tugs toward other men, temptations that tried to lull him into complicity.

That had been his destiny in every relationship, regardless of who his girlfriend was. Regardless of his fervency when his relationships began, his inner tugs would, in time, sabotage them.

Hunter *wanted* to be normal. He just couldn't find a way to get there.

With all his heart, Hunter wanted to be attracted to Kara. He wanted not only to find her attractive, but to *desire* her the way he knew she desired him. The way other men desired the woman with whom they shared a relationship. Though Hunter had tried to kindle that sort of desire on countless occasions, he wound up frustrated each time. His roots had anchored themselves so deep, not even sex could eliminate them.

Of that, Hunter was certain.

He had tried it once already.

It happened his junior year in high school, a few weeks after Hunter turned seventeen years old.

By that point, he had wrestled with doubts about his sexual identity for five years. He'd given it little thought at first. Growing up, he'd assumed he would get married and have kids. He'd had crushes on girls his age. As a young boy, he'd had girlfriends of the elementary-school type, where they would eat lunch together on occasion or dance together at the school's Valentine's Day party. Nothing had caused him concern.

Until the day curiosity hit. Hunter couldn't pinpoint when it happened; it camouflaged itself in a blur as it crept into his life. But at some point, he found himself wondering about the anatomy of other boys his age. By no means a fixation, it distracted Hunter, taking the form of images on which his mind would linger for a minute before he returned his attention to other matters. It seemed akin to a gnat weaving around his head on a hot summer day.

But his curiosity grew year after year. And by age seventeen, the notion of potential attraction to other males had caused him alarm. Yet he hadn't told a soul.

Hunter had given his life to Christ the year before. He'd heard stories of how some people, upon becoming Christians, experienced freedom from physical issues: a miracle healing or deliverance from alcohol or cigarette addiction. Hunter himself knew a classmate who'd had a penchant for vodka on the weekends but, upon receiving Christ, had lost the desire to touch another bottle. Hunter believed those testimonies were genuine and, in the case of the classmate, he'd witnessed firsthand the tangible evidence and the change in behavior.

So Hunter had wondered why, upon giving *his* life to Christ, *he* hadn't lost his curiosity toward the same gender. Not only hadn't he lost that curiosity, but he'd wondered whether God frowned upon him for experiencing the same attractions he'd experienced *before* becoming a Christian. He knew his conversion had brought significant change to other areas of his life—mental, physical, the way he treated other people—so he didn't doubt the impact of his faith. Instead, he concluded he faced a struggle that wouldn't end any time soon.

Nobody suspected he wasn't a red-blooded male. By his junior year in high school, Hunter had played baseball for years, and had dabbled in basketball, cross-country and other sports at leisure. He'd found his place with the jocks, the popular crowd at school, and had benefitted from the abundance of masculine connotations and assumptions that accompanied his status. Girls found his personality charming. They whispered about his brown hair and the golden specks in his green eyes. In the hallways, freshmen girls giggled when they found themselves the focus of his unintentional eye contact. Cheerleaders—even the gorgeous ones perched at the highest rungs on the slippery social ladder of adolescence—flirted with him, hinted at his taking them out. They wanted to be seen with him. They wanted a reputation as Hunter Carlisle's girlfriend.

No one suspected anything awry about Hunter Carlisle.

And Hunter did nothing to suggest otherwise. When it came to hiding his secret, he treated it like a baseball game, playing through an injury. Hunter laughed with the guys and flirted with the girls. When a beautiful girl sought physical contact, he would often oblige, within the boundaries he'd set for himself. Once he became a Christian, his confidence soared higher than it already had.

Jenna Coltrane was his first real girlfriend. A cheerleader Hunter's age, Jenna looked like a Barbie doll, with long, blond hair that shined on sunny days. Her bosom caught the attention of many teenaged guys. Yet Jenna possessed a down-to-earth nature which Hunter found appealing. Though she wasn't a Christian, she treated people with kindness. Hunter knew she didn't seek a relationship with him to build her reputation or to land herself a fairy-tale picture in the high school yearbook. In their time alone together, she asked him questions about life and held genuine curiosity about his views.

Hunter and Jenna's relationship began when they attended a homecoming dance together as friends. From there, they studied together in the evenings, spent weekends running around with their mutual friends, and, when the weather wasn't too cold, huddled together in front of bonfires in Jenna's backyard. Jenna had an inherent sense for navigating a high school relationship. Hunter, along for the ride, followed her lead. Though he held a secret, Jenna ignited self-confidence in him. When he was with her, hope emerged that his sexual struggle might dissipate with time, that he might awaken one morning free, banishing his secret to the past without further consideration, the way he would toss aside a bad dream.

That didn't mean, however, that Hunter didn't feel uncomfortable when Jenna started talking about expanding their physical border. He found the concept of sex frightening—not the act itself, but how he would accomplish such a feat with her. He found her attractive, but in a way that made him feel alive, not aroused. Sexual attraction toward her was absent. Not that he found the concept of intercourse with Jenna repulsive; rather, the concept struck him as bland. He simply felt ... nothing.

Besides, sex outside of marriage went against the teachings of his newfound faith.

Sex seemed unfair to Jenna, as though Hunter's consent would give her an inaccurate impression of what their future together might hold.

No, he thought to himself, *I couldn't do that to her.*

But it was her idea, right? He hadn't *asked* for it.

Maybe God could turn it around for good. After all, God wouldn't want him to remain attracted to other men, would He? When playing basketball, you couldn't always score alone. Sometimes you needed an assist.

One Friday night in February, Jenna's parents were out of town. Hunter's parents had given him a midnight curfew. Hunter and Jenna wouldn't need that much time.

Before leaving town, her parents had locked their liquor cabinet but had overlooked a few bottles of wine they kept in a refrigerator in the basement. By the time her parents would look through those wine bottles, they would assume they had drunk the missing bottle around the holidays and forgotten about it.

Instead of looking forward to losing his virginity and proving to himself that we was, indeed, a heterosexual male, a muffled anxiety churned in his belly. It lasted the entire week leading up to that Friday night. By the time he arrived at Jenna's house, Hunter still didn't have a clue how he would get through what lay ahead.

According to Jenna, it wouldn't be her first time. She'd done it once before, but nothing that would relegate her to the "slut" category. Hunter had confided about his virginity, to which Jenna had said she understood and would guide him, if that would help. That had removed some of his pressure. The alcohol helped numb his fears.

The evening played out faster than Hunter had expected.

Jenna had some of her favorite music playing, songs by Justin Timberlake and Rhianna. Though Hunter had spent countless hours inside Jenna's home, it seemed different that night. The furniture in the den, a reflection of Jenna's parents' taste, reminded Hunter he wasn't an adult. And when he followed Jenna into her bedroom, Hunter felt as though he'd wandered into another world. No matter where he looked, he saw signs of their youth: the book bag on the floor beside a small desk, a stuffed animal he'd given her on Valentine's Day, the blue-and-white pom-poms she'd used at football games.

Nervous, Hunter trembled. He felt tremors in his bones and prayed Jenna wouldn't notice, but how couldn't she? Even his teeth started to chatter before he forced them to stop.

Jenna removed his shirt and ran her hands along his chest. Hunter closed his eyes, tilted his head back, and breathed deep. He felt himself calm. The alcohol crept through his limbs and felt like sunshine radiating through his veins.

They wasted little time on foreplay. Before Hunter knew it, they'd removed their clothes and slid beneath the sheets. Though the furnace buzzed in the house, the sound of winter wind whipping outside the bedroom window sent Jenna into a shiver. Hunter ran his warm palms, back and forth, upon her shoulders.

Hunter felt relieved. The awareness of his nakedness in a new place and the chill of the sheet against his bare skin stimulated him as he hovered over his girlfriend. Yet he couldn't reach complete arousal. He said nothing. Jenna stroked him and it helped, but the fact that his sexual desire wasn't aimed toward her had introduced an invisible barrier, a force field, between his will and his physical ability.

Jenna's eyes were closed, for which Hunter was thankful. He feared his face might betray his concerns.

He grinded against her. He laid kisses upon different areas of her body. Nothing seemed to work for him. Desperate, Hunter started to panic inside. Beads of perspiration lined his brow.

He couldn't keep buying time. He had to enter her at some point, but she would notice if he wasn't fully aroused. Surely it would take away from her satisfaction. What could he do?

Hunter winced at the idea. But he had run out of options.

Shifting his mental focus from Jenna, he escaped into the corridors of his imagination. Hunter had always had a weak spot for his friend Randy and had filed away mental images of him from numerous occasions.

As Hunter concentrated on those images, blood rushed down to his torso and he felt himself increase in size. Hunter and Jenna, slick with perspiration, moved together in rhythm. Hunter's mind swirled.

And before he knew it, they finished.

Jenna relaxed. Exhausted, Hunter panted to recapture his breath. He rolled over beside her and felt his entire body go limp on her bed. She reached for his hand and entwined her fingers with his.

For the first minute after they finished, Hunter felt thrilled. The pleasure had proven different from anything else he'd experienced. He felt as though he had passed a milestone, conquered an undiscovered land.

But when Hunter considered the bigger picture of what he'd done—or, more accurately, *how* he'd accomplished it—guilt overwhelmed him fast.

He peered at Jenna, who had fixed her eyes upon his, a gentle yearning in her irises and the shape of her eyelids. In Jenna's eyes, Hunter could see her heart had bonded with his.

For Hunter, however, the bond felt lacking. Emotionally disconnected. Conflicted.

The truth was, he cared for Jenna from deep within his heart. She had trusted him, and he knew he had taken advantage of her trust. The realization sunk in the waters of his soul.

Yes, that night had been her idea. Hunter could try to justify it however he wished, but deep down, he knew Jenna's perception of what had occurred was in stark contrast to his.

She believed he had desired her, that he had focused on her as they moved together. Jenna had engaged in the presence of the moment, while Hunter's mind had strayed. While whimpers of satisfaction had escaped her lips, his thoughts had traveled elsewhere.

Jenna had focused on Hunter. Hunter had focused on another man.

You only get one opportunity to lose your virginity. And when Hunter lost his, it wasn't even real. The experience felt dishonest, as if he had taken something not only from Jenna, but from himself, as well.

Another secret he could never reveal.

He wrapped his arm around her and she cuddled against him. Her perspiration had evaporated, leaving the flesh of her upper arms clammy and cool. He planted a soft kiss on her temple because it seemed the right thing to do. After all, he didn't know what to say.

In the weeks afterward, despite his efforts to convince himself otherwise, Hunter knew his sexual encounter with a woman hadn't cured him as he had hoped it would. The realization left him more confused, more disheartened, than ever.

Moreover, Hunter found himself in spiritual anguish. Knowing he had trampled his values as a Christian—engaging in a sexual encounter outside of marriage—made him feel worse. He imagined Jesus looking down upon him from heaven. How displeased He must feel in him, Hunter thought. That was the hardest part of what Hunter had done: the feeling that he had let God down. Shadows of torment crept into his soul as Hunter recognized he could never rectify what he'd done—the deception, the lust, the disobedience to God.

After a month of shadows dancing in his soul, Hunter decided to do what he always did when he'd stepped outside of God's will: He returned to God. One night, unable to fall asleep and restless at the thought of going to school in the morning with a half-night's slumber, Hunter's mind drifted once again to his encounter with Jenna. He whispered from his heart to God's heart.

"Lord," Hunter whispered, "I really let you down this time. The hardest part is the wall I've constructed between You and me this past month. There's nothing I can do about the mistake I made, but I can't go forward with this guilt anymore. You said Jesus paid for it at the cross, so I'm trusting You to forgive me and take care of it."

Hunter sensed God's presence. In truth, that presence had never left him; Hunter had felt God trying to wrap His arm around him in the dark moments of the past month, but he hadn't opened himself to God's love and forgiveness. But that night, alone in his bed, as awareness of God's mercy flooded Hunter's heart, a tear of gratitude trickled from his eye and Hunter drifted to sleep in peace.

"Looks like the movie grabbed your heart after all," came

Kara's voice, soft.

Hunter startled, unaware he had drifted into memories past. "Huh?"

With two fingers, Kara reached over and brushed the tear that had escaped from his eye.

CHAPTER 10

The basketball hit the rim with a muted clang.

It deflected toward Hunter, who caught the ball, dribbled it several feet from the basket, then halted. With the ball in both hands, he swiveled at the waist to his left, then to his right. Jesse Barlow, mere inches behind his back, shadowed him. When Jesse, who was over six feet tall, spread his arms, their breadth limited Hunter's options. A drop of perspiration slid into Hunter's eye, which he wiped against his shoulder. Another drop trickled past his upper lip and brought the taste of sodium to his tongue.

Hunter faked to the right, then dribbled to the left, just fast enough to get Jesse off his tail. Hunter passed the ball to his friend Rex, whom Hunter had known since high school. Rex dribbled farther down the court, as two guys darted for him. At the moment one of them reached Rex, before the guy had a chance to extend his arm, Rex rocketed straight off the ground and launched the ball toward the basket for a three-point jumper.

"You did *not* just make that shot!" Jesse shouted in good-humored disbelief.

Rex shrugged. Jesse shook his head. Hunter and the other guys joined in the laughter. And with that, the six of them decided to call the pickup game to an end. They headed for a bench at the side of the court, where they had set their water bottles and phones, along with their keys and wallets.

On Saturday mornings like this, frequently Hunter and several friends met at the basketball court at Hunter's church to shoot hoops. Between these pickup games and his weekly Bible study meetings, Hunter had the opportunity to hang out with Jesse Barlow or Joe Garza a couple of times per week. The other three guys didn't attend Hunter's church. Having never had a faith-related conversation with Rex, Hunter couldn't determine where he stood on the matter. Hunter knew that neither Randy Gresh nor Matt Toenjes were Christians. Hunter had known Randy since childhood. Matt was a graduate student at Akron University.

Hunter wiped his face with his T-shirt, which was drenched with perspiration. The October air chilled his skin dry. His palms, coated with dust and grime from the basketball, felt caked. He could smell the basketball rubber on his fingers. Hunter associated that scent with invigoration, a scent that had proven one of the few constants in his life, regardless of his age.

Randy nudged Matt and said, "You coming tonight?"

"Definitely. Last week was crazy, man!"

"Where are you guys going?" Joe asked.

"Last Saturday night, we met up with a couple more guys and decided to hit some clubs," Randy replied. "The ladies, man, I'm telling you what …"

"Nice, huh?" Rex said.

"And at one place, we met two girls who'd shown up together," Randy spread his fingers, the way a bard might share an ounce of folklore with a captive audience. "These women had it all. One looked like a model, the kind of body you'd like to—"

"Randy got her number," Matt interrupted.

"What about you?" Hunter asked Matt.

"We'll sharpen Matt's skills tonight," Randy said. With that, he took a swig from his water bottle and leaned back on the bench, his head resting against a chain-link fence behind them. "If you're ever a bachelor in the near future, Carlisle, we'll need to take you to those clubs."

"Oh sure, because random hookups at clubs are right up my alley," Hunter joked.

Though Hunter fit in well with other guys, he said little. Once he graduated college, he grew more introspective and found less need for ordinary banter. As a teenager, he'd proven much more vocal about his opinions on women and other topics.

He couldn't explain why, but his mind now turned to a random Friday night as a teenager. Hudson had won its football game that night. High school students had packed into cars, grabbed french fries and shakes at a fast-food drive-thru, then parked at a strip mall on Streetsboro Street, where shops had closed for the night. A fall breeze nipped at Hunter's cheeks. He'd arrived with Rex, Rex's girlfriend, and two other guys, all crammed into Hunter's car. With a shout, the five of them climbed out and rested their butts against the car as they ate.

As more cars arrived and screeched to a halt, whoops and hollers from football players and others in Hunter's crowd combined in volume. Cheerleaders and other girls shrieked and cackled. Boyfriends and girlfriends groped. A car stereo blared, its subwoofer sending shudders along the asphalt pavement. Teenagers meandered from one car to the next, some to socialize, others in search of a significant other.

Hunter wasn't in a relationship at that point. He had dated a girl earlier in the summer, a fling which had dissolved after a few weeks. By the end of summer, his friends itched to hook him up with someone, but Hunter had resisted their pressure. As a result, by the time the school year started, girls considered Hunter one of the more eligible bachelors.

"I'm freezing out here!" Shelly Gruber ran up and threw her arms around Hunter, her thighs a cold pale under her short cheerleader skirt. She nuzzled against him. He opened his letterman jacket to allow her inside, then closed the jacket around her and held it shut with his arms. Her body brought welcome heat to his own, and he could feel her tiny tremors as her shivering began to subside. She had set her curly, sandy-brown hair in a ponytail and wrapped it in a ribbon of blue and white, the school colors. Hunter and Shelly flirted more often than they held normal conversations.

Hunter wished the embrace meant something to him, but he decided to play along anyway. Maybe it would cause the other guys to ease up on their remarks about his laxity in the romance department.

"Of course it feels frigid to you," Rex's girlfriend said to Shelly. "The game's over. Why don't you wear something over your legs?"

"I totally forgot them at home." Shelly bent one leg at the knee and lifted it a few inches to show Hunter. "I'm dying out here! Look, I've got freakin' *goosebumps* all over my legs, my arms—geez, I can feel them all over my *ass!* Hunter, I'm gonna need to borrow your pants, too."

The group howled with laughter, Hunter included.

"Yeah, Carlisle," Rex shouted with a clever grin, "what *does* it take to get in your pants?"

Another eruption of laughter, its volume double this time around. Hunter took the joke in stride, wondering if the lights in the parking lot could reveal whether he'd blushed. Rex had no idea how nervous such a comment made Hunter. Self-conscious, Hunter sought a way to deflect attention from himself.

"You did a great job tonight," Hunter whispered, holding Shelly's gaze.

She tilted her head and considered his comment. Her eyes swept across his face.

He picked up traces of spearmint on her breath as she leaned in to kiss his cheek.

Hunter now focused on the basketball net before him as he took a long drink from his water bottle. The church building sat about twenty yards away. The Saturday-morning sky had grown overcast, but he could see the sun's outline through the veil of clouds. Joe sat beside him on the bench. Grabbing the basketball at Joe's feet, Hunter twirled it on his fingertip.

He could smell perspiration on Jesse, who sat on Hunter's other side and bantered with Joe. Hunter looked over at Joe, whose forehead still had a wet sheen from his exertion during the game. Though he no longer needed to, Hunter wiped his face again with his T-shirt, taking his time. As he did, he turned his head a notch, eased his eyes toward his right, and caught a glimpse of Joe's arms. Joe must have started working out, Hunter figured, based on the extra tone to his bicep, which flexed slightly as Joe scratched his head. Hunter slid his eyes down to Joe's legs, which were toned, as well. They, too, shined with perspiration. Unaware of Hunter's attention, Joe, in an absentminded manner, reached down and brushed the sweat from his legs.

Regretful, Hunter shut his eyes, gritted his teeth at the knowledge that he had just checked out his friend, though it wasn't the first time Hunter had done so.

Ever since middle school, curiosity had challenged Hunter's friendships and taunted his conscience. Regardless of the innocence with which he began a friendship, Hunter would, for no particular reason, notice a physical characteristic he found attractive about that friend. Once that happened, unknown to the other person, Hunter's mind introduced another dimension to how he viewed that friend. With time, Hunter's curiosity got the better of him and he'd find himself wondering about the individual, picturing them in ways he knew he shouldn't.

On occasion, a friendship emerged and Hunter would survive several months without thinking such thoughts. He would hope it meant a pure, untainted friendship had materialized in his life. But sure enough, in time, he would take note of a physical characteristic, which would then set his imagination in motion; it had taken longer than usual, that was all. While others took friendships for granted, seeming not to give them a second thought beyond their face values, Hunter grew angry at himself for coupling friendship with an ulterior additive. He wished he could see his friends the unpolluted way they saw him.

He craved to be normal.

Sitting beside Joe and the other guys reminded Hunter of how, oftentimes, the activities he enjoyed came paired with a unique challenge. Hunter could endure it, as long as he didn't allow his mind to wander at the wrong time.

While growing up, Hunter spent countless hours in locker rooms before and after games and practices. He was used to the environment and the people surrounding him, many of whom had attended school together since kindergarten.

Those locker rooms always felt cold to him. And their environments—concrete floors and walls, the musty scent of socks, the cacophony of locker doors slamming and water dripping and voices echoing—all seemed to join forces to reduce the temperature a few extra degrees.

Hunter was a freshman in high school the first time he saw his friend Randy naked. They ran cross-country together. When they discovered they kept comparable paces, they ran side by side during practice to help motivate each other. As a result, they started and ended their runs at the same time.

Although the school year hadn't yet begun, practices had started several weeks prior, in early August. While Hunter found northern Ohio summers comfortable due to their lack of extreme heat and humidity, running for miles would cause anyone to sweat. By the time Hunter returned to the school campus at the end of practice, he was drenched. He slowed to a walk for a few minutes, his cool-down period, which eased his perspiration but also brought a cool, gluey quality to his skin. Randy's blond, wavy hair, now sticky and a shade darker with dampness, had plastered itself to his scalp.

Hunter and Randy had dodged the seniors and picked lockers beside each other for the season. At the end of their first cross-country practice, they made their way to their lockers in the last row, at the far end of the room, and maneuvered their combination locks. Hunter was exhausted, but Randy had run cross-country in middle school and maintained a trace of invigoration after the long run. Randy released a heavy exhale and sifted through his locker. Hunter needed a minute to recuperate. He took a seat on the bench to give his quivering legs a rest and rubbed the fatigue from his eyes.

By the time Hunter looked up, Randy was in his boxer shorts and ran his fingers under the waistline before giving the shorts a tug, letting them drop to the floor without a second thought.

Hunter had been Randy's friend for as long as he could remember. They had watched afternoon cartoons together as kids. They had built forts in the woods. They had had gym class together in elementary school and middle school, where they had simply changed shirts and shorts before and after. They had participated in many activities together, seen each other in countless contexts. But Hunter had never seen his friend naked.

Whatever innocence had existed to their friendship vanished in that instant.

Without warning, their world had changed. Randy didn't know it, but Hunter did. It caught him off guard. Another secret to bury.

Randy rummaged through his locker, sorting through items for the first time, unloading from his gym bag a few items he would store in his locker. From where Hunter sat, he could only see his friend from the back. He had considered himself physically comparable to Randy: They weighed about the same. Hunter was a couple of inches taller. Girls found both of them attractive. But now Hunter wondered how far the comparable characteristics went. And in a matter of seconds, he edged closer to a boundary, one from which, once crossed, he could never retreat. Once he saw something, he had seen it. He couldn't remove it from his mind.

Yet Hunter found his curiosity piqued.

Randy, preoccupied with his locker, wouldn't notice. But Hunter had to be careful. He had to be able to appear normal should Randy turn around unexpectedly. And Hunter needed to look preoccupied, as well, so he bent over at the waist and set a personal record for the slowness with which he untied his shoes. Then, without turning his head, he allowed his line of sight to inch in Randy's direction. At that point in his life, Hunter believed God existed but didn't know much about Him; nonetheless, he sent up a prayer that he wouldn't get caught. The seconds slowed to a crawl.

Randy's feet were the same size as Hunter's, but his toes looked more defined. His legs had a firm tone due to his regular runs. Earlier that summer, Randy's family had spent a week at the beach, so he'd developed a dark tan. His tan stopped just above his knees, where the length of his swimming trunks had ended, a solid border line between light and dark. Above that line, his skin color turned from summer to winter. His buttocks looked flatter than Hunter's, almost as though they didn't quite exist. As Hunter removed his shoes, he swept his eyes higher and noticed a few dark specks on Randy's back, which Hunter recognized. He had returned to familiar territory.

But Hunter had one more unanswered question. One quick glance upward to make sure his friend was still preoccupied. Then Hunter leaned forward and reached down, taking his time removing each sock but careful not to take so long that Randy would notice.

Hunter still couldn't see. He scooted forward, then leaned farther down, as if he'd simply approached his sock removal from the wrong angle. He glided his eyes toward Randy again and caught sight of what he'd sought. Like Hunter, Randy had entered puberty the year before, a conclusion he'd drawn when Randy's voice had deepened. His pubic hair was a shade lighter than Hunter's, which confirmed Hunter's suspicions, given Randy was a blond. Hunter concentrated on Randy's torso for a split second, made a mental calculation, and noticed Randy's penis was slimmer than his own, more vertical and shapeless, and was about a half-inch longer than Hunter's.

As soon as Hunter drew his conclusions, Randy whipped a tan towel from his locker and wrapped it around his waist. But Hunter now had a mental picture he knew he could never erase. The awareness of what Hunter had done brought a mix of stimulation and regret. He had satisfied a desire yet felt he had betrayed a friend.

Hunter felt himself stir beneath his shorts. He swore under his breath and closed his eyes, willed himself to calm, and managed to regain control of functions.

"Man, you're so slow," Randy said. With the towel covering his pale midsection, he looked tan from head to toe. "Practice must've worn you out."

Hunter looked up at his friend. Randy wore a broad grin, the same grin he displayed whenever he joked around. Hunter detected neither hesitation nor anger in his friend's eyes.

Hunter drew a breath of relief.

Randy hadn't noticed anything. Hunter was safe.

"You were right to start running during summer," Hunter replied. "I'll be in the routine after a couple of days, though."

"You coming?" Randy asked, nodding toward the front of the locker room where the showers were.

"Yeah, be there in a minute," Hunter replied.

With that, Randy disappeared around the corner. Hunter rose to remove the rest of his clothes. The cool air felt awkward against his bare skin, as if he'd entered unnatural territory. They hadn't showered after sports in middle school, so again, he prayed that, if there was a God, He would protect him from embarrassment in the minutes ahead.

Approaching from several feet away, Hunter could hear a dozen showers running and knew the room would be crowded. When he entered, he noticed a thin cloud of steam hung in the air, which meant other team members had occupied the room for a while. The humidity caused a sweat to break out along his brow. Students of all grades, from freshmen to seniors, filled the room. Shouts and laughter echoed against the tiles that lined the walls and floors. The room had an open layout. Shower spouts lined its perimeter.

Not far from the entryway, Hunter found an unoccupied spout beside Randy. Self-conscious after what had happened minutes earlier, the location near the entryway provided Hunter a security blanket, an easy escape in case he needed to make a fast exit. Randy's proximity might prove convenient in case he needed a quick distraction through idle chatter.

Hunter tossed his towel aside. The prickly coolness returned to his bare skin. When he turned on the hot and cold water knobs, the water felt ice cold and sent a chill up his spine. A torrent of goosebumps ripped across his flesh. Hunter sucked air and adjusted the knobs to locate a comfortable balance—another reminder he had entered unfamiliar territory. Randy, his blond hair drenched and dark, gave Hunter a nod as if to say, *Of course you're here. Nothing out of the ordinary.* Meanwhile, the neighbor to Hunter's right finished up, turned off the water, and departed, leaving the last spout along the wall unoccupied.

Howls of laughter erupted from the other side of the room and gave Hunter a jolt. He turned around to locate the source of the noise and found a group of juniors and seniors bantering back and forth. *What a difference two or three years makes,* Hunter thought. The guys must have worked out in the weight room throughout the year, judging from their sculpted upper bodies. Hunter felt insecure by comparison, then reminded himself that most freshman were as undeveloped as he. Tempted to look further, he gritted his teeth, and turned back to the task at hand, stifling his urge.

He hated that urge. Why did other guys get to enter environments like this without a second thought, while he had to struggle the whole time? While they joked around, he had to fight to maintain his physical composure. If he didn't, he knew the circumstances that followed would torment him for the next four years. What if he were to stir *right now?* If anything embarrassing happened, it would become a leech to his reputation, latching on and drawing rumor content as its lifeblood.

Even the smaller scale scared him: Assuming he made it through today, he would still face tomorrow … and a week from now … next month … next year. How would he survive? The odds didn't look good. Hunter groaned within himself at the notion of the constant battle he would face, day after day, for years to come. What was he supposed to do, quit? Sports were his passion, but that meant a price for him to pay—a price which, as far as he knew, nobody else in this room would ever know for themselves, a price they would never need to pay. At age fourteen, he already worried about how his own physical dimensions compared to his peers, those private details others might mention about him during idle chatter. And on top of that, he had to worry every day about whether his groin stirred at the wrong time? It struck him as unfair. Why did he get stuck with this?

This sucks, he muttered to himself.

Hunter saw a light shadow creep across the tiled wall at an angle in front of him. Keeping his eyes straight ahead, he focused on a patch of discoloration in the grout along the wall. He sensed the presence of someone else, and sure enough, he heard the water start. Gritting his teeth again, Hunter tensed.

He shouldn't look. He knew he shouldn't. He'd had enough for today.

Whoever it was, the guy didn't say anything, so Hunter assumed they had never met. He squinted, focused further on the wall tiles, increased his speed so he could put an end to his suffering for today.

One more minute. That's all he needed to do—make it through one more minute, then he could escape into safety and get the hell out of there. Randy had left already.

The temptation felt electromagnetic, tugging his eyes toward his right. Hunter fought to face forward. But he wondered who stood next to him. Casual, forcing himself to keep his eyes shoulder-level or above, Hunter glanced over and recognized the guy. A sophomore. Hunter was correct, they had never met, but he had seen the guy earlier. Had someone called him *Anderson?* His last name, probably. Of all people, though—Hunter hadn't just noticed him when practice started. A good-looking guy, Hunter had *wondered* about him. People appeared to like him, but he didn't carry an air of cliquish popularity. Once, when Anderson looked in his direction during practice, Hunter darted his eyes in another direction, well aware of the weakness he sensed within himself and afraid it might reveal itself in his eyes. Now the guy stood beside him. Droplets of water dotted his tan shoulders. The running water brought a sheen to his back.

Hunter's temptation returned. Over and over, a constant cycle, all within seconds.

Fight, Hunter! Fight it off!

Determined not to give in, Hunter grunted and turned the water knobs in front of him. The water shut off. He was almost in the clear. He wiped his face with his hands and ran his fingers through his hair twice to shed the excess water.

Damn it, don't do it!

The tug felt so strong. An invisible force of some kind. Hunter knew it wasn't physical, but it sure felt like it was. Resistance was so difficult.

Hunter felt himself weaken.

No! Stop!

It would be so easy to look. One quick glance. Nobody would know, right? It wouldn't cause harm to anyone else.

But no, Hunter was sick of this fight. He didn't want it in his life, so resist it. Fight it off.

The water kept running from Anderson's spout as he lifted his arms. Hunter clenched his jaw. The fight wore him down.

Oh, fuck it. It's just one look. Get it over with, then you won't want to do it again.

Anderson washed his face, his hands blocking his vision. Hunter turned to walk away but allowed his eyes to linger downward, toward his right, as he turned.

Another mental picture. Front, back. Hunter filed it away in his mind. Although he hated to admit it, he did like what he saw and, in that instant, felt lucky. He would never need to look again. He had a memory.

A few moments later, heading toward his locker, Hunter grimaced in shame.

Here on the church basketball court, Hunter had covered his lap with the basketball, but now felt safe to stand up. All felt normal below his waist.

Hunter grabbed his keys and said good-bye to his buddies.

Upon turning his back, his countenance fell.

His pace more sluggish than usual, he walked toward the parking lot and unlocked his car with his keychain remote. The car's alarm mechanism emitted a quick bleep.

"What's wrong with me, God?" he asked.

CHAPTER 11

On Monday, Hunter's mind returned to his conversation with Ellen the previous week. She, too, had wondered if Gabe was gay? Now Hunter was curious.

He should fix his attention upon his relationship with Kara, Hunter told himself, but a piece of himself felt drawn to Gabe. Hunter couldn't put his finger on why, but in the short time they had known each other, he found comfort in Gabe's presence, in knowing Gabe was near. Though Hunter wasn't accustomed to confiding in anyone, or sharing his concerns or passions, when he was with Gabe, he wanted to.

The best way Hunter could describe it was that Gabe possessed a quality Hunter needed in his own life, a puzzle piece that could fill a void.

What that void was, Hunter didn't have a clue. Or did he?

Ellen's remark about Gabe continued to pique his curiosity. He pondered details about Gabe and his background; whether he was, in fact, straight; and whether he'd had girlfriends before. Hunter wanted to know. There had to be a way to find out from

Gabe, but he didn't know how to ask without causing Gabe to wonder why he'd asked in the first place.

Hunter grew annoyed at the fact that he wanted to know. Deep down, he knew why he wanted to know about Gabe. He had traveled this road numerous times: one big cycle in his life, upon which he had treaded over and over again; the enemy in his life that never disappeared, the one he couldn't vanquish. Each time the cycle began, he tried to remain strong but, with time, weakness always settled in. Even now, Hunter felt his resistance crumbling and he resented it.

Yet he moved forward with it anyway.

After work on Monday, he drove to Gabe's clinic for his next appointment, which, Hunter admitted to himself, he could now classify as a weekly occurrence. In a recent phone chat with Kara, he'd finally mentioned his appointments with Ellen's therapist, and Kara hadn't given it a second thought. Hunter no longer felt awkward showing up at a massage clinic, not that he would admit it to anyone but Ellen and Kara. When entering Gabe's clinic, though, it was more like he *forgot* to worry about what people would think—at least *inside* the place.

"So yeah, when I first started, I was flat-out scared," Gabe said, as he worked the heels of his hands into the crevice between Hunter's shoulder blades. "A brand new business, not many clients." He paused and asked, "How's this feel for you, working between the shoulder blades like I'm doing?"

"Feels fine," Hunter replied. "So you started out from ground zero? No clients at all?"

"I had a few. Even though I'd worked at a hotel and served out-of-town guests for the most part, I still had several local people who showed up for weekly appointments. When I started my own business, they followed me here, and word of mouth spread. But with two business partners, we were able to spread the risk and bear the costs better."

"It still must have been challenging, though," Hunter said. "Even with partners, you would've had overhead costs before you opened your doors, right?"

"To say the least," Gabe chuckled. "The three of us emptied our bank accounts to invest in this place, but we believed in what we were about to do. We researched the facts and felt confident we could grow."

"As long as you grew before you went broke."

"Exactly." Gabe thought for a moment, then moved farther down Hunter's back with his fingers and thumbs. "God showed up for me in that situation. To this day, I look back and can't imagine how He did it. My client base grew on a slow, steady basis, but I had a full schedule before I knew it. I'd look at my appointment schedule week after week and shake my head. The clients seemed to multiply, yet I couldn't pinpoint where or how it happened. Kind of like that Bible passage, where Jesus multiplied the bread and fish to feed the multitude. So when I think about my clients and thank God for them, that's what I call it: my bread-and-fish situation."

Before the appointment started, Hunter had wondered what they would talk about. Given his sales career, Hunter found small talk easy. Once he located an effective ice breaker, he was home free. But when Gabe walked through the door, his eyes lit up, and Hunter could tell Gabe was glad to see he had returned. That dissolved Hunter's defenses and rendered conversation much easier. With Gabe, Hunter didn't need an ice breaker; the ice melted and evaporated on its own. It felt as if they had picked up where they had left off a week ago. Although they had known each other but a few weeks, Gabe felt like a friend, and Hunter sensed Gabe felt the same way toward him.

Hunter had never had a friendship like that, where he could speak without barriers, without worrying what the other person thought of what he said.

Hunter's male friendships now struck him as surface deep, a matter of hanging out and having fun. Those interactions involved a continual flow of talk, but not about things that mattered. They didn't *confide* in each other. And in light of this friendship with Gabe, Hunter realized he didn't know some of his own friends well at all. He could list their interests and behavioral tendencies, but he didn't know who they were, down in their souls.

Hunter also found Gabe's faith appealing. While some people spoke of their faith as a sidenote, a hula-girl ornament on the dashboards of their lives, Hunter recognized Gabe's faith as sincere and relevant. When Gabe spoke of God and God's role in his life, how God had come through for him in various scenarios, Gabe meant it. He verbalized the sort of relationship with a Savior that Hunter himself possessed in his own life. When Hunter spent time with Gabe, he sensed a bond with him as a fellow Christian.

"How about your job?" Gabe asked. "Any improvements over the last week? New clients?"

Hunter shifted on the massage table and found a new spot for his belly. "The good news is, I signed a new client last week—a small one, but I'll take anything."

Gabe stopped his work for a moment and spread his arms sideways, palms out, clearly excited for him. "Great news! It's a step in the right direction."

"Thanks. It doesn't do enough to save my butt on the job, though. You're right, it's a positive development and I'm grateful for it, but it doesn't erase all those months of deficit. Because it's such a small client, I'm concerned when my boss sees it, it will disappoint him. To be honest, I can't escape the feeling I'm in danger. I'm really worried I could lose my job—that's how bad it looks to me."

"Maybe you should talk to your boss, get his point of view, decipher what you're truly dealing with, rather than what you *think* you're dealing with."

"Maybe so. I hadn't thought of that."

"Do you interact with your boss often? Do you ask him for feedback?"

Such a simple notion to overlook, Hunter thought. His other friends didn't offer ideas like that, and neither did Hunter for them—their conversations never even ran *that* deep. "I've never leaned on my bosses like that. I suppose I've always gone my independent route and figured I'd find a way to tread water." Hunter shrugged. "But you're right, it's worth a try."

From his peripheral view, Hunter could see Gabe had furrowed his brow in concentration, not on Hunter's back but on something else, as though debating whether to put words to it.

"I hope you don't mind my saying this, because I enjoy having these conversations," Gabe said at last, "but I find it interesting that you confide all this in me and not your girlfriend. I mean, don't get me wrong, I'm honored." Gabe gave his words another thought and waved them off, shaking his head and covering his eyes with his fingers. He continued down Hunter's back. "Sorry, I didn't mean that the way it came out. Forget I said anything."

Gabe didn't appear suspicious of Hunter's motivation for coming here at all. Before he appeared embarrassed, he'd had a matter-of-fact expression on his face. Hunter didn't want to let Gabe's curiosity hang, so he considered how to respond.

"The truth is," Hunter said, "it's more than her travel, the physical distance, that keeps me from confiding in Kara. I don't know, maybe it's because when you're a guy, you think you need to put on a performance for people—the whole hunter-gatherer thing, the strong man. And then, when you run into challenges, you don't have many people to turn to because you've spent all those years building that stalwart image. You can't turn around and destroy the persona everyone has of you, the one you constructed."

Gabe nodded, said nothing.

"I'm talking in circles," Hunter said.

"No, it makes sense." Gabe considered Hunter's words. "Actually, I understand more than you know, but I could never figure how to describe it." He grinned, then added, "You have a way with words."

"I don't think anyone's accused me of *that* before," Hunter said with a glint in his eye. "Seriously, though, have you noticed we can't be real with many people? But *you're* genuine. It's like I can be real with *you,* and you won't judge me for whatever stupid things I say. I can lay things out on the table and I won't need to live it all down later."

Gabe moved his thumbs in a broader, circular motion. "I appreciate hearing that."

"Guys don't say thanks enough."

"They don't seem to. But if I'm not like others, it probably has more to do with the fact that I'm not much of a social butterfly."

Something in Gabe's words caused Hunter to pause. He maintained a laid-back tone in his voice and a nonchalant expression on his face, for Gabe's sake rather than his own. To let Gabe know he cared.

"Do you spend a lot of time alone?" Hunter asked.

"Let's say I have plenty of time on my hands. But I'm okay with it, so it works out fine."

Hunter didn't like hearing that. A chunk of his heart sank, like a link had gone missing from a chain that connects a boat to its anchor. Without that link, the boat would drift into isolation.

Gabe had an air about him that Hunter considered a blessing. How could Gabe's depth end up going to waste? Did people stay away from Gabe, or did he choose solitude? Hunter didn't find much comfort in solitude, but he knew people are different and had come across a wide range of personalities in his career, brief as it was. He couldn't imagine people keeping their distance from Gabe. If anything, Hunter himself wanted to spend *more* time around him, not less.

Then an idea dawned inside him. He didn't know how Gabe would respond, but it was worth a try.

"Just a thought," Hunter said, "but would you want to hang out some time? I mean, we're different, but we get along, right? The talks and all."

Gabe's countenance brightened. Hunter could tell that, even though Gabe guarded himself against looking too eager, Hunter's invitation had made his day. Hunter felt his own heart warm.

Gabe regarded Hunter for a beat. "Sure," he said, "let's do it."

"Would tomorrow night work? We could catch a game on TV at my house. No social-butterfly stuff to worry about."

"Sounds like a plan."

The more Hunter thought about the idea, the more he looked forward to it.

The massage continued. When Gabe reached Hunter's lower back, he incorporated his elbows, which he had not used in prior appointments. "I switched my technique here. How's it helping? Better?"

"I think so."

A minute passed in silence. Hunter felt a nerve snap and felt a release of tension as he exhaled.

"I think I *heard* that one," Hunter snickered.

"Yeah, I heard it too. I found a knot down here. I'll bet you feel better after that."

Hunter reconsidered Gabe's words about solitude and, once again, grew curious about Ellen's remarks and Gabe's past relationships. Maybe he could find a way—discreetly—to tiptoe around the topic, see what happens.

Hunter tried to convince himself he didn't care either way, but it didn't stop the nervous quiver in the pit of his belly. Gabe was a Christian. Chances were, he was straight. Then again, people would say the same thing about Hunter—yet Hunter and God knew the shades of gray that colored the truth. Maybe Gabe wrestled with the same secret undercurrent as Hunter. At least, Hunter hoped he did—a wish Hunter took back instantly. As a Christian, he felt convicted, wishing such hardship on anyone else. Hunter just yearned for someone who could understand. The whole misery-loves-company side of human nature.

No, Hunter thought. Gabe was, in all likelihood, straight. How could Hunter navigate around the question without ruining their new friendship and rendering himself unwelcome for a professional appointment? He wouldn't be able to look Gabe in the eye if he bungled this.

Yes, despite his reservations, he really did want to know. He just needed a Plan B to provide coverage in case Gabe grew suspicious.

If he asks, tell him you have some female friends and thought one of them might make a good match.

Perfect!

Hunter shut his eyes well in advance of asking. That way, Gabe wouldn't be able to read them. If Hunter made any fast or unusual eye movements, they wouldn't be noticeable. That relieved some of the pressure.

Because Hunter knew his true motive in asking, the quivers accelerated in his belly, but he fought to keep his voice steady.

Relax, Hunter told himself, taking a deep breath to usher in calm. He knew from past experience that if he allowed tension to reach his muscles, Gabe would detect the change.

Hunter entered the conversation through a side door. "Most of your clients are female, right?"

"The majority are. You're not getting concerned about *that* all over again, are you?"

"No, not at all. I was curious what your girlfriend thinks of you massaging other females. I know *you* realize it's a professional matter, but you know how girlfriends can get sometimes."

"The good news is, I don't need to worry about that. No girlfriend in the picture."

That intrigued Hunter. If his heart were connected to an EKG monitor, he could imagine the sudden, rapid spikes that would appear as his heart beat faster.

"Well, how about in the past?" Hunter said. "You've been doing this for several years."

Hunter felt Gabe's fingers slow down, then recover their normal speed, as if he had caught Gabe off guard but Gabe didn't want him to notice a change had occurred.

"Relationships don't seem to work out for me," said Gabe, "so I guess I lost heart. I gave up on dating back in college. Well, 'gave up' isn't accurate. I didn't make a decision. Things worked out the way they did, and I made peace with it."

Hunter could tell Gabe was an honest person. And after the openness of their conversations, he should have expected Gabe to give the candid answer he did. Yet he hadn't anticipated its transparency. It drew him toward Gabe's heart. Hunter wanted to listen. Opening his eyes, he turned his head toward Gabe.

"There's been nobody since college?" Hunter asked. "Not even one date?"

"I guess my heart never hooked up with it." Gabe looked Hunter in the eye for what seemed a moment too long, then continued working. "Besides, I don't think many women would be interested in a guy like me."

"That's hard to believe."

"It's true," Gabe shrugged, "but it's no loss, I suppose."

"It's *their* loss. You seem to have a great heart. You're a good listener."

"Thanks, but I don't think that puts me in a special club. Lots of people listen well."

Hunter didn't seem to have gotten through with what he'd meant to say, so he decided to try again. Perhaps it was the competitor in him, but for some reason, he wanted Gabe to know what he'd meant and how rare it was to find Gabe's qualities in other people.

"I didn't say it the right way," Hunter said. "It's hard to explain. You have a transparency about you. It's not so much something you do, but something you *are*. You have everything I've ever wished *I* could find in a relationship."

Hunter winced. He hadn't intended to make himself vulnerable and certainly hadn't planned to say *that*. Granted, he'd felt it in his heart, even if he hadn't found the words to describe it. Maybe it crept forth from his subconscious. Whatever the reason, he'd gotten too comfortable as they'd talked. Normally Hunter said too little. Now, the one time he made his best effort to open up, he'd said too much. But maybe it wasn't as bad as Hunter figured; after all, Gabe didn't know what had gone through Hunter's mind these past weeks. Holding his expression steady, trying to appear as if he'd meant nothing by his words, Hunter looked back at Gabe.

Sure enough, Gabe had noticed. Hunter could tell by the momentary, stunned look in his eyes, the way they flicked back and forth before Gabe refocused his attention on Hunter's back.

Did Hunter catch the slightest twitch of a grin at the corner of Gabe's mouth? He wasn't sure. Hunter clenched his jaw at his unanswered questions. How could he have said something so stupid?

"I just realized how that sounded," Hunter said, stumbling his way to a recovery. "What I meant was—"

"No worries. I understand what you meant by it. I appreciate the compliment, though."

Gabe nodded as though nothing out of the ordinary had happened, but Hunter detected new fervor—broader, deeper sweeps—from Gabe's thumbs. Gabe gave no signs of anger. For that matter, he didn't look offended at all.

As Hunter continued to gauge Gabe's reaction from the corner of his eye, Gabe peered in contemplation at Hunter's face once more. And to Hunter's surprise, Gabe's eyes lingered a second or two as he resumed his work.

Something had changed. Hunter could sense it hanging in the air, two feet between Gabe's face and his own.

Hunter's mind churned as he reflected on their past appointments and pieced together arbitrary details: The way Gabe's eyes had flicked back for a second glance the moment they'd met. The sense of disappointment that lingered when their appointments ended, and the way Gabe seemed to prolong them rather than simply end them.

Call it instinct, a sixth sense. It wasn't the actions themselves, but the sensations Hunter picked up in those moments. He didn't have tangible evidence, yet he no longer doubted.

The familiar nervousness, that bittersweet pang, returned to his gut.

Hunter wasn't the only one with something to hide.

Gabe felt something for him, too.

CHAPTER 12

That night, conflict roiled within Hunter's soul.

Earlier that day, he had left his appointment exhilarated. After all these years, Hunter was no longer alone. And not only had he found someone else in the same predicament, but that individual felt drawn to him, too. Hunter felt overwhelmed by the thrill of discovering another person, someone he found appealing, had responded with mutual, albeit unspoken, interest. He felt poised for a new adventure.

But as the hours progressed, Hunter considered the scenario further and shame arose in his heart. Soon Hunter felt he had entered a room he had no business entering.

Forbidden fruit.

Back and forth, Hunter veered between two extremes—thrill and remorse—for the rest of the evening. At its root, Hunter recognized it as the same inner conflict that had wrenched his soul since he was younger. And as excited as he felt tonight, Hunter viewed it as selfish. He couldn't shake the sense that he'd made God unhappy.

Hunter could hide from people, but he couldn't hide from God.

Shortly before bedtime, Hunter reclined on his side upon his bed, his Bible open before him. As was his custom this time each night, he quieted himself and allowed his heart to connect to God's. Hunter would read the Bible, then ponder what he'd read and let God minister to his heart. Whatever restlessness Hunter experienced during his days, these final minutes before bedtime brought refuge. Hunter considered God not only *God,* but also his closest friend, and their friendship grew stronger during these final minutes of the night. Some nights, Hunter could sense God speaking to his heart. Other nights, his personal study felt like mere reading. But Hunter dedicated himself to reading the Bible regardless.

Tonight, Hunter focused on the sixth chapter of 1 Corinthians. In the twelfth verse, he read, *"All things are lawful for me, but not all things are profitable. All things are lawful for me, but I will not be mastered by anything."*

Hunter paused. *All things are lawful.*

He considered those words in light of his current predicament. If all things were lawful, did he need to worry about his feelings for Gabe?

Then he considered the rest of the verse. *Not all things are profitable.*

Hunter's parents had raised him to believe that romantic attraction toward the same gender was inappropriate. His friends, pastors and role models, from churches to Youth Vision meetings to leisure activities, had reinforced that view over the years.

I will not be mastered by anything.

The fact was, Hunter did believe his attractions displeased God. So shouldn't he resist those attractions rather than give in to the power they seemed to hold over him?

That's what made the battle so confusing. That's what wore him down. He hadn't asked for this fight. He didn't *want* to be attracted to Gabe or any other guy in the first place. If God didn't want him to give in to the temptation—if neither God nor Hunter wanted it—why didn't God remove it from his life? Wouldn't that be the easiest route?

Hunter didn't have answers. Not for this.

So he continued to read. Soon he came across verse 19: *"Or do you not know that your body is a temple of the Holy Spirit who is in you, whom you have from God, and that you are not your own?"*

Hunter sighed. Not only did verses like that remind him he couldn't escape by ignoring his circumstances, they also caused him concern. He wanted to please God. He wanted God's will, not his own, to come to pass in his life.

With blurred vision, Hunter set aside his Bible and wiped away a film of tears from his eyes.

He needed God. Sometimes he simply wanted to draw near to Him.

Climbing off of the bed, Hunter planted his feet on the ground and stood still. With a hefty breath, he filled his lungs with oxygen, then exhaled. He closed his eyes and tilted his head toward heaven. Palms outward, Hunter lifted his hands to God and allowed a sense of God's presence to fill him.

His lips trembled. His voice shook. Although he felt defeated and weak, Hunter spoke aloud to God, his volume just above a whisper.

"Please heal me."

More tears sprang forth. He started to wipe them away, but they trickled in such abundance, he gave up and let them flow.

"I don't want this. I'm begging You," he said, "please heal me of this."

How often have I prayed that prayer? wondered Hunter. So many times over so many years, he had lost count.

"God, You know I love You."

Though he didn't hear audible answers when he prayed, he knew in his heart God heard him. If nothing else, Hunter kept the communication lines open between them. He could lay his heart on the line, expressing his feelings in the simplest way he knew. When he felt broken, Hunter ran to God.

Hunter grew quiet, then sat cross-legged on the floor and leaned against his bed, spending time in God's presence. He could tell God was there, so Hunter talked to Him like he would talk to a friend. Simple prayers in passing when fleeting desires flared up or when shame felt so murky and thick, he couldn't withstand it any longer. Moments when passion burned in him at night as he lay in bed. Moments of close calls where he had almost gotten caught.

Moments like tonight, when he felt so dirty … so lost … so alone … so helpless. Moments when the pain in his heart weighed so heavy, he would fall to his knees in tears at the side of his bed, in his bathroom, on his kitchen floor—wherever he was when the hidden monster emerged so overwhelming that Hunter felt miserable, disappointed in himself.

God was the only one who saw these moments or knew about them.

And what pained Hunter most was how his secret must break God's heart.

CHAPTER 13

"**M**y staff is drowning with work!"

The client sounded exasperated.

"Monday was bad enough, but it's Tuesday morning, and the software is bogging down our system. And because it's integrated into our own software, we can't work around it."

"I apologize, Sharon," Hunter said. "The software-development department has notified us that they expect to have it fixed by—"

"We're in a busy season and my staff is working at half its normal speed! If it continues, we'll need to pay overtime to get caught up. Plus, some of the reports we scheduled to run overnight stopped in the middle of processing, so we've had to run them during the day when everyone's using the system. That's slowing things down further. We need this fixed."

Over the weekend, the software-development department had applied a patch to the software's framework. In order to apply the patch, they needed to shut down their system for a few hours. Few clients logged into the system on weekends, so a

Sunday shutdown had minimized disruption. The development department's testing had gone well. When clients returned to work on Monday, however, they discovered trickle-down issues the development staff hadn't anticipated. Hunter couldn't control what the software-development department did or how they approached their work. Clients were supposed to contact the client-support department if they experienced any issues. Unfortunately, though, since clients liked Hunter personally and knew him as someone who could get things done, often they registered their complaints with him instead.

"I understand how frustrating that can be," Hunter said, "and I assure you, our people are working on it. They let us know they expect to have a fix in place before lunch."

"That's what they said yesterday."

"Tell you what: Let's give it a couple more hours to see if the tech folks can get the system fixed. I'll give you a call around midday to touch bases on where you stand, and we'll take it from there. Meanwhile, I'll submit a separate work order regarding the overnight reports. That way, if it turns out to be an unrelated issue, the work request will already be in the pipeline. Does that sound like a plan?"

He and Sharon ended the call in an amiable manner—as amiable as possible while a client was frustrated—and he entered the work order into the system as promised.

Glitches like these irritated him. He knew clients—and prospective clients—talk to each other. System glitches and inaccurate deadlines wouldn't enhance the software's reputation, nor would it help him secure new clients. Yet he couldn't fix the issues himself. It reminded him of when he worked as a waiter one summer: A short-staffed kitchen crew took longer to fulfill orders. He couldn't control the kitchen staff's progress, but the final impact of slow progress tended to manifest by way of a smaller tip from the customer.

Fortunately, his other clients had contacted the client-support department instead of him, so his morning had brought no other surprises.

Hunter's belly quivered. He had decided to take Gabe's advice and talk to his regional manager about his dry spell, but Hunter didn't look forward to it. So he procrastinated by scanning his email inbox. He opened a message from the technology team about the latest developments on the company's horizon. Not only did those messages help him clinch deals—he could inform potential clients of future benefits they would receive with the software—but it fostered the image of a company on the cutting edge.

Hunter scrolled through the message on his laptop, which informed him that the latest software updates were successful (yeah, right!), but that employees should inform the software-development team of any issues. He read a news bite about upcoming security changes. A tidbit on new rules considered by the Post Office that would impact the cost of mailing larger packages.

Another article announced a new partnership with a major client: Congratulations to Cassie Magellan, who had signed a regional distributor of newspapers and magazines. That article bothered Hunter, who had felt he could have secured that client. Months ago, he had *mentioned* the company as a potential client, but his regional manager had assigned Cassie to their trail when Hunter hit his dry patch. Hunter had taken that decision hard because it suggested his manager lacked confidence in Hunter's ability to secure the deal.

Enough stalling. Hunter grew tired of the fear or dread or whatever kept him from talking to his manager. He locked his laptop, took a final swig of coffee that had gone lukewarm, and headed down the hall. In the distance, he heard a telephone ring, which a muffled female voice answered. Plexiglass accented cubicles to help shield next-door neighbors from excess noise as they talked to clients. Several cubicle occupants were absent, probably on sales calls. Half of the individuals Hunter passed had their phones against their ears, while others had glued their eyes to their laptop monitors. Hunter heard the tapping of computer keys, muted phone chatter, and the slam of a phone returning to its cradle. Although windows lined the exterior of the office building, offices and conference rooms lined the perimeter, blocking most sunlight from the room in which Hunter worked. He had never counted cubicles but estimated 40 to 50 cubicles sat beneath the fluorescent lights of this room.

When he approached his manager's office, he found the door open. From several feet away, rays of sunshine emanated through the doorway and splayed upon the corridor floor. From outside, Hunter heard his manager's voice, words of parting, followed by a telephone hitting its cradle.

Hunter tapped on the door and poked his head into the office.

"Wayne, do have a few minutes to chat?"

"Have a seat," Wayne said with a wave. He had filled his desktop with stacks of paperwork, which Hunter perceived as organized piles, though he couldn't tell what hid within each. Wayne wrote some notes on a document, closed its manila folder, and stuffed it into a leather satchel. "I'm headed to Detroit this afternoon, then Milwaukee next week. This is the last you'll see me for the next couple of weeks."

"Would it be better if I stopped by after you return?"

"No, this is perfect timing. I can talk to you, then finish up some market analysis. What's on your mind?"

As Hunter took a seat facing his manager, he realized he didn't have a clue how to approach the subject. He didn't want to make himself look bad by pointing out his own flaws, but his flaws were the reason he sought Wayne's input. Hands in his lap, Hunter fidgeted where his boss, from his angle, couldn't see it happening. From chest height and above, Hunter sought to appear confident.

A fit man at 49 years old, Wayne aged as well as Kevin Bacon. Each day, Wayne ran eight miles before dawn. He was the plainspoken, no-nonsense type, an achievement-oriented individual who laid his challenges on the line for the purpose of annihilating them. A few years ago, when he started to experience significant hair loss, Wayne took a razor to his scalp and turned his curse into an air of cutting-edge chic, which ended up working to his benefit. Prospective clients assumed he understood modern technology because he *appeared* modern. He looked like a man on a coffee break as he reinvented the Internet.

Hunter decided to take a direct approach.

"I believe my recent track record could improve," Hunter began. "It's obvious to both of us, so I'd prefer to tackle it head-on."

Wayne stroked his graying goatee. "And you're looking to isolate the reason for it? Find the smoking gun?"

"I don't know what's going on with it. I haven't changed my approach, which worked well for me until earlier this year."

Wayne leaned back in his leather chair, gave his laptop a few taps, and began to scour a document he'd opened. He hit an arrow key several times, perusing the document at half-attention as he spoke. "I've kept up to date on the summaries you've provided every week. You're contacting everyone you should. You reach your weekly goals for cold calls and visits."

"And I'm not filling it with bad prospects to inflate my figures. I invest a lot of time upfront to identify solid prospects, where we'd have a genuine shot at getting their business. If I were doing that, I wouldn't be surprised at the outcome."

Wayne sat with his fingers interlaced across his chest as he examined Hunter eye to eye. Hunter sought clues as to what went through the guy's mind as he looked at his underperforming staff member.

"Do you have any feedback for me?" Hunter asked. "Anything you think I could improve, from your perspective?"

"I think you're doing all the necessary preliminary work. You've proven yourself adept at sales and have a bright future." Wayne tapped a pen on his desktop as he continued to observe Hunter. "Look, Hunter, we all hit these desert seasons when it comes to sales. All you seem to be missing is a little luck."

"I'd hate to think it boils down to luck," Hunter said. "Luck suggests we can't improve."

Wayne had trained Hunter in his current position. Hunter had gleaned valuable skills from him, adapted them to his own personality, and discovered his sweet spot for success. Yet Hunter had always found Wayne difficult to read. Even now, Wayne's words sounded supportive, but the man kept a poker face, one he had refined after two decades on the sales battleground.

On most occasions, Wayne kept his speech to a minimum; he chose his words with caution, speaking no more than necessary to accomplish the task at hand. Hunter assumed this was Wayne's way of never having his words come back to haunt him. But as a result, Hunter never knew quite where he stood with his manager. That hadn't concerned Hunter when he'd had a stellar track record, but now …

Wayne leaned forward, clasping his hands atop his desk. "As I see it, Hunter, the pinch for you seems to be in *closing* the deal."

"So I'm missing a detail?" Hunter grew hopeful. Perhaps Wayne had identified something concrete which Hunter could tweak.

"That's hard to tell without watching as you reach your point of closure," Wayne replied. "If I were in the office more often, I might have time to accompany you, help you troubleshoot. Unfortunately, that's not an option for me."

"But you think the issue comes into play late in the game? You don't think I'm making errors en route?"

"Everything that has fallen through has occurred during the final phase. Take your Pipeline Insurance project, for instance."

Pipeline Insurance. The major opportunity that had looked like a sure thing until his final meeting with Jake Geyer. Hunter cringed at the memory. Coming from his manager's mouth, though, the loss sounded even worse.

"That one took me by surprise." Hunter shifted in his seat, his forehead turning feverish. "My contact person had gone from talking about how they didn't need our product to talking about if a deal were to occur."

"So what happened, from your perspective?"

"I don't know. At our last meeting, I showed up ready for him to recommend me to his department director to start negotiations, and it's like my contact had a change of heart right there in the room. Suddenly he didn't need the software."

Hunter realized the conversation had gotten off its original course. He wanted to steer it back into positive territory.

"I've brought great ideas to the table for our team—successful ideas—that didn't end up under my realm of responsibility, like the deal Cassie Magellan delivered, the one they mentioned in the corporate newsletter this morning." Careful to show deference toward Wayne, Hunter remained calm and treaded with caution. "You might remember, I identified them as a ripe prospect, but you passed it along to Cassie to pursue and close."

Now Wayne shifted in his seat, crossing his arms across his chest, but remaining relaxed. "Well, that was a major client acquisition, and as you mentioned, you had hit a bump. There's a time for risk, and we couldn't afford to take a chance, given the environment we've faced."

"Actually," Hunter said, "that brings up another concern I had. Well, I don't know if *concern* is the right word, but … specific clients aside, the economy has hit another downturn. Companies are hawkish about their bottom lines—"

"That's for sure," Wayne chuckled.

"So they've cut back on what they might consider extras, the nice-to-haves. In talking to other sales people, we've all seen clients choosing their own in-house data maintenance over our software. It's more weight on their shoulders and higher staff costs, but they believe they'll see a net cost savings."

"You're right, I've seen the same thing. It's a challenge to convince them otherwise."

"This year, more and more of them have opted to terminate their contracts rather than renew."

Wayne nodded in concurrence. Hunter focused tighter on Wayne's face. Without intending to, Hunter lowered his voice a notch.

"That's started rumors of layoffs here. Just through the grapevine—you know how that goes."

Wayne blinked, then clasped his hands on his desk.

Hunter opened his mouth to speak further, then abandoned the words. He took a breather, tensed his jaw line, and leaned forward.

"I'm not sure how to ask this, so I'll just cut to the chase." Looking Wayne straight in the eye, he asked, "Wayne, do I need to be concerned about my job?"

Wayne's body grew rigid in his seat. "Concerned about ..."

"About losing it."

"We've had no layoffs among our sales team." Wayne's poker face remained intact.

Wayne's reply did nothing to ease Hunter's doubt. Hunter had learned to read between the lines. He knew from dealing with clients that, oftentimes, what a person *didn't* say held as many clues as what he *did* say.

What Wayne had said was accurate: No layoffs had occurred. But Hunter noticed Wayne had kept his response in the past tense. He'd said nothing about the future.

"Well, no, nothing has happened as of today," Hunter said, treading with caution once again, "but what does the future look like? Has word come down about any options the company might be considering?"

Wayne stroked his goatee with his thumb. "I've received no instructions to implement any layoffs."

I realize that, Hunter wanted to say. *Technically that's true, but what else do you know? What else is running through your mind?*

That poker face had begun to make Hunter uneasy. He could tell Wayne knew more than he had revealed, but didn't want to tell anyone. Clearly, Hunter's question had caught him off guard, as if he'd asked something about which Wayne hadn't had time in advance to construct a boilerplate answer.

"Okay. It just seems—"

"Hunter, you're doing your absolute best, right?"

"Yes, I am."

"Then worrying won't do any good. Things have a way of falling into place, don't they?" Wayne shrugged. "Sometimes in unexpected ways."

Beneath the table, Hunter cracked a knuckle.

CHAPTER 14

Hunter still didn't have firm answers regarding his job security. Then again, maybe Wayne had given a straightforward response. Perhaps the guy *didn't* know anything. Not only was Hunter concerned about himself, he didn't want to see his coworkers in danger, either.

Though disappointed by a lack of answers, Hunter's Tuesday improved by evening: Gabe had stopped by to hang out. With Kara out of town again, Hunter was glad to have company. Otherwise, he would have grown preoccupied with apprehension about his job to the point of ruining his evening. He knew he should trust God to take care of his future, but Hunter recognized that as yet another growth area for himself.

Hunter and Gabe had decided to grill burgers on Hunter's patio. On his way over, Gabe had stopped by the grocery store to pick up ground beef, along with a salad in a bag. The flames glowed with bright orange fervor on the grill as the evening sky transitioned to a mystic blue. Hunter's arms bristled at the chill in the October air, and as he reached across the grill to flip the burgers, the heat of the dancing flames ushered forth memories of bonfires. He set the spatula aside while the burgers sizzled.

Gabe moved toward the grill and let his hands hover over the top to warm himself. "Now I understand why you assumed the role of flipping burgers: to avoid the chills. I'm such a sucker."

"By all means, look like a fool and spread your hands over the barbecue grill," Hunter snickered.

"You never know if this'll be your last chance to grill outside while it's halfway comfortable." Gabe readjusted his jacket, pulling the sleeves over his wrists. "They're talking snow flurries overnight next week."

"What do you mean, 'our last chance?' You can grill in the middle of winter if you want to."

"Sorry, I don't dress in layers to cook." Gabe grabbed the metal spatula Hunter had set aside and shifted the burgers at an angle to accent them with crisscrossed grill marks.

Hunter felt his cell phone vibrate with a single pulse. He retrieved it from his pocket.

"It's a text message from Kara. I'll send her a quick reply." Holding the phone in both hands, he thumbed his way through a response and sent it on its way.

"Long-distance relationships." Gabe grinned.

"You're close," Hunter replied. "Texting is the main way we keep in touch these days. If she's in New York, phone calls work fine. But if she's in another country, factor all those time zones into her schedule and calling is no longer feasible. If she's in Hong Kong, she's eating lunch while we're asleep here."

Hunter gave the burgers a final check, judged them fully cooked, and started transferring them to a plate. Gabe turned off the propane tank.

"Did you talk to your boss?" Gabe asked. "I didn't know if you'd planned to do that today or not."

"I did."

"And?"

"Let's put it this way: Wayne and I talked. That much got accomplished."

"But no answers?"

"I have trouble reading him to begin with. He doesn't give any hints about what's going through his head. No facial responses, nothing. Plus, he was evasive."

"He dodged the questions?"

"More like he danced around them. He answered the questions I asked, but he picked his words in a way that told me things I already knew. 'No one has lost their jobs.' Well, of course not. But what about a month from now? They must know something. They don't turn on a dime; they plan things out and weigh their options. That takes time, so I'm sure they know things in advance—maybe not far in advance, but they start thinking about what-ifs."

Hunter put the last burger patty on the plate and led the way inside, where he and Gabe assembled a couple of burgers each, then added their side salads.

Hunter headed toward his living room and sat down on the sofa. Grabbing the remote, he turned on the television, then noticed Gabe standing beside the sofa, looking confused.

"Is there any place you want us to put the plates? I wasn't sure how you do things in your house."

Then it hit Hunter. "Oh geez, I headed in here out of habit! I tend to eat in front of the TV with the plate on my lap. Kara calls me a caveman. We can eat in the kitchen if you want, the way civilized people do."

Gabe laughed and took a seat. "No, that's fine. I didn't want to assume."

"You're one of those sophisticated people who always eats at the kitchen table, aren't you?" Hunter smirked.

"Habit. What can I say?"

Gabe sat down on the opposite side of the sofa, then caught himself losing his balance.

"I forgot to mention that cushion sinks in pretty deep," Hunter said. "A buddy of mine used to plant himself there years ago and managed to get it screwed up. Obviously, you're in a bachelor pad. It's probably hard to eat like that, though." Hunter motioned beside himself with his elbow. "Might be easier to eat if you sit on the middle cushion."

Gabe scooted over and settled within a few inches of Hunter. They set their beverages on the coffee table. As Gabe got himself situated, trying to grow accustomed to balancing the plate on his knees, Hunter couldn't help but find the sight a bit humorous. Though a minor thing, Hunter considered what it said about Gabe: He seemed like such a nice guy, willing to make himself uncomfortable to meet somebody else halfway. For Hunter, it served as another example of why he found Gabe a refreshing change from other guys in his life.

As Hunter opened his mouth to offer to pray, Gabe made the offer himself. They said a quick prayer of thanks over the meal, then took their first bites.

"Do you follow sports at all?" Hunter asked, aiming the remote control at the television.

"Not much, but go ahead and turn them on. It'll be a good learning experience for me," Gabe said in good humor.

Hunter settled on a baseball game. "It's post-season time in baseball. The playoffs are going on until it reaches the World Series."

"St. Louis at Atlanta?"

"See? You know more than you thought you did."

"I read the graphics at the bottom of the screen."

"Well, duh! I guess that works, too." Hunter crunched on a morsel of lettuce and swallowed. "What type of shows do you usually watch?"

"If anything, I think I use the TV for background noise. Most of the time, I'll turn on the news, or anything with comedy." With a nod toward the game, Gabe asked, "Who do you expect to win?"

"Atlanta has a better record, but a lot of pundits expect the Cardinals to win. The Cardinals seem to do their best when they're underdogs. They had a relatively weak year in 2006, then went on to win the World Series, so anything goes. In a way, at playoff time, a whole new season begins, because both teams start with a zero record. Atlanta gets home-field advantage because it had the better regular-season record, but that means nothing if they don't win."

"Too bad it's not Cleveland instead of St. Louis, huh?"

"Yeah, the Indians didn't make it to post-season. We're in the American League, though. This is a National League playoff game."

An Atlanta player walked up to home plate, loosened the muscles in his arms and neck, then took his stance to await the pitch.

"So if St. Louis wins, what happens next?"

"This is game two, and the first team to win three of five games moves on to the next playoff round. Atlanta won last night, so if they win again tonight, it eases the pressure on them. They'd only need one more win." Hunter took his eyes off the screen and looked toward Gabe. "But if St. Louis wins tonight, they're dead even, and then the two teams will need to slug it out for two more games, minimum."

At that, the sound of a cracking bat jerked Hunter and Gabe's attention back to the television. The crowd roared. Hunter held his breath and waited for what looked like a home run in formation, then eased again when the ball hit the wall behind center field. Though the baseball player could have rounded to third by the time a St. Louis outfielder grabbed the ball, the player stopped running and backed up to second base.

"What just happened?" Gabe said. "He could have made it to third base. Why did he stop?"

"If it hits the back wall, it's an automatic double. It's a rule of the game."

Squinting at the game before him, Gabe chewed his burger slowly as he considered Hunter's explanation, then shrugged. "Did you play any sports?"

"As a matter of fact, I sacrificed a lucrative career in professional sports so I could sell software to those in need."

"Whatever. I meant back in the day—school stuff."

"I played baseball at Hudson."

"Were you good?"

"I was decent. My brother was a lot better at it." Hunter placed his empty dinner plate on the coffee table. "I ran cross-country, too."

"That must've been the crowd you ran around with, the athletes?"

"Pretty much." Hunter reflected on those former days and, almost to himself, said, "Teenage years are strange, aren't they? The stuff that matters back then but makes no difference by the time you're an adult. The weird thing was, despite running with that popular crowd and knowing some of them since I was little, I never felt like I fit in."

"Why do you think that was?"

"I don't know. We had similar interests. I tried to feel like I belonged, but the opposite always nagged at me." Hunter considered it further, then added, "Actually, it wasn't so much that I didn't fit in. It was more like I never felt one hundred percent *comfortable*. Does that make any sense?"

"More than you know."

They grew quiet for a few minutes as the next inning began. Both Hunter and Gabe grew engrossed in the game as the count alternated between balls and strikes, culminating in a full count.

When the batter struck out, Gabe took the final bite of his dinner. Hunter eased forward with his right hand to grab his cola, unaware that Gabe had also reached forward with his left hand to put his plate on the coffee table.

When their arms brushed, Hunter's heart vibrated.

The contact occurred quick and weightless. A chance encounter. The light hairs of Gabe's arm swept against Hunter's arm like the stroke of a feather. Hunter felt himself stir below the waist. Before he had time to blink, the moment had passed.

Careful to act as though he hadn't noticed, Hunter angled his head and peered out of the corner of his eye to see whether Gabe's composure changed. Gabe appeared oblivious to the incident. Gabe didn't add space between them, nor did he draw his arm closer to himself to prevent a future incident from occurring. He remained focused on the television. Hunter wondered if Gabe thought nothing of what had happened, or if he kept his composure guarded the way

Hunter did. Then again, maybe Gabe hadn't noticed their contact at all.

For a few seconds, Hunter felt frustrated at the close call. While he dealt with this, fighting to cover up in such scenarios, other guys had the luxury of remaining carefree, plodding along without lending a another thought to the incident. Why him? Hunter shook his head, then caught himself and stopped.

Hunter remained a tad stimulated below his waist and, though it felt subdued, he prayed it wasn't visible to Gabe. It would be the kind of situation neither person would acknowledge, but both would feel awkward knowing what had happened. When he gathered the courage to assess his status, Hunter glimpsed his lap and, to his relief, discovered the stirring wasn't strong enough to alter the topography of his jeans. Plus, he noticed his shirt hadn't bunched together when he'd sat down, so it covered enough of his lap to keep it safe from view.

If only he could read what went through Gabe's mind.

"Braves are up next," Gabe said.

Hunter realized he'd stared at the television without noticing what had unfolded. He'd pondered the encounter for so long, he'd gotten lost in it while two more St. Louis players had struck out to end the inning.

"Looks that way," Hunter replied. "Not good for the Cards, huh?"

Hunter turned and looked at Gabe, and when he did, he saw something more in Gabe's eyes than a comment on the game.

Their eyes locked a split second too long. Hunter felt his pupils dilate and he noticed Gabe's fluttered, as well. Though it lasted a mere moment, Hunter sensed something cement itself between them.

In that moment, Hunter knew Gabe had indeed noticed their physical contact earlier.

And now, in spite of his attempts to disguise it, Hunter knew he had revealed a hidden part of himself to someone else.

CHAPTER 15

The café served everything from coffee to salads to hearth-baked, flatbread pizzas. Hunter munched on a vegetarian pizza at a corner booth. Though a meat lover, he favored this pizza, with its combination of goat cheese, white mushrooms, eggplant and other grilled vegetables. Hunter inhaled the sharp scent of its crust, the aroma of its grilled surface invigorating his senses.

He couldn't shake the previous night from his mind. Or, more specifically, the brief arm-brush encounter with Gabe. Afterward, neither had said a word about it; they had continued to watch the game until Gabe left a little past nine o'clock. Yet both were aware of what had happened. It had hung in the air between them the rest of the evening.

Hunter wondered if he had revealed too much about himself. Not that he had *intended* to. But at this point, did it matter? He couldn't change it, could he? He couldn't take it back. Still, Hunter remained anxious. He could picture the humiliation if Gabe said anything to anyone. Then again, Gabe was a

Christian, too. Others believed he was straight, right? If Gabe struggled the way Hunter did, he wouldn't want anyone to know about *him* either, would he? And Gabe was one individual, not thirty. It was a secret between them—a secret which, if revealed, would serve neither of them well.

Hunter breathed a sigh of relief. He was safe for now.

Forget about that moment, Hunter thought. *You get to move forward as if nothing happened.*

Brendan Pieper, Ellen's fiancé, walked into the café and scanned the lunch crowd. Hunter caught his attention and waved him over.

"You said you weren't sure when you'd get here, so I went ahead and ordered my lunch," Hunter said. "You don't mind, do you ?"

"Makes no difference." Brendan shed his jacket and laid it on the booth seat across from Hunter. "I'm gonna grab coffee and skip the meal anyway. I'll munch on an energy bar when I get back to the office." And with that, Brendan stepped away.

Brendan came from a wealthy family in town. Hunter's parents and Brendan's parents were acquaintances, though Hunter's family wasn't in the same economic scale.

Due to their age difference, Hunter hadn't known Brendan growing up, but he'd had a friend who'd lived in the same neighborhood as Brendan's family. As a kid, numerous times after school, Hunter had visited that friend's house, with its white siding and black shutters beside its windows. Like all other homes in that upscale neighborhood, the house was large, but to Hunter's perspective as a child, it towered over him. Back then, to Hunter, it resembled a palace, complete with tall, white columns that stood guard along the front porch. Located deep within the neighborhood, it took a five-minute drive to reach that home. Hunter recalled the broad backyard with its lush, manicured grass, never more than an inch high. The house sat atop a knoll, so the backyard featured a gradual, downhill slope, where the terrain seemed to roll toward a manmade pond below. Hunter and his friend had held countless somersault races to the bottom, then turned around and raced each other back to the top. They had played Frisbee on that lawn more times than Hunter could recall. The lawn looked straight out of a golf magazine, minus the risk of shattered windows from a wayward golf ball.

From the front and back, Hunter had thought that home looked so peaceful, so serene. In fact, he had once pictured a stray leaf fluttering in the breeze and bouncing against the front door. He'd wondered if such a disruption would set off the home's security alarm.

Brendan returned and dropped himself into the booth, his face flushed.

"Are you okay?" Hunter asked. "You look flustered."

"I've been rushing around all week. This is my first chance to sit down and relax, and it's only Wednesday."

"Wedding stuff?"

"Yeah, but Ellen's handling most of that. Work's been busy with customers gearing up to break ground on their new homes this spring."

"Don't they have a few months to figure it out?"

"They're making their decisions and picking out a lot of options before the holidays hit, before winter sets in and time gets short." Brendan took a sip of his coffee. His shoulders went lax. "Plus, Ellen and I have a big dinner event tonight. That's why I decided not to bother eating here."

"What kind of dinner event?"

"My parents signed us up to attend a charity gala with them. I'll need to leave work early. Come to think of it, maybe I shouldn't have left the office for lunch."

"What's the charity this time?" Hunter asked.

"A shelter in Akron for runaway teens. The charity does great work." Brendan shrugged. "Nothing against the charity itself, but I go to these events because my family expects it from me."

"Does Ellen look forward to going?"

"I doubt it. She hates these social functions. Once we got engaged, my parents started dragging her into all this. She wasn't thrilled." Brendan's mouth twisted into a mischievous grin. "You know how she is. Can you picture her in one of those gowns that go all the way down to her feet?"

Hunter couldn't help but snicker at the image. "Grab a snapshot with your cell phone."

"I hope you're kidding. She'd strangle me! The first time her photo hit the community newspaper with her dressed in one of those fancy gowns—I've never heard the end of it! *Every* time we've gone to one since then ..."

"I'm surprised she's never mentioned it to me."

"She hides her annoyance from my parents quite well. I'm impressed," Brendan said. "She'll do a little mingling once we get there tonight. Then, twenty minutes after we arrive, she'll sidle up next to me and mutter in my ear, 'Just shoot me now. Nothing permanent; just nick me in the leg, a little something to get me the hell outta here.'"

Hunter fought to keep his cola in his mouth, forcing himself to swallow before he burst out laughing.

"Sounds like something she would say," Hunter said.

"What do you mean, '*would?*'" Brendan's eyes went wide as he fell back against his seat. "Those were her words at the last event. Verbatim."

Hunter took a bite of his pizza, glad his family didn't expect him to play the type of social games Brendan's family expected of their son. One characteristic Ellen possessed to which Hunter related was her desire for the genuine—from others *and* from herself.

"Anyway," Brendan continued, "Ellen's so wrapped up in wedding plans these days, she can't think straight."

"What's she working on?"

"As far as I know, she's looking for a reception site. I just stay out of her way and show up when she tells me to. That way, I can stay awake and Ellen can do her thing."

"But I thought she said you have a wedding planner."

Pursing his lips, Brendan shook his head. "Ellen refuses to let her handle more than the bare minimum, and that's to keep my parents happy. She doesn't trust the woman to get it right."

"Surely a wedding planner has handled plenty of them before."

"My guess is, Ellen's a caterer and knows how one wrong move can screw things up beyond repair."

"Not to mention she's a control freak."

"Nothing she wouldn't admit about herself, right?" With that, Brendan drained his coffee cup, then excused himself. He wandered over to a small beverage station in the corner of the room, where he refilled his cup with a dark roast, stirring in cream and sugar.

When he sat back down, Brendan added, "Ellen's parents are so hands-off, mine can come across as overbearing by comparison. And it doesn't help that she's getting social pressure from mine."

"For what it's worth, Ellen puts up with an awful lot before she reaches her explosion point," said Hunter. "She has endurance I could only wish for."

"She keeps it all under control, but the wedding stuff has her so stressed out to begin with. Then Mom and Dad start nudging her, and I can tell something's bubbling beneath the surface. She won't come out and *say* it, though."

"Have you asked her about it?"

"Yeah, but independent as she is, she doesn't like to feel weak. Ellen wants enough space to figure it out on her own. You know that better than I do," Brendan replied. "Maybe what I need to do is figure out a diplomatic way to tell my parents to back off a bit."

Sliding his plate to the side, Hunter checked his watch. He had another ten minutes before he needed to head back to the office for a post-lunch meeting. "What's the latest on the house front?"

Brendan's eyebrows rose. "An unexpected development there." Leaning forward, he rested his elbows on the table and dropped his volume a notch, as if he'd gone into spy mode. "There's a guy I know in the industry, a builder. He owns some land and decided not to build on it. It's too small and out of the way for commercial development, so he won't try to get the plot rezoned. But he decided against building a house there." He sipped his coffee. "I don't know all the details yet, but it came up during a conversation. Ellen and I are supposed to check it out soon. Nobody else knows about it, so if we like it, we might arrange a private sale."

"Ellen mentioned the land when I talked to her the other day," Hunter said. "Does that mean you could reach your goal and get your home built by the wedding day?"

"Looks that way, if this deal works out and we haul ass to get it done." Brendan made a fist and landed a bump on Hunter's arm. "Has Kara tried to wrangle you into a wedding yet? Any end in sight to your bachelor life?" he joked.

Hunter dreaded that kind of question.

All through his teen years, the standby question was, *Any girlfriend on the radar?* Now, during adulthood, the question had morphed into, *Any plans to find the right woman and settle down?*

On the surface, those questions appeared harmless. Casual conversation. Inside, however, they had made him uncomfortable for as long as he could remember. Each time someone raised such questions, it reminded Hunter of his own uncertainty. The questions never ceased; they kept coming back, which reminded him that his own issues kept coming back, no matter how hard he tried to resist them.

To Hunter, the questions felt like small knife cuts in his heart. Not painful cuts, but clean slices, the work of a surgeon's scalpel, the kind where you felt nothing until the bleeding began. Their intimations left tiny wounds that lurked in the recesses of his soul and took several days to heal.

As a teenager, the girlfriend question had caused Hunter a momentary spike in anxiety that left him fearful of what the future might—or might not—hold for him. Fortunately, although Hunter hadn't kept a girlfriend in tow as often as his friends had, he'd managed to acquire them with enough frequency to provide himself cover with his family and friends.

It kept suspicion at bay and provided an escape route when interrogations arose. He'd resorted to tangent remarks, such as, *Well, the last relationship ended badly, so I'm taking a breather.*

Brendan stared at Hunter, an amused expression on his face, awaiting a response to his marriage jest.

Hunter drummed his fingers along the table and forced a humorous expression to mimic Brendan's.

"Way too early for that," Hunter said, "though I wouldn't put it past Kara to be thinking about it already."

"You've got that right." With a smirk on his face, Brendan shook his head in a male-bonding manner. "Women, huh?"

And with that remark from Brendan, Hunter knew he was on safe ground again. He breathed easier.

CHAPTER 16

The following evening, a vendor gave Kara tickets to see *The Music Man* at the Palace Theatre.

Hunter wasn't a fan of musicals, which struck him as dated and boring. When a director remade an old film, he could alter details in the storyline and place it into a modern context. With musicals, however, their songs formed the crux of the production. To Hunter, old musicals remained stuck in an era that time had forgotten.

Kara, on the other hand, loved them. On occasion, when they watched television at her apartment, she would turn on a musical she had recorded. A progress-driven individual, Hunter had noticed the story's momentum reached a standstill whenever the characters broke out into song and dance. So Hunter had learned that, when Kara left the room to use the bathroom, he could fast-forward through a song to move the recording along. She never knew the difference when she returned. He could understand why some people enjoyed such slices of Americana; he simply didn't relate to them.

While Hunter had never seen a live performance of *The Music Man,* he had watched the film version in the distant past and could recall the gist of the plot.

"Of all the musicals I've seen, *The Music Man* is my favorite." Kara eyed the closed curtain as she spoke, which came across as endearing, a child not wanting the curtain to open without her seeing it. "More than *Madame Butterfly,* and I loved that one."

"This one has a librarian in it, right?"

"You remember! And it's got the mayor and his wife—she always steals the show. And their daughter, the *ye-gods* girl. So funny."

Kara rested her head upon Hunter's shoulder, to which he responded by placing his arm around her.

"And the main guy is a salesman who leads a band?"

"He doesn't know a thing about music but figures forming a band for the kids in the town can make him money. He comes up with the idea on the spot. When people ask him, he tells them he graduated from some music school."

"Wait, I don't remember that detail. You mean he doesn't know what he's doing?"

"Nope. The man appears in the lives of the townspeople and forms an image of himself that he thinks the town will respond to. He's a man who isn't what he appears to be."

Hunter shifted in his seat.

"But when he falls in love with the librarian," Kara continued, "his secret comes to light."

Hunter nodded. "Then what happens?"

"A big brouhaha."

"Followed by a song and dance?" Hunter grinned.

"Of course. Wouldn't we all do it that way?" Kara replied, matching grin for grin.

Hunter took in the sight of the auditorium. The Palace was a historical attraction on Euclid Avenue in downtown Cleveland. Upon entering the lobby earlier, Hunter couldn't help but notice the carved stone and the staircase that expanded from bottom to top, open arms welcoming royalty. From their vantage point near the middle of the auditorium, Hunter lost count as he tried to estimate the number of seats padded in burgundy fabric. Carved décor surrounded the stage, from which rested a heavy, red curtain with intricate etchings that, for Hunter, brought Oriental calligraphy to mind.

Kara checked her watch, a child bubbling with anticipation, and whispered, "It's almost time."

Hunter felt a waft of heated air trickle past him. In its wake, a strand of Kara's hair strayed and landed upon her face. With his free hand, Hunter reached over and brushed it away with his knuckle. Their eyes locked. She searched his face, her eyes flicking back and forth, the way she did when she desired a display of tenderness from him.

Hunter focused on her face, tried to summon a more intense attraction toward her. Searching her eyes, he found it difficult to locate depth in them, one with which he could connect. He so wished he could. He *wanted* to desire her from the deepest part of his heart, but couldn't find a way to get there. Frustrated, he remained cool and kept a tender exterior in an effort to give to her what he *could* summon.

Leaning forward, he gazed into her eyes and laid a soft, protracted kiss upon her lips.

When they parted, Kara opened her eyes and smiled, her eyes shimmering in the theater's ambient glow. Her smile spoke of contentment, a heart touched.

"That was nice," she said, her tone soft and earnest.

Her words pinched Hunter's heart, a tinge of sadness as he looked into her eyes and realized, in a degree new and profound, that she hadn't the faintest suspicion of his lack of desire toward her. He had played his part well.

Hunter loved her. He truly did, in some shape or form. No doubt about it. His love for her emanated from his heart. And while he could sense it within, he couldn't identify which *type* of love it was. It resembled gentle compassion more than romantic urge, a quality that brought comfort but not invigoration.

Yet tonight, he stared into her eyes and continued to search, desperate to find an ember that could draw his soul to hers.

This is how I want to be, Hunter thought to himself. *I'm not gay. Keep it suppressed. Force it down, and the nightmare will go away.*

Granted, he had fought it this way for years without success, but maybe that's the way it was. Maybe it took years to see victory. Nothing more than a prolonged battle, a foe that took longer than others to conquer.

Just forget about it for tonight. You'll be fine.

The theater lights flashed twice to signal the program was about to begin.

He felt he should say *something,* express *something,* to her before the moment passed. Something genuine from his heart. But he wasn't sure what.

Retrieving his arm from around her shoulder, he took her hand in both of his. Her pixie-size hand looked diminutive when engulfed in his. He gazed into her eyes once again, one more try, and opened his mouth to see what words he could find.

Too late. The lights dimmed. Music boomed from an orchestra. Kara beamed, turning to face the stage as the overture played.

Soon the curtain opened to reveal a train setting. Hunter found the details impressive—the props, the costumes, the backdrop. It was amazing how much a curtain could hide. Hunter sank into his plush seat to enjoy the show.

Onstage, salesmen engaged in rhythmic banter, their speech gaining momentum to simulate train movement. Back and forth, the salesmen traded jabs and professional philosophies. In Hunter's opinion, their cadence sounded like roosters squawking a limerick.

Hunter enjoyed teasing Kara while they watched her musicals at home, poking fun at the nostalgia of yesteryear, so he decided to give it a whirl.

"Few people know this," Hunter whispered in Kara's ear, "but this was gangsta rap in its early era."

Kara didn't find his joke funny during a live presentation. She glared at him, then returned her attention to the stage.

With humor no longer an option, Hunter rested his chin on his palm and watched as the scene changed, as Iowan characters drifted into a song about their town. A place where life was simple, straightforward.

Hunter's mind drifted back to the kiss he and Kara had shared a few minutes ago. As he analyzed its details and his lack of authentic engagement in its affection, his frustration mounted.

He hated this battle. He hated it for the unsuspecting hearts that stood to get hurt in its wake.

Sleep eluded him that night.

Lying in bed, Hunter's eyelids felt heavy. And while he'd flirted with slumber several times tonight, he'd startled himself awake in the final instant, unable to relax enough to drift away.

Darkness. Hunter listened to the steady tick of his watch, which sat atop the dresser. A faint noise he would have overlooked in other scenarios. Tonight, however, each tick reminded him of how much closer the night crept toward dawn.

Lying on his back, with his lower-back muscles at rest, his mind wandered to his evening with Kara at the theater: Her porcelain arm in his as they treaded across the red carpet in the lobby. The sound of her gasps as she admired the ornate carvings along the walls. The way she had leaned into him in the auditorium as the storyline unfolded.

That kiss. The innocence in her eyes.

And his awareness that he had deceived her.

Hunter couldn't shake that notion. Despite the sense of love he held for her, he feared he could never surrender his heart to it. And that didn't seem fair to Kara.

It didn't seem fair to *him,* either. After all, he *wanted* to love her. He *tried* to love her.

He needed time. What was wrong with that? Didn't all relationships take time?

Then a more frightening thought emerged: Hunter wondered if he could ever give his whole heart to *anyone.* If not, should he settle for less? Is that what other people did? If you couldn't find complete happiness, was it possible to get 95 percent of the way there?

Hunter listened to the furnace hum as the heat kicked on. From a nearby vent, a faint, toasty draft tickled his face. Outside, a streetlight flickered in the distance. The moon cast its electric glow through the window, which created long shadows at perfect angles on the far side of his bedroom.

Hunter pulled his blanket snug beneath his chin.

Gabe.

Images of Gabe floated across his mind in a stream of consciousness.

Gabe's smile, the one that warmed Hunter's heart with the glow of a hundred candles and ushered in a sense of security. The openness in Gabe's eyes, which welcomed Hunter's honesty, eyes that wouldn't think less of Hunter for revealing a glimpse of his soul. Perfect, succinct ears that Hunter knew would listen to words he had buried since childhood.

Then his mind's eye skipped to Gabe's arms, the arms Hunter had noticed during his first appointment as Gabe had worked along Hunter's shoulders. The way the muscles flexed along Gabe's forearms. Deep crevices that lined Gabe's arms to form narrow moats between bone and muscle, which showed up whenever Gabe angled his arm in the midst of therapeutic motion.

Hunter knew he should stop right now. But he didn't. He allowed the images to run their course.

He concentrated with more intensity, adjusting the lens of his mind's eye to bring Gabe's arms into sharper focus. Hunter closed his eyes. He could feel Gabe's fingers make contact on his skin as they worked their way along his back, descending from his shoulders to where his shoulder blades converged, then farther down toward Hunter's waistline.

Hunter sensed himself stir below his waist. Heat emanated from his torso and sent a steady, electric current coursing through his veins. He thought of his own bare skin on the massage table, the vulnerability present when a towel had provided the only barrier between the flesh of his midsection and Gabe's sight. At that first appointment, the thought had made Hunter uncomfortable. But now, its mystery enlivened him.

Gabe's face came into focus as he worked through the routine, coming nearer to Hunter's skin as he concentrated on Hunter's back. Drawing closer, yet his chin or cheekbone never made contact with Hunter's flesh. Hunter had wished for contact, just one moment of it. He imagined the fever from Gabe's breath as it landed on his flesh.

Now, lying in bed, Hunter felt his resistance wear thin. The slide occurred in a gradual decline, the way it always did. Thought by thought, image by image, he peeled away layers of onionskin, one by one.

Hunter's breathing grew heavier, his gasps more desperate. He held each breath a full second before releasing it. He fought—halfheartedly—to endure this inner torture, to resist the pictures he had allowed to ambush his brain. Caught between the urge of his flesh and the desire to bring this thought pattern to a screeching halt right now, he winced. Of all the aspects of his battle, lust was the most difficult, the toughest obstacle to resist. God would want him to put a stop to these thoughts, he knew. Yet Hunter continued to tiptoe forward, brushing against the boundary line, nuzzling it.

Beads of perspiration burst across his scalp, soaking his hair at its roots.

Gabe's hands again. Strong fingers. Blue eyes like ice on fire.

Hunter curled his hands into fists at his sides, arms locked at the elbows, eyes aimed toward heaven, whispering for God's help. With every ounce of defense he could summon, he tried to fight the pressure.

Yet Hunter sighed as he felt his resistance crumble, sand washed from the shoreline during high tide.

His hand now rested feather light on his chest. He clenched his jaw. Bit his lower lip.

Fully aroused at his torso, he hurt from withstanding for so long.

The crack was almost imperceptible. A breaking in his will.

He allowed his hand slide down his chest … farther … farther …

Hunter tilted his head back. His fingers continued to slide until he experienced an involuntary jolt as they made initial contact with his midsection.

Images raced … raced … a flurry of sporadic pictures that melded into a blur.

And within seconds, it was over.

With his heart racing, his neck went lax against his pillow. He panted for breath.

Hunter felt an anchor drop in his gut.

He had been through this scenario countless times before. But not with Gabe on his mind. Now he had crossed *that* line.

Hunter couldn't deny it. He knew his attraction to Gabe was real.

Shame settled in. Part of him wanted to weep because he felt as though he had let God down. Another part of him felt a stronger pull toward Gabe. Incidences like this, these five-minute rollercoaster rides, had occurred before, ignited by thoughts of other guys his age, all the way back to when Hunter was a young teenager.

But this instance was different.

This time, the guy about whom Hunter had fantasized was someone he actually cared about, someone with whom Hunter felt comfortable opening up—a rarity in his life.

Unable to reconcile the incongruity, Hunter felt helpless.

Exhaustion overcame him. His breathing slowed. His heartbeat coasted toward its normal speed, and soon he drifted to sleep.

CHAPTER 17

Hunter knew he should have seen it coming. He should have listened to the nudges he'd sensed in his spirit.

But he hadn't.

The call arrived at 10:26 on Monday morning. Out of habit, as soon as he'd hung up the phone, his eye had darted to the lower-right corner of his laptop screen to note the time. A conscientious Hunter always noted the time a client called so he could create a journal record in his customer-relationship software, where he would summarize their conversation. Then, prior to calling a client or prospect, Hunter would scan the last few records of their interaction to jog his memory. If the client mentioned his kid would play third base in a softball game that weekend, Hunter would, during the next call, ask how the game went, how many stolen bases the kid had prevented, or the number of runs he'd scored.

But this call hadn't come from a client. When this call arrived, the phone's double-ring tone indicated it had originated from within the building. Hunter glanced at the phone's display screen.

Human Resources had summoned him. The *director* of Human Resources.

Gretchen Miller's voice had sounded askew in a way Hunter couldn't identify—not so much what was in her voice, but what *wasn't* in her voice. She had sounded pleasant, yet removed, a neutrality Hunter sensed as intentional. The sort of neutrality that preceded bad news.

Hunter wondered if the call would involve bad news about his manager, Wayne. Wayne had left for Detroit last week. He was supposed to continue to Milwaukee this week.

Wayne got on his flight to Milwaukee, right? Hunter wondered. Hunter assumed he had. Come to think of it, however, he hadn't received any phone or email messages from him today. For a man like Wayne, whose battle cry occurred in full force around daybreak, today's Monday-morning silence wasn't in character.

Hunter's tongue went fuzzy. He took a sip of coffee, which had gone cold.

As he pondered the situation, he caught himself chewing his thumbnail and ceased.

No, this definitely can't be good, Hunter thought. Wayne must be in trouble. Hunter had heard of the man's heated exchanges with other managers when he was tense. Had it finally come back to bite him, prompting Gretchen Miller to notify Hunter that, for the interim, he didn't have a boss? Or maybe Wayne had quit on the spot. *That* would fit his personality: a renegade who would spend two years planning his own business venture, line up a slew of clients, walk out on his job, and then, the next day, notify his former employer he'd become their major competitor.

Had anyone else received Gretchen's call?

He checked his clock again. 10:28 a.m. The foreboding continued, but he couldn't stall any longer. He'd better head to the first floor, he figured.

Hunter took the long way through his department. Instead of cutting through the narrow corridor between his cubicle section and the next, he walked toward the far end of his area, wrapped around the final row of cubicles, and headed up the corridor on the opposite side of the room. Along the way, he eyed various cubicles to see if anyone was missing, to get an idea of who else Human Resources might have contacted. He didn't hear a chain of ring tones, but maybe they had called him last. He noted a few absences but knew one of those individuals had called in sick. Another had mentioned a client visit first thing this morning. Close to the glass doors, one person was away from his cubicle—Hunter didn't know why—but his light remained on. Otherwise, the team appeared in place, no signs of abnormality. No one sneaking into a neighbor's cubicle to whisper. No muted chatter in corners of the room.

Taking the stairs to the first floor, he crossed the lobby, offering a brief wave to the receptionist on his way. The Human Resources office sat at the far end of the lobby, behind a pair of frosted-glass doors to convey confidentiality. Hunter entered the office, where the air felt five degrees cooler.

"Gretchen asked me to stop by," Hunter said to an executive assistant, his tone inquisitive, hoping she knew more about this than he did.

"Hi, Hunter. Yes, you can go on in." The same detached manner Hunter had detected from Gretchen on the phone. The executive assistant offered him a smile, but looked as though she'd forgotten to remind her eyes to follow suit. She returned her attention to her computer in what Hunter considered a bit too early.

Gretchen Miller wore a professional blazer-skirt combination of navy blue, with a white blouse and a power-red scarf worked into her outfit. Traces of gray highlighted her brunette hair. Hunter and Gretchen had enjoyed a cordial working relationship during his years with the company.

When he gave her open door a quiet knock, she peered over her eyeglasses, the tortoiseshell frames of which lent her nose a beaklike quality.

"Thanks for coming, Hunter." She gestured to a small table and chairs in her office. "Have a seat."

As Hunter took a seat with his back toward the door, he heard the door click shut as Gretchen closed it before joining him. He eyed the sole item in her arms: a glossy, dark green folder with the company logo embossed in gold on the front. Gretchen opened the folder before her, removed a section of paperwork, thumbed through its contents, then continued with the next section. She progressed with efficiency, a step-by-step routine practiced to perfection. Her eyes darted in his direction once. The same detached smile as the executive assistant's, but Hunter caught a hint of regret in Gretchen's eyes, as if her pupils had retreated to avoid the moment at hand.

Once she judged all documents intact, Gretchen sat with exquisite posture, her hands on the mahogany table with her thumbs and fingertips touching, a meticulous steeple toppling over in his direction. She looked him in the eyes and didn't begin to speak until he returned eye contact to indicate he'd yielded his full attention.

"As you know, Hunter," Gretchen said, "the company has had its challenges this year. The lagging economy has exacerbated the situation and tied the company's hands. I realize rumors have circulated, but we've held together the best we could and made our employees one of our top priorities."

Okay, he thought. He rested one elbow on the table and focused on Gretchen's words, his concentration so intense, he caught himself resting his index finger on his upper lip. He returned his hand to the tabletop.

"Each sales region was instructed to reduce its team by two people," Gretchen continued, her demeanor professional, her tone absent of emotion. "Those reductions are being implemented today."

Hunter offered no reaction but clung to every syllable, trying to identify clues as to what lay mere seconds ahead. But he cringed inside because he already perceived what Gretchen was about to tell him.

"Unfortunately, Wayne is out of town this week, so he wasn't able to be present today." At that point, Gretchen hesitated. Hunter noticed a subtle alteration in shape at the corners of her eyes and saw a trace of sorrow, which she tried, without success, to mask. She penetrated his eyes with hers; along their edges, he detected she didn't want to say the words that came next: "Your position has been eliminated as of today."

Hunter didn't say a word.

Lightheadedness settled in, causing him to feel as if he could doze into a nap. His chest felt heavier. To buy himself a few seconds, he shut his eyes. His eyelids felt feverish.

He'd suspected this day might arrive, but that changed nothing. No matter how inevitable it might appear as it draws near, you're never prepared to hear you no longer have a job. The words sound different, harsher, coming from someone whose mind you know you can't change, regardless of what you might say. At the moment, Hunter couldn't say anything. He wanted to vomit.

What Hunter *hadn't* anticipated in such a moment was an absence of emotion. What fascinated him was how *non-angry* he felt upon hearing the news. He'd pictured himself, were this event to occur, filling with righteous resentment, pointing out his faithful service, years of dedicated labor that had preceded a handful of unsuccessful months.

Instead, he felt deflated.

One thought ran through his mind in tickertape fashion.

I've lost my job.

Too stunned to speak, Hunter yielded to Gretchen, who, he now noticed, had developed a standard, step-by-step procedure for informing an individual that his roof was about to collapse and she would have the honor of taking the final swing of the sledgehammer. She would need to speak next, because he didn't have a clue how to navigate this mess.

As Gretchen Miller opened the shiny green folder with the gold logo, she provided a rundown of the severance package the company would offer him: Three months of health coverage. Outplacement services to help him locate another job. A lump-sum payment which, given alternate circumstances, would have looked like a nice reward. In this context, however, Hunter tried to calculate in his now-fuzzy mind how many rent payments the lump sum could cover. It's strange how far a dollar can stretch when it's not needed, and how little that dollar stretches when it's needed most.

Minute by minute, Gretchen's rundown wobbled through Hunter's head in a drunken blur. He studied Gretchen as she spoke, as she pointed to a printed bullet point, then made eye contact with him, followed by the next bullet point, then flipped to the next page. Gretchen explained the details as if he had a *choice,* as if he had selected this option a few weeks ago and the time had come to sign on the dotted line. But she and Hunter both knew he couldn't afford to say no. He was out of a job. Did the details matter?

Hunter kept his eyes on the paperwork, not out of interest, but because this scenario made him uncomfortable. The folder was the only object on the table and he needed to look *somewhere.* A jumble of hurt and embarrassment rendered him no longer willing to look at Gretchen's face.

Hunter listened further, then perceived a shift in his mood from embarrassment to betrayal. As Gretchen set one stack of papers aside and moved on to the next, she continued her spiel. Without flinching, Hunter raised his head again and stared straight at her, trying his best to hide any traces of anger or pain, replacing them with a confident façade. With the detachment of a scientist or psychologist, he observed the composure in Gretchen's eyes. He marveled at the precise, efficient manner in which she laid out how, exactly, they had opted to screw him over in the fairest way possible.

How could you operate with such mundane efficiency while, step by step, dismantling somebody's financial stability? Hunter wondered.

As it turned out, signing on the dotted line wasn't a cute saying. On the final page, there *was* a line on which to sign. Above that line was an agreement filled with legal verbiage that stated Hunter would receive his severance package in exchange for relinquishing all options to pursue legal action against the company between now and eternity. And the standard kicker: Hunter couldn't try to lure any employees from the company for the next two years. In Hunter's view, it felt more like they had wrapped their arms around his financial security, his food and bills, and held them hostage until he signed his name. Which he did.

A win-win scenario, as a seminar speaker might have called it.

With the formalities complete and the glossy, gold-embossed folder under his arm, Hunter returned to his cubicle, accompanied by Gretchen Miller, as if Hunter posed a threat and required an armed guard. And as if the situation weren't humiliating enough, Gretchen had given him two empty boxes to carry up the stairs and down the hall, past the cubicle rows, boxes he could fill with his belongings. Everyone who saw him walk down the hall with her would know what had happened.

Voices hushed. Individuals stared at their laptop screens, yet Hunter could sense their stares jabbing against his back. From the corner of his eye, he caught a young woman rise from her desk and saunter into the hallway, probably to light the grapevine on fire. He could have predicted the scenario before he arrived on his floor.

Gretchen sat down in a nearby chair, crossed her legs with one knee high over the other, and kept guard as Hunter emptied his desk and filled his boxes.

Among the files in his desk, Hunter kept personal files, such as performance reviews and trade-industry articles. If Hunter packed a folder or binder into his box that appeared confidential, Gretchen would raise her eyebrows to summon forth an explanation, to which Hunter would open the item and explain it was material from a recent industry-training seminar or another non-threatening source, material he would like to keep since he had recorded helpful notes in it. Gretchen would grant permission, and Hunter, the convicted criminal, would add it to his box.

Ten minutes later, with both boxes in tow and the glossy, gold-embossed folder sticking out at the top, Hunter walked out the front door of the building and loaded the boxes into the trunk of his car.

He checked his watch.

11:48 a.m.

It wasn't even afternoon, yet in the course of an hour, his entire day had emptied.

Hunter climbed into the front seat, where ordinary noises now sounded louder.

The slam of his car door. The squeak of driver's seat. The click of his seatbelt.

Stopping short of turning on the ignition, Hunter placed his hands on the steering wheel and stared straight ahead at a giant tree whose trunk blocked his view.

So now what? Hunter asked himself.

CHAPTER 18

Turning onto Route 91 in Solon, where businesses and small shopping plazas dotted the periphery, Hunter noticed the street had started to grow busier with noontime traffic. He was a few blocks from his office—or, rather, his former office. Hunter couldn't help but laugh at the depressing irony before him: A sea filled with drivers rushing around to return within an hour, while Hunter had nowhere to go.

Kara didn't believe you could exist without thinking *something.* Like Hunter's past girlfriends, she figured your mind is in a perpetual churn. And if it's churning, then thoughts must be present. So when Kara or another girlfriend asked what was on his mind and Hunter would respond by saying, "Nothing," they refused to believe him. He'd insist his mind was blank, perhaps in relaxation mode, and they would insist he was wrong.

But now, driving along Route 91, Hunter knew without a doubt that your mind could, in fact, be absent of thought, because his mind had drained. Hunter didn't know *what* to think. At the same time, he sensed pressure mounting by the minute as cinder-block walls closed in around his brain and darkness crept in.

From behind his sunglasses, Hunter looked toward heaven.

"God, what am I supposed to do now?" he asked, one friend to another.

No matter how bad his circumstances had appeared in the past, he'd held peace that God would work out the details on his behalf. God had never disappointed him, and Hunter had confidence He would come through for him in this new phase of life.

Nonetheless, that confidence was a long-term assurance. It didn't annihilate the cinder-block walls of the moment. And the truth was, it didn't make him feel any less like an asphalt patch on the shoulder of Route 91.

He would need to tell Kara, but he didn't want to feel weak before her any earlier than necessary. Besides, he didn't want to get her concerned about his predicament before *he himself* knew how concerned he should be. She would want to stop by his house immediately after work, while he would want a few hours alone. He could call her in an hour, let her know what had unfolded, and she could swing by later that evening if she wished. She didn't understand every aspect of how he operated, but she knew he held much inside. Maybe she would respect his need for time.

Yet, at the moment, he didn't want to be alone, either. He craved proximity, someone who could be near him without trying to solve his problem or unleash a long list of questions to which Hunter didn't have answers. Somebody who didn't have a vested interest in whatever his next decision might entail. Someone who understood the value in just being there. No games, no façades, no walls.

Unfortunately, he didn't have such relationships in his life. Everyone Hunter knew was accustomed to his holding everything inside.

Except one.

As he approached a traffic light at a familiar four-way intersection, Hunter decided where to go. Jerking his car into the left lane at the last second, he heard a quick screech from his tires. With a glance in his rearview mirror, he waved an apology to the driver behind him.

Hunter walked into Gabe's clinic, scanned the reception area, and noticed a client paging through a magazine while she waited. She might be someone else's client, Hunter figured. It was worth a try. Even if she was Gabe's next client, Hunter could wait. He had all the time in the world today.

"Is Gabe available?" Hunter asked the same sunny receptionist.

With a furrowing of her eyebrows, she checked her computer monitor before returning her attention to him.

"Hello, Hunter. I'm sorry, were you scheduled for an appointment?"

"No, I … thought he might have a few minutes to talk, that's all." On second thought, Hunter started to turn around and added, "I can talk to him later."

The receptionist rose and said, "I doubt that's necessary. He's finishing with a client now, but he should have a few minutes when he's done. Have a seat."

As Hunter waited, reality began to hit home. He had no immediate answers. By this time tomorrow, where would he be? What would he be doing? He could call a handful of contacts tomorrow, but beyond that, he didn't have a plan.

Emotion rose inside, a powerful wave of grief, and Hunter detested how vulnerable it made him feel. He gritted his teeth and squelched the sadness, forced it down. His stomach quivered, but he feigned a steady countenance. Only in private did he let emotions seep out. Behind the walls of his house, where no one else could see.

A few minutes later, Hunter heard the click of a door and he raised his eyes. A middle-aged woman departed Gabe's appointment room, waved to the receptionist, and walked out the front door. Hunter's palms grew moist.

The next door swung open, and through the doorway, Hunter caught a glimpse of a small office. When Gabe emerged and saw Hunter sitting in the reception area, his eyebrows furrowed to match the receptionist's initial reaction. In Gabe's reaction, however, Hunter caught not only confusion, but a hint of welcome surprise.

"Hey, Hunter," Gabe said, "did I forget about an appointment?"

Rising from his seat, Hunter forced a smile. "No, you didn't. I just—do you have a few minutes to chat? Is that okay?"

"Sure." Waving Hunter into the appointment room, Gabe said, "My office is tiny and cramped. Want to meet in here instead?"

Hunter nodded and followed Gabe inside, closing the door behind him.

"That was my last appointment before lunch," Gabe said with a gesture of his thumb toward the reception area. He removed the sheet from the massage table, leaving its surface bare. "I was gonna change the sheets and clean up, then eat lunch in my office. But I can do that later."

Hunter sat on the massage table—at least *that* familiarity remained in his life—and forced a smile. He believed he hid his grief well until Gabe gave him a second glance and leaned toward him, studying Hunter's expression. Hesitating at first, as though deciding what his next action should be, Gabe bit his lower lip with determination and took a seat beside Hunter on the table. At that, Hunter knew Gabe had picked up on his need for proximity. He'd figured he would. Gabe was a rare breed that way.

"Are you sure you're okay?" Gabe asked. "You look shaken."

"I thought I'd hidden it well."

"Your face looks red, like you're flustered. Is it because of what you wanted to talk about?"

"Yeah."

"Is Kara in town?"

"She's at work. I can't talk to her right now," Hunter said, fixing his gaze on his knees and his dark dress pants. He had bought this suit two weeks ago. The credit card bill hadn't even had time to arrive. Had he known what would develop today, he wouldn't have made the purchase. "I need to talk to somebody I can be myself with. I mean, let my guard down or whatever."

"That's fine." Gabe's voice was muted, the murmur of a close listener. "What happened? Are you on your lunch hour?"

"I lost it," Hunter said.

"Lost what?"

"I lost my job."

Gabe grew wide-eyed. "What? When?"

Hunter checked his watch. "I left the office twenty minutes ago. My stuff is in the trunk of my car."

Gabe's shoulder's grew limp, deflated. "Oh man, I hate to hear that." He waited a few seconds, then said, "I thought you talked to your boss."

"I did, last week. He tried to convince me I was in good shape." Hunter's eyes felt heavy, as if a day's worth of energy had drained out of them in the last hour. His eyes met Gabe's before Hunter returned his focus to his knees. "He looked at me and knew this was coming, but let me believe he didn't have a clue—encouraged me that I was doing everything I could do, the whole bit. Then he left town, and they made cutbacks today." Hunter increased the pressure of his palms against the table, dug his fingers into it, tried to release his tension and frustration while holding himself together. "I knew he was holding back, like I told you later. He said things like, 'The company hasn't made any cutbacks.' And I thought, 'Well, no, not yet.' I tried to dance around the present tense and future tense, but he kept his mouth sealed about the future. He had to have known this was coming down the pipeline. He would have chosen who to let go. He'd probably already submitted his names to Human Resources before I walked into his office that day." Hunter's chest grew heavier. He could feel his ribs along its surface. "Man, I'm so stupid."

"You're not stupid."

"Stupid, gullible, whatever. How could I have trusted my boss?"

"You have a good heart. You gave him the benefit of the doubt, trusted him to be straightforward with you. Some people take advantage of that."

Hunter paused. "Now it's all over. The months of failure, the humiliation of having to admit I lost deal after deal, finally came to an end."

From the corner of his eye, he saw Gabe's steady gaze remained focused on him, and Hunter couldn't find words to express his gratitude for a listening ear that didn't judge him, for another human being who wouldn't give him odd looks because he laid his honesty on the table.

"After all this time, I'm just plain worn down, the way you feel when you've fought hard and finally achieved your goal. But this isn't exactly an achievement to be proud of." Hunter rubbed his eyes. "I don't know how else to explain it, but I'm not used to defeat. I'm a competitive person; I'm not used to feeling like I've lost. I wasn't raised to lose, I—"

Hunter stopped short when he heard his own voice quake. All at once, a list of failures arose in his heart and flashed in a slideshow through the recesses of his memory: his job ... his failed relationships ... the way he fell far short of the type of Christian he so desired to be ... and the gender attraction he found so hard to resist. Suddenly, all the hurt he'd suppressed on his way to this building reached the surface and broke through.

A tear spilled from Hunter's eye.

Embarrassed, immediately Hunter wiped his eye with his thumb, angry at himself for allowing that tear to escape, but it had come before he could block it.

He glanced at Gabe, then drew his own shoulders inward.

"I never let anyone see me cry," Hunter said.

Hunter sniffed, then pursed his lips and let out a long breath through his mouth.

Hunter said nothing. Gabe said nothing.

Silence hung in the air between them, which Hunter considered a relief. He didn't need anyone to speak empty words. He needed to know someone cared enough to be there for him, just for who he was, not for who he could be for them.

The next minute stretched to triple its length. He heard the muted sound of traffic through the window.

Finally, Hunter broke the silence.

"I don't know what to do next. I can't even see far enough ahead to think."

Another beat passed, then Gabe patted Hunter's knee.

"It's going to work out, I promise," Gabe whispered. "I believe in you."

It's going to work out. I believe in you.

Those were the two things Hunter had wanted to hear since childhood, the whole time he had buried his horrible secret.

When he turned to Gabe, he found him gazing back at him. Gabe held his countenance steady but without expression, intent on supporting Hunter. And once again, Hunter recognized the compassion in Gabe's eyes, that unceasing quality with which he had grown so familiar.

But now, as time slowed, Hunter perceived a depth in Gabe's eyes he'd never noticed. Hunter squinted, focused on those eyes, found himself drawing nearer by the millimeter. The movement would have been imperceptible to anyone who might have watched it unfold, but Hunter felt the pull. Their eyes remained locked.

In retrospect, Hunter would reconsider that episode for years to come. He would ponder what had happened between Gabe and him, and what might *not* have happened had the moment ended one second sooner.

Perhaps they had focused on each other a split second too long. But that extra tick in time—one frame on a film reel— proved enough to cement something between them.

Hunter couldn't put his finger on what caused it to happen, but a deadbolt unlocked inside his heart.

Before he could catch himself, before his defenses took control, Hunter flinched. Leaned closer. Just an inch.

Gabe leaned an inch closer, too.

And before he knew it, before he could register what would transpire at 12:37 p.m., Hunter closed his eyes. Gabe's lips brushed against his. The sensation bubbled in Hunter's fibers the way saltwater foamed along the Atlantic shoreline.

Hunter's hands found their way to Gabe's biceps and lingered there.

And for the next few moments, Hunter breathed deeply, peacefully, as he melted into the most tender, satisfying, electric kiss he'd experienced in his life.

PART TWO

FACADE

TRUST

CHAPTER 19

That evening, Hunter pulled a frozen Hawaiian pizza from the freezer, unwrapped it, and set it on a baking tray while the oven preheated.

Were the event at Gabe's clinic not etched into his brain, he could have dismissed it as a dream, a figment of his imagination. The problem was, the experience had included a tangible aspect, which had left concrete reference points in its wake. If he closed his eyes, he could still feel the brush of Gabe's upper lip against his.

But that kiss boded worse for Hunter because the experience had unleashed another event, one that frightened him even more.

It had blown Hunter's disguise. Somebody else knew his secret.

The kiss replayed itself on his mental movie screen, over and over, in an endless loop. He couldn't stop it. And as the reiterations played, a range of emotions coursed through him.

Confusion about whether he understood all facets of his identity.

Nervousness, wondering how he could look Gabe in the eye again.

Concern about what this meant for Kara and him, and whether one kiss—with no long-term viability—meant he should end his relationship with her.

Anger at allowing vulnerability to creep in, poison his judgment, and reveal what hid beneath the mask he'd perfected.

But most of all, Hunter felt scared.

Scared because, in the darkest corner of his heart, Hunter knew he'd *enjoyed* that kiss.

Following the kiss, Hunter could hear the tick of every timepiece in Gabe's clinic—the clock on the wall; Hunter's watch; the beat of the music that, due to the silence in the appointment room, he could hear from the reception area on the other side of the door.

And yet, time had screeched to a standstill in Gabe's clinic.

At first, Hunter had felt too stunned to react. At the end of the kiss, he'd sat there, wincing, his shoulders still inclined halfway toward Gabe, not wanting to open his eyes. When he'd drawn back and opened his eyes, he'd discovered Gabe had reacted in a similar fashion. The familiar compassion had fled Gabe's eyes, and Hunter could read the shock and hesitation that had skulked in, their shadows lurking.

In Gabe's eyes, Hunter recognized the fear was mutual.

Neither one said a word after the kiss. Each man had dropped his gaze, each trying to catch a glimpse of the other in his peripheral vision. Each trying to gauge the other's reaction and see whether the other possessed the same awareness—and the same guilt—of having fulfilled a desire, one which neither felt prepared to face.

The longer the knowledge dripped between them, the more awkward the scenario felt.

Hunter, as if by reflex, had slid from the table and planted his feet on the floor.

"I need to go," Hunter had said, avoiding eye contact with a fervor he wished he'd engaged before the whole mess erupted.

With that, he'd hurried out of the room. And Gabe hadn't stopped him.

The oven beeped. When Hunter opened its door, a 425-degree blast hit his face and made his eyes water. For an instant, Hunter wondered how hot hell is, but brushed away the thought before it could take root.

Overwhelmed, he shoved the pizza into the oven, then took a seat at the kitchen table and rested his head in his hands. When he raised his head again, he noticed a CD sitting at the corner of the table, the corner closest to his back door. As preoccupied as he'd been when he'd arrived home, Hunter hadn't noticed it earlier. He saw a note sticking out from underneath the CD.

He retrieved the note and recognized the paper from a stack he kept in a kitchen drawer. Before reading a word, he recognized Kara's penmanship. Upon leaving Gabe's clinic, he had given her a call and relayed the news about his job, if for no other reason than to get his mind off of what had occurred with Gabe.

In her note, Kara had reiterated how sorry she was to hear the news. As it turned out, at the last minute that morning, she and her boss had booked a flight to Chicago. Kara had taken two hours that afternoon to race home, pack an overnight bag, and head to the airport. On her way home, however, she had picked up the CD—*Moondance* by Van Morrison, an album Hunter loved but had never bought—as a surprise to help lift his spirits. She noted she had let herself in and hoped he didn't mind.

That incident left Hunter conflicted. On one hand, her effort to cheer him up was a sweet gesture. Despite her limited time, she had gone out of her way to give him a boost.

On the other hand, Hunter wasn't sure how comfortable he should feel about Kara having let herself into his house. He knew she was honest; he harbored no concerns that she would steal anything. And even though she had a key, she never took advantage of it. This marked the first time she'd entered while he wasn't home.

If she made a habit of it, which he doubted, then they would need to have a chat.

The doorbell rang. When Hunter opened the door, he found Gabe, hands in his jacket pockets, standing on the front porch.

"We should probably talk," said Gabe with a tentative glance.

Hunter hesitated for a beat, but then, with a nod to Gabe, he opened the door wider to allow him inside.

He led Gabe into the kitchen and gestured toward the table. Compared to the living room, Hunter noticed, the oven brought palpable heat to the kitchen and a welcome sense of comfort. Gabe shed his jacket.

"Have a seat," Hunter said, trying to sound casual, and well aware he didn't sound that way at all. And because he didn't know what else to say, he added, "I've got a pizza in the oven, if you want a slice."

"Thanks," Gabe said as he settled into a chair across from Hunter, "but I ate dinner on my way over."

With the formalities out of the way, Hunter didn't know how to proceed. Part of him didn't want to discuss what had happened; the other part of him knew he couldn't ignore it. He respected Gabe for his attempt to face it head-on.

Both men stared at the kitchen table, which contained the CD, a stack of paperwork, and nothing else, minimal evidence of domestication and all the evidence of a bachelor pad. Hunter sensed Gabe catching glimpses of him to decipher what went through his mind—and Hunter followed suit. Hunter felt nauseous and ashamed, but curiosity accompanied the shame, as if he stood on the cusp of the answer to a question he'd asked for years.

Finally, Gabe lifted his head, and Hunter noticed a glint in his eye.

"Well, *that* was unexpected," Gabe said in reference to the kiss, an obvious attempt to bring humor to a thorny scenario.

"I've never exactly … *done* that before …"

"Neither have I …"

"Kind of awkward."

"That's one way to describe it," said Gabe. He shifted in his seat. "It gets more interesting from there, doesn't it?"

Silence resumed. Hunter didn't know which was worse: speaking to the man he associated with the shame he felt or allowing the shame to churn in him all alone. Gabe laid his hands on the table and rubbed his fingers over his fingernails.

"So this … *thing* that happened today," Hunter began. "What does it mean?"

"I don't know," mumbled Gabe.

At least we're on the same page, thought Hunter.

"You uh … when we, you know …" Hunter said at last, "you kissed me back, right?"

"Yeah, I think I did."

A grin twitched at the corner of Hunter's mouth. Then, in an instant, he started to fidget, still angry he had put himself into this situation. With one quick decision to keep up his guard earlier that afternoon, he could have avoided it. He could have shown up at his next scheduled appointment, he and Gabe would have engaged in their usual conversation and humor, and everything would have remained normal. A nice, comfortable status quo. A *predictable* status quo. But that option had evaporated in a minute, one for which Hunter hadn't even thought to prepare himself.

He hadn't moved the CD from the corner of the table, but now he wished he had. One look at the CD, and his thoughts veered toward Kara. Hunter's nausea increased.

Should he tell her? At this point, Hunter didn't know. He felt humiliated enough. It didn't seem fair to reveal this to Kara when he himself didn't understand it fully. After all, he *wanted* to want her. And after his failed attempts at romance in the past, he didn't want to sabotage another one because of a stupid lapse in judgment.

Hunter forced a calm demeanor as panic crept in.

"It was a big mistake," Hunter said. "That's all it was, right?"

"It wasn't planned, if that's what you mean."

Their eyes locked. How could Hunter rationalize what had happened? Could he make Gabe understand the kiss was a lapse in judgment, not a pattern of behavior? It was real, but it wasn't *real.*

"What happened, it isn't me—or it's never been me." Hunter mustered as much sincerity as possible. "I don't even know what to make of it."

"You've never had feelings like this for someone else?"

In Gabe's eyes, Hunter recognized the desperation, the weariness of an endless search for a companion. Eyes that long to know someone else understands your inner turmoil. The yearning to know you're not alone.

Hunter sighed to himself. "I have, but I've never acted on those feelings before. Nobody has a clue about me."

"Yeah," Gabe rubbed his eyes, "nobody knows about me, either."

"Then this isn't something we need to tell anyone—please," Hunter said. "Neither of us has this figured out. It would devastate *both* our lives. People would ask questions we don't have the answers to. Is it worth disrupting our lives for something that might not even …"

"… have substance to it?"

"Right."

Each man retreated to his thoughts. For the time being, with Gabe on board to remain quiet, Hunter knew he would have a chance to figure out the impact that day's events would—or should—have on his life.

Their eyes met again, and Hunter asked, "So where do we go from here?"

Palms open, Gabe shrugged and said, "We can't pretend it didn't happen, can we?"

Hunter paused. "Do you *want* to pretend it didn't happen?"

"No," Gabe replied, his voice tentative. He studied his hands before raising his head again. "I guess we just live. Take it day by day."

"No pressure on us. We can figure out what it means on our own timetable."

"And if there's something there, we'll take whatever steps we need to take."

"We won't cause stress for anyone without knowing there's anything to stress about with … with whatever this is …"

"… and we'll see where it leads." Gabe paused, then glanced at Hunter once again. "That is, if you want to."

Hunter breathed deeper, then looked into Gabe's eyes and found in them the compassion that had drawn him from the beginning.

CHAPTER 20

On Sunday morning, Hunter heard drum beats reverberate as he approached the church building from the parking lot.

He never had trouble getting to work or an appointment on time, yet week after week, he arrived to church a minute after the worship service started. With its large congregation and a music segment at the beginning of each service, though, individuals like Hunter could trickle in without anyone noticing their late arrivals.

When he opened the door to the worship auditorium, the music's volume doubled in his ears, the audible equivalent of a blast of heat. A greeter who stood inside the door, a man Hunter had never officially met but had seen for years, gave him a wide smile and a pat on the back. Hunter found an open seat near the middle of the room.

Nearly a thousand people sang the lyrics projected on the wall. From listening to Pastor Chuck's sermons and getting to know him personally over the years, Hunter knew his pastor sought an environment of freedom in worship. Some individuals clapped to the music, some closed their eyes while others kept theirs open. Many individuals across the auditorium lifted their hands in praise, while the occasional person leaped in place or danced with joy in the aisle.

Rather than singing this morning, Hunter observed the environment around him.

Along the auditorium's walls hung fabric-covered rectangles to absorb sound, along with framed photos illustrating the church's history. Dimmed lights, which hung overhead and along the perimeter, ushered a cozy ambience into the room. At the front of the room, on a large platform, the worship band consisted of about ten members: a lead vocalist and several background vocalists; an electric guitarist and a bass player; an alto saxophone player, a keyboardist, and a drummer. The band represented a wide range of ages, yet found common ground as they played an upbeat, contemporary song about God's love that had set them free.

Hunter loved Sunday mornings in church. He could see the elation in people's eyes, people from all walks of life whose relationships with Christ had changed their lives. To Hunter, church felt like a celebration. It reminded him of how glad he'd felt when he'd given his heart to Jesus Christ. He recalled the relief he'd felt, no longer dragging chains of failure and overwhelming guilt. And over the years, as Hunter looked back on his life and compared it to how he'd felt *without* a Savior, he'd grown more grateful.

Today, Hunter felt as welcome in church as he always had. He perceived the same sense of joy and wonder among the people who had gathered together. The song lyrics still resonated in his heart. Since becoming a Christian, whenever Hunter stepped foot in a church service, he held an awareness of his personal struggles. He knew he was far from perfect, as was everyone else around him.

Yet today, Hunter had arrived with an altered perspective.

Last week, Hunter had come to church aware of his attractions, but with the knowledge nothing physical had occurred. It had remained a mere temptation, just as it had every week of his faith life.

As he stood in the worship auditorium this morning, however, he did so with the knowledge of what had occurred between Gabe and him earlier that week.

Today, the contrast lurked in the recesses of his conscience.

The sense of guilt reminded him of how he'd felt before he'd become a Christian, back when he'd given minimal thought to God or religion. And on the occasions he *had* wondered about God, he'd had no idea how to reach out to Him or connect with Him.

Now, in the midst of a sea of other believers, Hunter felt alone.

The final upbeat song came to a close. From their various seats around the auditorium, individuals clapped or gave spontaneous shouts to God. Beyond God's ability to meet needs and keep the whole world in order, the facet of God that Hunter found most fascinating was that He was a *loving* God. He was a God who noticed each individual, who knew each person intimately. A God who looked at each individual with compassion, loved that person in a manner beyond comprehension, and truly cared about the details of that individual's life.

The band changed musical keys and transitioned into a slower, worshipful song. As the tone grew tender, Hunter yearned for a connection between God and him. He closed his eyes and shut out the people around him, focusing on the sweet melody and lyrics of the song.

As the music washed over him, Hunter ruminated on his relationship with Christ, who had rescued Hunter from his own devices and set him on a better course than he would have dreamed otherwise. Jesus had set him free. Hunter had received forgiveness for his sins.

But though he had received a clean slate in his life, his struggles and temptations hadn't vanished, had they? Though he had hope, his problems hadn't disintegrated.

Unfortunately, while Jesus had liberated him from sin, Hunter hadn't experienced the smaller miracle he'd sought.

This morning, as the keyboard-driven worship song continued, Hunter's mind wandered to the electricity he'd discovered when he'd kissed Gabe. Growing more aware of God's presence amid the worship—of Hunter's sin compared to God's holiness—a wave of shame rushed over him. Here he was, worshipping God while he held secret desires for Gabe. A pang hit his heart. Tears formed behind his closed eyelids and seeped out onto his cheeks.

When God looked at Hunter, which one did He see: the genuine Hunter who worshiped God from the depths of his heart, or the Hunter who had succumbed to his weakness?

The truth was, Hunter cared *very much* about what God thought of him and how his faith reflected on others. So where did God stand on this struggle? And in light of that, how was Hunter to reconcile his feelings for Gabe?

For Hunter, the question wasn't about God's love. Rather, he likened it to a child who cared about what his father thought of him, who wanted to bring gladness to his father and make him proud of him.

He knew God loved him. That security had provided an anchor for his heart since he'd turned to Christ at sixteen years old. Besides, he knew from his Bible reading that God even loved people who hated Him or didn't believe in His existence.

The question was, Did Hunter's feelings and actions bring *shame* to God or this church?

Was Hunter a hypocrite for standing here worshipping while knowing the secrets he hid inside? God knew about his struggle. Was it anyone else's business? Or was he a hypocrite for *not* confiding in someone, for keeping the issue private between God and him?

The worship song continued, the lyrics of which spoke about God's grace. Hunter recognized the songwriter had based the lyrics on Psalm 139, a chapter to which Hunter had turned so often in his Bible that the page corner, already thin as onion skin, showed wear marks. When Hunter hit rough times in his life, he read that psalm because it reminded him of God's presence regardless of where he turned. The psalmist pondered whether there was a limit to where God could reach him, and couldn't name one. Even if he made his bed in hell, the psalmist said, God would remain beside him.

Hunter returned his attention to the music. If he lost his chance to worship with believers around him, his next opportunity wouldn't come until the midweek service, and he needed this hour's worth of refuge.

Yet he couldn't remain focused. He couldn't shake the feeling of slipping slowly down a muddy cliff toward a valley, toward unknown territory where answers evaded him.

God's grace.

God's grace was the focal point of Hunter's faith in Christ. Sin brought a penalty, but Jesus had paid that penalty on Hunter's behalf. When Hunter had given himself to Christ, it had brought him into the family of believers, and Christ's payment now covered him, the way an insurance policy might cover all members of a family.

But how far did God's grace reach?

Hunter had never examined that question in such an applicable way. Like everyone else, Hunter sinned in his life. Most of those sins, however, were one-time failures. They didn't carry with them long-term ramifications or strong emotional components.

Where did God's grace begin and end? How much did it cover? Did it cover past mistakes only, or current struggles? Did grace come by the act of *asking* for forgiveness, or did grace already exist to the fullest degree in a heart that belonged to Christ? Was it a step-by-step provision, or did Christ's sacrifice cover *everything*—past, present and future—to free Hunter from having to ask for God's forgiveness detail by detail?

Hunter didn't know the answers to those questions, nor did the Bible seem to state them outright. At least, not as far as Hunter could find in his reading.

And Hunter's torment resided in that absence of knowing.

Most of all, he craved to know where God's grace *ended*.

As far as Hunter could tell, whatever actions that might ensue with Gabe entailed a series of choices, and once he made a conscious choice, Hunter didn't know if God's grace covered it. Could one decision today doom him for eternity? Hunter's salvation had come from a heart response, not physical works.

The Bible said a man's actions could never earn his salvation; rather, salvation came as a free gift, by grace through faith, lest any man should boast.

If Hunter's actions couldn't *earn* his salvation, could his actions *sever* his salvation?

God knew Hunter's faith was genuine. God knew how much Hunter loved Him from what felt like his whole heart.

Where does God draw the line between heart and actions?

Hunter's torment mounted. He was confident he was safe so far. Nonetheless, he wondered if any actions with Gabe might serve as baby steps toward losing his salvation. If he consented to his feelings for Gabe, would he risk his own heart straying from God? Would he step outside the canopy of God's protection? Is it possible for someone to wander so far, he falls out of grace? Could Hunter wind up in hell, forfeiting his salvation for eternity, and trace its root to involvement with Gabe or another man? Was Hunter on the verge of setting into motion permanent damnation before he understood the full consequences and without hope of recovery?

An image flashed through Hunter's mind—an image of himself floating in darkness, writhing in pain as the fires of hell burned away his soul and worms ate at his body, knowing a reprieve would never come and the agony would last forever. Fear of what would come with each instant. Loneliness in knowing God had departed, the notion that he could never again feel the comfort of God's embrace.

Fear shot down Hunter's spine, a terror so severe, he wanted to thrash his head from side to side, desperate to shake the frightful thoughts from his mind. But he remembered where he was—surrounded by people—so he forced himself to settle down, despite the fact that his stomach wrenched and his jaw now felt sore from its clenched state.

This wasn't the first time such images had traveled through his mind. Hunter had considered those pictures year after year, and he had endured them alone.

In moments like these, Hunter turned his attention back to God's love, the love that had accepted and welcomed him years ago. God had known Hunter's challenges and had wanted him anyway. Hunter trusted that love. He trusted that, somewhere along the way, mercy had to be available for someone like him. Not because he deserved it, but because it matched the nature of the God he knew.

With his eyes still closed and another heartfelt worship song fading into the background, Hunter lifted his hands, tilted his face toward heaven, a grateful man worshipping his Savior who sat high on His throne. Tears came forth in such abundance, he gave up on trying to wipe them away. Besides, he wasn't the only one who wept during worship.

To anyone who might have noticed Hunter, they would have assumed this was a simple moment of worship, which it was. But it was also more than that.

For Hunter, it was a desperate cry for God to show up and give him wisdom: hands open and arms outstretched, the arms of a child racing into his father's embrace. Pleading for his father to never abandon him.

CHAPTER 21

"Well, here it is," said Ellen, unlocking the door on the passenger side as Hunter shifted the car into park. Together they climbed out and sauntered toward a view of, what appeared to Hunter, nothing.

The secluded property sat in Brecksville, a suburb located in what Cleveland-area residents called the west side. To reach the property, Hunter and Ellen had exited a freeway, driven through a series of main roads, then twisted and turned for another ten minutes along numerous side roads. Taking a deep breath of early November air, Hunter scanned the grassy plot of land with his eyes. He noticed it stretched several acres wide and about two acres deep, before hitting a thick, wooded area at the rear of the property.

If secrets took a physical form, Hunter mused, *this would be the perfect place for them to hide.*

Hunter zipped up his winter coat. The air felt unseasonably cool. Snow flurries had swirled outside his window the night before. Once December arrived, Hunter knew, any snow that fell would accumulate on his lawn and remain there through winter. It wouldn't start to melt until March, and by then, he knew the pile would measure at least three feet in his front yard.

"We closed the deal on Saturday morning," Ellen said, squinting her eyes and examining the property as through the lens of a dream. "Two months ago, we knew nothing about this land."

"How did you find out about it?"

"The owner was a homebuilder. Brendan has worked with the guy on a bunch of projects over the years, so they cross paths on a regular basis. The guy owned this land and intended to build a house on it, but for several years, nothing happened."

Hunter recalled, during his youth, when he and his family had considered moving and searched for homes around this area. They had looked at a couple of homes built by builders and had noticed a significant difference compared to other homes on the market. Unlike the standard features of a typical home, many builders had avoided neighborhoods and opted for standalone plots of land. They had poured money into all the details of the home and purchased the best of options which, as Hunter's father estimated, the builders had bought at cost.

"Why did he give up on building the house?" Hunter asked.

"It wasn't him," said Ellen. "It was the guy's wife who nixed it. After they'd owned the land a few years, they got a divorce. The wife got the land in the divorce settlement and decided to put it on the market. We bought it directly from her, a for-sale-by-owner thing. The guy mentioned it to Brendan in passing. Next thing we knew, Brendan was on the phone with the wife. Or ex-wife, I should say."

"I wonder why they never built the house in the first place," Hunter wondered aloud. "Why'd they wait all those years without doing anything?"

"I was curious about that too." Ellen swept her foot along the grass, which hadn't grown out of control but needed a final mowing for the season. "When she showed us around the property, we got to talking, and I asked her that question."

"What did she say?"

"She doesn't harbor cozy feelings toward her ex-husband, of course, but her explanation threw me. She said she'd felt trapped inside the marriage and couldn't bear the thought of building a house to fill with lies. A house where the façade looks ideal and the fixtures are everything she'd dreamed of, but behind the front door—between those walls—the lies mount higher and higher. Finally, the day would come when she'd suffocate and die inside."

"Sounds harsh."

"Scared the hell out of me, that's for sure. That's how she put it, though: The lies would build inside that house till she'd suffocate and die. No way was she gonna let that happen—build a pretty house and put on her best show for the public, while inside, she'd crumble from the pressure between the walls of her lies. So after years of trying to gloss over the problems in their marriage, she told her husband she didn't want what he wanted. All the deeper issues between them rose to the surface and escalated from there. Next thing you know, they got a divorce."

Hunter drew his shoulders together to bring his coat tighter against himself.

"I never want one of those in my life," Ellen murmured.

"Don't want what?"

"A fucking house of lies," she replied, no expression upon her face.

A gust of wind blew and the chill in the air seemed to plunge. Hunter shoved his hands into his pockets and glanced at Ellen, whose face had grown ashen in the cold. Rosy patches had bloomed on her nose and cheeks. She appeared lost in reflection as she stared at the broad land before them.

As he pondered Ellen's remarks, Hunter considered his relationship with Kara in light of the feelings he'd developed for Gabe. When honest with himself, Hunter had to admit he felt much more attracted to Gabe than to Kara. Yet, on the other hand, his relationship with Kara made sense: a woman, a wife, a family … a future. And if not with Kara, with another woman. What was he supposed to do? Sabotage another relationship? Give up on the future he desired in his heart, a course he believed wiser, because of attraction to someone else—an attraction that might prove fleeting in the end? He wanted to treat Kara with kindness. If she knew the whole scenario, what would she say? Would she *want* him to give up on her? Given a different work schedule for Kara—less travel, more face-to-face time—perhaps the situation would be different. Perhaps this was a season of weakness, Hunter tried to tell himself. A temporary period, like the dry season at his sales job.

Yet, at some point in the future, a choice would be inevitable, Hunter knew. Kara or Gabe. Regardless of *why* he'd grown more vulnerable in recent months, a moment of decision would come. But maybe it wouldn't come soon. Maybe he needed time to sort everything out, a season in which the best answer for everyone would emerge with clarity.

"When do you start building?" Hunter asked Ellen.

"We'll break ground in the spring, as soon as possible, then shift as much as we can into high gear."

"You're starting *this* spring? When do you plan to complete it?"

"September."

"Isn't that your wedding date?"

"We'd finish the house around the same time. It'll be a tight fit with work, wedding plans, and now building a new house. Talk about pressure."

"Pressure doesn't always serve you well."

"You can expect me to be a crazy bitch by the time it's all over. But I know you'll love me anyway, so you're kinda screwed."

With that, Ellen burst out with a raspy laugh, the kind you'd normally expect from a chain smoker. Hunter chuckled along with her because he knew every word she'd uttered would come to pass.

"But in the end," Ellen said, "we'll have a sparkling home ready to move into after the honeymoon—if he keeps me around after my crazy phase, that is."

"So what happens next?"

"Now that we know the exact dimensions of the lot, Brendan can get blueprints drawn up. That'll involve a lot of back and forth, but we have a general idea of what we're looking for."

"Since Brendan speaks their language and understands the regulations and code requirements, shouldn't the process move along faster?"

"We hope so. In the meantime, he and I need to pick out everything from siding to fixtures to carpet. All the options you take for granted: How many cars we want the garage to fit for the future. Paint colors, shingle colors, roof style. Everything."

"Kind of like planning your wedding, only ten times bigger."

"Geez, it all seems to grow bigger the more I talk about it," Ellen said. "One enormous hot-air balloon in my face."

Ellen tapped her foot nonstop.

"But it's *good* pressure," said Hunter. "I mean, you're happy, right?"

Ellen paused. "Yeah … yeah, I'm happy." After another beat, she shot Hunter a mischievous grin. "I'm sure I'll feel like crawling into a corner once all the pressure sets in, but yeah, I think I can say I'm happy. I have someone to love. Life doesn't get better than that, does it?"

Ellen wrapped her arm around Hunter and gave him a hug from the side. And with that, the two old friends, shivering in the northern Ohio wind, headed back to the car and closed themselves into its warmth.

CHAPTER 22

The next day, Hunter had a job interview with a small company in Aurora, a community adjacent to Hudson's eastern border. The interview, which he hoped had gone well, wrapped up by the middle of the afternoon. Since he was so close to home, he decided to head back to his house, where he would spend the rest of the afternoon researching job openings online.

As he drove down Hudson-Aurora Road, Hunter passed his old high school on his left and peered out the window. The school day had ended minutes earlier. Swarms of teenagers departed the building. Cars snaked through the parking lot and lined up at the exits. It reminded Hunter of one February morning at that school, during his junior year.

Hunter's lunch period arrived around 11:30 a.m. that semester. Randy and several other friends had the same lunch schedule. Each day, they met at the same table in an atrium known as the Commons. Through the windows that lined one side of the Commons, Hunter could see the parking lot filled with students' cars. Mounds of white lined the perimeter of the lot, snow that had fallen that winter, which the maintenance crew had plowed to the side and now sat several feet high. A cool, gray sky hung overhead, an entity with eyes that observed and saw everything that occurred under its watch, which, for Hunter, ushered in feelings of imprisonment.

Teenagers sat around small, round tables that speckled the large, airy room, while several other teens approached and hovered around those who sat. Some who hovered munched on a bag of chips; others killed time, skipping out of study hall while claiming a trip to the restroom.

The tables seemed to reflect unwritten rules about who sat with whom. Hunter noticed he could summarize each table with a label: jocks, choir members, band members, future MIT alumni. While Hunter hung with the athletic crowd, he made an effort to talk to individuals regardless of their activity interests or social statuses, and he never understood why middle and high school students gravitated toward social segregation. Beneath their layers, Hunter supposed, they all shared similar insecurities, fears and struggles. At least, he *hoped* he wasn't the only one who possessed them.

Voices echoed throughout the atrium, their sounds bouncing from the walls and performing acrobatic maneuvers beneath a ceiling that stretched two stories above the ground.

Hunter turned his attention to Randy and the others at his table, a few football players Hunter knew. Hunter couldn't say he had a particular fondness for the players with whom he sat, nor did he consider them friends per se, but they ran with the same crowd of athletes as Hunter and Randy. The players wore letterman jackets of blue and white, which sounded like rubber when they stretched their arms or slapped each other on the backs in jest. Randy had taken a seat on Hunter's left. Tom Fisher, a mouthy defensive end with strong legs and arms, sat across from him. Between Tom and Randy sat Alex Keller, a tight end. On Hunter's right, Grady McEvoy, a running back who had stacked up an impressive record of pass receptions for the season, sat with his girlfriend, Gina, on his lap. Hunter had always liked Gina, who, although she tended to flow with the crowd rather than stand her ground, never failed to treat Hunter with genuine kindness.

Hunter knew Tom had the hots for Gina. The guy had spent the past year salivating for the day she might tell Grady to hit the road. Most of the student body considered Grady and Gina destined for marriage, a classic fairy tale of high school sweethearts that would receive special mention in their senior yearbook. For the time being, however, Tom had to settle for taking his macho behavior an extra mile in Gina's presence to try to capture her notice. Hunter didn't understand why the guy didn't move on to someone else.

Grady cracked a remark about the tie their chemistry teacher wore that day, a throwback to what they had agreed upon as the hippie era, and Tom retorted with a comment that sent his tablemates into laughter. When he noticed Gina had found it humorous, Tom kicked his efforts up another notch. Each remark vied for dominance over the last, one degree higher in volume and wit. Soon they erupted into explosive laughter that boomed around the atrium, despite the room's overall noise level.

Hunter grew a tad embarrassed at the loudness. Tom's, in particular, struck him as borderline obnoxious. Well aware of his status atop the high school social ladder, Tom seldom paid attention to how well he kept his behavior in check.

When Tom's voice boomed, Hunter peered at tables in his vicinity and, sure enough, he caught a reaction. A few tables away, a group of bookish types had looked over in shock, trying to identify which loudmouth had all but sent the piles of snow outside into an avalanche. Once they pegged Tom as the source, they returned their attention to each other, rolled their eyes, and shook their heads in disgust as they resumed their conversation. Hunter wondered whether the root of such reactions was jealousy or if, in actuality, those students were more confident in their own brainpower than the athletes were in their physical prowess. Oftentimes, when he looked into their eyes, Hunter had a hunch the brainiacs knew something the jocks didn't— like who would work for whom in twenty years.

"You should take notes from Hunter," Gina remarked to Tom as she fluffed her blond hair, which fell in curls halfway to her waistline. "He knows how to behave in public."

With that, she gave Hunter a nod of acknowledgment, then retreated into giggles as Grady nibbled her earlobe.

Tom looked irritated at the display of affection, of having to suffer watching Grady accomplish what Tom would give his starting position in the next season opener to have a shot at.

With his jaw line set so firm, it couldn't have protruded with more prominence along the edge of his face, Tom glanced over his shoulder at the table behind him, where one student sat alone. Christopher Patton nibbled on a crinkled french fry as he fingered through a large book with *How to Succeed in Business Without Really Trying* printed on the front. Hunter presumed it was a script. Last week, Hunter had heard Christopher—never

Chris—won a supporting role in the upcoming spring musical, and now he looked immersed in the process of memorizing his lines.

Christopher hadn't always sat alone.

On occasion, others still sat with him, but Hunter noticed Christopher had grown more withdrawn in recent months. Rumors had circulated about him since one week in late October, earlier that school year.

Ever since middle school, people had suspected Christopher was gay but never had proof. Their suspicions had lingered in the hallways and traveled through whispers, text messages, and phone chats. Whether Christopher realized it or not, Hunter couldn't decipher, but the guy possessed a handful of stereotypical, effeminate qualities that provided fodder for those suspicions—qualities like the frequent limp wrist; exquisite posture when he sat; loose gestures of his head, holding his hands close to his chest, when he spoke with passion; and a lilt to his voice which, compared to his peers, seemed to have one fewer ounce of masculinity. Nothing blatant in his qualities, but off-kilter enough to produce subtle reminders of why the suspicions existed in the first place. A tall, skinny redhead, Christopher hung out with the band and choir crowds. He had bold taste in clothes, as demonstrated by the vivid pink polo shirt he wore today, a shade Hunter wouldn't have the guts to carry to a cash register much less wear in public.

Unfortunate timing back in October confirmed the student body's suspicions about Christopher.

Rehearsals for the fall play had begun a few weeks earlier. Because rehearsals were in their early stage, the schedule called for a focus on particular scenes in the afternoon after school and additional scenes in the evening. Such an approach allowed the cast to develop each scene at a slower pace as they learned their lines, acquainted themselves with stage blocking, and adjusted to each other's dynamics. Once November arrived, they would rehearse entire acts from beginning to end, followed by full dress rehearsals.

On that fateful October date, Christopher's rehearsal occurred in the evening, when the rest of the school building was dark and empty. The fall play required a small cast to begin with, and the director had scheduled only seven cast members to attend that evening's rehearsal. Christopher's presence wasn't required on stage until the next scene. Neither was that of Sheldon Horvath, a fellow cast member.

Stories fluctuated on what led a third cast member—one not even involved in that night's rehearsal—into the dressing room. Most students concurred that he had left his script behind by accident and needed to retrieve it from his dressing-room locker.

According to the stories, upon entering the side of the dressing room nearest the hallway, the cast member thought he heard whispers and rustling. The main area of the dressing room was well lit, but he saw nothing. The sounds seemed to come from the darkness around the corner, near a doorway that led to an inner corridor, one that opened into the backstage area.

Curious, the cast member forgot about his script and decided to investigate the rustling, so he crept toward the far end of the dressing room. The room's fluorescent glow cast a trace of light into the dark corridor.

That trace of light provided all the cast member needed. Stunned, he froze at the sight.

Christopher Patton and Sheldon Horvath.

Together.

In the dark.

Versions of the story varied regarding what the cast member saw, with descriptions ranging from innocent to graphic. The story evolved and spread over time. Its most common iteration, however, painted Christopher and Sheldon in an embrace, whispering in each other's ears, trying to keep their rendezvous covert. Hands in motion as they felt each other up in the blackness.

It took a few seconds for Christopher to notice the presence of another individual, an anonymous silhouette surrounded by incoming light. By the time the pair jolted apart, the intruding cast member had vanished into the light of the dressing room. The cast member grabbed his script, slammed his locker door shut, and fled the room.

Neither Christopher nor Sheldon heard anyone mention the incident that evening. The cast member didn't approach them and didn't appear to talk to anyone else for the remainder of the rehearsal. But at some point, the cast member talked to *someone,* because the next morning, gossip buzzed throughout the school hallways.

Everybody knew Christopher Patton's secret.

Many students—including Hunter, who, as a Christian, had felt like a hypocrite at the time—had already avoided interacting with Christopher Patton due to mere *suspicions* about his sexual preference. But the eyewitness account eroded his social status further. A few of Christopher's friends stuck with him and didn't appear disturbed by his preference, but most of his acquaintances—individuals Christopher had once called friends—fled his presence and never returned.

Hunter couldn't imagine his own friends standing beside Hunter himself in such a scenario, either. Not because they were bad people, but because he was sure their awareness would render them too uncomfortable to engage in conversation or stand in close proximity to him, as if reputation were contagious. Besides, Hunter had an "in" status to lose, whereas Christopher hadn't had much status to lose in the first place.

In a way, Hunter envied Christopher's luxury.

Now Christopher sat alone at a lunch table behind Tom, and Tom was in the mood to impress Gina with his hotshot wit.

Tom turned around and jabbed his thumb toward Christopher's script. "Another musical?"

Christopher looked up. Hunter could see a hint of caginess in Christopher's eyes, any trace of which Christopher tried to hide. Instead, he offered a smile in return. Hunter had always known Christopher as a gentle individual. He'd never heard him speak a negative word about others.

"It's for the spring," Christopher replied, holding his place with one finger as he showed Tom the cover. "I'm trying to learn my lines for it."

Hunter heard Grady snicker under his breath. Tom maintained a straight face.

"Want me to help you read your lines?" Tom asked with obvious insincerity in his eyes.

Hunter could see where this was headed. Judging from how rigid Christopher now sat in his chair, he had detected the insincerity as well, and had begun to brace himself for whatever would come next.

Christopher offered another casual smile. "Thanks, but I'm fine."

"You don't think I'd be helpful? Come on, man, I want you to do a great job in your play."

"I do better learning lines on my own. I appreciate the offer, though."

Christopher returned his eyes to his script a smidgen too soon, and Hunter could smell blood in the water. He knew Tom could smell it, too.

Tom brought his face a bit closer to Christopher's and kept his voice just loud enough for his own tablemates to hear.

"Is it true you guys wear makeup when you do your plays?"

Grady's snickers grew louder. By this time, Gina fought to stifle her laughter, though her furrowed eyebrows suggested she vacillated between finding humor and taking pity.

Christopher drew in his shoulders, kept his eyes riveted to his script. Hunter noticed the guy's feet had broken into a nervous jiggle under the table.

Christopher ran his fingers through his gel-styled red hair and replied, "Yes. For the spotlight. The bright light bleaches out your face. The makeup makes you look normal."

The legs of Tom's chair squeaked as he scooted within a few inches of Christopher.

"I mean it, man, I'd like to help you learn your lines," said Tom, his voice still loud enough for his own tablemates to hear every word. When Christopher angled his shoulder away, Tom added, "No, seriously. We'll get together, sneak a few glasses of Chablis …"

More snickers from the table. Alex and Randy had joined in.

"… maybe find a place to park, turn on some tunes …"

The giggles grew louder.

Gina covered her eyes and muttered under her breath. "Oh, my—"

That reaction fueled Tom further.

Tom leaned in and tried to keep from bursting out in laughter. He put his arm around Christopher, who glued himself against the back of his chair as if it would provide an escape hatch. He looked small and wiry engulfed in Tom's thick, muscular arm.

"Tell you what," Tom murmured into Christopher's ear, "I'll even let you give me a hand job, okay? I've gotta nice package here—you've seen it, remember? The locker room? Phys Ed class freshman year?"

At that, Hunter's table exploded with laughter.

"Shit, Tom …" Grady muttered as he hid his face in his hands. "You're a perv, man!"

"You're such an ass," Gina said through a stifled giggle, trying not to look at Christopher.

Hunter's stomach jumbled as he tried to paint a grin upon his face. He felt sorry for Christopher. At the same time, though, Hunter felt relieved he himself wasn't the butt of Tom's harassment—which Hunter knew he could be if Tom discovered the truth.

Hunter joined his group with a chuckle. In truth, he faked the chuckle, trying to make it look as though he found the situation funny. Meanwhile, Hunter felt his arms shake from nervousness. He didn't want to be part of this. He felt horrible for Christopher, yet he also feared if he stuck up for him, Tom would immediately ask why *he* was so bothered by the remarks, then crack a suggestive joke about Hunter's own sexuality in retaliation. Who knew what would mount from there? As a new Christian, Hunter lacked the confidence to stand up for Christopher, yet he grieved because he knew God wanted him to say something to defuse the situation.

But Hunter remained silent and watched what he feared could happen to himself.

Christopher's face turned the shade of a mild sunburn, which rendered his freckles more prominent. He refused to look at anyone laughing at his expense. Eyes fixed on his own table, he snapped the script shut and shook himself free from Tom's arm. As he did, Hunter noticed a sheen upon Christopher's eyes that reflected the atrium lighting.

Were those tears in his eyes?

Christopher didn't take time to pack his book bag or locate its shoulder strap. With his script in one hand, he bear-hugged his book bag with his free arm, arose from the table, and left his lunch tray behind. As he did, Hunter saw the first tear had, indeed, trailed along his cheek.

"Asshole," Christopher mumbled as he rushed past Tom.

"You're more familiar with 'em than I am!" Tom shouted back at Christopher, at which Hunter winced. One final twist of the knife. Tom never let the last word go to waste. By that point, however, a few seconds had passed. Christopher had managed to put fifty feet of distance between them already and hadn't heard the insult.

Hunter could only imagine how hurt Christopher must have felt. The physical contact from Tom must have left him feeling dehumanized. The humiliation of public ridicule, where the perpetrator had surrounded himself with supporters as pillars to hold him up, while the victim had nobody.

Hunter recoiled not only at what he'd witnessed, but at the awareness that he'd allowed it to continue. Moreover, he found another aspect of Tom's actions—and the support he'd received from his cohorts—disturbing: Their ridicule seemed effortless.

The activity had proven genuine fun for his friends, who had no idea what it was like to deal with the thing they mocked. Meanwhile, little did they know Hunter, who sat in their midst and tried his best to ride out their laughter, was scared to death—scared they would figure out that another Christopher Patton sat in their midst, and his name was Hunter Carlisle.

Self-conscious at that concept, Hunter avoided any glances from his tablemates. Too afraid to utter a word, he hoped to fade into the background for the next few minutes. He angled his body forward, hid his quivering arms and hands beneath the table the best he could. He had lost his appetite; the sight of his greasy, breaded chicken patty sandwich made him queasy.

In that hour, Hunter learned a lesson he would carry with him from that February day forward.

He could never confide in his friends about his secret.

Trust no one.

Hunter would need to bury his secret deep inside his soul. And he'd better take *even further* precautions to hide any shred of its evidence from his life.

That day, surrounded by his social crowd, Hunter felt utterly alone.

Today, arriving home from his job interview, Hunter pulled into his garage and turned off the car engine. He didn't move. Instead, he stared at the steering wheel as the memory of Christopher Patton consumed him.

Hunter had never forgotten that guy. Oftentimes, as the years passed, he had wondered what happened to Christopher. Did he suffer permanent emotional scars from that lunch incident or that school year? Once he reached adulthood, did he go on to live in happiness, or had life gotten worse and left him wounded?

The moment someone discovered him in the dressing room, Christopher's life changed forever. And it all happened in an instant, without warning. That's what alarmed Hunter most, that he could take a wrong step and wind up an outcast and abandoned. All for a reason he couldn't seem to shake from his life.

To this day, Hunter wished he could apologize to Christopher Patton, not simply out of decency, but as someone who understood the fight and fear. As it turned out, Hunter's inaction that day in the Commons had ended up one of his biggest regrets in life. Hunter would give anything to retrieve that moment from the grip of the past and have another shot at protecting Christopher.

Hunter tapped the steering wheel and sighed, then whispered a prayer.

"God, please let him be okay. Let him know he's not alone, that somebody cares."

Dismayed, Hunter shook his head.

Christopher Patton dealt openly with his issue—albeit against his will—and paid a hefty price for it, while Hunter hid in the shadows with the benefit of a social buffer. It didn't seem fair.

And while he reconsidered Christopher Patton's interests and mannerisms, a new realization hit him.

As an adult, Christopher might have grown up to become an equivalent of Gabe Hellman.

Suddenly, Hunter's regret grew more personal. He wondered what aches might lie in Gabe's past, the unspoken hurts he might hide.

The light of the garage door opener flicked off. Hunter didn't move a muscle.

CHAPTER 23

The first thing Hunter noticed in the dining room was the restaurant's expansive view of Lake Erie, courtesy of windows that lined three of the room's walls. Around six o'clock in the evening in mid November, twilight had set in, but he could picture the gentle lapping of water beneath an afternoon sun.

As the hostess led them to their table, Hunter scanned the dining room, on the lookout for second glances or signs that anyone might wonder why two young men had shown up together for dinner at a nice restaurant. From what he could tell, nobody had noticed yet. In fact, most patrons appeared too engrossed in their own conversations to observe who entered and who left the dining room.

The hostess placed two menus on a small table for four, a square table with one chair on each side, a table angled beside a window. Before Hunter could say a word, the hostess gathered the two unneeded sets of tableware and glasses, leaving Hunter and Gabe catty-cornered and, in effect, sitting next to each other. As she gathered the items, the glasses clinked and tableware clanged at a volume that made a self-conscious Hunter uncomfortable, not wanting to attract any more attention than he envisioned might occur. Rather than shift his place setting to an alternate position, Hunter decided to act as though all was normal and take his seat. Gabe was mere inches away, close enough for Hunter to feel his warm breath settle onto his arm.

Hunter wondered about the arrangement the hostess had maneuvered. Had she seated them so close to each other as part of the restaurant's standard procedure, to facilitate easier conversation between two patrons? Or had she assumed he and Gabe were in a relationship and wanted a romantic setup? Hunter tried to gauge her facial expression, but she remained neutral, wished them a nice dinner, and departed. He could drive himself to the brink of insanity worrying about what people thought of him. Hunter realized such concerns were childish, but by the time you're twenty-six years old, long-ingrained habits can prove hard to break, especially when rooted in insecurity.

He and Gabe perused their menus, which featured a wide selection of seafood dishes.

They had picked a restaurant in the suburb of Lakewood, west of Cleveland and far northwest of Hudson, where they were confident they wouldn't cross paths with anyone they knew.

Their goal was to dip their toes in the water, to discover how an actual first date in a normal restaurant might feel. Hunter had proposed going on a weekday evening, when restaurants were less busy, with fewer people around to take note of them. Gabe had countered that idea, suggesting that fewer patrons meant less opportunity to blend in, which might render them *more* noticeable. So they compromised on a Friday evening far from home. And to play it safe, Hunter and Gabe each brought a portfolio to set beside himself on the table so it would look like a dinner meeting to end a workweek that had gone too late. For extra coverage, they had decided to request separate checks.

Their alibi didn't do much to ease Hunter's nervousness. Tonight was a new experience for him. Yet Hunter wasn't uncomfortable because he didn't *want* this experience; rather, it was akin to the jitters he felt his first day on the job after graduating college: an apprehension that accompanies the unknown. The kind you feel when you try to appear collected and hope no one else can tell the difference.

But regardless of alibis, regardless of how well Hunter could succeed in looking confident to the patrons in this restaurant, *he and Gabe* both knew this was the first same-sex date either had experienced. Judging from Gabe's sideways glances and the way he kept rubbing his fingertips together, Gabe felt as nervous as Hunter.

They placed their napkins on their laps and continued to examine entrées—in part, to keep themselves occupied. Gabe cleared his throat.

At least Hunter knew the person whose company he kept this evening. He found comfort in that familiarity. This wasn't a blind date. And he had to admit, Gabe looked handsome in his chocolate-brown sport shirt, which brought out a richness in his eyes that Hunter hadn't noticed prior to tonight. Peeking over the top of his menu, Hunter appraised Gabe's eyes, which Gabe had trained on his own menu. Searching for the perpetual compassion in those eyes, Hunter caught a trace of it, which steadied him as he resumed perusing entrées.

He drummed his fingers on the tablecloth. Gabe set his menu down and looked up.

"Nervous?" asked Gabe, his voice subdued.

"Yeah. You?"

"Somewhat."

Hunter paused, debating whether he should be honest and admit what was on his mind. He decided to go ahead and say it so Gabe wouldn't take his reserved manner personally.

"It's not you," Hunter said at last. "I *want* to be here. I guess it's … maybe I care too much about what anyone thinks."

Gabe offered no response except a nod to let Hunter know he had his attention.

Hunter grunted, then set his menu down. "It's stupid, I know. But I've always cared what people think of me. I've always tried so hard *not* to stand out—at least, not unless I control *how* I stand out."

"Why's that?"

"Less attention means maybe people wouldn't suspect anything about me." Hunter gave Gabe a tentative stare, then added, "I'd feel better if I knew you understood."

Velvet warmth filled Gabe's countenance. With a gentle laugh, he leaned forward an inch and looked at Hunter with affection, the tenderness a father would offer a child who had come to him for reassurance.

"I understand. I'm a bit uneasy about that, too," Gabe said. "It's probably less bothersome to me, though: I'm used to not fitting in too well to begin with."

At that, Hunter realized much of their interaction had focused on Hunter—his back pain, his job loss, his attempt to make sense of his relationship with Kara. Gabe had spoken little about himself. Hunter wanted to know more about the individual who sat beside him.

Their server, a man in his late twenties with ash-blond hair bound in a short, metro-stylish ponytail, stopped by to take their orders. Although Hunter's stomach felt fine, he opted for grilled tilapia, figuring its delicate flavor wouldn't unsettle him if his nervousness increased. Gabe ordered shrimp scampi. They had discussed wine earlier, but had figured glasses of wine might reveal this date for what it was, and splitting a bottle would have looked even more obvious. In the end, each stuck with water for his beverage, and the server departed.

With another glimpse around the restaurant, Hunter confirmed no other patrons sat close enough in proximity to overhear their conversation. Gabe's last comment had renewed his interest in getting to know more about him.

"A few minutes ago, you said you're used to not fitting in. What did you mean by that?"

Gabe opened his mouth halfway, then stopped, as if Hunter had caught him off guard in mid-sentence. One more glance toward Hunter, in which Hunter thought he caught a plea for reassurance.

Finally, Gabe shrugged, regained his confidence, and replied, "I never fit in well with other guys my age."

"I hate to hear that. You have a great personality."

Gabe furrowed his eyebrows. "The personality didn't really *match,* though. The way I relate to people seems different from the way other guys do. I think guys detect it early on, and before long, that's how others know you. They identify you that way."

"I think we have that in common, the not-relating thing. Somewhere along the way, I found a way to downplay it and act like my peers, but I always sensed the disparity."

Gabe grinned. "So we're similar, only different."

"Looks that way," Hunter chuckled.

"Of course, the fact that my interests were different from other guys didn't help my cause, either. A lot of guys aren't interested in drama or aren't comfortable with it."

Hunter thought for a moment. "When did you sense you were different from other guys? What made you feel like you didn't fit into everyone's normal box?"

"I discovered early on that I had no interest in sports. That was key for me. That's when I realized I had no chance of fitting in, at least not completely."

"What didn't you like about sports? Not that it matters today, but I'm curious."

"Some of the sports that guys play are physically rough—football, hockey. The idea of getting battered around or knocked in the teeth didn't appeal to me. And when it came to the other sports like baseball or basketball—well, no offense, but I didn't see it as a game. I saw it as throwing a ball back and forth. That didn't fascinate me at all. So, since I didn't have an interest in those activities, I never practiced or became good at them. That exacerbated the problem, because all it did was make the difference more obvious.

"I enjoyed the idea of *life,* the things that make people who they are, and wanted to explore *those* things instead. When you're a young kid in elementary school or middle school, and all the guys you know take off to play ball every chance they get, that leaves you with female company most of the time. Eventually, the other guys don't know how to relate to you, and it leaves you isolated. So in the end, you just want to be accepted. Between that and a dad who died in combat before you got a chance to know him, you just want someone—someone who knows what it's like to be you—to wrap his arm around you and let you know you're … well, that you're loved. That you're wanted."

"And you never felt wanted?"

Gabe thought for a moment. "Every time you overhear someone use a slur like 'faggot' or 'homo' or whatever, even if it's in jest and they don't mean it, even if they're talking about someone else, it reminds you that you don't fit in. It reminds you of how solitary you feel inside. It reminds you that you'll *never* fully relate to your peers; you'll *never* be cared about first, then talked to later. So you get used to being alone."

Hunter recalled the slurs he'd heard on countless occasions. To escape all risk of suspicion from his peers, *Hunter himself* had uttered those slurs in jest. Yet each time, regardless of who spoke, the words had cut through his flesh and reopened the wounds in his heart. Those words and the motives behind them had pushed him farther into his corner of fear.

As Gabe spoke, Hunter realized that he and Gabe *did* share one quality in common: Both knew the pain of traveling through life lonely on the inside.

"Didn't you feel like drama was a match for you, though?" Hunter asked. "I saw you perform only once, but I remember how good you were at it."

"I loved it from day one. And I was never shy," Gabe chuckled. "In fact, drama held a special irony: Growing up, when I tried joining in soccer or some sport just to relate, or those situations like gym class, where you're forced to play, I felt like I was on a stage for everyone to see and find humor in my inability, or in maneuvers they took for granted in themselves but saw absent in me. Drama gave me a stage—literally—where I could excel."

"A place to play to your strengths."

"And to my personality."

Their server returned with their entrées, then refilled their water glasses. After asking if he could bring anything else, Hunter and Gabe declined, and the server made the rounds with his other tables as the restaurant grew more populated.

Hunter and Gabe prayed over dinner and took their first bites. Hunter glanced at Gabe, who appeared deep in thought as he twirled a shrimp in circles with his fork. Taking inventory of those around them, Hunter noticed a woman who sat with her husband a few tables away. When Hunter shifted his head in her direction, he could have sworn she'd stared at him and turned her head abruptly. He wondered if the woman could tell he and Gabe felt attracted to each other. Did she recognize their dinner as the date it was? Or did they look to her like two buddies?

Next, his eyes darted toward one corner of the room, where his server chatted a few moments with a female server. Each glanced in Hunter and Gabe's direction for a second, caught his glance, then broke eye contact. The female server pursed her lips, angled her chin toward the ceiling, and shook her head before checking on one of her tables. Had Hunter and Gabe kidded themselves by thinking nobody would recognize what was going on here?

Hunter almost didn't ask his next question, but he believed the answer might bring a degree of comfort. He dropped his volume a notch.

"Did you ever try to … escape your interest? In other guys, I mean. Like, did you ever try to get, I don't know …"

"Cured?"

"Is that the best way to put it?"

"I don't know quite how to put it. However I say it, it seems too simple or inaccurate. Unfair, maybe."

"Like it doesn't tell the whole story of what you're going through," Hunter said.

"Exactly."

Gabe took a bite of pasta, chewed it slowly as he pondered their discussion further. Once he swallowed, he furrowed his eyebrows in concentration, then speared a shrimp with his fork.

"I saw a therapist about it," Gabe finally said.

Hunter felt his jaw begin to drop but tried to hide his reaction. He hadn't expected this revelation. He hoped he hadn't given any signs of surprise that might make Gabe feel awkward. Gabe still appeared in full concentration, though.

"When?" Hunter asked. "That is, is it okay for me to ask?"

"You're okay," Gabe replied. "It happened two years ago. I'd thought about it back during college, but wanted to keep it private from everyone. So I waited until I was out of school, no longer under my mom's insurance plan so she wouldn't know. I didn't want to break her heart."

Hunter found himself enthralled at the idea of therapy. He could only imagine the freedom in letting all your concerns off of your chest, of having someone in whom you could confide without worry of risk.

"What made you take the step?"

"It was a combination of things. Same-sex attraction was one of them, plus insecurities that had lingered since childhood. Never knowing my dad too well. All sorts of stuff. But the attraction issue was my biggest concern. I felt bad holding that inside me while I was a Christian. So I figured I had nothing to lose in seeing a therapist. It might do me some good."

"Did it help?"

"It helped to talk about it all. I staked a lot on those therapy sessions, hoping I'd get cured of my attraction to other guys. I wanted to move past it—but then again, maybe part of me didn't, I don't know. Maybe it was my own fault. But obviously, here I am, still in the same boat. In the end, after a couple of years of therapy, I ended up so disappointed, I don't know which felt worse: struggling *before* therapy, or the pain of going through therapy, then feeling let down—the hopelessness I felt in the months afterward. And maybe still feel today."

Hunter nodded as he listened to Gabe's story, felt his heart go out toward Gabe. Though Hunter himself had never sought therapy, he related to the discouragement that came with trying to escape his inner battle and winding up defeated. How many times had he tried to quit his 'habit,' as he'd once called it? How often had he hungered for liberation from the torment, from what felt like invisible slavery, from what felt like aimless wandering at midnight down a long, dark road?

CHAPTER 24

"What about you?" Gabe asked as he twirled pasta around the prongs of his fork. "Did you ever try therapy?"

"No," Hunter replied, sipping his water to buy himself a few beats, "I never did."

"Wow." Gabe's eyes widened. With a blink, he added, "So when you say you haven't told anyone, you literally haven't told *anyone*. Not even a professional anyone."

"It crossed my mind years ago. The load started to feel so heavy, I craved to release it. When I considered talking about it, I was a college student like you, and the church I attended near campus had a counseling ministry. The darkness in my soul got so thick, the thought of finally coming clean and letting someone in on my secret seemed like an oasis in the desert: After all those years fighting, maybe I could get a drink of water. If I could get just one sip, I believed I could make it through."

"What happened? Did you make an appointment?"

As the memory resurfaced, Hunter felt anger rekindle, but he stifled it and allowed forgiveness to settle in, as he had done countless times before.

"I couldn't go through with it," Hunter said. "I was on the verge of calling them up, but then I abandoned the idea—ran as far away from it as I could."

"Why?"

Hunter took a bite of his tilapia. He peered out the window at the lake where, amid the darkness, he noticed lights shining from a boat as it drifted farther from shore, toward the peaceful, endless horizon. He returned his attention to Gabe, who focused on Hunter with eyes of concern. Hunter preferred to let the memory die with the past. Then again, Gabe had confided in him, so he might as well open up, too.

"I was in the lobby talking to a few other students after the church service ended. I knew them from a Bible study and sat with them at church on Sundays. After we said good-bye, I headed to an information table to find out about an upcoming event. While I scoured the flyers on the table, I overheard two people talking. I recognized one of the women as the lady who worked as the office assistant in the counseling office—staff or volunteer, I don't know what she was. I didn't eavesdrop, but you know how, sometimes, you're so close in proximity that you overhear conversations whether you want to or not? Well, it was one of those situations. I tried to ignore the conversation and find my flyer, but the woman was loud enough for me to hear. And by the time I realized what they were talking about, it was too late."

"Too late for what?"

"Too late for me to trust that counseling office with my secret. Because of her position, the woman was privy to what was going on in the lives of people who made appointments for help. She was whispering about some man who had called the counseling office the week before, about how the guy had discovered one of his kids was using drugs. The kid's habit had started to cause problems in the family, and the guy—the father—had run out of ideas. So he'd talked to the office to get general information, maybe schedule a family session, that sort of thing. Maybe the woman had talked to him herself, or maybe she had filed the paperwork and read notes in the file. Whatever happened, she knew specifics about what was going on. Apparently it was a family that had gone to church there a long time and were well-known. And this woman was revealing their secrets behind their backs. I mean, picture that dad: There he was, in the middle of a struggle and at the end of his rope, desperate for help for his family. He'd confided in someone at a church counseling center and trusted them to maintain his privacy. He'd probably shown up to church that day, putting on a brave front, feeling relieved he'd gotten honest and reached out for help, thinking his information had remained confidential. So there he sat in church, thinking nobody knew. Meanwhile, who knows how many people that woman had told, and how many people *they* had told? For all he knew, while he sat there relieved, people might have been looking at him from all over the room with the knowledge of his private matters."

Hunter shook his head. To this day, he marveled at what had happened, that someone entrusted with a ministry of care could behave in such a self-absorbed manner. Had she stopped to think how she would feel if someone had revealed *her* personal affairs to others?

Gabe's eyes revealed a mixture of disappointment and anger. "I'm sorry to hear that. I'm sure not all churches are like that."

"You're right, they're not. And I realize it's not necessarily the churches, it's individuals—bad apples, or whatever the appropriate term. But the thing is, you don't *know* which churches or individuals or counseling offices are like that and which aren't. Once you've discovered untrustworthy staffs exist, you don't know who you can trust. And with an issue so personal and embarrassing—the type people love to gossip and joke about—I shut myself down to that option. One more reason to keep everything hidden. If they can't keep it private, why would you bother confiding in them? Doesn't it defeat the purpose of confidentiality?"

"I'd never considered that. To be honest, I can't say I would've responded differently than you."

"Can I fill your glass with more water?" came the server's voice from behind Hunter's shoulder.

Hunter's heart jumped, then he cringed. Had the server overheard anything? No, Hunter realized, if he had approached earlier, Gabe would have seen him coming and peered up.

Hunter settled again as the server filled their glasses and departed.

Gabe studied Hunter, as if to reconsider a past remark. "You've never told me much about your family. Are you close to them?"

"I'd say we have an average family relationship. We're not the tight-knit variety you might see out there, but we're not strangers, either." Hunter paused. "I don't think they understand me."

"What makes you say that?"

"One factor is my faith. I wasn't raised in church and, to this day, they've never expressed an interest in faith-related things, so I think they wonder about why it's so important to me." Not used to opening up to this degree with another person, Hunter set down his fork and began to fidget with his fingers before forcing himself to stop that habit. The sincerity in Gabe's expression invited Hunter to trust him. "I've always felt on the outside with my family. It's like I never found my place. I was there, but I guess I wasn't as much a participant as, say, my brother."

Creases formed along Gabe's brow, which prompted Hunter to clarify his remarks.

"Remember how you mentioned your dad died in combat, so you couldn't have a relationship with him because he was never around?"

"Sure."

Hunter had never translated his perceptions into words. Now he searched for the best way to describe them. "Well, obviously, your situation was different from mine. But I can relate to not seeing your dad much. My dad traveled a lot—like Kara does— and I rarely saw him during the week, even many weekends."

"So you didn't have much opportunity to interact with him? That would make it difficult to bond with your dad."

"The thing is, though, my brother found a way. He and my dad were close—well, closer than *I* was to Dad."

"Did they have similar personalities?"

"All three of us do. But Bryce, my brother, is eight years older than I am, so while I was a little kid, Bryce had already reached the point where Dad could interact with him on an equal level. And Bryce was a gifted athlete."

"It doesn't seem like athleticism should make a difference."

"But with Bryce, Dad had somebody to live through vicariously. You see, Dad was a gifted athlete while growing up, too—a stellar football player in high school. Even when he was in middle school, he'd caught the attention of the high school coach. By his freshman year, he was good enough for varsity, but he was behind other players in his growth, so the coach kept him on the junior varsity team, where he excelled. According to the coach's plan, he would be their star player at that level, then by his junior year, when he'd grown bigger, they would advance him to varsity. Everyone could see he'd go on to play in college and maybe have a shot at the professional level." Hunter paused, then added, "But that never happened. He never played varsity, never played college ball."

"Why not?"

"He calls it his career-ending injury. During one game his sophomore year, another guy tackled him illegally. Dad hit the ground hard, and at the wrong angle. Blew out his knee. He went through rehab for it, tried everything he could, but his knee never recovered well enough to avoid the risk of it shattering on him. He never played again. And if you think about it, you need your knees for almost every sport, so he didn't try anything else. He could play on a casual basis but not on a team level. And that was Dad's *dream*. For as long as he could remember, people had told him what a great player he was, how he'd play for a university one day. And he'd bought into the idea. Then, in one game, it all crashed down on him. His dream died. From there, the rest of his life seemed like second best. That's the way he's described his career, his potential: He calls it his second best."

"It hurts to put a dream on the shelf temporarily," Gabe said, "but to say good-bye to it permanently—I can't imagine. But didn't it give you something in common with your dad? The sports, I mean. He must've been proud of you."

"That's where my brother found a way to bond with Dad. I enjoyed sports, but wasn't a stellar athlete. Bryce, on the other hand, was like the second coming of Dad, minus the injury. He played varsity football and baseball, then went on to play college-level baseball for Kentucky. When I was seven years old, Bryce was already fifteen, so he and Dad could challenge each other without dumbing it down like they had to do for me. Dad got to compete with someone who could play at an equal level in the backyard or at the park, and I think he could see himself in Bryce. Bryce had the potential to fulfill Dad's dream, to grab the baton in life's relay race and carry it to the finish line. And like Dad, Bryce's talent started showing up when he was young. It became a fixture for the two of them before I was born.

"So by the time I was interested in it, they had their routine and, as far as I could tell, it was easier for them to do their thing without me. It didn't occur to them to include me. I don't think Dad or Bryce meant any harm by it. Sometimes, that's how things work out.

"I have a random memory that replays in my mind year after year: It happened one Friday afternoon when I was eight or nine years old. Dad had been out of town all week and hadn't gotten home yet. We lived in a two-story house, and I was in my bedroom, which was in the rear of the house, overlooking the backyard. A short while before dinner, I heard noise coming from the backyard. People shouting. I stopped what I was doing and headed toward my window. As I got closer, I realized the noise was a mixture of shouts and laughter, and recognized Bryce's voice. I heard a second voice shout back to him, and when I opened the blinds, I saw it was Dad. He'd taken off his suit coat and tie, set them on the patio, and had started playing catch with Bryce before dinner, before Dad had even walked into the house to let Mom and me know he was home.

"I remember standing there, looking out the window, seeing how much fun they had together. Each one tried to challenge the other with how they threw the ball—fastballs, curveballs, breaking balls—to catch each other off guard. And I remember how much I wished I could be part of their club, wishing I could toss better, throw higher, do whatever it took to be one of them. I felt hurt that they'd started their game without me that day, without even thinking of including me, but I also knew it was the norm. I was a kid; I didn't know how to change the norm. I wanted to go down and join them, ask them to let me play anyway. But then I heard Mom's voice calling us, telling us dinner was ready."

Hunter stared at the tilapia on his plate, which he no longer had the desire to eat. At the corner of his eye, he felt an inkling of a tear, which he wiped away by pretending to scratch an itch.

"I've never told that story to anyone," he added.

Raising his head, he met Gabe's eyes, focused on him with full concentration.

Hunter forced a quiet chuckle. "Dumb thing for a kid to get hurt about, huh?"

Outside the restaurant, a small boardwalk ran along the edge of Lake Erie. After dinner, Hunter and Gabe lingered beneath the night sky, strolling without a destination in mind. Several other restaurants dotted the boardwalk, each one close in proximity to the next, yet far enough apart to provide a stretch of walking space between them. Hunter noticed a few pedestrians on the boardwalk, who shoved their cold hands into their pockets and hurried from restaurants to the parking lot, seeking refuge in their cozy vehicles.

"We should've ordered some hot coffee to go," said Gabe. Peering up at the sky as he spoke, he looked as though he had cast a wish toward heaven.

Hunter zipped his leather coat, which felt snug the way it enveloped his chest. While on any other occasion, he would have considered the air too chilly to loiter, tonight he enjoyed the crispness of late autumn. Flurries swirled in the breeze, plump white clusters dancing against the navy-blue horizon: Hunter's personal snow globe. He took a deep breath and savored the invigoration that accompanied cold air burning his lungs. As Gabe exhaled, Hunter watched his breath appear, then dissipate.

They strolled side by side. When Hunter took a moment to listen, he realized he detected no sounds from restaurants, boats or pedestrians. Complete silence, save the thudding of Hunter and Gabe's feet on the boardwalk and gentle laps of water that teased the shoreline.

"It's so calm outside," Gabe said, his eyes roaming from star to star.

"It's like the world slowed down," Hunter said, his voice gentle. "Tonight was good. I'm glad we decided to do this. This is the most peaceful I've felt in a long while."

Gabe eased to a halt and Hunter followed suit. Gabe's eyes widened, the way a child opens his eyes in wonder while watching a butterfly for the first time.

"Listen," Gabe said, then paused. He didn't seem to look at anything in particular. "Can you hear that?"

Hunter listened a moment, but heard nothing unusual. "Hear what?"

"Your coat. Listen."

Cocking his ear toward his own shoulder, Hunter discovered if he listened closer, he could hear the faint patter of snowflakes as they landed on his coat. Gabe relished details in life that Hunter took for granted. Fascinated at what he now heard, Hunter listened to a few more snowflake taps, then couldn't help but grin. Without a need for words, he felt accepted and secure in Gabe's presence. Together they continued their stroll along the boardwalk.

With no other pedestrians close enough to overhear them, Hunter and Gabe conversed at normal volume in this public setting. For Hunter, the freedom came as a relief.

Gabe gave Hunter a hesitant glance. As time stood still, Hunter noticed a rarity in the expression on Gabe's face. Gabe appeared unsure about something.

"Did you ever consider a same-sex relationship before?" Gabe asked.

Though the question caught Hunter by surprise, it didn't set him as far off-kilter as he would have expected. Yet he couldn't muster the confidence to answer the question. Instead, he opted for the easier route, punting the ball back to Gabe.

"Did you?" Hunter asked.

Gabe considered the question, nodding his head to the rhythm of their footsteps. He bit his lower lip as he contemplated his answer. "I hadn't considered a *relationship,* per se. But I never felt comfortable around females in a romantic setting. I tried dating females in the past, and each time I was on a date, I'd find myself shrinking back. We'd have great conversations, but it's like I'd withhold a piece of myself. I couldn't bring myself to fully engage in the conversation. Each woman would try to draw me out of myself by asking me deeper questions. I think they sensed something was awry but marked it as shyness, so they tried to get me to open up. But the more they tried, the more I shut myself down. I didn't do it on purpose; it was more like a subconscious reaction, a kneejerk response. It happened before I could decide to stop it *or* allow it. My heart couldn't engage—that's the best way I can describe it." Gabe held his thumb and forefinger close together: so close, they almost touched, but didn't quite make contact. "A disconnect. The way an electrical socket goes out when a wire comes loose. It can be one millimeter off, but it's all you need to prevent the connection."

Hunter studied his own feet as he walked, watched his breath disperse before him as he exhaled. In spite of their divergent personalities and backgrounds, Hunter recognized similar aspects in the secret they had in common.

"In my heart, I knew I'd be more comfortable with a male. I'd have an easier time relaxing if I felt … wanted in that way, I guess," Gabe continued. "But as a Christian, I didn't consider it an option. So once I realized the female romantic scenario wouldn't work out, I expected to spend the rest of my life alone. That sounds melodramatic, but it was reality for me. You always have Jesus walking with you as your permanent companion; at the same time, though, you crave that human partnership, someone who will love and accept you for you. But like I said, it didn't fit my faith, so I never considered getting to know another guy as more than friends. And as lonely as it made me feel, I had come to terms with it." He glanced over at Hunter, and the hint of a smile formed along Gabe's mouth. "Until you entered the picture, that is."

Hunter nodded at Gabe, who kept pace at Hunter's right side. Hunter kept his portfolio under his left arm and hugged it closer against his side.

"So, what about you?" Gabe asked. "Have you ever considered a relationship with another guy?"

"I never even allowed myself to *think* of it." Hunter studied another pedestrian in the distance, who came in and out of view as she passed beneath the lights of a restaurant. "In those seasons where I felt myself drawn to other guys, I knew being drawn to them was different from *acting* on those inclinations. So when the mental pull toward another guy tried to draw me in, I didn't allow myself to cross that initial line. I refused to let myself imagine *doing* anything with him. Any time the thought of a relationship with another guy entered my mind, I'd shut it down immediately. I told myself, 'No, you're not that person. That's not who you are.'"

"Like a tug-of-war inside your soul."

"That's exactly how it feels. I spent so many years fighting it. To an extent, the fact that I also felt attracted to females—however strong or weak that attraction was—eased the struggle for me and provided coverage. I tried a bunch of heterosexual relationships over the years, not to hide, but to deny the shame of admitting to myself what was askew in my life. I knew how to *perform* on a date—the conversation, flirting, humor, displays of affection. But crossing over into a long-term relationship and the vulnerabilities that came with it—that's what tripped me up. Once she'd want to move the relationship into the next phase, my heart would start to distance itself from her, as if I'd sabotage my relationship before I needed to get too honest with her.

"But even though I never ventured into long-term territory, I had enough short-term relationships to keep myself moving on the treadmill, cycle after cycle. As a result, I managed to hide my secret so well, I didn't *need* to consider a same-sex relationship. I'd gotten by, day after day, by playing the game the way everybody expected me to."

Hunter stared out at the water, honed in on the lights of a dinner-cruise boat, and listened to the lapping of waves below. He inhaled. The air had grown sharper as the minutes passed.

"I lied to myself for so long," continued Hunter, "denying the truth that lurked under the surface, that I convinced myself nothing was wrong. One day, I told myself, I'd be cured; it was a matter of time, that was all. And if that was the case—if I'd be cured—then why *consider* a same-sex relationship? Why consider the pariah factor, being labeled a misfit and treated like an outcast, if it would all disappear from my life anyway? So I stifled it the best I could."

They reached the far end of the boardwalk, where the last restaurant, a small bistro, sat. Turning around, they headed back toward their starting point, where Gabe had parked his car near the seafood restaurant. For a while, neither Hunter nor Gabe spoke. The steady rumble of their footsteps continued along the wooden planks. The fabric of Gabe's winter coat swished as he moved his arms. Hunter gazed upward, pondered their conversation and considered the individual who walked beside him. As he counted, once again, the years of burdens that had gone unarticulated until tonight, his stomach grew rigid as a wave of anxiety pulsated through him. Overhead, the moon glowed bright; from behind a veil of clouds, the ghostly moon illuminated their edges with electric fire.

Gabe's romantic touch didn't feel the way Hunter had expected, at least not the way he'd imagined it happening beneath the sunlight or on a hot summer night. Tonight, after a ten-minute stroll, both men's hands felt frigid. Yet Hunter couldn't mistake the touch of Gabe's fingers against his own.

With no one else around, Gabe had taken a quick, fleeting opportunity to stroke his fingers twice along Hunter's hand. He had kept the action brief enough to where, if anyone witnessed it, they would have assumed Gabe had made random contact, a natural byproduct of two people walking side by side as they conversed.

But Hunter and Gabe knew better.

Chancing vulnerability, Hunter peeked up at Gabe, who stared straight ahead but pursed his lips to disguise a grin.

Hunter's heart softened.

Somehow, Gabe's touch felt right, a perfect fit. At first, it sent Hunter's belly into a nervous ache and his arms into a quiver; but like a sweet aftertaste, it settled within him in a delightful, welcome way. It rendered in him the desire to spend more time in Gabe's presence, as if Hunter was *supposed* to be with him. In that moment, he felt as though he had come home.

Hunter's tranquility screeched to a standstill.

Squinting, he tried to get a better look and told himself it couldn't be them.

But sure enough, as they stepped out beneath the exterior lights of an Italian restaurant, Hunter recognized his parents a mere five hundred feet away.

They weren't supposed to be there. That's the whole reason Hunter and Gabe had driven so far from Hudson—to *avoid* running into anyone they knew.

Paralyzed from the shock, Hunter went rigid for a few seconds. He flipped through scenarios in his mind, a desperate search for options, as he tried to determine what to do next.

Gabe halted when he realized Hunter had fallen out of step. Hunter forced himself to resume walking.

"What happened?" Gabe had a concerned look on his face. "What's wrong?"

Careful not to gesture or appear abnormal, Hunter located his voice at last. His first syllable came forth in a croak.

"Those are my parents over there. Leaving the Italian place."

Gabe kept pace as he turned his attention to the couple from the corner of his eye.

At first, Hunter wondered if he and Gabe might escape the situation without his parents noticing them. That would prove the easiest scenario. As they walked, though, his hopes diminished when he saw his mother squint and lean forward, her hand shielding her eyes from the restaurant's lights so she could better see the boardwalk in the distance. When she did, she nudged Hunter's father, and the duo sauntered toward Hunter and Gabe at a casual, yet eager, pace. They had recognized him. His father carried himself with an air of indifference, as if to say, *Why* wouldn't *we run into you here?* The expression on the face of Hunter's mother, however, exhibited innocent curiosity.

The couples were now two hundred feet apart. Hunter's parents closed the distance. His time grew shorter. He had to make a decision.

"We can't exactly make a run for it," Gabe whispered, his eyes focused straight ahead. "Any ideas?"

"I'll handle it," Hunter murmured. "Play it cool and follow my lead."

Not that Hunter had a plan. He had no desire to fool anyone. In fact, he would have given anything to drop the façade. At the same time, he knew his parents weren't ready to hear the truth. For that matter, Hunter himself wasn't ready to tell them. The purpose of tonight wasn't to commit to a choice, after all. Its purpose was to appraise how well one option might fit, a first step to discover whether Hunter or Gabe could even consider a second. They needed time while God worked on their hearts and helped *them* understand how to navigate through their questions.

Now Hunter's parents were close enough to see his eyes. Hunter readied his poker face, his defense mechanism. His body stiffened as extra stress settled into his lower back. In his peripheral vision, he caught sight of Gabe and was relieved to find Gabe maintained his steady composure.

"What a surprise!" his mother called out from a few steps away. "Your father thought it looked like you, but I told him, 'It couldn't be. Hunter wouldn't have come all the way up here!'"

Hunter's parents arrived arm in arm. His mother looked like a stereotypical suburban wife, with short blond hair and a figure that indicated she had birthed two children but had kept an admirable balance afterward. Under the lights that lined the boardwalk, Hunter could see his father's cheeks had already reddened in the outside air.

"Chilly night to wander around," said his father. "You here for dinner?"

"Just grabbed a quick bite to eat," Hunter said with a dismissive wave.

"Kinda far north."

"Oh, you know how it is when you're in the mood for seafood. Remember how I always loved that place?" Hunter nodded toward the seafood restaurant. "I've had a craving for years, so I finally bit the bullet and went."

"We decided to try the Italian place back there," said Hunter's mother. "We'd heard wonderful rumors about it—all true, by the way. Where's Kara?"

"Traveling for two weeks. Isn't she always, right?"

His parents chuckled, well aware of Kara's career and the schedule that accompanied it.

"So I'm a bachelor for the weekend, hanging out, living a life of boredom," Hunter continued.

His mother turned to Gabe with a smile of greeting. "Who's this?"

"Oh, I almost forgot. This is Gabe. He's a buddy from the office, from my old job." Hunter winced. He wasn't a liar and, under normal circumstances, would have found it difficult to tell a white lie, much less a blatant one like this. "Gabe meets a lot of people and offered to help me polish my resume." With that, Hunter remembered the portfolio he held under his arm, which he grabbed and waved, grateful for the implied evidence. Gabe followed suit, waving his own portfolio with a nervous laugh.

"Hi, Gabe. I'm Cindy, Hunter's mother." She reached out and shook Gabe's hand.

While Gabe handled himself well, Hunter sensed the deception made him uncomfortable, too. Gabe revealed no outward signals of discomfort, but over the course of tonight's date, Hunter and Gabe had begun to communicate on a common wavelength.

"Ed Carlisle," said Hunter's father without a smile, which Hunter knew to be a feature of the man's detached exterior. Nothing personal against Gabe. Hunter also knew people misinterpreted his father's detachment as displeasure. The man had a shaved head which reflected the boardwalk lights.

Ed offered a handshake, and though Gabe had large hands, Ed Carlisle's hand seemed to engulf Gabe's in his own. The man had gained a few pounds over the years, yet his build contained remnants of a football player from a bygone era. His voice had a gruff edge to it, and he had an unintentional habit of staring down any person to whom he spoke. All of these qualities projected the misleading first impression that Ed Carlisle was an intimidator. Gabe retrieved his hand from Ed's grip as soon as he could. Gabe offered Hunter's father a polite half-smile, then immediately shifted his focus to Hunter's mother, who came across as the more charming of the two.

"Tough job market out there," said Hunter's father.

"The right position will come through," his mother chimed in. "You never know who will cross your path and what it might lead to. Right, Gabe?"

"You're right about that." Gabe tucked his portfolio back under his arm and shoved both hands into the pockets of his coat, then peered off into the distance. Hunter couldn't tell if Gabe felt cold or if his actions were meant to buy himself a chance to become invisible.

Hunter's mother patted Gabe on the arm. "Thanks for helping Hunter out. I know he appreciates it."

Hunter's father exhaled, his breath spilling forth in a massive cloud. Hunter picked up traces of oregano and dry, red wine.

"We'd better get going, Cindy. I'm sure these guys are as cold as we are."

With another round of nice-to-meet-you greetings, Hunter's parents waved good-bye and headed in the opposite direction. Hunter kept his eye on them as they trekked, but not once did either parent take a second look behind them to reassess their son or his buddy from work.

Hunter and Gabe stood still, watching as Hunter's parents rounded the corner and out of their lines of sight. Though relieved, Hunter had a sick feeling in his gut. He stared at the spot in the distance where he last saw his mother and father before they disappeared.

By this time, Gabe had dropped his defenses and appeared awkward. He glanced over at Hunter, no doubt unsure how to break the silence.

"Your parents seem nice."

"Yeah," Hunter said. "They've never suspected a thing about me."

Hunter paused. His cheeks now felt chapped. A mass of clouds overtook the moon and concealed its glow.

"They'd be devastated if they knew."

CHAPTER 25

Fatherhood and the role of family.

Such topics were standard fare in a men's Bible study group and proved helpful. Given Hunter's recent circumstances, however, he had grown uncomfortable listening to the discussion that occurred in his midst this Thursday evening.

While not all group members were married, they operated under the assumption that most of the group's unmarried men wanted to marry one day, so the topic remained applicable. Hunter found it curious that the Apostle Paul, a bachelor who wrote most of the Bible's New Testament books, believed it more beneficial to remain single, yet today, Christians often felt pressured to settle into a family.

For as long as he could remember, Hunter had considered marriage and fatherhood part of his future and had dreamed of it since childhood. He'd never questioned it. He loved the notion of becoming a father. And though he hadn't related to his own father as well as he had wished, Hunter believed in new beginnings and determined to make himself as accessible as possible to his own children.

Sitting on the sofa tonight, a thought dawned on him: What if a same-sex relationship turned out a comfortable fit for him—to such an extent, he could never be happy in marriage to a woman? How would that impact his prospects of becoming a father?

Hunter's stream of consciousness flowed from there. He considered himself a man of perpetual hope. With that in mind, what if, down the road, he found himself free from attraction to his own gender? Suppose he found himself fixed one day, no longer tempted toward other men. Suppose he desired a heterosexual relationship and marriage with his whole heart, with everything within himself. At that point, what if anyone discovered his current inclinations? What if he and Gabe entered a relationship, and others found out about it after it ended? Would it render Hunter damaged goods? Would any woman want him after that? Would any woman want to live her life tormented by lingering doubts *she* might have about his sexuality?

The flipping of book pages brought Hunter's attention back to the group meeting.

"And so, in marriage, God gives us a picture of His relationship with the church," explained Dan, the group leader. "When we read about that husband-wife relationship in the Bible, the love the husband has for his wife and the affection the wife has for her husband, we see Christ's love for His church, for His people, and the love we hold for Him."

Hunter looked at Joe Garza, who sat on his left, and Jesse Barlow, who sat on his right. As they read the next paragraph in the study guide, Hunter scanned the entire group of men, who sat in a circle which, Hunter now mused, resembled the shape of a wedding band.

What would they say if they knew about him? He and Gabe had experimented with a first date. Hunter felt confident no one else in the group had experienced what he had. Albeit exploratory rather than a firm step toward a relationship, in his heart, Hunter knew he and Gabe had crossed a demarcation line. Now, sitting among these men, Hunter harbored a new secret. Nobody suspected anything, but he was sure they would disapprove of what had occurred. They wouldn't want his secret in their presence. He didn't want to keep it a secret, either.

He felt like a hypocrite, sitting with a Bible open in his lap while hiding a major aspect of his life, a feeling of shame in his heart, albeit a shame that also came with unconditional acceptance from another individual. The first date had done nothing to ease the conflict that roiled inside him and tormented him.

They think I'm living one way, but I'm living another way.

Hunter couldn't shake the notion. He felt unworthy sitting in this wedding-band circle of Christians who must have their lives together so much better than he.

Desperately he wanted to confide in someone and release the pressure, the way he'd confided in Gabe. Romantic enticement aside, the whole reason he'd started talking to Gabe was because he felt so alone.

Advice would come quick if he spoke up. How easy to advise someone to snap out of depression, for example, when you've never awakened each morning under the weight of its chains. And gossip comes easier when you haven't endured the experience in question. People have good intentions of keeping matters confidential, but when faced with the temptation to talk, sometimes they give in—even Christians, as much as Hunter hated to admit it.

His sexuality represented the most private, most sensitive facet of his life. Confessing its details carried significant risk, more so than the admission of an individual who had quit smoking but sneaked a cigarette in isolated moments of stress. That confession wouldn't ruin the individual's reputation; Hunter's confession would. What if he confided in someone and that person broke his confidence? What if word spread, people abandoned him, and he wound up alone—the very thing he'd sought to avoid in the first place? What if he wound up not only alone within himself, as he felt tonight, but also physically alone from the company of others as a result of his honesty? What comfort would that bring? Yes, he would still have Jesus, and Jesus was all he needed. But in the Bible, God Himself had said it wasn't good for man to be alone. That was why He had created not only Adam, but Eve, as well.

As the group moved through its list of discussion questions, Hunter glimpsed each individual in the circle, one by one. Dan the group leader ... Joe Garza ... Jesse Barlow ... Ross the college student. Each one a Christian. Each one a mystery.

Isn't there someone I can trust?

Other group members had confessed struggles during these Bible study meetings and nobody had judged them. Ross had admitted to cheating on an exam. Another individual had admitted he'd checked out pornography on the Internet— only to discover several members of the group had done the same thing at one point in their lives and broken free from the tendency. They prayed for each other, respected each other, and moved on. They had tested the group members' willingness to listen, but hadn't necessarily tested their trustworthiness or the boundaries of their support. They hadn't confessed anything as shocking—or as scandalous—as Hunter's revelation.

Then again, perhaps he *could* trust them. They hadn't proven themselves *untrustworthy*. These were his brothers in Christ, after all. Maybe he should take a risk. He hated the mask, the hypocritical feeling. Maybe he should take a bold step, end the torment right now, and open up his heart to this group.

Hunter felt his defenses drop. Already he sensed a wave of relief in anticipation of the burden that would disappear from his shoulders in a few minutes. If he could trust anyone in this life besides God, it should be the people in His church.

Okay, here we go …

Hunter awaited a break in the discussion, a lull between wrapping up one discussion point and moving on to the next. But the group had detoured into one of its tangent discussions with no end in sight. Hunter's stomach somersaulted. In his nervous state, his eyelids felt hot, but he gathered courage. He needed to set himself free.

Just interrupt the discussion and get it over with. They'll understand.

"But what about high divorce rates and blended families?" said Ross, the college student. "Wouldn't that make it even harder for everyone involved?"

"How would it make it harder?" asked a guy across the circle.

Hunter measured their words and tried to find an inkling of a breather in which he could speak up. His arms trembled.

"My parents stayed together, but I always wondered what the transition must be like for blended families," Ross answered. "I mean, what's it like for a kid? In a way, he has two father figures, right? A father and a stepfather."

"Better than two *dads,* though," Joe chuckled. Because he sat beside Hunter, his voice sounded forth in a sudden boom, louder than the other voices in the room.

"Two dads?" asked Ross.

"Yeah," Joe replied, his eyebrows now raised, a smirk on his face as though he found the conversation amusing. "Like in those gay relationships where they adopt."

"Do you know anyone like that?"

"Of course not," Joe snorted. "I'm just saying, that's all."

By this time, every group member had fixed his attention on Joe and Ross, back and forth, as the verbal tennis match played out before their eyes.

"But that's different from what I'm talking about," Ross said. "That's two equal fathers, not a father and stepfather. The kid with two gay dads knows his dads from birth, so right or wrong, it's at least been consistent."

"Consistency isn't exactly what I was talking about," Joe said. Another smirk, another chuckle.

"Okay, then what's your point?"

Joe straightened his posture. "I'm thinking more about the *environment*, where the two dads are … well, the *perversion* of it, you know? Think about it: Eventually the kid is gonna wonder why each dad chose to be with another dude instead of with a woman …"

Hunter froze. No way could he say anything now, given the direction in which the conversation had veered and the flippant way in which Joe had spoken of people who struggled like Hunter. Hunter locked himself down in fear.

Motion startled him, but he recovered in time to suppress an outward reaction. The movement had come from Jesse Barlow, who sat on Hunter's other side. Jesse sank back into his chair, arms crossed, but said nothing. Just listened.

Hunter pondered Joe's last comment, a rusty nail which punctured Hunter's heart. A new wound formed.

Hunter knew his attractions wouldn't be met with approval, but now, Joe's words revealed a harsher truth, one Hunter had never considered: Some people wouldn't see Hunter as merely shameful; they would regard him as *perverted*.

The word sounded both glib and horrible at the same time.

Some people wouldn't see him in a conflict. They would look at him as an individual who awoke one morning, made a conscious choice, and started a new life as, in their view, an evil person.

Hunter had never looked at his struggle as *perversion*. He had always thought of perversion as the result of a long road of intentional, specific actions—a series of *desired* choices, things people *welcomed* into their lives. Yet Hunter's battle felt *nothing* like a choice, and he certainly never considered it welcome.

In fact, Hunter's feelings had little, if anything, to do with any type of sexual encounter. Rather, it felt more like a need for acceptance, a desire for companionship with someone who could understand him.

He didn't know why the need was there. It just was.

Of all people, the individuals in this Bible study group were the ones that should feel like a second family to him, in whom he could confide and find help. But now, he realized it was a mirage: He could *never* open up and trust them. They could never *begin* to understand him.

And once again, with that fresh awareness, he felt alone.

Dan's voice interrupted Hunter's contemplation.

"Hey, guys, this discussion has really drifted off course. Why don't we move on to the next paragraph in the book?"

Heads nodded, followed by scattered *Yeahs* and *Okays.*

"Thanksgiving and Christmas are coming up, so this is our last meeting until January," Dan added. "We might as well try to make it through a full chapter in the book *once,* right?"

Hunter peered down to discover his knee jostling as fast as his heart rate. It resulted from bouncing the ball of his foot upon the floor, a frequent reaction when he felt anxious and didn't catch himself in time. He put an immediate halt to his fidgeting, maintained his poker face—he almost hadn't stopped his eyes from widening the moment he'd noticed his knee in motion. Hunter begged God that nobody else had noticed. Looking around, he doubted anyone had; they appeared too enthralled with Joe and Ross's conversation to have noticed anything else around them.

He mouthed a word of thanks to God, then bit his lower lip as a shroud of sadness settled over his soul.

"Hey man, you okay?" A whisper.

Hunter looked beside him. Jesse Barlow remained sunken back in his chair, arms still crossed. Jesse had leaned so far back, Hunter had to crane his neck farther and look over his shoulder to meet Jesse's eyes.

From the corner of his mouth, Jesse had managed to whisper soft enough, discreetly enough, to make sure no one except Hunter heard him.

Jesse Barlow, the minister's son. Talk about a guy who had fought through some rough years. Hunter didn't know the whole story, nor had he tried to find out. He'd always felt Jesse should have a right to privacy.

Jesse had disappeared to California for more than a decade. Apparently, along the way, he had made some choices that had caused him severe regret. When he'd returned to Ohio, Jesse had found out his high school sweetheart had given birth to a son—*Jesse's* son. Nowadays, Jesse found himself in the process of trying to raise a pre-adolescent.

Yes, Hunter figured, Jesse must have seen some hardship of his own. No wonder the guy hadn't jumped into Joe's discussion a few minutes ago. He'd seemed as if he didn't even want to hear it.

Hunter gave him a discreet nod.

"Yeah, I'm fine," he whispered from the corner of his mouth.

Fine, thought Hunter.

If only.

CHAPTER 26

Hunter didn't have answers. Nor did he have a solution. He found it difficult to reconcile his feelings for Gabe and didn't know what his next step should be. But his guilt continued to rise, strengthening by the day—the sense that he had begun to string Kara along.

Along this unfamiliar road, Hunter discovered the presence of many unknowns. But he did know this: His feelings for Gabe had grown and had now replaced any feelings he'd had—or *convinced* himself he'd had—for Kara. It didn't seem fair to her. Besides that, her travels and absences for long stretches of time only made resistance to Gabe that much tougher. Yet Hunter and Kara's relationship hadn't lasted all too long, so asking her to set aside her job for the sake of their relationship didn't strike Hunter as fair, either.

He'd given a lot of thought to tonight's location, but no matter which option he considered, he knew Kara would interpret it as a date setting. He wanted to take this step in the kindest manner possible; doing so at her home seemed insensitive, and his own home provided specific memories of romantic evenings.

He had settled on a small winery. He knew Kara loved the place, which meant he could offer at least one pleasant aspect to an evening that might otherwise prove thorny.

In season, dozens of individuals packed the patio on Saturday nights. In late November, however, Hunter knew the winery's population would be sparse, which meant a private setting. Although it was too cold to sit outside, the owners had added at one end of the building a small annex, with beautiful tiled floors and a gas fireplace made of polished stone. The winery crew had unpacked the Christmas decorations early, and over the fireplace hung a row of stockings with a staff member's name etched on each. Seasonal music played overhead—steel drum music, which Hunter pegged as a reminder of warm weather, a cue for visitors to return to the winery when summer rolled around.

A Christmas tree sat beside the fireplace. On either side of the tree, Santa Claus and Mrs. Claus figurines, each the size of a toddler, stood guard with smiles on their faces. The figurines' hands were clasped, as if delighted *someone* had finally come to visit them. Tonight, the room was empty aside from Hunter and Kara, who sat at a table near the tree.

Hunter tried to savor the scent of bread fresh from the grill. He munched on a hot panini of turkey and artichoke, while Kara nibbled on a gourmet grilled cheese sandwich. Hunter also felt a bottle of wine might help keep Kara relaxed—if possible— as they ended their relationship.

How could he transition to that topic? Cutting to the chase struck him as cruel, and he didn't want to hurt her. So he had started the evening with light conversation and proceeded with care, vigilant not to use words or actions that would lead her into a romantic mood.

"By the way, we never talked about Christmas," Kara said. "I hope you won't be disappointed, but I promised my family I'd travel home to see them in Minneapolis. That means I can't be here for our first Christmas together."

Maybe he could transition from there. "I understand. When you think about it, we haven't been together long enough for Christmas to be a given, have we?"

"You're right. We're in that in-between zone. No black or white."

"Have you booked your flight yet?"

"Not yet, but I'd better get around to it before the flights fill up. I get a free ticket with my frequent-flyer miles."

"No shortage of those," Hunter smirked.

"Plenty more points where those came from, for sure." Kara took a bite of her grilled cheese. When she wiped her hands on her napkin, her fingertips left behind little butter imprints. "Do you have plans for Christmas?"

"Mom and Dad are visiting Bryce and his family in Boston."

"Are you going with them?"

"That was the plan," Hunter said, "but when you're between jobs, suddenly a plane ticket seems like a budget buster. I could always drive, though."

Once those words left his mouth, Hunter stopped. He wondered what Gabe was up to for Christmas. To his recollection, Gabe hadn't mentioned leaving town, and he knew Gabe's only family in town was his mother. Maybe Hunter should invite them over for fun.

"I haven't decided for sure if I'm going to Bryce's house," Hunter said. "I might keep it low key, conserve my budget, hang out with a friend in town."

"Who?"

"Just a buddy. You haven't met him."

At that, Kara shrugged, then sipped her wine.

Yes, this relationship factor had gotten harder. Kara didn't suspect a thing—neither his lack of interest in her, nor his attractions toward anyone else. And now he had allowed their conversation to drift away from anything leading to a breakup. Hunter couldn't identify a good way to steer the conversation back onto his intended course, so the direct route seemed best.

He looked down at his dinner, which he hadn't touched in several minutes and had gone lukewarm, and realized his appetite had departed. He shifted in his seat, procrastinating amid the inevitable.

"Kara, this isn't easy," he began, forcing himself to look into her eyes, "but I need to talk to you about something."

Creases formed along Kara's forehead. An expression of concern overtook her face. Despite the music playing overhead, the space between Hunter and Kara had grown eerily quiet. Hunter could hear her swallow her wine.

"You look so serious," Kara said. "What's wrong?"

He didn't want to do this to her, but it seemed selfish *not* to. Kara's big, blue eyes had the innocence of a child. Though he struggled to maintain eye contact, he felt she deserved that much, considering he was about to break her heart. He wished she hadn't grown attached to him as fast as she had.

"I, um, I can't find a good way say this, so maybe I should lay it on the table." With a deep breath, Hunter said, "I think it would be good for us to … take a break."

In a split second, though anyone else would have missed it, Hunter saw something fall in her pixie stare. The first tear of the fabric upon her heart. Her eyes flinched with a look of dejection, the kind where you search for an inkling of hope—evidence that you had misunderstood what you'd heard—before giving up.

Kara peered down at the tabletop, ran her fingernail along its diamond pattern, before looking up again. Her expression appeared hopeful but revealed hope had gotten shot in the heart.

"By 'take a break,' you don't mean … to go away together somewhere? As in a break from Ohio?"

True to form, Kara had believed the best about him. Numbness waded into Hunter's stomach.

"No," he replied, his voice above a whisper, "I mean a break… from us."

"Oh …"

Hunter could understand her lack of response. Yet silence didn't seem fitting. He felt responsible to talk, to say *something,* if for no other reason than to keep her from feeling self-conscious. So he trudged forward.

"I don't know if the answer is to take a step back and see other people—"

"Is it something I did?"

Hunter held out his palms to stop her from blaming herself. "No, it's not you. I *promise* it's not you. It's me."

"What do you mean, it's you?"

He didn't know how to answer that. After all, *he* didn't even know what was going on inside himself or why. How was he supposed to find words to explain it to *her?*

"For some reason, my heart can't quite, well, *get there.*" When Kara blinked at that statement, Hunter hurried his next words in an effort to protect her. He could sense his sincerity coming through as he spoke. "Look, Kara, I care about you very much. I enjoy our time together. The best way I can explain it is, my *heart* can't seem to get in sync with ... *us*. Not in a way we both know would be necessary for a long-term relationship."

He considered sipping his wine, then decided against it.

"Maybe it's a proximity factor," Hunter said. "With the travel your job requires, you're rarely in town."

"You never mentioned this before. Suddenly it became an issue?"

"Not suddenly. But consider how little we see each other. Thinking long term, is that enough for us to build a lasting relationship?"

"So, this is *my* fault?" Her expression turned from hurt to confusion. "My career has become a problem?"

"No, it's not your fault. And your career hasn't become a problem. I'm just saying—wondering—if that lack of connection makes it harder, at least for me, to ... *get there*. I know how important your job is to you, and it should be. I can't ask you to change your career in order to suit me. That wouldn't be fair to you."

Hunter found this scenario all too familiar. Regardless of how deep or shallow his romantic relationships, he managed to sabotage them every time. Maybe, beneath the surface, he was scared of being found out.

More likely, however, his need to sabotage his relationships were tied to proximity. But though he had told Kara he struggled with *lack* of proximity, Hunter wondered if the opposite was true: Perhaps he *feared* proximity. If he allowed a woman to get too close, she might find a way to his heart.

Despite his desire *not* to be attracted to the same sex, was it possible he didn't *want* a woman to find a place in his heart?

That notion took Hunter aback. Now that he thought about it, whenever he sabotaged a relationship, though he felt a sense of failure, he also felt relieved. Ending relationships removed a load of pressure from his shoulders as he tried to sort through the feelings he repressed and make sense of the commotion inside his soul.

Nonetheless, those self-sabotages left him confused. They left the females hurt and, perhaps, *more* confused than he.

Kara certainly looked that way.

But wasn't this route, bringing closure to their relationship, more compassionate than stringing her along?

"Is there someone else?"

Kara's words startled him. Hunter kicked himself for allowing his thoughts to drift.

"Huh?"

Kara leaned closer. She looked him straight in the eye. Her eyes now possessed pointed determination, one which sought answers. "I said, is there someone else?"

"No," he answered, his voice firm, "there's no one else."

Technically, that seemed true, Hunter told himself. He and Gabe had only had one date—if you could call it a date—to test the waters. Neither he nor Gabe could define what existed between them. Therefore, Hunter didn't *know* if there was someone else. Even if he were to fall in love with Gabe, Hunter didn't know how far he could allow himself to dive in.

Nevertheless, he felt a twinge of guilt because, in his heart, he knew he had told Kara a little white lie.

Yet he *couldn't* tell her the whole truth. He wanted to, but he hadn't confided in anyone about this, and it was *his* personal issue to wade through. Kara would understand if she knew the dark truth, but Hunter wasn't ready for anyone to know—because as soon as they did, he knew his life would turn upside down.

Kara appeared stunned. She must have felt humiliated. After all, his words had caught her off guard. But what else was he supposed to do? Let her waste her life by living a lie with him?

Once again, Hunter felt the responsibility to fill the silence. He had started this mess; navigating their way through it was the least he could do.

"Maybe after the holidays pass—in the new year—we can talk about where things stand," Hunter suggested, an effort to soften the blow rather than an authentic proposal. Even to Hunter, as he listened to himself, his words sounded lame.

Kara just stared at him, pursing her lips, prolonging the moment—a moment Hunter wished would come to a merciful end.

Hunter continued to fill the vacuum of silence. "Maybe we need to see other people to—well, maybe we're not as compatible as we first thought."

Oh geez, he was making it worse, he could sense it. He wanted to shut his mouth and quit insulting her intelligence. He knew her well enough to know she could see through these emotional bandages.

Verbal clumsiness aside, Hunter had entered this evening concerned about Kara, not himself. But regardless of what he said tonight, she would interpret his words and actions as a personal rejection. She wouldn't recognize the larger story at play.

Hunter stopped talking. Just stopped short. Folding his hands on the table, he let his gaze fall to his knuckles, which he rubbed in an effort to distract himself from the mental acrobatics in his mind.

Steel drums continued to fill the room, this time with a Caribbean rendition of "A Holly Jolly Christmas." In spite of his efforts, Hunter realized, he couldn't have picked a worse place for Kara and him to part ways. So sprightly and sweet, Kara seldom spoke an unkind word. Knowing he had broken her heart made him feel awful.

Kara looked away, focused on the flames that lashed inside the fireplace. When she returned her attention to him, he lifted his head and their gazes met. A film of tears had rinsed over her eyes. From the way Kara tensed her jaw, Hunter could tell she had used all her might to force the dam to remain in place. He would never see her cry.

Finally, Kara spoke.

"So this is it?" Resignation, thick as coconut oil, dripped from her voice. "We're done?"

Hunter wanted to reach out and hold her, offer her comfort, but he no longer possessed that privilege. At this point, he was the last individual from whom she'd desire consolation.

Hunter held her gaze once more and absorbed her brokenness.

"Yes," he whispered.

Kara bit the inside of her cheek, her habit when she grew nervous, then nodded.

"Hunter, please take me home."

CHAPTER 27

On Friday afternoon, Hunter rapped his knuckle on the door to Ellen Krieger's apartment. He'd left his coat and tie in the car. Dressing in a suit today had given him a surge of confidence he hadn't expected to return while out of work.

No answer. He knew Ellen often spent weekday afternoons working in her apartment, so he gave the door knocker a couple of *thunks*. From somewhere within, he heard the words, "I'm coming, one sec!"

When she answered the door, she appeared frazzled, her face flushed a dark shade of pink. Dressed in jeans and a white apron, strands of hair had escaped her brunette ponytail. She looked like she'd stuck her fingernail into an electrical socket.

Hunter took a step back and extended his arms toward her, palms out, to feign a reaction of fear. "What happened to you?!"

"Come on in," she said with a gesture of her head. "Lock the door behind you," she said in afterthought as she made a beeline for her tiny kitchen.

Upon entering her dining room, Hunter's attention settled on a table filled with what looked like entrées and side dishes in progress, all uncooked and sitting in disposable serving pans. To his right, he perused Ellen's kitchen and found the counters littered with cutting boards and containers, as well as celery, carrots and other raw vegetables, two of which he couldn't identify by sight. He noticed stalks that looked like overgrown green onions. Had Ellen called them leeks?

Ellen took her position at the counter beside her sink, where she resumed mincing an onion on a wooden cutting board. Two wadded dish towels, one dry and one wet, sat within reach on the counter. To Ellen's left, a waste basket stood in sentry position, guarding her leg.

"Never mind the mess," Ellen said. "It's my busy season. Everybody's holding their holiday parties. Thanksgiving, Christmas ... *in between* Thanksgiving and Christmas ..."

At first evaluation, Hunter thought the scene looked like a disaster. But upon second glance, he began to recognize a semblance of organization. Vegetables sat beside vegetables; items destined for the oven or refrigerator sat near each other. When he realized Ellen had set an authentic plan into motion— and, having savored her cooking, he knew what the end result would be—Hunter had to admire his friend's forethought and stamina. She had endured this type of pressure for more than a year.

Hunter flicked the leaf of a celery stalk, then crossed his arms. "I'd say the whole holiday season landed in your apartment at once," he snickered.

"I have two catering jobs this weekend: a small company party tomorrow night, and a social function on Sunday evening.

Each one requires two entrées and several side dishes." With her knife, she gestured to his hand. "And don't touch the celery without washing your hands first, unless you're ready to lose a finger."

Hunter didn't acknowledge her remark, but chuckled to himself. "Sounds like a full menu. What about desserts?"

"Those too. And of course, they wanted different menus, which means I can't make larger batches and split them between the two jobs. So today, I'm getting as much prep work done as I can. Tomorrow morning, I'll be baking like crazy."

"Didn't you tell me you had an assistant for large jobs?"

"I pay a Kent State student to help when needed, but she called yesterday to bail on me."

Ellen stopped working. Her shoulders drooped as she took in the spread of food, her eyes roaming from left to right, then right to left.

"What was I thinking?" Ellen shook her head. She compressed her lips so tight, they disappeared from view. "Why did I agree to all this? This is insane."

"Looks like you'll need an extra oven or two."

"Don't laugh. I was going to hit you up for yours tonight after dulling you with a few glasses of wine. Brendan plans to help out tomorrow. Believe me, he'd be thrilled to help me take over your kitchen if it stops me from going bitchcakes on him this weekend."

"You can help yourself to my kitchen if you need it," Hunter said. "No alcohol required."

With the blunt edge of her knife blade, Ellen slid a mound of onion shavings from her cutting board into a bowl, then resumed mincing.

"How's the job hunt going?" she asked.

"Wrapped up an interview a few minutes ago, right before stopping here."

"No wonder you're all dressed up. You could use a tie though," she said with a wink.

"I left it in the car."

Ellen stopped mincing and wiped her brow against her shoulder, which left a dark spot on her shirt fabric. She'd broken a sweat in the process? She was under more pressure than he'd figured. Ellen protracted her exhale to twice its normal length and scanned the array of food once again.

"You're hired," she blurted.

"What?"

Reaching into the cabinet beneath her sink, she retrieved a white apron identical to the one she wore. One quick whip to unfold the apron, then she waved it before Hunter as if to tantalize him.

"Say hello to this little guy. He'll help you make your next rent payment. You're gonna help save my ass."

With that, she tossed the apron to him, which he caught before he could give it a second thought.

"I don't do aprons."

"Do you want to get tomato juice splattered all over that sexy outfit?"

"But I don't know much about cooking. Nothing official, anyway."

"I'll teach you what you need to know. I've always wanted to give you orders."

Hunter rolled his eyes, followed by his sleeves. He lifted the apron's loop over his head.

"Fine," he joshed, "but only if we work naked under the aprons."

"Don't make me go bitchcakes on *you,* Carlisle. I'm surrounded by knives."

An hour later, the kitchen felt more crowded to Hunter, if that were possible. He worked beside the sink while Ellen worked several feet away, at the opposite end of the counter. So far, she had assigned him simple tasks like washing and cutting vegetables. He had minced onions and diced tomatoes. Now he julienned peppers, slicing them into thin, vertical strips of green, yellow and red. He'd never thought about how many ways you could cut vegetables into pieces. Left to his own devices, he would have chopped them up and thrown them into the mix without a second thought.

Ellen had also taught him a cutting technique whereby he curled his fingers atop the vegetable as he held it with his left hand, which allowed him to rest the blade of the knife against his knuckles and slice faster while avoiding injury. At first, the technique felt awkward, but after several minutes of practice, he had grown more comfortable. The feeling of progress sent a rush through him.

"I knew you were an awesome cook," said Hunter, "but I never knew the details that went into it."

"It's an art form."

"Green peppers are definitely the new Monette."

"You mean Monet?"

"Whatever," he winked. "But it makes me realize I never asked you much about it. I've just devoured your—your *art*, I should say—and moved on."

Hunter noticed Ellen had grown less flustered since he'd agreed to help her. He could sense that tension had dissipated from the kitchen. Between ovens at her apartment, Brendan's apartment, and Hunter's home, she assured him everything would come together on time.

"What keeps you busy when it's *not* the holiday season?" Hunter asked.

"I get lots of orders for cookies, specialty cakes and cupcakes, giving the corner bakery a run for its money."

"Yeah, but they've got a store location. How does word get around about you?"

"People discover my desserts at a catering function and crave them afterward. Word gets around. They place orders for their own parties and offices, or just for themselves—guilty pleasures."

"You're the queen of guilty pleasures."

"That's what I can call my business: Queen of Guilty Pleasures! Thanks Hunter, you're such a help," she said with a tease.

"Sheer talent, what can I say?"

"Speaking of guilty pleasures, what's Kara up to? You and I haven't crossed paths for a few weeks. Bring me up to speed, but keep it to the point. I'm a busy woman, as you can see."

Hunter tilted his head in reaction but kept his eyes focused on his work to prevent cutting his finger. Safety provided a convenient excuse to avoid her scrutiny.

"We're no longer together. We ended things last week."

"She ended things?"

"I did."

Ellen stopped working for a moment, gave him a precursory once-over with her eyes—to gauge how well he'd handled the breakup, no doubt—then resumed cutting through a raw chicken.

"I'm sorry to hear that."

Hunter winked at her. "Sure you are."

"Of course I am!" she said, shrugging her shoulders with feigned innocence. "Seriously! I'm your friend and I care about you. Granted, I wasn't Kara's biggest fan, but she wasn't a bad person. I just couldn't get the poor girl to shut up at times!" Another glance at Hunter, then she said, "Look, I don't want you to have a broken heart. That's the important thing. But you sure seem okay, unless you're hiding it well."

"I'll admit my heart wasn't fully in the relationship. We enjoyed each other's company and tried to make a relationship work, but sometimes it—"

"—isn't meant to be?"

"Right," Hunter replied. "Besides, as much as she traveled, we spent more time apart than we spent together. So, as strange as it sounds, my day-to-day doesn't feel much different today than it did when we were together. She's gone, but she's no more absent than she was three weeks ago."

"But you're okay? Promise me you're okay."

Hunter grinned. "I promise I'm okay."

Ellen examined his face, then looked confused. She placed her fist on her hip the way she did when she knew the details didn't match.

"No, you seem *too* okay." She squinted for a moment, as if to examine him closer, then her eyes grew wide. "What a sly little Valentino you are! You have another woman on your radar already, don't you!"

Hunter felt his eye muscles expand and his pupils dilate before he took control of himself. Ellen tilted her head in one direction but kept her eyes trained on him, expecting an answer.

Nonchalant, Hunter replied, "No ladies on the radar at the moment." Technically true. "I might take a break from the dating scene, save my money till I find a new job. That's not a bad idea, right?"

Ellen stared at him, stabbing him with that suspicion in her eyes.

"Speaking of love," Hunter said, scurrying to deflect her attention, "what's the latest on your wedding plans?"

Ellen returned to her raw chicken, its flesh pallid, a trickle of blood escaping here and there. After a beat, she gestured with her head toward the array of food.

"Look at all this food," she murmured, almost to herself. "Tons of details, each dish begging for attention. Racing the clock to get it all done. I've done my best to organize everything, to keep it under control. But it still feels like it's teetering, on the verge of erupting into a hot mess."

Hunter glanced over his shoulder at her.

"That's how planning the wedding feels, along with everything else happening around it," she said. "Part of it is due to my busy catering season, plus trying to get all the factors worked out for the new home. Everything is coming together at the same time as this wedding …"

Ellen stopped her work. She gave him a cautious glance, as if to reconsider what she'd said.

"I'm supposed to *enjoy* planning my wedding, right? I'm twenty-six years old, in the prime of my life. I don't know what it is, but I'm not … happy. And it bugs the hell out of me because I can't figure out *why*."

Hunter didn't know what to say. Though their friendship had lasted years, Ellen seldom confided in him. Her strong exterior served as her trademark, a trait he took for granted until it dissolved on rare occasions like this afternoon.

"You know what scares me the most?" Ellen continued. "I don't want to be the woman who sold us the property."

"The property you and Brendan bought to build your house?"

"Yeah. I'm scared of becoming that woman."

"What do you mean? What about her?"

"That woman felt so trapped thinking she'd made a mistake with her marriage, mistaken who she was, afraid to build a house anywhere that would remind her of her regrets. What if *I* enter this marriage, then figure out ten years later that I made a mistake? Not because of who Brendan is, but because of who *I* am?" Ellen said. "You know me, Hunter. I can do anything without being afraid. But marriage—that's not a thing, it's a *life*."

"Have you talked to Brendan about this?"

"Yeah, but he thinks it's stress and wedding jitters. And he knows what to say to calm me down when I get stressed out."

"But you *don't* think it's stress and wedding jitters?"

With a shrug of resignation, Ellen bit down on her lip.

"I don't know what it is." She pursed her lips and curled her fingers, focusing on her cutting board as if it would reveal her answer. "It's like this tiny seed sits trapped inside my soul, surrounded by darkness, hidden inside me. But it doesn't grow into a tree; it just lingers as a seed—a seed of doubt. Nobody can see it because it's not a giant tree. But that doesn't change the fact that it's there, reminding me of all I stand to lose with love, all the people I could hurt if I make a critical mistake. It's a small, hidden question, but it weighs me down and pulls at my attention. The rest of my life is fine, but that damn seed still lurks beneath my skin. And nobody else can remove that seed from my life."

Ellen paused in thought, then continued slicing away at the chicken before her, working much slower than before. Hunter knew her thoughts resided elsewhere.

Ellen shook her head. She mumbled under her breath, words Hunter wasn't sure were meant to reach his ears.

"That damn seed …"

CHAPTER 28

On Monday night, as Hunter drove the car, he could tell Gabe felt nervous. Gabe couldn't keep his hands still, interlocking his fingers, then kneading them, one by one. He would rest his hands in his lap for a few seconds, then repeat the process all over again. Hunter didn't think Gabe was even aware of it.

Peering over at the passenger side, Hunter asked, "You're okay meeting them?"

"Sure, nothing wrong with meeting new people," Gabe replied in a casual tone, the way someone overcompensates to hide the fact that they're nervous. "I meet new clients all the time, right?"

Despite his normal air of confidence, Gabe struck Hunter as a lone wolf. Gabe had mentioned he *didn't* feel like he fits in, so Hunter figured an evening with the guys might help him stretch. Beyond that, Hunter wanted to test the waters to see if his friends would notice or say anything about this new person in Hunter's life, but test it under the guise of a new friendship.

He'd decided to treat it the way he would add hot water to a lukewarm bath, a gradual increase, imperceptible until, at some point, he'd reached full temperature.

Could it be that simple?

Hunter wondered if this was his way of seeking permission, of getting approval for something he'd grown up hearing others teach him is wrong.

When they reached the apartment building in Twinsburg, a community north of Hudson, Hunter parked the car and they climbed out. He waved for Gabe to follow him up the stairs.

"You're sure they won't mind my showing up without an invite?" Gabe asked.

"They won't care. They're a laid-back group of guys," Hunter said with a knock on the door. "Good guys. I know one of them from church, the others from elsewhere. On Saturdays, I shoot hoops with some of them. Somebody said he might bring along another buddy or two tonight, too."

Gabe shoved his hands into his coat pockets. "If they're okay with my coming, then so am I."

Randy Gresh opened the door. Dressed in a hooded sweatshirt, his five o'clock shadow made him look older than he was.

"Hunter Carlisle!" Randy boomed, an open bottle of beer in his left hand. He gave Hunter a knuckle bump with his free hand and opened the door wider with his elbow.

"I brought my buddy Gabe along. Hope that's okay."

"Of course," Randy said, "the more the merrier. Come on in."

Hunter made his way inside with Gabe close behind. In the living room, Randy had already placed the chairs from his dining-room table on each side of his sofa, all arranged in a semi-circle around a flat-screen television. The deep, crisp voices of two sports broadcasters emanated from the surround-sound speakers as they called plays for a Monday night football game, which had begun a few minutes earlier. The Cleveland Browns would play this game on the road in Kansas City.

The living room was sparse, true to form as a bachelor pad. Joe Garza and Matt Toenjes sat in two chairs on one side of the sofa. Two other friends of Randy's had come and occupied the other chairs, guys Hunter had met in the past but whose names he'd forgotten. He figured he'd pick up their names as the game continued and they bantered back and forth. On most occasions, Hunter knew, Randy sat on the sofa, taking the seat nearest the door. Since Hunter knew everyone, he decided to take the middle seat on the sofa to reduce any discomfort for Gabe. He sat down and removed his coat, and Gabe followed his lead.

"Browns doing okay this season?" Gabe asked of no one in particular.

"If they win all their remaining regular-season games and two other teams suffer losses, we'll eke out a wildcard spot next month in the playoffs," Matt replied.

"Miracle of miracles," Joe chimed in.

A sudden round of shouts and hand claps interrupted Joe's comment as the Browns completed a 16-yard pass. The receiver managed to carry the ball a few more yards before the Kansas City defense forced him out of bounds and the game clock stopped.

"Hunter or Gabe, you guys want a beer?" Randy called from the kitchen, where he searched inside his refrigerator.

Gabe gave a polite decline. When the broadcast entered a commercial break, Hunter met Randy in the kitchen and retrieved two colas from the refrigerator. He handed one to Gabe and settled back onto the sofa. Though Hunter kept his words at a minimum tonight, he hadn't disconnected himself. On the contrary, he intended to gauge his friends' responses to Gabe and would step in if the interaction grew awkward. That might provide Hunter with clues about what he would be up against down the road if they were to discover him in a relationship with Gabe.

After a long drive and several failed attempts to deliver the football into the end zone, Cleveland settled for a field goal on fourth down. Though it generated a tepid response from the guys in the room compared to the touchdown attempts, Hunter offered a halfhearted handclap at the effort.

"Did any of you guys play football back in the day?" Gabe asked.

Two of the guys gave a finger wave but remained focused on the television as a commercial ended, kickoff occurred, and Kansas City managed a 28-yard return.

"You?" Matt grunted.

"No, not me," Gabe chuckled. "I was one of those drama geeks. I was always better at *playing* a football player than actually being one. I left sports to the guys who were good at them."

A nod from one of Randy's friends. Other than that, the guys remained silent as the broadcast blared from the television. Hunter could hear Joe shift in his seat. Though Gabe sat inches away, Hunter could sense Gabe had gone tense. Gabe lifted one eyebrow as he concentrated on scratching his index finger against his thumb. Hunter assumed the guys had gone silent as they tried to predict how Kansas City would set up its next play. He hoped their silence didn't reflect a lack of interest in Gabe. He also looked to see whether anyone's glances flicked between Gabe and him, but noticed nothing.

Why am I so paranoid? Hunter wondered. *I know these guys. Joe, Randy and Matt are my friends.*

Gabe eased back against the sofa and watched the game. Other than the occasional fidget, he seemed fine once again.

Kansas City attempted a touchdown on fourth down, but wound up short. They returned the ball to Cleveland. On first down, Cleveland executed a running play for two yards. On second down, the quarterback's pass attempt went incomplete. On third down, Cleveland succeeded at a running play of eight yards, one that appeared sufficient for a first down. When the referees pulled out the chain link and measured the progress, however, they ruled the ball inches shy of a first down at Kansas City's 46-yard line.

"Think they'll go for first down?" Hunter asked.

"No way. I think they'll punt," Randy replied. "It's still early in the first quarter. They have no reason to go for it."

"Yeah, but Cleveland's gotten more aggressive this year," Matt chimed in. "Plus, they need to win tonight to have any hope of making it to the post-season. I think they'll try to rack up as many points as possible early on."

"Okay, stupid question since I don't watch many of these games," Gabe said. "If they just went for a play and got eight yards, why wouldn't they make a play to get these last inches? If they don't make it, they can try again like before, right?"

Immediately Joe stifled a smirk. His pointed glance hopped from Hunter to Randy. Without a word, Joe and Randy had communicated a message.

"You get four downs—four attempts—to make it ten yards," Randy replied in a matter-of-fact tone. "If you make it, the downs reset at the new spot."

"But if you don't make it, you lose the ball to the other team—at that exact spot," Joe added.

"Oh, okay, I see," Gabe said. He leaned forward in his seat and relaxed his shoulders in a manner that struck Hunter as a tad too loose for a male. "But if our fourth-down attempt failed, what would be the problem if the other team got the ball?"

More shifting glances. More hidden smirks.

"Well, they're halfway down the field," Randy said. "If we punt, the other team will catch the ball, maybe run it a little, and let's say they end up at the 20-yard line. They'd need to travel 80 yards for a touchdown."

"If we went for the fourth down and failed," one of Randy's friends interrupted, "our best-case scenario is that K.C. would get the ball at their 46-yard line. K.C. would only need to travel 54 yards to score, then we'd be down 7-3."

Gabe thought for a moment, then nodded. "Oh, okay."

Gabe's face underwent a subtle change to a light pink, which only Hunter could notice since he sat close beside him, and Hunter knew Gabe had grown embarrassed. He wanted to wrap his arm around Gabe to protect him, but given the context, he knew such a gesture would mean trouble for Gabe. And Hunter, too.

Cleveland opted to take its chances. A round of groans from the living-room quarterbacks ensued. Joe slapped his hand against his forehead. The team lost 15 yards, ending up deep into its own territory when Kansas City sacked the quarterback.

"*Shhhhhhhit!*" Randy shouted, then nodded at Gabe and added, "Or, your quarterback tries a surprise passing play and doesn't get rid of the ball in time. Then you're screwed!"

The game faded to a commercial break. Gabe excused himself for a quick run to the bathroom. From that distance, the television's volume overpowered voices at a normal conversation level. Joe spoke first.

"Who *is* that dude, Hunter?"

Okay, here we go.

Hunter couldn't mention the massage appointments. He'd never hear the end of it.

"Just a buddy of mine," Hunter punted.

"How long have you known him?"

"A few months. He works in Solon."

"He doesn't seem to be into anything you're interested in. How'd you start hanging out?" asked Randy.

"We crossed paths at his work, started shooting the breeze, then started hanging out. Good guy."

"Is he straight?" Randy asked with a tone of derision.

Hunter grew nervous. His pulse rate spiked. Suddenly, he realized trying to hang out with the guys with Gabe around would prove tougher than he'd imagined. He would need to fight to maintain a tight grip on what information he allowed them to learn.

Joe rolled his eyes and glared at Randy. "Dude, why would you ask him that? Of course the guy's straight."

"Hey, I'm just saying!" Randy said, palms out, fingers spread, two beers already in his system. "It didn't seem like he—"

A click from the bathroom door and the voices stopped. One broadcaster spouted a piece of trivia about Kansas City's star wide receiver as the team set up its next play. To Hunter's relief, Gabe padded back into the living room. He'd only left the room for a minute, but to Hunter, that minute had stretched much longer.

"Did I miss anything?" Gabe asked with a nod toward the game.

"Not a thing," Randy replied. Nonchalant, he waved a hand in the air in *Whatever* mode. "Just talking shit while K.C. sets up its next play."

Hunter sank so far back into the sofa, they could have used the cushion to cast a mold of his body.

CHAPTER 29

Only once before had Hunter come anywhere near the border of a same-sex relationship.

Hunter was a junior in college at the time. The difference between Gabe and the guy back in college was that Hunter and the college classmate shared similar interests. That's how it all started between them.

Hunter had found himself in the midst of a vulnerable season in his life. Before returning to school for the fall semester, he had ended a relationship with yet another girlfriend. Unknown to the girl, Hunter had experienced a loss in confidence, and she had fallen victim to his self-sabotage tendency. And while Hunter always felt bad after ending a relationship under those circumstances, where he knew more about his rationale than the other individual, this particular breakup had hit him harder than usual.

This time around, Hunter underwent a lot of internal evaluation. He felt like a loser, as he usually did when he sabotaged a relationship: He had failed both his girlfriend and himself through his dishonesty, and by involving both of them in a relationship he knew was doomed before it had begun.

For the first time, however, this particular failure left him afraid about the future.

For the first time, he wondered if winding up *alone* in life was a real possibility. He couldn't force himself to yield to a heterosexual relationship. But he also couldn't bear to consider the possibility that his attraction to the same sex was *not* a temporary phase that would disappear.

And so, that August, Hunter returned to school with an intense sense of loss. He felt like he'd started to outgrow his fraternity activities, so he minimized his time at the fraternity house and lent more time to his studies. For social interaction, he opted for intramural sports. He involved himself in sand volleyball until October, then indoor volleyball until spring.

Hunter met Lance on the sand volleyball court. Lance exuded sheer confidence in demeanor and agility. The first thing Hunter noticed about him was his legs, bronzed from the sun and carved with precision after years of exercise. From behind his sunglasses, Hunter would study Lance's legs in motion on the sand, racing closer to the net, then flexing before he reversed course to prepare for the volleyball's return. Hunter gave no indication of his own interest. And although he couldn't pinpoint where the masculine Lance's attractions resided, Hunter had to assume the athletic guy was straight.

Their association began innocently enough. They played on the same team. Hunter would set the volleyball for Lance to spike over the net, or they would crash into each other as both chased a ball the other team had lobbed over the net faster than expected. The ball would sail past their arms and leave them shrugging their shoulders, laughing.

Hunter and Lance also shared similar personality characteristics, including compatible senses of humor, and within a few weeks, they bonded. In the weeks and months that followed, on most days, they met each other at the campus recreation center, where they ran a mile or two before dinnertime.

They talked sports and business classes. Lance wanted to go on to law school after graduation. After classes, oftentimes they sneaked into the law school library, where, unlike in the student commons, they could study without distraction from fraternity guys who walked past. Sometimes Hunter and Lance would look up from their books and engage in spontaneous conversations about inane topics, speaking under their breath in the law library.

"I have an affinity for leather-bound books," Lance would whisper in jest as he glanced at the reference shelves around them. "And fine mahogany tables, and lamps with these little green shades," he would add, flicking a banker's light with his index finger.

The cunning expression on Lance's face as he joked around kindled Hunter's affection, yet for all Hunter knew, he meant nothing more to Lance than anyone else in the room. So Hunter would respond with a tone of equivalent humor.

"I have a sudden urge to smoke a pipe filled with the finest tobacco," Hunter whispered above a snigger.

Hunter enjoyed those moments. Because the library enforced a strict policy of silence, he and Lance had to lean toward each other to whisper. Though he refused to admit it to himself, Hunter grew weak at Lance's green eyes, which seemed to wink whenever he smiled. He admired the natural way Lance's hair parted on one side, and the tiny scar over his eyebrow, which Lance attributed to a hockey incident as a kid.

One evening in early December, Hunter stopped by Lance's apartment to study for final exams before they caught a basketball game on television. Lance's roommate had left for a study date at his girlfriend's apartment.

As game time approached, Lance turned on the television. Side by side, they sat on the floor, backs against the sofa, where they continued to study. Soon they veered into one of their typical back-and-forth jabs involving random, personal trivia.

"Pancakes or waffles?" Hunter said.

Lance thought for a moment.

"Waffles," he replied. Then, with a glint in his eye, he said, "Ocean or mountains?"

"Mountains."

Lance looked surprised. "I didn't expect you to say that."

"Why not?"

"I guess you seem more like a beach type of person. The waves, soaking up the sun ..."

"I like the ocean too," Hunter said. "Given a choice, though, I'd get submerged in nature, up in the mountains where it's silent and you're surrounded by trees and wildlife."

Lance grinned, then angled his head as if to examine Hunter's face closer.

"I guess I learn something new about you every day," said Lance.

For Hunter, though the television remained on, the room quieted down. As Lance studied Hunter's face, Hunter returned his stare. Soon their eyes locked, their gazes lingering a bit too long. Hunter felt a magnetic current tighten between his chest and Lance's, and he sensed Lance had picked up on the connection, too. Lance's pupils fluttered larger—ever so slightly, but Hunter caught sight of it.

Lance leaned in. Hunter responded on instinct and, before he could give it a second thought, leaned into the magnetic current.

One kiss.

Hunter had never kissed another guy before, and on the slim chance it were to occur, he'd always envisioned a queasy feeling would settle into his gut. What he *hadn't* anticipated was his reaction upon kissing Lance. Peaceful confidence overshadowed the nervousness he'd expected. Rather than shame, invigoration coursed through his veins. The kiss reminded him of neon-orange sparks on the Fourth of July.

The shame followed later.

As Hunter lay in bed that night, recounting the kiss in Lance's apartment, the acid of guilt washed over his soul. Hunter realized he now had another secret to hide. More than that, he wondered if he had failed God. Hunter felt ashamed by the temptation he faced, because he knew, given the same opportunity, he would engage in that kiss all over again.

After that night, Hunter decided his best course of action would be to avoid Lance altogether. Since it was the last week of the fall semester, he had no difficulty accomplishing that feat.

Hunter never touched bases with Lance during winter break. When they returned for the spring semester, Hunter switched to intramural softball. He avoided the law school library. Hunter retreated into the backdrop of the university's large campus.

He and Lance never crossed paths again.

But in spite of his efforts to deny the temptation, Hunter couldn't erase the memory of that kiss, the one that challenged who Hunter had thought he was.

CHAPTER 30

Hunter ran a finger between his tie and his neck. Normally ties didn't bother him, but the context of a stuffy uniform made it feel tighter than usual.

Ellen had rented the uniform for him. Its black jacket and pants mimicked a tuxedo. His white shirt felt so starched, Hunter swore he could hear it crinkle when he shifted his arm. Ellen had furnished Gabe, who stood beside him, with an identical uniform for her catering event.

Ellen had arranged a buffet-style layout for the evening. In keeping with how organizers had planned the room's décor, she had designed her menu with an upper-echelon feel. Oftentimes when she catered, Ellen plated each course, which the event's servers would deliver to guests at their tables. Tonight's event, however, called for a cocktail hour and silent auction, after which guests could make their way to dinner tables at will. The buffet layout had struck her as a fitting match for the evening's schedule, and organizers had agreed.

Ellen had assigned Hunter the primary duty of slicing honey-roasted ham upon request. She had taught him the precise method by which she wanted him to slice the portions. For his part, Gabe sliced roast beef. Throughout the evening, they had also acted as runners, replacing serving pans of side dishes and an assortment of desserts they had plated in advance. Before the event began, Hunter and Gabe had helped Ellen prepare and deliver the food. When the evening ended, they would help her clean everything up. Throughout the evening, in addition to replacing items along the buffet line, Ellen had floated around the room, filling in gaps and helping tend the open bar when the bartender got busy.

Though dinner service had ended, Hunter and Gabe remained in position at the serving line in case any no-shows decided to arrive late. Taking a breather after refilling some desserts, Ellen stood beside Hunter, facing the dinner tables. Hunter knew Ellen had pasted a smile on her face in case any guests happened to look back at a random moment.

"So, Gabe, Hunter wrangled you into helping me? You're such a sucker." She gave him a wicked grin. For an extra jab, she added, "And you're not even getting paid. Go figure."

"Well, you've given me enough referrals. I think I owe you something," Gabe joked back. Ellen had, in fact, offered to pay him, but he'd turned down her offer. "Thanks for the tux uniform, by the way. It's spiffy."

Hunter snorted under his breath.

"I have to say, I knew the massages would do Hunter some good," Ellen said, "but I never expected the two of you to become friends out of it. How did *that* come about?"

Hunter felt his heart rate rise. They would need another cover story. Would he spend *years* covering things up? The pressure had begun to weigh on him. But then he considered the alternate scenario, of people finding out and opening *that* Pandora's box.

"Oh, you know ..." Hunter shrugged, "we started talking, had a few laughs ..."

"Yeah, I've told Gabe plenty about myself the last couple of years. You just hope he can keep a secret, know what I mean?" she said with a wink.

"I'm still standing right here," Gabe joshed, leaning over from the far end of their threesome. "Good to know you think I'm a double agent trading secrets, Ellen."

"I apologize for doubting your loyalty." Ellen turned to Hunter. "Don't even think about gaining blackmail material from him about me, Hunter. Gabe doesn't play for both teams. Only mine."

If Hunter were sipping champagne, he would have choked at Ellen's remark. Perhaps he could find humor in this after all.

They stood in the rear of a hotel ballroom. Guests had mingled over cocktails in the hotel's inner terrace before heading into the ballroom for dinner. From Hunter's view, he saw a range of circular tables covered with white tablecloths and a crowd of two hundred people, most of whom he estimated as his parents' ages or older. The men had dressed in tuxedos or black suits, the women in formal gowns or dresses. At the front of the ballroom sat a podium where, after dinner, the evening's host would perch. Classical music played overhead, a concerto from Vivaldi's *Four Seasons,* which Hunter recognized from a music-appreciation course in college. The hearty scent of roast beef now sent hunger pangs through him. He'd grabbed a chicken sandwich for dinner a few hours earlier, but now he craved a bite of red meat. It took extra ounces of self-control not to sneak a sample. Then again, a mental image of Ellen's wrath served as a deterrent.

"What is this event, anyway?" asked Gabe.

Through her pasted smile, Ellen replied, "It's an auction to benefit a charity in Cleveland, one that offers extracurricular programs for underprivileged kids." With a gesture of her head toward the guests, she said, "See all those people sitting out there?"

Hunter and Gabe nodded.

"Most of them donate a lot of money to the place. Some don't donate anything yet, but they're wealthy enough to give a lot, so they got invited, too."

"How'd they select you for this catering job?" Hunter asked.

"Brendan's mom is on the charity's board of directors and recommended me for the gig. I suspect she had an ulterior motive, though: I think she hoped to hear people rave about her future daughter-in-law's cooking."

As if on cue, a woman rose from one of the tables and made her way toward them, her hair a perfect shade of silver, wrapped in a bun fit for a gala. The woman wore a full-length gown and held aloft a glass of white wine in one hand.

"Speaking of my mother-in-law-to-be, here she comes," Ellen murmured, donning a facial expression more chipper than she'd worn thus far.

As the woman drew near, a married couple approached her and engaged in a brief conversation before accompanying her to the buffet line. The couple looked close in age to Brendan's mother, their demeanors modest.

"Hello, Ellen," Brendan's mother said. Her skin looked so smooth, it defied her age. Hunter wondered if her hair color was prematurely gray like Steve Martin's.

When she and Ellen greeted each other with European-style kisses on each cheek, Hunter almost burst out in laughter. Oh, he could tease Ellen about this for years to come. From the corner of his eye, he could see Gabe, too, trembled from stifled laughter. Hunter nudged Gabe with an elbow to the ribs to get him to stop before it became contagious.

"Ellen, I'd like you to meet Ron and Julia Napoli," said Brendan's mother, a picture of graciousness. "This is my future daughter-in-law, Ellen Krieger."

A cordial Ellen shook hands with the couple. "How nice to meet you! This is Hunter Carlisle and Gabe Hellman, friends of mine who offered their assistance tonight."

"I'm Joyce Pieper," said Brendan's mother to Hunter and Gabe. "Thank you for taking care of my Ellen."

Pleasantries and shaking of hands all around. When Joyce held her wineglass aloft, Hunter noticed lipstick marks on its rim.

"I'm going to boast a little about my future daughter-in-law," Joyce said. "She designed the menu for tonight and prepared the meal."

Ron and Julia responded with genuine *Ah!* expressions as Joyce beamed at their reactions.

"Have you been involved with this charity long?" Ellen asked the couple.

"We've supported it for the last few years. A wonderful organization," Ron said. "You and I have something in common, Ellen."

"Really? Do tell."

Do tell? By Hunter's estimation, Ellen's response to most people would have been "Get outta here!", and chances were fifty-fifty she would have thrown in an expletive for good measure.

"I assume you began your catering business from scratch," Ron said.

"I did indeed, sir."

"I began my business from scratch, too. I used an old family recipe to create the pizza sauce."

"Ron and Julia own the local Napoli Pizza restaurant chain," Joyce chimed in.

Ellen blinked once, the way she did when someone had impressed her, but she kept her cool.

"I'm sorry, I didn't put two and two together," Ellen said. "I can only imagine how it must have felt to see your restaurant grow from one location to—"

"The second-largest chain in northern Ohio," Julia said, her lips pressed together. "The opportunities for expansion are prime. I'd like to see us move quicker than we do. Ron prefers to keep the intimate, family feel."

"So you and your husband make all the business decisions together?"

"Oh heavens, no, dear."

"Julia involves herself in full-time charity work," Joyce Pieper said. "In fact, she's one of our most critical friends here. We couldn't benefit the youth of Cleveland to the extent we do without her support."

"So you volunteer with the children the charity helps?"

"Julia helps us make important decisions for how we *operate* the charity," Joyce said. "We'd like to have her on the board one day, but I've yet to convince her."

"How wonderful for you, Mrs. Napoli," Ellen said with another winning, plastered smile. Julia pressed her lips together into a tight smile in return.

Julia Napoli sent chills across Hunter's flesh, and from the telling look in Ellen's eyes, he suspected she affected Ellen the same way. The more Hunter listened to them talk, the more he realized Julia knew her husband's business as well as he did. Much like a first lady married to a president—no official position, but perhaps greater influence than the most trusted advisors. For his part, though, Ron Napoli seemed rather kind, a grandfatherly type. Julia, however—well, Hunter couldn't see kids as a thrill for her.

Hunter looked toward the floor and noticed Ellen's foot squirming against the carpet, out of sight of her mother-in-law and the Napolis. If given the chance, Hunter knew Ellen would have bolted for the door.

"If I may inquire," Ron said to Ellen, "where do you base your operations?"

"For my business? I handle everything at my home for now."

"Nothing wrong with starting out in your home. Julia and I—this was decades ago—lived in a tiny apartment above our first little location in Parma. The pizza oven helped keep the apartment warm." Ron's eyes gleamed as he reminisced. "Those were quite the days."

Hunter had no doubt Ron Napoli, a successful businessman, must possess a firm edge to manage his operations and employees while fending off his competition. Yet he also had an air of childlike innocence. Hunter wondered if Ron even suspected he had received tonight's invitation due to his capacity to write a hefty check. His wife, on the other hand, appeared fully aware and absent of complaint.

"We should probably return to our seats," Joyce cut in, checking her watch. "The program will begin in a minute or two."

"In that case, I wish you the best in your endeavors," Ron said, shaking hands with Ellen, then with Hunter and Gabe. His wife followed suit, switching her wineglass from right hand to left. Ron's handshake felt warm and fleshy, while his wife's felt wiry and cold, chilled by the glass of wine.

"It was lovely to meet you!" Ellen called as they parted ways. Julia peered over her shoulder and offered one taut blink of the eyes.

Once again, the room offered nothing but the loud hum of indiscernible voices. As she gazed upon the crowd, Ellen maintained her professional smile, which impressed Hunter.

"I hate games," Ellen murmured. "I love to cook—that's why I enjoy my business. But the fawning and behaving like someone I'm obviously not …"

Hunter watched as Ellen examined from a distance her future mother-in-law, who floated from table to table, exchanging pleasantries. The tap on a microphone sent a low boom throughout the room and drew Hunter's attention to the podium, where the host asked if everyone could please take their seats for the evening. He would announce the winners of the silent auction in a moment, but first, he offered a word of thanks to Joyce Pieper for organizing the event with such finesse. A polite round of applause followed, to which Joyce responded with her best Queen Elizabeth wave.

When Hunter returned his attention to Ellen, he found her stare frozen in place, a longing in her eyes, the longing of a child reaching out for help.

"This is my future with Brendan's family. These are the games they'll expect me to play for decades to come," Ellen said to Hunter. "Someone shoot me in the leg right now."

"Brendan isn't like that, though, is he?"

"No … but being expected to act that way to please my in-laws, to avoid embarrassing them at this function or that one—isn't that living a lie? Trapped into being someone I'm not?"

Hunter gazed to his left, where Gabe had overheard Ellen's words. His eyes darted from Ellen to Hunter and back to Ellen.

From the podium, the host continued with the results of the silent auction.

"The first item for sale was an original painting by a local artist …"

CHAPTER 31

Hunter could smell the dampness of snow melting on his winter coat as he and Gabe stepped through the garage door and into Hunter's kitchen, where they left their wet shoes on the doormat and tossed their coats on two chairs to dry. Both men shivered from the December cold. Once inside, Hunter felt his fingers begin to thaw.

They had returned from a Christmas Eve service at Gabe's church, a large church like Hunter's. The Presbyterian environment featured a culture different from that to which Hunter had grown accustomed over the years, but its traditional feel seemed a perfect match for Christmas. Hunter hadn't recognized a soul there, and Gabe, the quiet type who tended to engage in social interaction only when necessary for business, had waved hello to a few individuals but engaged in little conversation otherwise. For those with whom Gabe had spoken, he introduced them to his friend Hunter. They had extended to Hunter an affable welcome absent of suspicion.

Now Hunter made his way to the living room, where he built a fire in the fireplace. Gabe retrieved from the pantry a jug of apple cider, which he emptied into a pot to simmer on the stove. After a quick search through the kitchen drawers, he found a ladle. When steam began to rise from the pot, Gabe fixed two mugs of cider and brought them to the living room, where a fire crackled to life in the fireplace.

Gabe handed Hunter a mug of cider. They settled onto the sofa, where Hunter grabbed the television remote and flipped through Christmas programs. From their view through the front window, where Hunter had opened the curtains, they watched snowflakes fall in clusters.

When Hunter came across *A Christmas Carol* with George C. Scott, Gabe put his hand on Hunter's to stop him from surfing channels.

"I love this movie!" said Gabe. "George C. Scott is the ultimate Scrooge."

Hunter couldn't help but smile at Gabe's childlike manner, the way his face lit up. "Is this your favorite Christmas movie?"

Gabe considered the question, then said, "I like the older version better overall, the one in black and white. It doesn't get better than those old classics." His visage softened as he peered into Hunter's eyes. "Okay, your first-impulse answer: Favorite Christmas movie of all time?"

Hunter chuckled. "I'm more of a *Christmas Vacation* comedy guy."

"What! That's not a Christmas movie! I mean, it *is,* but not really."

"It's the best Christmas movie of all time!"

"Oh, please!"

"I'll meet you halfway: Chevy Chase as Scrooge."

"Now *that* would be awesome!"

With that, they shook hands to seal the deal.

"Is it strange not being with your family at Christmas?" Gabe asked.

"It's different." Hunter replied, then reconsidered his response. At first, he grew shy and had trouble meeting Gabe's gaze, but when their eyes locked, Hunter found comfort. A desire to speak words of honesty rose within him. "It's *better*," he clarified.

Gabe's eyes softened. "That was nice," he said. Another beat, then he asked, "Didn't your family wonder why you didn't come along, though?"

"With the job loss, they know I haven't been in a party mood. I told them I'd find a friend to hang out with."

"You knew you'd spend Christmas with me before *I* did, didn't you!"

"Yes." Then Gabe's question about family triggered in Hunter another consideration. "But what about your mom? Won't she think it's odd you didn't spend Christmas Eve with her?"

"No, she won't care. Mom never does much on Christmas Eve. Maybe it's a holdover from losing Dad all those years ago, when she tried to get through the holidays without him. Maybe shortening the Christmas celebration into one day helped her cope. Anyway, with Mom, it's all about the *actual day,* no previews. She'll head to her church for a midnight service. She knows I went to my church tonight."

They sipped cider and watched as George C. Scott spoke to a giant ghost adorned in a green robe and curly, shoulder-length hair, at which Hunter felt tempted to poke fun, but opted against it.

"Oh, we almost forgot!" Hunter set his mug on the coffee table with a clink.

"What?"

Scurrying over to the Christmas tree nestled beside the fireplace, Hunter sat cross-legged and waved Gabe over to him. "Gifts!"

Two wrapped gifts lay underneath the tree. One gift each, a twenty-dollar limit, as they had agreed upon a few weeks before. Hunter lifted one of the gifts and handed it to Gabe. The package was a small rectangle about an inch thick. Hunter tried to hide a smirk; he couldn't have timed this better if he tried.

"Merry Christmas," said Hunter.

Gabe took his time, running his finger along the edges before sliding it between the layers of paper. At the bottom of the gift, where Hunter had taped one flap, a bulge stuck out, soft as a pillow. Hunter had wound up with a bit too much paper and had tried to tuck it all in to make it look presentable.

"Nice wrapping job," said Gabe with a witty purse of his lips.

"It's not my forte."

"Are these Christmas candles printed all over the paper?"

"You're one of the most perceptive people I've met. They're birthday candles." Hunter shrugged. "I wrapped it right before you got here earlier. All I could find in my house was birthday paper. You're lucky it was wrapped. Usually, I leave it unwrapped on the person's table by accident and forget I left it there, then they find it and want to know why the thing's sitting on their table. Kinda takes the fun out of the surprise."

"I can imagine." Gabe smirked and continued unwrapping his gift. When he discovered its contents, he rolled his eyes and laughed. "It's scary how ridiculous you are."

Gabe held up two blu-ray discs: *National Lampoon's Christmas Vacation* and *A Christmas Carol* with George C. Scott.

"Maybe God has a sense of humor," Hunter said.

"Whatever." Gabe gave him a playful punch on the arm. "I love the gift. Thank you."

"You can return them if you want to."

Gabe held them against his chest in mock protest. "Not at all! They're a piece of you. Straight from your heart—especially the Chevy Chase movie, that's particularly touching," he said with a wink. Grabbing the remaining gift from under the tree, he passed it to Hunter. "Your turn. Hope you like *Gilmore Girls*."

"How'd you guess?" Hunter joked back. The gift wasn't much larger than the one he'd given Gabe, but it felt heavier. He noticed slight flexibility when he tried bending it at the edges. He felt Gabe watching him as he tore back the paper with care.

When Hunter discovered what Gabe had placed inside, a sweet ache hit his heart.

Hunter fanned the ivory-colored pages, each one lined and empty, awaiting his input. The journal had a leather cover the color of mocha. But what touched Hunter's heart wasn't the gift or its binding, but the word Gabe had embossed on the cover in sturdy, gold letters:

S A F E

"Safe?" Hunter said.

"It's a journal," Gabe explained. "When you don't want to bottle things up, you can put them into words on paper. It stays between you and God, but you get to release the pressure by getting the words out of you. It's a safe place." He gave Hunter a look of evaluation, then added, "I also wanted you to think of me whenever you look at the journal. You're safe with me. I wanted you to know that."

"I … I don't know what to say."

Hunter stared at the item, held it in his hands, ran his thumbs along its textured, leather surface. If he could sum up Gabe's impact on his life, he would use this gift as a symbol. With this gift, somehow Gabe had peered into Hunter's soul, past all the complexities, and boiled it down to who Hunter truly was. Who Hunter truly wanted to be.

All Hunter had ever wanted was to feel safe.

And as he considered this gift once more, Hunter knew, without a doubt, Gabe had accepted him for who he was.

Hunter shook himself from his daze and managed a hug for Gabe. Emotion overwhelmed his heart but he held steady.

"I needed this," Hunter said, referring to everything about the gift *except* the leather and paper. "Thank you."

They sat in silence for a minute, neither knowing what to say next. Hunter gazed at the fireplace, listened to snaps and crackles as the flames waved in all directions. Hunter and Gabe's shadows flickered on the carpeted floor.

"What's going through your mind right now?" Gabe whispered.

Hunter grew enraptured with the tiny white lights strung upon the Christmas tree. From his close proximity, their glow caused his skin to tingle. Though he couldn't find words to express what ran through his heart, those lights captured the essence of the comfort he felt, the relief and security.

"I was just thinking," he replied at last.

Sitting cross-legged, Gabe scooted closer so they sat eye to eye. Their knees touched. "Thinking about what?"

Hunter sought for the words but wound up short. He shrugged, wanting to speak yet holding back. Gabe gave him a gentle nudge with his arm.

"I was thinking that this feels right. Thinking about how good it feels to finally, *finally* have someone I can talk to who... who understands me," Hunter said. "I'm not used to being free that way. I'm not used to talking about what I feel inside. So I was thinking of how good it is to find somebody you can be honest with and not need to hide, where there's no need to put on a mask or be on guard."

Gabe listened, staring into Hunter's eyes with that familiar compassion Hunter found so comforting. His smile welcomed Hunter to say more. It told Hunter he *wanted* to hear more.

"It's different from how I've ever allowed myself to live," Hunter continued, "and it's such a relief." He felt tears well up in his eyes and savored the respite he felt in knowing he didn't need to wipe them away, didn't need to feel ashamed of his feelings. Not in this individual's presence. Not with Gabe. Hunter sensed boldness arise as he peered into the depths of Gabe's eyes. "It's been so many years of private heartache and secret struggle. And tonight, sitting here with you, it hit me: To whatever extent, the torment is finally over. The seclusion is gone ... and I'm no longer alone.

"When this year started, I never would have pictured myself saying these things. I didn't go looking for this. Yet tonight, I feel like I've received a gift—a *valuable* gift, one I've awaited for decades but never thought I would find. And what I've finally come to terms with is ..."

Hunter allowed his thought to linger. He turned his head toward the Christmas lights again, focusing on their glow. Such a tiny glow, yet so bright. Gabe gazed at him with expectancy, a look by which Hunter found the strength to unlock the rusty deadbolt of his heart.

"Yes?" Gabe whispered. "What did you finally come to—"

Hunter turned his head back toward Gabe, and before Gabe could finish asking, Hunter said, "… that I love you."

Gabe blinked twice. His eyes widened, and for a moment, Hunter feared he had scared him away.

But Hunter knew better.

"I love you, Gabe," he said, wiping a tear from his eye. "I do."

A look of subdued rapture overcame Gabe's face. The corners of his mouth turned upward into a smile. And without a word, Hunter knew Gabe felt the same way.

Hunter had simply spoken first.

The logs in the fireplace continued to snap. Firelight lit Gabe's countenance and danced in his irises. He reached forward and wiped away another tear from Hunter's eye.

Gabe leaned forward. Hunter met him halfway. And when Gabe's lips met his, Hunter's body filled with warmth and security, an anchor to steady a ship that had finally found its way home.

CHAPTER 32

Gabe's mother looked nothing like Hunter had pictured. She didn't make a negative impression upon him; rather, Hunter had expected her to look like Gabe. To Hunter's surprise, Gabe looked like his mother had *adopted* him. Instead of Gabe's Scandinavian skin tone, reddish-blond hair, or icy blue eyes, Mrs. Hellman's features possessed a South American quality with her mocha skin and a rich tone to her brown eyes. Gabe must have looked a lot like his father.

"So this is Gabe's friend Hunter!" she said when she opened the door to her home on Christmas Day. The term *friend* sparked within Hunter a mixed reaction: He felt the safety of a secret intact, yet the inaccuracy of the word *friend* left him with a feeling of imbalance, the sense you get when something has fallen short of the goal. Clearly, Gabe hadn't said a word to *his* parent, either.

Mrs. Hellman exhibited Gabe's confidence but not his subdued manner. In fact, she struck Hunter as a downright extrovert.

Hunter and Gabe removed their shoes so they wouldn't track moisture into the house. Mrs. Hellman took their coats and left the foyer to hang them in a closet. Upon stepping through the front door, Hunter felt the normal awkwardness of entering a stranger's home for the first time, but within minutes, he felt at ease. For that matter, already he felt more at home here than he did at his own parents' house, though he couldn't put his finger on why.

Gabe waved Hunter into the dining room, where they stood beside a table prepared for dinner. Hunter's attention rested on a honey-baked ham, which he had smelled all the way from the foyer. The sight of it made his mouth water with anticipation. A pineapple ring rested atop the entrée. Side dishes rounded out the table, which Mrs. Hellman had covered with a festive tablecloth and place settings.

"I felt so bad when I heard you would be alone for the holiday," came Mrs. Hellman's voice from the kitchen.

"Don't feel bad," Hunter called back. "I could have gone with them to Boston. I didn't feel like a big family reunion, answering questions while I'm between jobs, trying to make sense of things myself."

"Well, you're always welcome here." Mrs. Hellman walked into the dining room holding a square present in her hands. She had wrapped it in cherry-red paper and tied a white ribbon around it. "This is for you."

She took hold of Hunter's hands and placed the box into them. Hunter kicked himself. How could he have forgotten to bring her a gift!

"No, please," he said, "somehow it slipped my mind to bring a gift."

Gabe's mother threw back her head and emitted a staccato laugh. "Don't be silly, Hunter. It's a gift, not a reward. Besides, it's not impressive, so don't expect to find a Rolex inside."

"It's a deal," Hunter said as he unwrapped the package. He opened the box and pulled from it a latte mug decorated with earthy, coffeehouse hues. The mug had a masculine appearance, and on its face, he read a Scripture engraved in block letters: "*The LORD's lovingkindnesses indeed never cease, for His compassions never fail. They are new every morning; great is Your faithfulness.* — Lamentations 3:22-23."

The comforting words of a lamenting prophet. And the promise that, regardless of Hunter's own shortcomings, God's mercy continued to await him.

He thanked Mrs. Hellman for the gift and realized that, for the next few hours, he had come home for the holiday.

———————

After finishing dinner, the trio sat around the table drinking coffee and eating cranberry-apple pie. From a stereo shelf system, Bebe and Cece Winans's *First Christmas* CD had completed its run, and now, a Vanessa Williams Christmas CD began with her rendition of "Do You Hear What I Hear." Williams's recording began with crystalline tones of simplicity; by the end, it morphed into an arrangement of vibrant, African-tinged inflections. Upon this first listen, Hunter added the song to his mental playlist of favorite Christmas recordings, a status he attributed to his current context as much as to the track itself.

"Maybe I'm growing senile," said Gabe's mother, "but I don't recall hearing about you until recently, Hunter. Have you known Gabe long?"

Gabe swallowed with caution, his eyes glued to his plate. Hunter could tell he felt guilty and hoped this subject of conversation would fade fast.

"Not long," Hunter said. "I worked in sales before my company downsized. I'd hit a hard season and had stress-related back pains, so a friend of mine recommended Gabe. He's her massage therapist."

Mrs. Hellman looked pleased, the way mothers do when they hear compliments about their kids. "Well, that explains it. I've heard more good things about my son's work. He's always made it his aim to take care of people. I lost count of how many times he made me breakfast in bed when he was a young boy."

Hunter shot Gabe a knowing smirk. Gabe stuck a fork into his pie, but given the way he raised his eyebrows as he listened, the conversation must have amused him. Either that, or he could sense Hunter eyeing him.

"How do you think he got to be that way?" Hunter asked, delighting in the opportunity to talk about Gabe as if he weren't sitting at the table with them. At the same time, though, Hunter had a genuine curiosity about Gabe and wanted to know more about him.

"When his dad died, I believe he grew up quickly, whether he needed to or not. He wanted to make sure I was safe. A little boy trying to fill the role of a man." She sipped her coffee and closed her eyes to savor it. "Being mature for his age, he never fit in well with the boys around him."

Gabe shrugged as if to say it was no big deal. But when Gabe lifted his coffee cup to his lips, Hunter noticed a change in Gabe's eyes: Gabe had buried roots of ache yet unspoken. No doubt, now that the humor has passed, he felt weird being talked about as though he wasn't in the room but didn't have the heart to ask his mother to stop.

"I'll tell you one thing about Gabe: He always had a heart for God, even as a little guy," Mrs. Hellman said. "And when he told me he'd decided to start his own business, I wasn't surprised. He's the type to take initiative on almost anything."

Gabe's face turned a shade of pink from embarrassment. "Mom, I don't think Hunter wants to hear all this."

"Oh, you're wrong," Hunter teased, trying to reinstate the humorous aspect of the conversation, "I want to hear it all!"

"Good, because I'm enjoying this jaunt down memory lane!" said Mrs. Hellman. "Did you know when Gabe was in kindergarten, he'd dress up in his dad's old military fatigues and pretend to lead a brigade of troops?"

Hunter couldn't stop himself from laughing at that. "I had no idea! Imagine Gabe hiding such a juicy detail about his life!"

Gabe rolled his eyes, shook his head, then scraped the top of his pie with the tongs of his fork. He shot his mother a kindhearted look, and she winked at him in return. Hunter found it obvious a bond existed between this mother and her son.

In the midst of the lightheartedness, a plume of smoke crept into Hunter's conscience.

He took another look at Gabe's mother, the joy that brought a gleam to her countenance, to this Christian woman who had welcomed him into her home. Regret sunk into his heart, the knowledge that both he and Gabe had engaged her in a charade. Not that they had lied, per se, but they had withheld the full truth.

Gabe's mother had kind, trusting eyes. Unsuspecting eyes. Little did she know her son and his friend held a secret, one that might devastate the dreams she likely harbored regarding her son and how his future might unfold.

One day, this woman would learn their secret.

One day, she would look back on this Christmas Day in her home with a different perspective. She would know Hunter had looked her in the eye and lied to her—or withheld the truth—the first time he'd met her.

Why did his personal struggle need to hold devastating ramifications not only for himself, but for the innocent individuals in his life?

The thought sickened Hunter's stomach. He knew the situation was more complicated than that; his reasoning was understandable. His *intention* wasn't to deceive or mislead her.

Yet something didn't seem fair. This caring woman had welcomed a stranger simply because he knew her son. She deserved the truth. But would the truth bring more pain to her heart than a buried secret?

CHAPTER 33

The first Thursday of the new year, Gabe stopped by Hunter's house for the evening. Most Thursdays, Hunter would have attended his Bible study meetings, but the group remained on its holiday break until the following week.

Sitting on the sofa, Gabe had tuned in to a sitcom on television. Hunter sat on the floor, at Gabe's feet, with his back against the sofa. Hunter clicked away on his laptop, which he had set on the coffee table, and searched job listings online. He had closed the window curtains after sunset.

Every so often, Hunter would reach up and rub Gabe's knee or run his thumb along the lower half of Gabe's leg to acknowledge he remained on Hunter's mind. Gabe would return the gesture with a pat on the shoulder or by running his finger against the back of Hunter's neck. Hunter would reach up, their fingers would intertwine, and they would hold hands for a few seconds before Hunter resumed his work.

"Is it me," Gabe blurted, "or is the grandmother character in these sitcoms always one step shy of a loony bin?"

Hunter considered the question and said, "Maybe it's vicarious living. Maybe young writers fear growing older and create older characters that remain ageless." Hunter continued typing. "Can you imagine your grandmother hitting on your best friend?" he added, just to see if he could make Gabe snicker, then basked in the sound of success. He loved to hear Gabe laugh.

Before he knew it, Hunter grew absorbed in his job search and the minutes ticked past. When he realized time had passed without his saying anything to Gabe or reaching out to make contact, he looked up from his computer and noticed Gabe had settled back into the sofa. Arms crossed, Gabe had turned his head upward, looking anywhere but at the television. It was Gabe's thinking position. Hunter recognized his concentration from times past. What Hunter didn't expect, however, were Gabe's next words.

"I'm feeling guilty."

Hunter stopped typing. The words crashed into him with a *thud*.

This can't be good.

Whatever Gabe was about to say, Hunter sensed it involved him too, and that put Hunter on guard.

"Guilty about what?"

"Maybe we should say something."

"You mean … about us?"

Gabe's face grew weary. He shook his head. "This secret—maybe it's not a good thing. It's getting harder to keep it inside."

Those words sent bolts of fear through Hunter's fibers. Immediately he felt a sweat break out across his brow. He fought to remain calm and talk Gabe through this.

The television now impeded Hunter's ability to process his own thoughts. He turned down the volume.

"What brought this on?" Hunter asked.

"I don't know. I can't shake it," Gabe said. "I feel like a fraud. A phony. Like I'm lying to people."

"So you want them to find out and judge you?"

"No, I *don't* want that, but ..."

Gabe's face contorted. Hunter could hear fatigue in the way Gabe exhaled.

"It's starting to keep me up at night," Gabe said.

"Why does it matter if random people don't know your secrets?"

"It's not random people." Gabe pressed his fingers against his forehead and massaged his temples. "It's my mom. I don't think I can keep lying to her. It's not a white lie, Hunter—I'm *lying* to her. I'm the only family she has, and I'm lying to her face. It doesn't seem right to me. I don't want to hurt her."

Hunter understood why Gabe felt that way, yet he felt the situation slipping from his grasp. A flood of unknowns rushed against him. Granted, Hunter knew if he continued down this relationship road with Gabe, the truth couldn't help but find its way to light—in its own due time. But he hadn't expected it to collapse so fast; he'd anticipated a step-by-step process, a slow fade into reality.

He didn't know what to do next, but the sudden pressure paralyzed his ability to think, so he asked more questions. Maybe a solution would emerge.

"Why didn't you say anything before?" Hunter asked.

"I didn't have an issue with it before."

"So what changed? How long have you felt this way?"

"Since Christmas," Gabe said. "That's when it hit me."

Hunter's knees turned to putty. He pushed himself from the floor with his hands and sat beside Gabe on the sofa. Hunter fidgeted with his hands, watching one finger interweave with another. Resignation started to seep in, which scared him. He tried to fight against it.

"I'll admit, I felt the same way facing her at Christmas," Hunter said. "I didn't intend to lie. It seemed better than the alternative, though."

Hunter got up from the sofa and started to pace the room. His stomach felt too jostled to sit still. When seated, he felt like he might vomit. His arms went into a nervous shudder. He had to find a way to convince Gabe to keep their relationship quiet; otherwise, their status quo would explode. More than anything, Hunter feared the loss of control.

"You can't say anything. *Please,* Gabe."

"Hunter—"

"I haven't told my parents, either." Wringing his hands, Hunter paced faster.

"That's different. You yourself said you're not close to your family. My situation's different."

Hunter took another look at Gabe and realized their conversation wasn't about family, not when they dug down to its root.

"This is bigger than family, isn't it?" Hunter said.

Pacing. Pacing.

"It feels like my walls are closing in on me from all sides." Gabe's shoulders slumped. From the way he rested his head against his tented hands, Hunter could see Gabe felt he'd disappointed Hunter.

Compassion for Gabe flooded Hunter's heart. He didn't want Gabe to live fettered.

"Gabe, listen. I know we can't make this all about what's convenient for me. But I don't even know where *I* stand on things yet—not everything, at least. I'm not ready for everyone to find out about me. Are you ready for them to find out about you?"

As Hunter approached, Gabe shot up from the sofa and placed his hands on Hunter's shoulders. Hunter stopped pacing. When Hunter looked into Gabe's face, their eyes held. Gabe's voice grew softer, more caring.

"I don't have all the answers either, Hunter. This is new to me, too." Gabe's eyes grew more sincere. "I need to confide in someone. I'm not looking to tell a bunch of people, but I need to take an honest step with my life. I'll keep it under control. I promise."

Hunter couldn't stay focused on Gabe's face. He allowed his eyes to wander. Then he felt the gentle touch of Gabe's finger on his chin. When Hunter looked up, he found Gabe searching his eyes, drawing him in.

"Do you trust me?" asked Gabe.

Fear aside, Hunter sensed strength in Gabe's eyes, an anchor, like a part of him had found solid ground. Without another word, Hunter sighed, closed his eyes, and rested his forehead against Gabe's. All memories of their conversation vanished. In that moment, Hunter's world contracted to this room, to Gabe and him. Neither had answers, yet in Gabe's eyes, Hunter had found genuine love.

With his eyes still closed, Hunter rested his head a moment longer. He could hear Gabe breathing. He sensed the nearness of Gabe's lips.

Hunter brushed Gabe's lips with his own. Gabe's mouth felt warm against his.

He listened to Gabe's exhale. Soon Gabe relented, and their lips met in a soft, tender kiss.

Until now, Gabe had felt like a companion. They had shared a heart connection but seldom engaged in physical affection. An invisible border had stood between them, its existence unnamed and unspoken. Tonight, however, Hunter felt drawn to Gabe, like they were in this struggle—this relationship—together. And he sensed Gabe felt the same way.

Gabe sought Hunter's lips again and kissed him fuller this time. They inhaled deeper. Slower.

Gabe slid his hands toward Hunter's lower back, which sent a pleasant chill up Hunter's spine. A sweet, nervous ache settled into Hunter's belly at Gabe's touch. This was new territory for them. Uncharted waters.

Hunter began to lose himself in the moment. By instinct, he drew closer to Gabe, running his hands beneath Gabe's shirt and lifting it up from the back. Without a word, Hunter discovered he and Gabe were in sync. Gabe wriggled his way out of his shirt and for the first time, Hunter saw Gabe's shoulders and the full length of his bare, slender arms.

Their lips continued to meet. Their hands continued to explore from one direction to the next. One layer of clothing departed, followed by another. Hunter felt himself stir below the waist as the bittersweet ache now sent flutters through his belly. Gabe ran his hands along Hunter's biceps.

When they reached their undershorts, Hunter hesitated. He had grown fully aroused and could see Gabe had, too.

Gabe leaned his head forward, rested his cheek against Hunter's, and kissed Hunter's neck. This sent a rush of strength through Hunter's veins. Hunter detected a musky scent upon Gabe's flesh.

Gabe glided his hand toward Hunter's waistline, where his thumb brushed across a sensitive spot along Hunter's lower belly. The sweet ache increased; Hunter's belly quivered in response, but he recovered with more vigor than before and placed his hands over Gabe's.

Hunter breathed deep. This would mark the first time they had seen each other undressed. Even at the massage appointments, Hunter had covered himself with a towel. But tonight, a different context existed: an invitation.

Hunter decided to trust. And in a flicker of boldness, Hunter stepped out of his undershorts, waited a beat, then ran his fingers along Gabe's waistline until his shorts fell to the floor.

Another kiss, passionate and full. Hunter knew their situation would grow more complicated after this, yet he found it difficult to stop. The frustration he'd pent up for so many years began to rush forth in an honest release. He immersed himself in the heat of Gabe's mouth and the security of Gabe's touch.

Hunter almost didn't hear the key turn in the front door. It seemed like the entry of an unexpected, unfitting character in a dream. But less than three seconds later, the front door opened.

Hunter froze. Gabe froze. Gabe looked up, his face stricken with fear.

With his back toward the front door, which led into the living room, Hunter looked over his shoulder.

Kara stood inside the door, staring at Hunter and Gabe, her mouth agape. Too stunned to move a muscle.

Hunter's mind felt paralyzed. His immediate response was to stand in front of Gabe and shield him from Kara's view.

Hunter kept his back turned toward the door, unable to face Kara or acknowledge the truth.

It was too late.

Too late to get dressed. Too late to pretend nothing had happened.

His secret was out.

PART THREE

STAIN

MERCY

CHAPTER 34

"**W**hat were you doing, letting yourself into my house!" Hunter shouted.

Gabe was gone. Hunter had dressed. Kara stood with her arms planted on her hips, her shoulders aimed in his direction, ready for a fight.

Hunter felt as furious as Kara looked. Her flesh had boiled to a shade of crimson. In the midst of the breakup and his concern for Kara's feelings, he had forgotten to retrieve her key to his house.

"I left a scarf in your garage when I was headed out your door one night," Kara yelled back. "Today I remembered where it was, so I came by to grab it and leave the key behind!"

"Why didn't you give me the key when we broke up? Why didn't you return it back then?"

"Gee, Hunter, I'm sorry if I didn't cover all my bases when you pulled the rug out from under me," Kara replied in a sarcastic tone. "I was too humiliated to look at you or your house, where I'd *wasted* so many evenings of my life!"

"So you decided tonight was the perfect night to stop by?"

"It's Thursday night! You said you have Bible study on Thursday nights! Were you lying about *that* all this time, too?"

Hunter stumbled at her remark but recovered. "No! Don't you dare try to change the subject on me, like this is *my* fault! And what does it matter, anyway? You decided to walk right in! Didn't it occur to you to knock?"

Kara furrowed her brow, rubbed her finger tips against her temples. "I didn't think you'd be here! I was going to grab my scarf, then leave a note on your kitchen table letting you know I locked the door and left the key under your doormat!" she yelled. "I was avoiding a confrontation, not sneaking behind your back! Then again, it doesn't look like *I'm* the one who's been sneaking around behind anyone's back!"

Hunter froze at Kara's words. Regardless of what she had intended to accomplish tonight, it had gone wrong—dead wrong. Kara had altered his life forever.

She turned and threw her hands in the air. With a grunt of frustration, she started to pace the living room, away from Hunter.

"How could I not see this coming?" she shouted. "I must be stupid! Or clueless!"

He had to admit, he felt bad for her, yet his anger lingered. Determined to restore peace, he took a deep breath and gritted his teeth. In a calm tone, he said, "It isn't what you think."

Kara whipped around and darted back in his direction. Hunter thought she would plow into him until she stopped a few inches away.

"It isn't what I *think?*" she said. Her voice had grown calmer, but Hunter could still hear her seethe beneath her words. "What

I *think?* It couldn't be more obvious what's been going on," she added, with a suggestive hint to the tone of her voice. Her eyes narrowed. She shot him a look that indicated he'd mistaken her for a fool.

"We didn't plan that," Hunter said. "What you saw—it just *happened* that way."

Kara let out a soft chuckle and shook her head. "You wouldn't even have sex with *me!* You said you'd lost your virginity but never had sex since. You told me you were waiting for marriage."

"That was all true," Hunter replied. "I never had sex with anyone else, and not with Gabe, either. We'd never gone as far as we did until tonight."

"*Gabe?* His name is *Gabe?*" Kara mimicked. "So how long have you and *Gabe* been together?" She paused. A knowing glare shrouded her eyes. "This is why you broke up with me, isn't it! It was *him!*"

"Kara—"

No sooner had he spoken, Kara started pounding her little fists against his chest. Though her punches didn't hurt him, he figured he'd best stop her before she lost control and started to throw things. Careful not to hurt her, he grabbed her arms at the wrists and held them still.

"Kara, listen to me—"

She wriggled to get loose from his grip. Hunter pulled her closer so she wouldn't twist her wrists and hurt herself.

"Let me go!" Kara shouted.

"Kara, listen to me," Hunter said, struggling to keep a grasp on her arms until she showed signs of composure. His voice reminded him of a father nudging his child toward rational behavior. "You need to … calm … down."

"I don't need your advice! You've screwed me over, Hunter!"

"Kara, it wasn't you—"

Hunter grimaced, holding on as Kara yanked him to her left, then her right. Finally, she thrust herself against his chest with a blast of force and broke free. Hunter watched rage burn in her blue eyes. She jabbed her index finger against his chest.

"You're a liar, Hunter," she said. Her voice had subsided to eerie composure.

Kara stepped back, took one long look at him from toe to head, and Hunter knew she meant every word she said. Wary, he watched each move she made. Not only had she recovered her composure, but he perceived a strange confidence about her, one which pointed to trouble ahead.

Lips pursed, Kara crossed her arms. She examined him once more.

"I don't ever want to see you again," she said. To Hunter, her words sounded like a statement of fact rather than emotion.

And with that, Kara turned around. She grabbed her purse from the floor—she had retrieved her scarf and put it in her purse while Hunter and Gabe had gotten dressed—and didn't bother to wait for Hunter to let her out. She slammed the door behind her. The house thundered. Even the glasses on the coffee table clinked and shook. The house key, Kara's former key, pinged on the coffee table and fell to the floor.

The ensuing stillness struck Hunter as foreign in the wake of their fight. His living room was silent except for the next sitcom on the television, which, amid the uproar, nobody had thought to turn off. A wave of audience laughter erupted. Hunter seized the remote control and shut it off.

CHAPTER 35

He didn't know where to turn, but he knew he must turn quickly. Otherwise, he stood to lose whatever remnant of control over his circumstances he might salvage. Hunter foresaw a hailstorm ahead. Kara was furious and had no reason to keep quiet after last night's fight. People would find out about Gabe and him in no time.

Hunter craved another Christian on his side who wouldn't judge him.

Earlier that morning, he had called Pastor Chuck to see if he was in the office and to ask whether he had time to talk. Hunter had avoided mentioning the topic. Chuck had suggested Hunter come to the church around lunchtime. The more Hunter considered Chuck's suggestion, the more he liked it: Fewer staff members would be in the office during lunch. At least Hunter could preserve *some* degree of privacy, no matter how fleeting it might prove within a few days.

Hunter stomped his feet on the doormat to shake the show from his shoes. As he entered the church building, he realized

Pastor Chuck wouldn't have heard about Gabe and him yet. He pictured Chuck's potential response to Hunter's revelation, the disappointment in his pastor's eyes.

Hunter knew Chuck wouldn't relate to him firsthand. But maybe he'd be willing to listen.

Hunter listened to the shuffle of his own footsteps along the carpeted floor of the deserted hallway. The church office was on his right.

He didn't find the church secretary at her desk—out to lunch, he supposed. Since Chuck expected him, Hunter sauntered to his office and knocked on the frame of the open door.

Seated at his desk, Chuck looked up from his computer and lifted his eyebrows. His visage brightened. Instantly, Hunter felt welcome.

"Hey, Hunter! Feel free to shut the door if you want."

Hunter was glad to do so. He shut the door and took a seat across from his pastor. The man wore a long-sleeved sport shirt and jeans, which complemented his graying hair in a way Hunter couldn't put a finger on. Chuck carried a few extra pounds around the belly but not enough to cause concern about his health.

"I hope you don't mind my stopping by," Hunter said. "I don't usually do this."

Chuck waved off the remark with his hand. "No worries. Has it stopped snowing out there?"

"Flurries, nothing else." Hunter decided to break the ice with casual chitchat. "Could be worse, right? We could be the Browns playing outside in Green Bay on a Sunday."

"That's for sure. They came so close to the playoffs, didn't they?"

"There's always next year."

"You're looking at a guy who believes in miracles," Chuck grinned and leaned back in his chair. "How's the job hunt going?"

"I'm plugging away. Interviews here and there, but nothing has worked out yet."

"God has it figured out. He'll carry you through to the other side. He's been faithful to you all along."

"Yeah, He has." Hunter stared at his hands folded in his lap. His heartbeat accelerated and his palms grew moist. He gave Chuck a second glance. One last opportunity to back away, before he steeled himself and made the decision to trust. Hunter resolved to move forward. He returned his eyes to his lap, tried to appear casual as he wiped the perspiration from his hands.

"There's something I need to talk to you about," Hunter said.

Chuck smiled again, the type that ushered kindness to his eyes.

"Something happened …" Hunter began, then determined that was the wrong way to approach the subject. He decided to start over. "Ever since I was a kid, I've had these … feelings."

Chuck said nothing. As he leaned forward, his chair squeaked, but he made a clear attempt to keep the noise down. He laid one hand over the other before him on the desk.

Hunter took note of his pastor's eyes, which remained fixed upon him. They weren't judgmental eyes, nor were they angry eyes. They were *watchful* eyes, the eyes of a protector. A guardian. A shepherd who cares about his flock.

When he perceived this aspect of his pastor's gaze, Hunter found confidence to take another step forward. Though he felt uncomfortable, he also realized if he could muster the courage to talk, he would find support.

Resting his eyes on his hands, Hunter couldn't yet bring himself to make eye contact as he spoke. Baby steps.

"I don't know exactly when these feelings started, but it was back when I was a kid. And I don't know *why* I feel this way. I just … I get … I get attracted to other guys, and …"

Hunter paused. He felt his eyes grow moist but forced it back. From his peripheral vision, he watched for a reaction from Chuck, but his pastor remained still, listening. So Hunter continued.

"This isn't something I've told anybody. I'd hoped it would go away, like a passing phase. So I ignored it—the best I could—all this time. I dated girls over the years to try to get myself cured, and also because of the fear—I mean, fear of anyone finding out. But it didn't work; it didn't fix me. And I don't know what's wrong with me or how to make it better." Hunter took a breath. The words weren't coming through the way he wished, but it was the best he could do. "I never had anyone I could tell. I was too humiliated to tell anyone, because it's one of those things where nobody can understand unless they've been there …"

As Hunter considered what he'd said so far, a wave of embarrassment washed over him. He raised one hand toward his eyes, to shield them.

"I thought it would go away with time," Hunter continued, "but instead, it got tougher and tougher, bigger and bigger. And before I knew it, it became a mountain, too big for me to think I could ever confide in anyone. As the shame got worse and worse, I felt weaker and weaker, tired from the battle. It's been a heavy burden to bear, keeping this inside, not telling a soul. And I wouldn't have said anything *now*, except I finally hit a moment of weakness. I wound up in a situation where my ex-girlfriend caught me with another … guy …" Hunter hated the way that word sounded as he spoke it. "Now word will get out. And I didn't know where to turn, so I came here …"

Hunter trailed off without finishing his thought. Perhaps he should have come into this meeting with a plan, a rough outline of what he would say, the way he would have handled a sales call. In the stillness of the room, he heard the hum of Chuck's computer as the seconds passed. The heater kicked on for another round and Hunter detected a waft of warmth from a nearby vent.

Chuck broke the silence.

"That's a long time to hold a secret," Chuck said, his voice mild and even.

A voice of compassion, Hunter noted.

"But everybody has secrets," Hunter said. "Why should this one be any harder than anyone else's?"

"Because this isn't a matter of having one rough experience on an isolated day, then moving on," said Pastor Chuck. "This is a struggle that occurs *inside* you. It affects you body, soul and spirit. If the enemy can isolate you and keep you locked up in shame, he can hinder you from moving forward with God's call on your life."

Hunter considered Chuck's words. "You're right when you said it's not just physical. It's got all these mental and emotional sides to it, where it stays with you 24-7." Although Hunter grasped for accurate words, he discovered new freedom here. Finally, he was able to talk and someone was willing to listen.

"I don't want these attractions. I want to be normal like everyone else," Hunter said, "but it keeps hanging on my life. I can't shed it. It feels like an addiction—but worse, because you can never escape it. It's not like a cigarette addiction you're trying to shake, where you can remove a product from your house and endure a few rough days without it. You might crave those cigarettes, but if they're not physically in your house, it's *impossible* to smoke them because they're not there. But these feelings inside me—I can't escape them. The thoughts are in your head, and the attractions are in your heart. You carry them with you wherever you go. So it goes on and on, your whole life. You feel tormented, but you don't see room to hope anything will ever change, so you never find a place to land. You spend your life drifting."

Hunter paused, drew a deep breath, then continued. To his own ears, his voice sounded subdued.

"I can't remember the last time I lived in peace—*actual* peace, the kind where you can totally rest. I must've been a little kid the last time I felt that way. Usually, there comes a point where you can see a light in the distance, and you know if you can just make it that far, you'll reach the end and your problem will be resolved. But my feelings are different. There's no end point. It's like living in permanent purgatory, year after year, and there's no relief. Ever."

Hunter sensed hesitation in Chuck, as though his pastor wasn't sure whether to offer input or merely a listening ear.

"You might not know the right words to say," Hunter said, "but that's okay, Pastor Chuck. As embarrassing as this is, I thought pressing through and talking about it would help me process it. I didn't know what all I wanted to say, but it's a relief to take my time and sort through the complexities. Unlike analyzing it alone, running in circles and getting nowhere, maybe a listening ear would mean progress. Is that okay?"

Chuck blinked once and held steady. "Of course that's okay."

That simple allowance brought Hunter respite.

"God and I have had many conversations over the years," Hunter said. "Sometimes I wonder if God made me this way. It seems easy for people to take a view on this: Some people will tell you you're made that way; others tell you you've made a choice. And it's confusing for *me* as the one going through it. If it's a choice, then why does it feel like I never got an *opportunity* to choose? A thief who decides to burglarize a house—that's a choice. But in my case, it feels more like an addiction that developed after someone laced a dessert with a drug: I didn't even realize I was consuming anything, but wound up in a challenge I never would have sought if given a choice."

Hunter realized he'd forgotten to keep himself in check when he felt tears spilling from his eyes. Now he sensed his face flushing and felt ridiculous for letting another man see him cry. He brushed the tears away. In his peripheral vision, he saw Chuck with his eye steady upon him, and regardless of all Hunter had said, he continued to sense compassion as his pastor listened. Hunter's shoulders felt lighter as the weight of a long-borne burden dissipated. Yet, at the same time, what he had revealed to another soul settled in, the knowledge that his revelation conflicted with his pastor's theological views.

Hunter felt emotionally deflated as he shook his head.

"God must be so disappointed in me," Hunter said.

Chuck stopped him. "You're wrong," he said. "Dead wrong."

Given the silence in the room and how still Chuck had sat as he listened, the sudden sound of the minister's deep voice broke an invisible barrier and startled Hunter. Speechless at first, it took a moment for Hunter to respond.

"Wrong about what?" Hunter lifted his head and found Chuck looking him straight in the eye. Despite all Hunter had confided, Chuck didn't appear afraid to talk; he seemed neither angry nor displeased. He was approachable. And though the man's countenance remained steady, Hunter thought he caught a glint in his pastor's eyes.

"God isn't disappointed in you," Chuck said, "and He's not angry."

Hunter searched Chuck's eyes for signs of insincerity, indicators that his pastor's words were empty or patronizing. But Hunter found none.

"He's not?" Hunter said, unable to downplay his wonder at what he'd heard.

"God's with you in this, step by step," Chuck said. "He sticks with you forever. He puts His arm around your shoulder."

Hunter's nose had started to run. He reached for a tissue from Chuck's desk.

Without intending to do so, Hunter had wrapped his arms around himself in a hug. Maybe it made him feel more secure as he considered his pastor's response. To Hunter's fascination, his tears represented neither sadness nor joy. Rather, he felt as though a cleansing process had initiated within him, whereby his tears ushered years of pain and rubbish out of his soul. He wiped his eyes with the tissue.

"An arm around my shoulder: Would you believe that's all I've really wanted?" Hunter chuckled to himself. "When you boil everything down to the essence of what I feel, that's what I've always craved, ever since I was a young kid. I've just wanted somebody's arm around me to accept me for who I am. The arm of someone who knows me and wants me to know I'm loved. It's the thing I longed for most and, strange as it sounds, the one thing I never received for as far back as I can recall."

Hunter reflected upon his own words. Though he had the company of another individual sitting across from him, Hunter still felt the pang of isolation because, in the end, he knew he would leave Chuck's office with the same struggle he'd faced when he'd walked through the door. Yes indeed, in times like these, he craved an arm around his shoulder most.

From the other side of the desk, Chuck studied him with the expression of a father watching over his son. Chuck looked as though he were considering his course of action, the next words to say.

"Tell you what," said Chuck, "we can take care of that right now. Would that help?"

Would it help? Hunter mused. *It would mean the world to me.*

Hunter couldn't muster the words to respond, so he nodded instead. Yet that was all his pastor needed.

Chuck didn't hesitate to make his way around the desk and hold out his arms.

If a stranger had made such a gesture, it would have struck Hunter as creepy. But coming from his pastor, something about the current circumstances fell into place. A trace of respite, however fleeting, hung within Hunter's reach. Though Hunter never would have thought to ask for this, Chuck, as a pastor, must have sensed how to respond to one member's unique needs. Yet another fact impacted Hunter more: Chuck, while knowing the truth about Hunter, wasn't afraid to reach out and make contact with him.

Hunter's father was never affectionate. Perhaps now, Chuck sensed Hunter had needed fatherly affection his whole life.

Regardless, Chuck's gesture fostered relief within Hunter's soul. He didn't have a chance to think about it or talk himself out of it. Before he could catch himself, he responded.

Hunter got up and stocky Pastor Chuck wrapped him in a bear hug. Hunter responded likewise, allowing himself the freedom to fall into the embrace, the innocent bond between a father and son. The affection Hunter had craved as a child. Hunter trembled as he allowed his defenses to fall.

They clung in their bear hug for a minute or so until Hunter began to calm. Soon Hunter drew a deep breath. Chuck patted him on the back, then returned to the other side of the desk. Each man took his seat.

"A little better now?" Chuck asked. "I know it doesn't solve everything."

"It's better," Hunter said. His muscles relaxed. The fear of looking into his pastor's face dissipated. "Thanks, I needed that."

Chuck picked up a pen, turned it back and forth in his hand, then set it back down. "Can I ask you something?"

Hunter nodded his permission.

"Why did you feel you needed to harbor this anguish inside rather than talk to someone?"

"I was never sure who I could trust," Hunter shrugged.

"Not even in church?"

"I thought about it. I looked around at my Bible study group and wondered which ones I could trust, but you never know for sure," Hunter said. "People have good intentions, but when rubber meets the road, that's when people reveal who they truly are. And that's what my secret would bring to light: What happens when people hear about something that conflicts with the status quo, especially when they disagree with you or get to be the first ones to spread your secret? Some people will jab their fingers at you and make you feel worse, but never offer to listen to what's going on. Other people gossip, but they pretend to do it in a caring way. They say things like, 'You might want to keep Hunter in your prayers—oh, you haven't heard? Yeah, it turns out he's held this secret.' And this secret of mine was too personal, too humiliating, to take that chance. So I kept it between God and me."

"As a pastor," said Chuck, "did I do or say anything that made you feel you couldn't come to me until today?" The sincerity in Chuck's face let Hunter know Chuck's words weren't meant as a challenge. Rather, it reflected Chuck's concern that he might have taken a wrong turn while leading his flock.

"No," replied Hunter, "but I figured you'd be disappointed in me. You saw me as a genuine Christian, and I *am* a genuine Christian, but it wouldn't appear that way. I'd look like a hypocrite—I *must* look like a hypocrite, because I *feel* like a hypocrite."

"I know you, Hunter. I know you're not a hypocrite. Why would you feel that way about yourself?"

"Because dealing with being gay—gay isn't considered part of what Christians usually stand for." Hunter shook his head as his eyes retreated toward his knees again. "I've often looked at myself as the worst Christian in the world. It seems my life should be in better shape. Instead, I've concealed this dark side of me, whether I wanted to or not. I've kept quiet about this since I was young, and when I became a Christian, I thought I'd get cured. Jesus is supposed to change your whole life, right? So when I gave Him my heart, I'd also hoped it would eliminate my feelings and remove the issues from my life."

"I wish I could tell you it would. But the truth is, not all of our struggles disappear when we give our lives to Christ," Chuck said. "Some do disappear, but others stick around. They become part of our journey, a journey we need to walk through whether we want to or not. As a Christian, you won't have a perfect life, but you'll have God's peace as you voyage through it. You mentioned you can't remember the last time you lived in peace. I understand what you're saying; but at the same time, you've made it this far, haven't you? You've found peace knowing you're never alone. Sure, you might have felt alone with your peers, but you've always held Jesus close. Even in the darkest, lowest moments, you've known in your heart of hearts that He's with you. Am I right about that?"

Lately, Hunter had felt so bogged down with shame, he had overlooked God's love. Even when he couldn't run to anyone else or talk to them, he had kept his communication open with God because he knew he could trust God. As Hunter considered his pastor's words, he found reassurance in them.

"I suppose you're right about that," Hunter said. "I've never thrown in the towel and given up on life. I guess I trusted God enough to keep hanging on. I kept drawing close to Him when the battle got fierce."

"The truth is," said Pastor Chuck, "you're never alone. God knows your battles, He knows your shortcomings, and He loves you in the midst of them. He also understands."

"It's hard to believe God can understand. He's perfect, isn't He?"

"Jesus experienced life on earth as a human being with flesh like ours. When He rose from the dead and went to heaven, He went there as our high priest. He reminds God the Father of our vulnerabilities. He tells God—from firsthand experience—what it's like for us as human beings, who try our best but don't live up to perfection, and He reminds God that Jesus Himself paid the price for our shortcomings. That's why the Bible tells us in the book of Hebrews that we have a high priest who *understands* our weaknesses. Does that make sense?"

"It's comforting, but it doesn't change the isolation you feel while you're step by step on your journey."

Chuck paused, smiled once again. "Hunter, look at me."

Hunter raised his head and met Chuck's gaze.

"You're never alone," said Chuck. "I promise."

CHAPTER 36

Hunter looked forward to tonight's conversation least of all. But he knew they deserved to hear the truth from him before word spread through the grapevine. He murmured a quick prayer to God for strength.

After leaving Chuck's office, Hunter had called his parents to make sure they would be home tonight. He had something important to discuss with them, he'd said.

It was Friday night. If his news caused them insomnia, at least they wouldn't need to rise early for work the next morning.

Heading to their front porch, a blast of winter breeze made Hunter feel encased in an ice cube. He let himself into the house and shed his coat. Compared to the frigid air outside, he almost broke a sweat in the heated foyer. With his first breath, he detected the familiar scent of home, a combination of dinner and his mother's favorite potpourri, which she placed on various tables throughout the house.

From the foyer, he heard clinking in the kitchen, where he found his mother loading dishes into the dishwasher. He leaned down and planted a kiss on her cheek, a gesture he'd picked up as a youngster, a routine more than a display of affection, something they exchanged without thinking. She wiped her hands on a dish towel and gave him a hug. Between his parents, Hunter had always felt more comfortable around his mother, and her hug ushered in a sense that he'd come home.

His gut quivered. She hadn't a clue what the next hour would hold. This period in the kitchen would be the easiest and most peaceful of the evening.

"It's about time you stopped by," she kidded. "How long has it been? A few weeks?"

"Something like that. Sorry, the job hunt got me distracted."

"Well, at least you're keeping busy. That's a good thing. How about a glass of wine?"

"No thanks," Hunter replied, trying to maintain a casual tone.

"I'm going to have a glass of wine," she said, and proceeded to pull a bottle of Riesling from the refrigerator. She poured herself a glass. "Do you want to talk in here?"

Hunter glanced at the kitchen table, where the chairs sat in close proximity. Much too close. As difficult as this talk would be, he preferred more space, where his face wouldn't be inches from theirs when the inevitable awkwardness emerged.

"How about the living room?"

"Fine. Your dad's working on the computer downstairs."

Upon reaching empty-nester status, Hunter's parents had finished the basement, one room of which his father had converted into a man cave. Leading the way out of the kitchen, his mother poked her head through the door to the basement stairs.

"Ed! Hunter's here!" she said, then headed into the living room without waiting for an answer.

When his mother took a seat on the sofa, Hunter opted to sit in the armchair, close enough but not too close for comfort. If they erupted with anger, at least he wouldn't be engulfed from both sides. Hunter heard a pair of feet thudding up the basement stairs. Hunter's father stopped halfway into the living room. Even in the middle of winter, Ed Carlisle went barefoot around the house. He had tucked a short-sleeved polo shirt into a pair of shorts in a manner which, to Hunter, resembled that of a gym teacher. He looked every bit the former athlete who could have gone professional.

Hunter didn't expect his father to handle the news well. His mother, on the other hand, would try to show Hunter her support, he figured, to whatever degree she might muster. But after some tough minutes, he felt confident both parents would give him reassurance. Whenever he'd made a mistake growing up, they had come around in short order. When nobody else accepts you, your family does. Or should.

"Hunter, want a beer? I'm gonna grab one."

"No thanks, Dad."

"You don't drink beer anymore?"

With a shrug, Hunter replied, "I do. I just don't feel like having one right now." Not that Hunter *didn't* suspect he would crave a glass of alcohol by the time this evening ended.

When his father returned with a can in hand, he cracked it open, sat beside Hunter's mother, and rested a foot on the opposite knee. "What's the big news?"

Hunter wondered how many of these awkward conversations he would endure in the months and years to come. How many relatives, friends and church acquaintances would ask? One by one, how many times would he need to recount his story and the background behind it? Maybe it would become routine. Maybe the repetition would numb him to the point where he could itemize the details while, in his mind, escaping the conversation.

Hunter's eyes dropped to his knees because he knew his parents would look straight at him. He didn't want to catch sight of the disappointment in their eyes. This was hard enough.

"I don't know how to put this," Hunter said as he kneaded a few of his fingers. "I, uh, didn't think you should hear this from anyone else ..." No doubt, talking to his parents was much tougher than talking to his pastor. "Something happened. Something ... well, a romantic something, and I don't think it's something you'll be thrilled about."

Hunter said nothing further, hoping he could gauge their reactions one step at a time. He eyed his parents, who stared at him with blank expressions on their faces, until revelation dawned upon his mother's face and her eyes widened.

"Oh my—Hunter, is Kara pregnant?"

Her interpretation bewildered him. "What? No, it's not—"

"Hunter, if that's what happened, we'll do what we can to help."

"Of course we will. You know that, son," his father chimed in.

"Is she okay?"

Hunter grew frustrated and held up his hands, palms out. "Hold on. Kara's not pregnant. She's fine."

"You two made such a cute couple. I know you mentioned you split up, but have you considered getting back together?"

"What? We're not getting back together."

"You never mentioned why you broke up, did you?"

"She was a go-getter, that's for sure," his father said. "A spunky little thing."

"Yeah, she is, but—"

"So you found another girl?" asked Hunter's mother. "I'm sure any woman would love to have you. Maybe you should consider—"

"Wait, stop! You don't understand!" Hunter grunted in the sudden confusion. His frustration peaked. Exasperated, he brought his hand to his forehead, across his eyebrows. "I don't *want* another—look, I think I might be gay."

Uh-oh.

His stomach sank. He hadn't meant to blurt it out.

His parents clammed up before he had a chance to take his next breath. His mother's eyes had fallen to her lap now. She kept her head tilted, the way she did when she found herself trying to comprehend how someone's words had blindsided her. His father hadn't moved a muscle, but a pointed look surfaced in his eyes.

His mother shook her head. "Wait a minute, I—*gay?*"

"I didn't mean to say it that way."

"I don't think there *is* a good way to say that," his father said. "How did this happen?"

"It's complicated. I don't even know. And I didn't say I *am* gay, I just said I *might* be. I mean, I'm sorting it out."

His mother looked up. He had anticipated the incomprehension in her eyes. He *hadn't* anticipated the pleading look that accompanied it. Tears began to well up in her eyes, and Hunter could see she fought to hold them back.

His mother's tears. He'd made his own mother cry. That knowledge pricked his heart.

"This doesn't make sense," she said. "You've *always* liked girls, Hunter."

"I have, but there's been another side to me that doesn't make sense to me either. I've tried to fight it."

"Obviously, you have a little more left in the fight," his father said, "because gay isn't acceptable. That's not how we do things in this family."

"How we *do* things?" Hunter said. "How *we* do things? This battle is all mine—believe me, it's caused me plenty of grief."

"How long have you known?" said his mother in a tiny voice that suggested she wasn't sure she wanted to hear the answer. "I don't know how this works. Did you decide a few months ago? Is that why you and Kara broke up?"

"I didn't decide anything. I don't know how to describe it. It's just *been there,* ever since I was young."

"How young?"

"I don't know. Middle school, maybe. It's just something that showed up. Or phased in. I didn't exactly welcome it with open arms."

With a sigh, his father grimaced, then closed his eyes and rubbed them with his thumb and forefinger. "You said something happened. A few minutes ago, that's what you said—something romantic *happened.* What happened?"

"Kara found me with someone. Last night."

"She *found* you?"

"She still had a key to my house and let herself in, and we were—together."

"Who's 'we'?"

"Just someone."

"Someone *male?*"

Hunter sunk further into the chair. "Yes."

His mother looked toward a corner of the room and ran her finger along the bottom of her eye to remove the tear. "And was this a person you …" Her voice trailed off.

"Nothing happened between us before, nothing like you're thinking. I'd reached a dark season in my life, and this developed. I don't even know *how* it developed."

"It seems there are a lot of things you don't know about this." His father.

"Does he have a name?" asked his mother.

"Mom, this is already difficult. I don't want to go into every detail—"

"I'm your mother. The least you can do is give me a name, don't you think?"

"Gabe."

"Gabe," she whispered to herself, nodding, as though repeating the name would make the truth easier to accept. "Gabe." At that, she stopped, and a look of awareness swept over her face. "Wait a minute, wasn't that the name—when we ran into you outside the restaurant that night, so far away from here—wasn't that boy's name Gabe? Was that him?"

"Yes."

"So this *Gabe* person, the one we *met,* the one you looked us straight in the eyes and said was a *friend*—you *lied* to our faces?"

"I didn't want to. We were trying to make sense of what was happening."

"And this Gabe is what," his father asked, "your *boyfriend* now?"

"He's not my—neither one of us expected this. We're figuring it out."

"Well then, that's just great, isn't it." His face a deepening red, Hunter's father shook his head. "I didn't raise you this way. You're not some Daisy Mae faggot. You're my kid."

"Ed!"

His mother's rebuke toward his father arrived several words too late. The blade had already reached Hunter's heart.

Pastor Chuck had handled Hunter's news well. Then again, maybe he had heard this revelation from others in the past. Hunter's parents hadn't—at least, not from one of their sons. Hunter noticed his parents had retreated from full eye contact to the occasional glance, where they didn't focus on him for long. It was the kind of attention you forced yourself to give to someone because you needed to, not because you wanted to. Among the trio sitting in the living room, not one of them was comfortable.

"So Kara found you," his mother said. "What happened afterward?"

"We got into a major fight, then she stormed out the door."

"Did you ask her not to tell anyone?"

"She caught me off guard when she walked into my house. I wasn't exactly thinking several steps ahead—"

"You can say that again," his father tossed in.

"—so no, I didn't think of asking her. Not that she would've listened. I think Kara will do whatever Kara will do. *She* wasn't thinking clearly when she left, either."

"I can imagine." His father crossed his arms over his chest. "This wasn't the smartest thing you've done. If you weren't interested in Kara, I don't understand why you didn't just wait it out and find another girl you *are* interested in."

Hunter found it fascinating how easy his situation appeared to those who had never experienced the fire of its pressure.

"So it's as simple as that? I just *choose?* How was I supposed to *choose* another girl that interests me?"

"The same way you chose this Gabe person. You weren't interested in guys before. If you snapped into it, you can snap out of it."

"I didn't snap into it. It's been going on for years. I was worn down to the point where it was hard to fight against it."

"Then you keep fighting anyway, Hunter. That's the way we do things in this family. We fight it off."

"Dad, this isn't helping." Hunter didn't know which was worse: derisiveness, by which he could read his father's reaction, or silence, where he wouldn't know where he stood in his father's eyes.

"The whole community will find out," said his mother. "How are we supposed to handle it when people ask about it? They're going to whisper. People we've known for *ten years* will gossip about us."

Hunter realized they could spend hours asking what-if questions, worrying about every possible scenario and every potential consequence. Hunter himself had spent most of his life in torment over such things.

He didn't know how to navigate through this conversation in a way that would bring resolution. He gathered his thoughts before speaking again.

"I don't have all the answers," Hunter said. "I know you aren't happy with me right now. Maybe you don't even want to look at me." He paused. His father wouldn't look at him, but he managed to catch his mother's eye. "I'm not asking you to understand me. All I'm asking is to know you're here for me."

It took a few moments, but his mother's painful expression transitioned into a look of maternal concern. She rose from the sofa. Though her steps were hesitant, more cautious than usual, she made her way to her son's side. She wrapped one arm around his back, nuzzled her nose against the top of his head the way she did when he was a child, then planted a kiss there.

"You need to understand this is hard for me," she said, "but you know I'm here for you. I'm your mother. I don't stop being your mother just because I don't understand what's going on."

Hunter felt an initial hint of relief. His family wasn't the closest-knit he'd seen. Yet, whether rooted in love or insecurity, he cared much about what his parents thought of him.

Hunter realized his father hadn't said a word in response. He looked up at his father, who still had his arms crossed and now stared at his own calloused feet, shaking his head in wonder.

"Dad?"

His father grunted under his breath, at a clear loss for words. "This isn't something I want to talk about. Sorry."

"Dad, I'm sorry I ruined your image of me as your son. But I don't think I'm going to live up to everything you wished I'd be. I've tried—I've honestly tried to be the son you wanted—but I can't. I'm not that person, I'm me."

"I want time to process it. I—" He stopped speaking, rubbed his temples, then he got up from the sofa. On his way out of the room, he said, "I can't deal with it now."

Hunter had forgotten his mother still had her hand on his back until she patted him again. She didn't say a word about his father, nor could she have said anything that would have removed the knife slice Hunter felt make its way down his heart as he watched his father walk away. His father's shoulders had never communicated anger to the extent they did as he left the room that night. The floor shuddered, small tremors of thunder as Hunter listened to his father descend the stairs to the basement.

Hunter hadn't expected a perfect outcome. He had, however, hoped to walk out of his parents' house knowing he had *both* parents' assurance.

The winter breeze had intensified into a bluster. As Hunter walked out the front door and into the icy night, the lack of closure with his father brought ache to his soul.

On second thought, that wasn't it. Rather, it brought a fresh burn to the ache he'd felt for as far back as he could recall.

CHAPTER 37

The next morning, Hunter pulled into a parking spot in front of Gabe's apartment building and left the engine running. He thumbed through a text message to let Gabe know he'd arrived. Overhead, the cloud cover seemed to thin, as if sunshine might find a way to break through for a few minutes. Hunter turned up the heat another notch and waited for his toes to thaw.

Saturday morning. A mere 36 hours had passed since Kara had discovered their secret, but it felt like two weeks.

Another minute passed and he watched Gabe make his way down the wooden staircase with his hands stuffed into the pockets of his jeans. He had dressed in a hoodie and a well-worn baseball cap. The cap didn't boast a sports team; instead, it was the sort you would find at a casual clothing store.

He climbed into the car and shut the door, rubbing his hands together and blowing into them to warm them.

"Where are we going?"

"Nowhere in particular," Hunter replied, pulling out of the parking lot. "I needed a drive, if that's okay."

"Fine with me." Gabe paused, then morphed into a wry smile. "Trying to escape the upcoming gossip, eh?" An awkward attempt at humor.

Gabe turned on the radio and settled on a Gavin DeGraw song, but kept the volume low enough for Hunter to hear the rhythm of the tires on the pavement. Within a few minutes, they had merged onto a freeway heading west. At a few minutes past eight o'clock on the weekend, Hunter was glad to find the traffic sparse. He felt like he had breathing room. Neither he nor Gabe needed much conversation. They needed each other's presence. Hunter wanted the proximity of someone whose support—whose *degree* of support—wasn't in question.

"I talked to my parents last night," said Hunter after several minutes of silence. "I told them everything."

Eyebrows raised, Gabe turned his head toward him. "How'd they take it?"

Hunter's mind traveled back to the final minutes in his parents' living room, up to when his father stormed out.

"Needless to say, they were stunned," Hunter replied. "I can understand why, though: I don't think it's what any parent wants to hear their son say. It's not exactly what I wanted to tell them. It's not what *any* of us wanted to confront."

"Did it end on good terms?"

"My mom started to come around. It was hard on her. No doubt, it'll continue to be difficult for her to sort through." With a smirk, Hunter glanced at Gabe. "Join the club, huh?"

Gabe grinned in return, though his lips remained pressed together. The grin of someone smiling through heartache.

"At least she's willing to stand by my side," Hunter said. "That's all I can ask. I don't need her to understand. She couldn't understand even if she wanted to. But there's a measure of peace in knowing she's with me." Hunter ran his thumb along the steering wheel. "Which is more than I can say for my dad."

"What happened?"

"He didn't take it well at all. He didn't explode on me. I had that image in my mind before I got to the house, where he'd get angry and start yelling."

"But he didn't?"

"He didn't yell, no. Then again, he seldom shows emotion. Keeps it all hidden inside, much like I do." Hunter pictured his father's face right before leaving the room. "He didn't need to go ballistic for me to see the anger in his eyes, though."

"Anger?"

"Anger ... resentment ... disappointment at the knowledge his son will never turn out the way he'd hoped." Once again, Hunter heard the rumble of his father's footsteps as they descended the stairs to the basement. "He walked out of the room, said he couldn't deal with it right now. He told me I'm his kid and he didn't raise a faggot."

Gabe grimaced. "Hunter—"

Hunter focused on the freeway ahead of him, the hypnotic blur of the lane markers as he sped along. "It's no big deal, right? That doesn't mean it didn't sting when he said it, but he's disappointed with his own life. Why should I expect anything more from him?"

"He's your father, Hunter."

"And this is how my dad handles things. It's who he is. Maybe I should've let them hear it through the grapevine. That way, I would've gotten a phone call from them and we could've discussed it without looking at each other."

"You did the right thing."

"Maybe so."

They stared at the freeway and listened to the undulation of the tires as they spun. Hunter passed a moving van, the roar of its engine diminishing to a whine as it retreated in Hunter's rearview mirror. Sara Bareilles's "I Choose You" played on the radio.

"Do you plan to tell your mom?" asked Hunter.

"I already did. You and I both had an eventful Friday night."

"How did she handle it?"

"It sounds like she took it better than your parents did. Lots of questions, but she didn't seem angry at me. No harsh words. I could see the disappointment in her eyes, though." He gazed out the passenger window. "That said, I couldn't help but think she saw this coming, like she sensed something was wrong, the way mothers can pick up on things. I think she was waiting for me to say it. She'll look to God to comfort her." Gabe peered at Hunter. "Did your mom cry too?"

"Yeah."

"That's the hardest part of the conversation," Gabe said, "watching your mom cry and knowing you were the one who busted her heart."

Hunter understood too well.

"How'd things end up with you and Kara on Thursday night?"

"Not good. A big fight, as you saw. We haven't spoken since and probably never will."

"You know, it'll be a matter of days before a lot of people hear about this. The world has a way of shrinking when news buzzes."

Hunter nodded.

Gabe leaned back in his seat. He tilted his head against the headrest and stared at the dome light above him.

"So where do we go from here?" asked Gabe.

Hunter felt his jaw grow rigid. He increased his foot's pressure upon the gas pedal. As the car accelerated, the lane markers blurred faster, combining into solid gashes of white.

Hunter shook his head.

"I wish I knew."

CHAPTER 38

On a Sunday morning two weeks later, Hunter sauntered across the parking lot beneath an ice-rink sky. He hadn't seen the sunshine in three weeks. A normal January condition for where he lived, and one to which he'd never grown accustomed.

Word had begun to spread around the area. While leaving the house that morning, he had found a hate note taped to his front door. On Friday night, someone—a group of teenagers, he assumed—had TP'd the tree in his front lawn.

Hunter had skipped church and Bible study meetings in the last two weeks since his secret had gotten blown. As ridiculous as avoidance had struck him, he couldn't bring himself to face the people. At a minimum, he knew one friend of Kara's was a member of his church, so he was confident people his age had heard about him. No doubt, word had spread. The only question was how far. Yet he knew a return to church was inevitable.

Besides, he had yearned for the worship time. As close as he felt to God during his times of personal prayer and worship, he grew invigorated worshipping God in the midst of other believers. To Hunter, it felt like drinking water from a fountain of life. So, this morning, he'd forced himself to return and trust God to take care of the rest. He would do this, he determined. Even if he had to do it humiliated.

Hunter had timed it so he would arrive a few minutes after the worship service started. By that time, the auditorium lights would have dimmed. He hoped people would be too preoccupied with the songs to notice him. Plus, a thousand people attended each church service from several communities, too large for Hunter to know each individual on a personal basis. That meant, by his estimation, plenty would attend who *hadn't* heard about him.

Still, he couldn't help but look for responses as he entered the church auditorium. The doors muffled the music inside the room, but when he opened one door, the audible blast hit him at full volume. At first, he stood at the rear of the room. An usher, positioned on the other side of the door, smiled at him with a nod. Hunter nodded in return and pretended he felt normal.

At the front of the room, an array of overhead lights lit the platform on which the worship band played a joyful, upbeat song. The rest of the room was dim, yet illuminated enough for Hunter to see faces. His eyes darted in every direction on a search for reactions, particularly from people his age, to determine whether he was safe. Was it childish to think that way? After all, would people spend their lives focused on *him?*

Maybe so. From the corner of his eye, Hunter caught sight of a few young adults, male and female, huddled together along a wall toward the far side of the auditorium. He recognized one guy from his Bible study meetings. The guy had started attending the meetings a few months ago and Hunter didn't know him well. In fact, Hunter didn't know any other individuals in the huddle.

The individuals in the huddle appeared to have engaged in conversation before the church service started and hadn't settled into seats yet. It wasn't an unusual occurrence, given the massive number of people in the room and the loud music that drowned out any lingering chatter. These church services began with an informal ambiance.

But the individuals in the huddle kept glancing at him. They chatted, then appeared to stop as one or two eyed him before turning back to the group, the way people do when they want to get a clear visual of the gossip subject—*There he is! That's the guy! Did you hear what happened?*—but are too polite, or scared, to make it obvious by a physical gesture. None of the individuals walked up to him. Finally, Hunter turned his head and looked at them directly. They averted their gazes. Now he *knew* he was their subject of conversation. Either they gossiped about him, or they were afraid of what he—or others—would think if they were seen *talking* to the pathetic pariah. Hunter wondered which was more childish: his concerns about what others thought or their seeming pleasure in his humiliation.

Hunter felt the clap of a hand upon his shoulder: Jesse Barlow, Pastor Chuck's son, Hunter's friend from Bible study and Saturday morning basketball.

Jesse sidled up beside him, a calculated grin on his face.

"Come on," Jesse said with a gesture of his thumb, "you're sitting with me today."

Until now, Hunter hadn't realized how alone he'd felt the last two weeks. He had planned to walk in unnoticed, but a friend's company proved a welcome relief.

Jesse led him to a seat in the middle of the auditorium, where they blended into a sea of people. Knowing Jesse, he'd intended his invitation as a deliberate, bold gesture in case anyone had a problem with his friend Hunter. But the people who surrounded them continued to sing and lift their hands in worship. Most had their eyes closed. When Hunter realized these people *weren't* focused on him, he shed his coat and started to relax. He wished he hadn't stayed away on recent Sundays. He shut his eyes and shut out the world around him.

Within a few minutes, the band transitioned to a slow, reverent song of worship. The lights dimmed further: an atmosphere of intimacy. For Hunter, the moment belonged to God and him.

First he listened to the lyrics, which spoke of God's rescue, of His love and undeserved forgiveness, all of which Hunter had experienced firsthand at various junctures in his life.

As he pondered the lyrics, gratitude overwhelmed him. A broken Hunter lifted his hands toward heaven. He didn't feel as though he deserved to lift his hands to God. Then again, thought Hunter, he *never had* deserved it. That was the whole reason he had given his heart to Christ in the first place—because of what Christ had done on his behalf. Hunter had found pure love in Christ, pure acceptance, and He had never expected Hunter to earn it. Hunter had received it as a free gift. The notion fascinated him: a huge, eternal God who cared about a speck like Hunter. Now Hunter soaked in God's presence—the way he had for years, both at church and during his private encounters with God—and joy filled his soul. Joy from the Lord.

But soon a shift occurred. Hunter's thoughts drifted again toward his struggles, and the conflict that tugged him, back and forth, between his faith and his desires. The knowledge crept into his mind like a thief trying to steal his intimate moment with God.

At a loss on how to reconcile his circumstances in light of his faith, Hunter grew disappointed in himself. He wondered if he had made Jesus look terrible. After all, people knew he was a Christian. Those same people had also heard some Christians— though Hunter was not among them—speak harsh, angry words about the mere *hint* of same-sex attraction. Would they consider Hunter a fraud? Would they consider *Jesus* a fraud because of him? Would they conclude Hunter had kept quiet so he could appear religious? The truth was, he never would have harbored the secret if he had felt like he could confide in someone. The hurtful words spoken by other Christians had helped drive him into himself. Hunter wondered at the irony. And now, the thought that others might reject Jesus because of Hunter tore at his soul.

He wondered how God could love someone with Hunter's shortcomings and regrets. How could Hunter, surrounded by people in this moment, feel so isolated, as if God were his only true friend?

Hunter was sick of weeping, tired of the tears. He had wept more in the last few months that in the last few years put together. Yet here they came again, filling his eyes and spilling out as he lost himself in the beauty of the worship song. At least his were honest tears, he figured.

Then he remembered he *wasn't* alone. Hunter opened his eyes and glanced to his left, where Jesse stood beside him. Hunter remembered the teardrops on his cheeks and pretended to scratch his face as he wiped them away. Yeah, right. Who was he fooling?

Jesse turned his head toward Hunter. In Jesse's countenance, Hunter found an air of compassion, like someone who had stood in Hunter's position before. Then again, Jesse had. Although Jesse hadn't experienced the particular challenges Hunter faced, Jesse, by his own admission, had spent years falling short of God's perfection and had found a fresh dose of God's forgiveness. Maybe Jesse understood the pariah factor after all.

Awkward with the knowledge another guy had seen him weep, Hunter scratched his face again to ensure the tears were gone.

"It's okay," Jesse said as he leaned toward him. "You do what you need to do right now. Let God love on you for a while."

That acceptance, the assurance from someone who had faced struggles of his own and come forth—scarred but safe—ministered to Hunter's heart. Hunter closed his eyes and resumed worshipping God.

Just God and Hunter.

A glimmer of freedom emerged.

———————————

"So, how have people treated you?" Jesse asked. "I haven't seen you at Bible study to ask."

After church, Hunter and Jesse had grabbed burgers at a fast-food restaurant in nearby Twinsburg. The simplicity of the environment, funny as it seemed to Hunter, was one less thing with which he needed to concern himself.

He swallowed a bite of his burger and said, "You mean since—well, since I got found out?"

"Yeah."

"The stuff you'd expect to happen. It started last week, but for the most part, I figure it's kids having fun. The tree in my front yard got TP'd. Some prank calls. Random whispers when I walk by. This morning, I found a note taped to my front door telling me how abominable I am." Jesse shrugged. "It's all harmless stuff, people enjoying themselves at someone else's expense. After all, *they're* in great shape these days."

"Makes you feel like shit, though."

Hunter hated to acknowledge it. "I shouldn't let it, but it does."

Jesse took a bite of his burger. "Everyone's got shortcomings. Some people may not *realize* they have them, but they do. Look at me: My minister dad would be thrilled with my choice of words a minute ago, huh? But one step at a time."

Jesse smirked, and Hunter couldn't help but return the gesture. He was grateful for Jesse's genuine air.

"How have other *Christians* treated you?" asked Jesse.

"I've avoided church and Bible study until today. But generally, they avoid me when I see them around the grocery store or wherever. A few people have made a point of expressing kindness. I haven't gotten much by way of text messages or emails, though—most people went silent. Maybe they need time. Maybe they don't know how to respond or are afraid to get too close to me," Hunter said. "I want to give people the benefit of the doubt, but I'd be kidding myself if I believed there wasn't gossip going around. I've seen it in action before, even inside the church walls, when other people dealt with stupid, minor things. My deal is much bigger—and much more fun to talk about."

Jesse gave him a tentative look as he chewed a french fry, then said, "Look, man, I've been places myself. I'd be a liar if I said I understood firsthand what you're dealing with, but I'm here for you. Even if things go south and you have nobody else, you have *me,* so that's *at least* one other person on your side." He paused, then added, "And just so you know, this isn't me being a preacher's son. My dad didn't have a chat with me and ask me to talk to you. This is me being your friend. I've been through enough shit—whoops, there I go again—enough *stuff* of my own, and I know how alone it can make you feel."

Hunter froze at Jesse's understanding. Then he noticed Jesse hadn't sat catty-cornered from him to maintain his personal space, or for fear he would give Hunter any clues of interest to misinterpret. He had sat across from him as though nothing had changed. Hunter felt a chain break loose in his heart: He could trust the friend who sat across from him.

"I keep thinking how disappointed in me God must be," Hunter said.

"I don't think it caught God by surprise."

"What do you mean?"

"The way I see it, God already knows everything," Jesse said. "He knows what will happen in the future, right?"

"Yeah …"

"If He knows what's coming in the future, then He knew *this* was coming. Apparently, He loved you enough to create you anyway."

Hunter had never considered God from that perspective. Sure, he understood God is all-knowing. He believed God had a plan mapped out for his life. But Hunter had only considered God's omniscience in terms of His overarching plans, large-scale events around the world, or chaos that might erupt in individuals' lives. He had never considered that God knew in advance where Hunter would fall short. Peace arose in Hunter's soul as he pictured God's love in light of Jesse's perspective.

Hunter caught sight of two young parents in the parking lot, leading their toddler to their car. He watched the parents wriggle the toddler into the carseat before returning his attention to Jesse.

"This doesn't make sense to me," said Hunter. "I'm not a bad person. I love Jesus from deep down in my heart. All I wanted was for somebody to love me, and for me to love that person back. I don't *want* to be different. I didn't want to hide anything; I felt like I *had* to. And I'm afraid I'll tarnish God's name, that people will lose respect for Jesus or Christians because of something I didn't even want in my life," Hunter explained with a pang in his gut. "That's what I wish I could say to everyone: 'Don't stop pursuing God because of me.' That's what always scared me more than anything else: the possibility that my feelings could hurt someone else's faith."

"Maybe you're being too tough on yourself," Jesse said.

"It worries me, that's all. I don't want to cause anyone harm."

"But maybe God already had this figured out," Jesse said. "If God already knows everything, and if He already knew this was coming—that you'd deal with whatever feelings you have inside, and that your situation would get found out by other people— then don't you think God also factored it into His whole plan? Don't you think God knew our struggles and shortcomings, and knew how He would cover those circumstances? Don't you think He already had a strategy for how He would work it out for you and everyone else, including how to guard other people's faith?"

Hunter didn't know what to say, so he remained silent, but Jesse's words settled into his heart.

"I've learned God isn't like people," Jesse said. "He doesn't abandon you when life gets you down."

Jesse's remark sent through Hunter a wave of intensity. A surge of hope.

"He's still here," Hunter said. "You're right, I can feel Him working on my heart, especially when I feel alone."

Jesse shrugged, then finished the last of his french fries.

"Maybe we worry too much about letting God down," Jesse said. "Maybe we try to walk on air across the Grand Canyons of our lives, when all the while, God has a big safety net stretched out under us."

Hunter considered Jesse's words.

Maybe.

CHAPTER 39

By the middle of March, Hunter felt more balanced than when his secret came to light two months earlier. Though he felt awkward at the weekly Bible study meetings and now spoke less at them, he continued to attend. While Ellen and Gabe had stuck by his side, along with Jesse Barlow, others had kept their distance. But his life had returned to routine—not its former routine, but a routine, nonetheless. The pranks on him had proven short-lived. He still heard occasional, derogatory remarks from individuals around town he'd never met, but who recognized him from years past.

Hunter branched out beyond the microwave-powered meals of bachelorhood and began cooking from scratch. He believed the influx of fresh meats and vegetables had made him feel more vibrant in recent weeks.

From the produce section at the grocery store, he selected a vivid, purple eggplant, the sight of which made his mouth water, and added it to his cart. He'd come across an intriguing recipe online and was eager to attempt it tonight.

A gallon of milk from the dairy aisle would complete his shopping. Listening to the rhythmic click of wheels along the floor tiles, he pushed his cart past a range of vegetables, past their fusion of yellow, green and orange.

"You're Hunter Carlisle, aren't you?"

Hunter turned to find a middle-aged woman with platinum-colored hair wrapped in a small ponytail. He didn't recognize her, but perhaps they had met at one point in years past.

"Yes ma'am. Have we met?"

"I'm Mindy Rodham. You played baseball with my son Garrett when you were teenagers."

"Nice to see you again, Mrs. Rodham."

"I remember him mentioning you're a Christian. You were in Youth Vision together."

"Sure, I remember him. He was a good guy."

"I saw you from the apple section over there," she said with a glance behind her. "I wondered whether I should say something, but I couldn't help myself."

"Say something about …"

Mindy Rodham peered to her left. Reassured no one was within earshot, she lowered her voice to a mutter, as though she still didn't want anyone to hear. One side of her mouth remained still, while she spoke through the corner of the other side.

"Didn't you *think* before doing what you did?"

"What I did?"

"With that—whoever he is. Your relationship with that other man. I don't understand how you can call yourself a Christian and do something so disgusting. Don't you realize you're making *all* Christians look bad? And for what? For a good time with—with *him?*"

"Mrs. Rodham, I didn't intend—"

"It's horrible, and there's no excuse for behavior like that. I hope you get down on your knees and repent and beg God for mercy on your soul. You'd better find a way to get that trash out of your life, because that behavior does *not* please God." With a final glance around her, she gave her cart a push forward and parted with the words, "*A Christian.* You should be ashamed of yourself."

Stunned at first, Hunter couldn't move a muscle. In the last month, two other individuals had taken the initiative to unleash their anger upon him in moments he didn't expect. But frequency didn't ease the rope burns their words produced on the surface of his heart. Each time it happened, he tried to let the person know he hadn't meant to hurt anyone. He wanted to explain that his feelings emanated from the loneliness he felt inside. If only they could see the sincerity of his faith and the genuine concern he harbored. But these individuals were not like Jesse Barlow, who listened. These individuals either cut him off as he tried to explain, or didn't seem to hear what he said, as though they had already decided in advance what they would believe about him. In the Bible, Hunter read that Christians are to walk in love, not bite and devour others. Yet Hunter marveled that he felt *less* loved now than he'd felt while his secret was intact.

At the same time, Hunter had to admit, he wondered what the years might hold ahead. How might the future look for him? He had tried to find happiness with the opposite sex, but no female had made him feel as content as he felt with Gabe. What if, for the remainder of his life, he could only find happiness in a homosexual relationship? Or suppose he dove into a serious relationship with Gabe and it didn't work out? Would he pursue another same-sex relationship? Or would he *ever* find fulfillment?

Hunter also bore safety concerns regarding the risk of disease, such as HIV. He knew Gabe hadn't had a sexually-active past, but what about any future relationships? He wondered if he could trust any future partners to tell him the truth about their past, or if they would even *know* whether their past partners were infected. What if a partner had caught a virus that didn't show up until years later, after they had lost touch? Could Hunter catch a horrible disease and seal his own early death?

But worst of all, Hunter wondered if a homosexual relationship would put distance between God and him. Hunter couldn't imagine life—or eternity, for that matter—apart from God. That notion tormented him most.

On his way toward the dairy section, with his mind focused elsewhere, somebody darted out of the cereal aisle and stopped short of a collision with Hunter's cart.

"Hunter! Sorry about that, man. I'm kinda in a rush here." Randy Gresh, one of the guys with whom Hunter had played basketball on Saturday mornings. They hadn't played since the winter weather arrived, before Hunter's incident.

"I haven't seen you in forever," Hunter said. "Where have you been hiding out?"

"Here and there. We need to get our Saturdays up and running again in a few weeks. Spring is almost here."

"Will do."

"Listen, man, I heard what happened and just want you to know we're still friends, no matter what."

"I appreciate that."

"It sucks the way people started preaching against you, like you're the worst thing that ever happened. You'd think church people would be nicer to each other."

"Preaching against me?"

"Yeah, a buddy of mine goes to that church just before you enter Stow. You know, that tiny little church on the side road with the stained-glass window of a shepherd and sheep? Been there forever. It's the one you always notice when you drive past."

"I've seen the church. Never been there, though. What about it?"

"My buddy rarely goes, but he had relatives in town and his parents twisted his arm into showing up at church last Sunday for the family's sake. He told me the minister there suddenly decided to preach a month-long sermon series on homosexuality and that all gay people are going to hell or whatever. My buddy says the preacher didn't mention you by name, just talked about 'some individuals in our community,'" Randy said, curling his fingers into quotation marks.

A second comment to render Hunter speechless, both in a single trip to the grocery store.

"I used to serve that preacher years ago—remember when I worked at Beckindale's restaurant? Yeah, he used to come in there a lot. I'll never forget him. Real mean guy. Didn't tip well, either. He actually counted out pocket change to get it right at 15 percent if I was lucky. Then he'd wish me his blessings or whatnot, I don't remember. After getting screwed on my tip, I was never in the mood to hear anything the guy said. At least he never mentioned Jesus at the restaurant, right? How embarrassing would *that* be for him: 'Hey, get Jesus and become a cheap-ass like me.' But anyway, that's the preacher I'm talking about. I'm not a church guy, but at least Jesse Barlow's dad seems like the real deal, you know what I mean?"

But Hunter's mind had halted at the words *preaching against you.*

CHAPTER 40

"I haven't been here in a week," Ellen said as she shut her car door. "I finally got a breather between jobs."

Hunter climbed out from the passenger side of the car and stopped short. Ellen stood still, her eyes fixated on her home in progress. She appeared dumbfounded.

"What's the matter?" Hunter asked.

"I didn't realize they'd already started putting up the walls," said Ellen in a manner that seemed like a passing thought, as though she stood there alone.

Hunter peered ahead. It looked like a typical house under construction to him, no different from any other such house he had driven past during his life.

"It's just the framework," he offered, at a loss for something more adequate. "The walls aren't up yet."

"Won't be long, though."

Hunter followed Ellen to her new house, where beams of wood now stood in a clear pattern. As far as he could tell, the builders had completed the framework for the two-story home.

Upon closer inspection, the wood looked clean and flawless, its color a few shades darker than ivory.

When they reached the space where the front door would reside, Ellen stopped. She touched the framework. Standing beside her, careful not to pick up a splinter, Hunter ran his palm along a wooden beam that, by his guess, would outline a window.

"Come on in," she said with a wave. Although she still seemed a tad distracted by something—whatever it was—she had, for the most part, recovered. "I'll give you the grand tour of the first floor."

Hunter sauntered behind her, beneath the threshold and into the foyer. He took a deep breath and tried to detect the scent of lumber, but the cool air had chilled his nose and masked the aroma. The construction process fascinated him, the way a house began with a basement, followed by a simple wooden frame. Without the walls, he could see through every room unhindered, all the way to the forest behind the house. As a kid, he would have paid cash for this type of X-ray vision. At the same time, the depth of framework, layer after layer as he peered toward the rear of the home, resembled an optical illusion, one designed to skew his perception of where one room ended and another began.

"That's the dining room on your left, and the living room on your right. We're walking through the foyer now." Ellen took cautious steps ahead. She swept her finger back and forth across a series of steps that stretched above their heads. "This is the main stairway. There's another stairway in the kitchen."

Ellen turned to her right and crept down another narrow corridor. The main hallway, Hunter deduced. When they reached one end of the house, Ellen pointed to a room on their right.

"This will be a guest bedroom," she said.

Although he could see right through the framework into the room, Hunter found humor in the fact that, out of habit, he poked his head through its doorway anyway.

"And here," said Ellen as she ran her finger along a threshold so tight, at first Hunter didn't realize it lined an open space, "is a linen closet."

The closet sat before them at the end of the hallway, at an angle perpendicular to the guest bedroom. It reached as high as where the ceiling would sit. Judging from its threshold, the closet would require a door of full-size height but half the regular width, the same size as the linen closet at Hunter's home.

Ellen stared at the closet. She smirked while examining it, as if she knew something this linen closet didn't. Rubbing her thumb along one side of the doorway, Ellen slinked inside the closet and turned around to face Hunter.

The closet was so narrow, when she pressed her hands against the sides of its framework, her arms remained bent at the elbows. Her body filled most of the empty space. In fact, with her body inside, the closet left only enough room for her hands to reach an inch or two away from her body. Once the builders finished the walls and shut the door, Hunter imagined, a person might suffocate inside that linen closet.

Ellen stared at the horizontal beams above her. Hunter watched her and couldn't help but grin. As cramped as she was, she looked like a little girl trying to squeeze herself into a dollhouse. A modern Alice in Wonderland, too gargantuan for her own surroundings.

"Have you ever noticed how life does this to you?" said Ellen.

"Life?"

"Life tries to fit you into a box," Ellen continued, as if she hadn't noticed Hunter's reply. One by one, she gazed at the wooden beams that surrounded her. Scrutinized them. "It builds walls like these. And you want to shout, cry out, release all the shit that stacks up around you and smothers you. But you can't say anything, because not even you yourself can figure out what's wrong. You just know something isn't right."

She traced the manufacturer's inked imprint on one beam and continued, "So you can't let anyone know because, even if you wanted to, you couldn't find the right words." She turned her head and looked into Hunter's eyes. "Do you know what that's like?"

Hunter stared into her eyes.

"Yeah," he murmured, "I think I do."

Hunter studied his friend, the sincerity in her face. She sounded neither discouraged nor stressed. For that matter, Hunter couldn't detect *any* expression in her demeanor. If anything, she seemed as cool as the breeze that swept through this naked house.

"Ellen, is everything okay?"

She pondered his question a moment, then said, "What if I don't love him?"

"Brendan?"

"Yeah. I mean, I love him, but what if I don't love him like I *should?* What if I'm making a big mistake getting married? Is it possible I said yes to him because I *should,* simply because it made sense? Sure, I said yes for myself. But what if it was more because it would make *him* happy?"

Hunter weighed whether he should say more, dig into why she had made those strange observations.

"Ellen, you can talk to me if you want to."

With her lips sealed tight, she twisted her mouth into a smile, then rolled her eyes.

"Wedding jitters," she said. "That's all it is."

"Are you sure?"

"I promise." She blinked her eyes once in a speed that made time look like it had slowed. "I'll figure my way through. Always do."

"And you love Brendan, right?" he asked, perhaps for his own reassurance more than hers.

"Of course," she said, her confident demeanor on the rebound. "I'm fine. You have enough going on in your life, Hunter. Don't worry about me."

And with that, she gave him one of her trademark winks.

CHAPTER 41

Hunter couldn't shake his curiosity about the preaching Randy had mentioned at the grocery store. So that Sunday morning, when Hunter left for church, he headed in the opposite direction than usual. Turning from Route 91, he weaved along a side road and made his way to the little church with the stained-glass window. The building had resided there long before many residents had moved to town. It had a whitewashed exterior. A skinny steeple sat atop its roof.

The tiny parking lot wasn't paved. Gravel crunched beneath the tires of his car as he drifted into the lot. At the sound of gravel pinging against metal, he cringed, hoping he wouldn't discover nicks along his car's finish. A smattering of vehicles sat parked around the lot, and he pulled in beside a beige sedan. He checked his watch again and noted the time as 9:24. Sure enough, the service was about to begin, but the only people walking into the church building were a couple who looked, from this distance, in their late fifties.

The heaviness of the church's ornate front door took Hunter by surprise. Solid oak, he guessed. When he walked through it, he discovered two ushers standing on the other side, engaged in conversation. The nearest one, a somber man with close-cropped hair, seemed hesitant to smile, preoccupied with his conversation, but handed Hunter a bulletin and, in what struck Hunter as an afterthought, offered him a frosty handshake. Neither usher seemed to recognize him. Hunter thought he caught the word *budget* in their conversation, but he didn't want to eavesdrop, so he sauntered through the next set of doors.

The silence in the sanctuary struck Hunter as eerie. He detected a draft coming from above, not enough to make him uncomfortable but sufficient to keep him from dozing. He slid into an empty pew toward the back. Straight ahead, behind the altar, he located the familiar stained-glass window depicting a shepherd and sheep. Given the scarcity of cars in the parking lot, he was surprised to find the pews half full with people. Then again, the room wasn't large. If he closed his eyes, he could picture the comfort of a rural church.

The blast of a pipe organ startled him. The congregation rose to its feet, pulled hymnals from their slotted nests beneath the pews, and paged through them. Hunter turned to the hymn noted in the bulletin, then studied the people in the sanctuary. Most of the men wore suits and ties. Hunter, dressed in his typical Sunday sport shirt and khakis, wondered if he should have called ahead to inquire about the dress code. Although the majority of the congregation looked past retirement age, Hunter saw a few young kids and a couple more school-age individuals sitting with their parents. Back in school, Hunter had several friends who belonged to churches but seldom attended. Maybe that explained the lack of young people here today. The older kids looked less than thrilled to be here. Then again, Hunter wondered how excited the adults were, since none of them smiled as they sang. He concluded it was a sign of reverence.

In one row, toward the middle of the sanctuary, he noticed a teenager who looked the age of a high school student, a lanky guy with an aquiline nose and blond hair pushed to the side. The teenager looked toward his right, which provided Hunter a glimpse of his face. Hunter couldn't put his finger on what was wrong, but he sensed the young man was unhappy—not about sitting in church, but about life. He looked the way Hunter had often *felt* at his age: alone. Hunter wondered if the guy dealt with the same issues Hunter did. Probably not. Regardless, Hunter felt compassion and whispered a quick prayer for the guy.

The hymn ended and the congregation sat down. They followed a litany of Scripture readings and call-and-response affirmations, followed by another hymn on their feet. Hunter found the entire church service structured in his bulletin. Though it was a Christian church, the environment felt foreign to him. Yet when he looked around, the congregants appeared to know which words to say, as if from memory, and he figured many had engaged in this style of church service for years. He could understand the comfort such tradition might bring.

Upon completion of the latest hymn, the minister stretched out his arms and motioned for the congregation to be seated. A tall man, he had dark hair well into the graying process. Donned with a clerical collar and a long, white robe, he matched the stereotype Hunter had held of a minister before Hunter had become a Christian. Near the middle of the minister's chest, a cross, three or four inches tall and made of polished silver, hung from a chain around his neck. When the minister turned at a particular angle, the cross reflected a light that shined from above the pulpit. Hunter had seen such giant crosses before, but on rare occasion, and had always been suspicious that the size of the cross was meant to distract people from noticing other, less flattering details about the wearer. He didn't mean to judge the wearer; he just couldn't shake the curiosity.

The minister smiled little, which, to Hunter, helped explain the lack of smiles he'd noticed since his arrival here. He couldn't determine if the congregation had followed the lead of its pastor, or vice-versa.

The minister began preaching in somber tones, but as he progressed through his sermon, his bass voice grew in intensity and echoed off the hard walls and floors. He seemed to conjure extra inflection or fervency when he was about to reach key points.

But Hunter's mind didn't focus on the eloquence of the man's speech or the flawless weavings of his robe. Sure enough, as Randy had said, the man preached about homosexuality. And while Hunter hadn't expected the minister to express approval in his sermon, he also hadn't expected the sermon to sound laced with anger. The man's words left Hunter aghast. They came forth like gunshots to Hunter's soul, their shrapnel biting into his skin, as various sermon phrases rang in his ears.

"… abominable acts in our community …"

"… issue that has infected people for millenniums. God destroyed two ancient cities, Sodom and Gomorrah, because of homosexuality …"

"… don't need to be patronized. They need the Law, God's Law. Before we can give them the good news of grace and forgiveness, we need to present them with the Law so they will recognize their sinfulness and repent of their actions …"

"… won't like hearing what I have to say, but it's necessary. First the Law, then the Gospel …"

Hunter shifted in his seat. From the corner of his eye, he searched for clues on how the parishioners responded, yet they remained chiseled marble sculptures, silent as they stared straight ahead. The teenager Hunter had noticed earlier sat with his arms crossed and his attention focused on the pew in front of him.

The sermon ended. More call-and-response litany followed. Hunter tried to pay attention, but the minister's words echoed in his mind. His struggle had never been about a lack of desire for God or a lack of respect for Him. Hadn't Hunter tried to find a resolution for years? Hunter hadn't tried to persuade anybody to follow in his footsteps and, for that matter, wouldn't wish the struggle upon anyone else. Had the minister ever *talked* to anyone who dealt with this? He'd spoken to neither Gabe nor Hunter. If he had, he would have discovered the *painful* aspect of such desires. For Hunter, it wasn't a matter of theory or of finding the right words to preach away his inclinations. On the contrary, the struggle was tangible. Real.

A final hymn occurred before the church service concluded. At the sound of the organ, the congregation turned pages in their hymnals and began to sing of how the world will know they are Christians by their love. Hunter tried to sing, but a sour sensation emerged in his belly. He recalled the Bible verse that served as the basis for this hymn. Hunter *believed* that verse. He had tried to live by that verse, treating people with love.

Yet, in this context, the song sounded rusty, corroded. After hearing such harsh words aimed against him by a man who had never met him, listening to this hymn made Hunter feel *unloved*.

Hunter wasn't a guy trying to corrupt a community or disrespect people around him. He was just a guy dealing with a challenge, like the rest of the people in this sanctuary.

The service ended 45 minutes after it began. "Go forth with joy," the minister had instructed them, and they filed out to the dreary sounds of the organ.

Too confused to move a muscle, Hunter hadn't stood to his feet yet, his thoughts concentrated instead on what he had heard as he repeated the phrases to himself, over and over. When he looked to his left and noticed a line of people had filed out of the pews, Hunter shook himself to attention and joined the end of the line in the center aisle, which progressed in a slow fashion. He looked ahead at the main doorway to which the line led, the doors through which he had entered the sanctuary, where the minister now stood, shaking hands with congregants. The man remained solemn, thanking the congregants for coming and offering them his words of blessing. Hunter couldn't bring himself to look at him. He doubted the minister would know who he was by sight, but Hunter would know.

Hunter peered over his shoulder. In the front corner of the sanctuary, beneath an *Exit* sign, he noticed a small door which led to the lawn at the side of the church building.

One more glimpse of the minister, then Hunter strolled toward the side door and departed the sanctuary.

The lawn felt mushy from melted snow and left mud streaks on his shoes, but at this point, Hunter didn't care. He could wipe them off later. In an attempt to remain casual, he made his way across the lawn as if he weren't the only one who had chosen to take that exit, then quickened his pace across the gravel parking lot.

When he climbed into his car, he checked the time. His own church's service hadn't begun. A second church service in one day would provide the perfect lift to his spirits, he decided. After the last 45 minutes, Hunter needed to connect with God.

———————————

The next attempt to help Hunter—if you could call it that—arrived that evening in a phone call.

Hunter had known Al Brickman for a few years through the weekly Bible study meetings. A father of two in his late forties, he and Hunter had prayed together on several occasions. Al had prayed for Hunter during critical junctures in his career and relationships, and had encouraged him as he grew in his faith. Hunter, for his part, had prayed for Al the best he could, though he didn't know from firsthand experience how to pray for people to have strong marriages or to be good fathers. Nevertheless, he had prayed from his heart and trusted God to take care of the answers. Hunter knew Al was a genuine Christian and valued his perspective.

"How are you doing these days, Hunter?"

Hunter turned off the stereo shelf system in his living room and switched his cell phone to speaker mode. "It's okay."

"Didn't see you at church today," Al said in a tone that suggested he didn't want to prod into Hunter's privacy.

"I got there a few minutes late, that's all." Hunter decided not to mention his visit to the other church that morning since it would accomplish nothing.

He heard Al hesitate before saying, "Hunter, I wanted to call to say I stand by you. I mentioned it to you a while back at Bible study, but I thought it worth saying again. I love you, man— you know, in a Christian way."

"Thanks, Al. I appreciate that." Hunter's muscles relaxed. He sat cross-legged on the sofa.

"Not an easy situation, huh?"

"No, but I have a few people in my corner letting me know they're here for me. That means more than you know."

"Glad to hear that," Al said. "I'd imagine it's a lot to process."

"It is. Seeing your status quo come crashing down around you takes you by surprise. It's not something you'd wish for."

"You're a good guy. I don't know of anyone who would wish trouble on you," said Al. "Of course, technically, you did make a choice here, and—"

"A choice?" Hunter said, careful to maintain an even tone. "What do you mean, a choice?"

"A choice in the sense that you chose it somewhere along the way, right? You didn't choose to have things come to light the way they did. But the deeper issue—we both realize that's a choice, right?"

Hunter found the direction of Al's conversation perplexing. Was it intended as a phone call of support, or was it to counsel him in some way? "I've heard people say it's a choice, but I have trouble finding where I was given the opportunity to choose it."

"Well, I don't think you were *born* that way, do you?"

The conversation took Hunter off guard and made him feel awkward.

"I don't know *how* I wound up dealing with this," Hunter said. "Sure, I chose my actions with Gabe, if that's what you mean. But I didn't choose to be *attracted* to him. Or to anyone else, for that matter. I don't remember making a choice. You're attracted to your wife, but I doubt you woke up one day and decided to find her attractive. Wasn't it something that just happened?"

Al kept his tone casual in response, but Hunter perceived this wasn't how Al had intended their chat to unfold. "I've heard some people say it's what you concentrate on. Could that be a factor?"

"All I know is it showed up somewhere along the way in my life. I tried to deny those … attractions. I tried to stifle them. I tried to pray them away. Believe me, I didn't *want* this. It sucks. It's been torture ever since I was a kid. I *wish* I'd been given a multiple-choice test—I would've picked another option."

At an obvious lack of answers, Al paused. "Is it possible you just need more faith?"

In his heart, Hunter knew that wasn't the case. If anything, he had drawn *closer* to Christ during his years of nonstop introspection. Nobody knew about those personal times Hunter spent—just God and him—soaking in God's presence … worshipping Him … telling Him how much he loved Him … seeking a closer walk with Him. Hunter sought closer proximity to God's heart simply because he *loved* God, not even to *receive* anything out of it. Hunter knew, without a doubt, his faith was sincere and full of ardent fire. But he kept that day-to-day intimacy with God unspoken to others.

"I don't think it's a matter of faith, Al. My faith hasn't changed. It's as fervent as it was a few months ago, a few *years* ago. Granted, I don't have it all figured out, but it's too simple to call my feelings a choice. I'm not sure this is something I can change."

"Look, Hunter." Hunter picked up frustration in Al's voice, as though the man had hoped to solve everything in one phone call but had collided with a situation more difficult than he'd anticipated. "I want what's best for you, so I'm trying to help. And as hard as what you're going through might seem, it *is* a choice. The fact is, God made Adam and Eve, not Adam and Steve—"

Hunter's jaw almost dropped. "I can't believe you resorted to a cliché."

No doubt, Al meant well and possessed genuine concern for Hunter. At the same time, however, this illustrated why Hunter had kept a secret for so many years. Couldn't people see him for who he was, consider the notions that churned in his heart, and quit jumping to conclusions about *why* he felt the way he did when *he himself* couldn't figure it out?

"I appreciate your concern, Al. You're a good person. But let me explain something most people don't seem to understand," Hunter said. "This isn't a cliché to me. It's not a witty play on words. This might seem like a game to people, a debate to win, but this is *my life* we're talking about. You might be able to make a clever remark and move on, but *I'm* the one who sheds tears at night. *I'm* the one who's trying to come to terms with my core."

Hunter paused a beat.

"Look," Hunter said, "it's been a confusing few months—years—*life*. Do you think maybe we could talk about this later? I appreciate your trying to encourage me. It means a lot. But I don't think I'm at a point where I can talk to many people about it. Can you respect that?"

"Sure, Hunter."

Thankful to end the call on good terms, Hunter set his phone on the coffee table.

Doesn't anyone out there have a clue what this is like? Hunter wondered. *Someone who's been in my shoes besides Gabe?*

CHAPTER 42

It felt like treading on foreign soil. The little church with the stained glass window had expanded decades earlier via a brick wing on one side. Unlike the oak door he had opened two days earlier, the door that led to the church office was white with decorative trim, the kind you would find on an ordinary house.

Hunter didn't know why he had come. But if the minister intended to preach about him, Hunter felt the man should, at least, meet him. Maybe he wanted the minister to know Hunter Carlisle wasn't a bad person.

"May I help you?" asked the church secretary, who looked like a soccer mom with hair that curled not far below her ears.

"I wondered if the pastor is in. If we could talk, please."

She examined Hunter and asked, "Are you a member here?"

"No ma'am, I'd simply like to talk with the pastor, if that's okay."

Before he'd finished speaking, a door opened behind the woman and the minister walked through. Hunter caught sight of bookshelves in the room on the other side of the doorway.

Dropping a file folder into the inbox on the secretary's desk, the man regarded Hunter.

"Can I help you, young man?"

Young man?

Hunter glanced at the secretary, who continued to focus on him as well, now grafted into the conversation by virtue of their stances beside her desk.

"I listened to your sermon on Sunday," Hunter said, "and had some questions, I guess."

At the mention of his sermon, the minister straightened his posture a tad. A pleased look entered his eyes.

"Come in," said the minister, extending his arm toward his office. He followed Hunter in and closed the door. "Have a seat."

Though he had shed his white robe for the week, the minister wore a standard clerical collar with a black shirt. The man had switched crosses since Sunday and, today, wore a wooden cross with metal trimmings, also three inches long. A nameplate on his desk read, *Rev. Dr. Rodney Harper.*

"I'm Reverend Harper," he said with a handshake.

"Hunter Carlisle."

No reaction from the minister at the mention of Hunter's name. Perhaps he knew Hunter and Gabe by reputation alone, not by name. At the man's invitation, Hunter took a seat in front of a large desk. Facing Hunter from the opposite side of the desk, Reverend Harper pressed his fingertips together into the shape of a steeple. The man kept his posture rigid as he sat.

His penetrating stare made Hunter uncomfortable. Hunter questioned whether he should have come at all. Then again, getting up and leaving seemed ridiculous.

"You mentioned Sunday's sermon."

"Yes. Your sermon—series. Well, I thought maybe your sermons came about because of … rumors about a … *couple* … in town."

Was *couple* the right word? Even today, it sounded odd to Hunter.

"I saw an issue in the community that needed to be addressed, yes."

Hunter tensed, scratching the back of his neck. How should he go about saying this?

"Well, sir, I'm the person you're preaching about."

Motionless in his chair, the man reduced the tension in his fingertips but kept them steepled. Though he didn't break his stare, Hunter watched as a pointed look crept into the man's eyes. He remained silent, waiting for Hunter to say more, so Hunter decided to forge ahead.

"I guess I wanted to stop by your office and let you know I'm not a bad person."

Reverend Harper considered Hunter's words.

"Well, Hunter, I'm sure you're a good person," he said, "but God is clear on how He feels about homosexuality."

"To someone wrestling with it firsthand, your words on Sunday sounded a bit harsh."

"It's a harsh subject. As I said on Sunday, God destroyed two cities because of homosexuality: Sodom and Gomorrah."

"I've been thinking about what you said. I don't know why, but as a Christian, it doesn't sound like the God I know, to single out one thing and treat it as worse than the others. To destroy a group of people because of one sin when He sees *all* sin as what separated people from God."

Reverend Harper swiveled in his chair and retrieved a Bible from a bookshelf that loomed behind him.

"Let me show you something, Hunter." The minister paged through the Bible and opened it to the book of Genesis, chapter 18. He ran his finger down the page as he scanned the text, then pointed to a verse, turning the Bible so both he and Hunter could read the text. "Verse 20 says, *'And the LORD said, "The outcry of Sodom and Gomorrah is indeed great, and their sin is exceedingly grave"'*—*exceedingly grave*, God says." The minister paged forward. "The Bible gives us a view of what that sin was, the night before God destroyed the city in chapter 19. Two angels came to the city dressed like regular men and came to stay at the home of a righteous man named Lot: *'Before they lay down, the men of the city, the men of Sodom, surrounded the house, both young and old, all the people from every quarter; and they called to Lot and said to him, "Where are the men who came to you tonight? Bring them out to us that we may have relations with them."'*" He gave Hunter a direct stare. "Do you know what the men were talking about when they said, 'have relations?'"

"Yes, I do."

"They were men seeking to have relations with other men. That's why God destroyed the city. God spared Lot and his family; those other men were dead by the next day. And God does not want that event forgotten. He recalls it in the book of Ezekiel."

The minister paged more than halfway through the Bible, stopping at the book of Ezekiel.

"Chapter 16, verses 49 and 50 show us God considered their actions not mere sin, but an *abomination: 'Behold, this was the guilt of your sister Sodom: she and her daughters had arrogance, abundant food and careless ease, but she did not help the poor and needy. Thus they were haughty and committed abominations before Me. Therefore I removed them when I saw it.'*"

Hunter stared at the page, poring over the verses again and again, searching for some sign of God's mercy, the mercy Hunter had come to know so well. The familiar feelings of pain and guilt sank into his gut, the way they had when he'd read those verses many times before.

Reaching the end of the verses, he started over a fourth time, biding his time, hating the awkward silence in the room.

Then, as he read the words phrase by phrase, a thought occurred to him.

"Wait," Hunter said. "It doesn't mention anything about homosexuality."

"What?"

"Look here." Without intending disrespect, Hunter pointed to the verses. "There's nothing sexual on the list. It gives a whole list of reasons why God destroyed the city, though. So isn't it saying God destroyed the city because of lots of different sins, not just one?"

Reverend Harper smirked. "We can deduce sexual sin from the verses in Genesis."

"But weren't there women in Sodom and Gomorrah?"

"Of course there were, Hunter. That's the point: The men rejected relations with women for relations with other men."

"No, I mean, the *whole cities* were destroyed. That means the *women* got destroyed too, right? The Bible doesn't say *they* committed anything sexual with other women—it only mentions the men did that. So if the women were also destroyed, the destruction *must* have been because of more than just the men's sexual relations, right? Like it says in these verses: arrogance, haughtiness, not caring for the poor—"

Hunter looked up. The minister appeared stunned.

For once, Hunter began to find an inkling of relief for his soul.

"Didn't God know we would have our shortcomings?" Hunter said. "Everyone has issues they deal with. Doesn't He walk through them with us? When I look at how Jesus treated the Samaritan woman at the well, the one who had a sordid past, I can see He didn't point a finger at her and He didn't try to destroy her.

"Or how about the woman caught in adultery, when the religious leaders were about to stone her? Or Mary Magdalene—rejected by others, but she ended up being the first person Jesus appeared to after He rose from the dead. It seems to me that Jesus is patient, walks with us, cheers us on as we press through. We aren't perfect, but we take it step by step—like the Bible says, we work out our salvation with fear and trembling. We make mistakes, but we love God and have reverence for Him in our hearts."

Hunter hadn't meant to unleash a stream of thoughts, but he found it encouraging. It didn't answer all his questions or resolve his challenges, but sitting there, it brought him hope.

With pursed lips and creases along his forehead, Reverend Harper looked as though he wasn't used to someone tying together Scriptures from the other side of his desk. Hunter wondered if he had gone too far with what he'd said to the man. Hunter hadn't tried to argue with a minister; rather, he tried to sort through the questions that had swirled in his soul for years. He wanted to help the minister understand that people who struggle don't always *want* to struggle.

At last, the minister leaned back in his chair, which released another squeak in the stillness of the room. He grinned at

Hunter, but the man's lips remained sealed, and the smile didn't make its way to his eyes or the rest of his face.

"Our doctrine can be difficult to understand," the minister said. "It's a doctrine of right and wrong."

"But what about the doctrine of love?" Hunter pleaded. "It seems God gives us guidelines on how to treat people: How about the Bible verse that tells us love *covers* a multitude of sins? Or the verse that says to love our neighbor as ourselves? Would you want someone to step up to a pulpit and announce *your* vulnerabilities, but never mention how difficult they are and that you might need *support* from other Christians? It seems to eliminate the aspect of loving people when we point a finger and then drive away, leaving them stranded to deal with the humiliation it creates."

"God's Law is clear," Reverend Harper said. "I don't want the people in my congregation to condone behaviors that violate God's Law."

"But isn't there a place for *mercy* without condoning anything? Isn't that how *Jesus* treated people? Wouldn't you rather encourage people to treat others with love and let *God* lead them in how to interact with people they disagree with?"

"God shared the Law first, then the Gospel of Christ," the minister replied. "If you're in sin, you need the Law. You need to be shown the error of your ways so you can repent."

"But the Bible says it's God's *kindness* that leads us to repentance."

Reverend Harper leaned back into his chair and crossed his arms.

"Do you attend church here, Hunter?"

"No, sir."

"The people who attend church here trust me to shed light on Scripture for them. If anyone in my congregation is in error, it is my responsibility to show them how their error violates God's Word."

Hunter thought back to the church service he had attended on Sunday. He pictured the stoicism in the faces around him.

"But sir, I don't think it's possible to change people by *controlling* their thoughts and beliefs, rather than letting God work on their hearts," Hunter said, careful to communicate a tone of respect. As he thought back to the lack of detectable joy among this minister's parishioners, Hunter ached for those who might be in the midst of private pain. "When you try to control them, you either make them feel like they'll never measure up, or they want to shake themselves free of that total control. But you can *help* them by showing them they're loved. That's what people want more than anything: to know someone cares about them. They don't need anyone to tell them they fall short of perfection—they already know that about themselves."

A smirk returned to the corner of Reverend Harper's mouth.

"Thank you for your advice, Hunter, but I did spend four years in seminary. With all due respect, I think I'm a little more qualified to lay out Scripture than you might be. You've read the Bible, no doubt. But there's a difference between reading the Bible and being a serious student of it."

At that, Hunter paused. A minister had never pulled rank on him before. He didn't know rank existed among Christians; he thought ministers' first concern was to help people, not position themselves as experts.

Hunter recalled the Bible's instructions in chapter 13 of 1 Corinthians, on how to treat people with love, even if he didn't receive corresponding treatment from others. Despite the stern expression on Reverend Harper's face, Hunter couldn't help but feel compassion for the man. Granted, this minister's preaching and latest insult had made Hunter feel horrible. This minister hadn't considered the *roots* that might underlie Hunter's struggle. But regardless, this man was, to borrow a phrase from Jesus, Hunter's neighbor. He was still Hunter's brother in Christ.

At the same time, Hunter remembered the Bible's words instructing him, if possible, to be at peace with all men as much as it depends on *him*. Reverend Harper might not *respond* with peace, but Hunter knew God held Hunter responsible for making the effort. At this point, Hunter assumed he couldn't persuade the minister to reconsider his approach in dealing with others, so Hunter decided to end the meeting in peace.

"Thank you for your time, sir."

Hunter extended his hand, reaching halfway across the minister's desk, then reaching a few extra inches to make his sincerity clear. They shook hands.

"You're welcome, Hunter."

Hunter rose from his seat and headed for the minister's door, scared for anyone in the man's congregation who might have questions about their sexuality or any other issues that weighed heavy upon them.

If they couldn't find hope in their church, not even with their pastor, to whom *could* they turn?

CHAPTER 43

One week later, Hunter didn't know why the meeting with Reverend Harper continued to bother him, but it did.

What had he hoped to accomplish by trying to change the man's mind? He couldn't tell if the minister thought he was a good person or not, but the man's lack of mercy, his unwillingness even to *try* to understand the private pain, illustrated why Hunter had never wanted to confide in anyone. Hunter felt as alone as he was now—in a physical sense—as he stood at the site of Ellen's new home. He wanted to spend an hour away from his house. Away from the world. Somewhere nobody would find him.

The construction workers had left for the day. Hunter knew Ellen wouldn't care if he stopped by. Lingering in front of the house, he noted how it loomed over him.

The walls had gone up. Hunter could no longer see through the structure.

He walked through the front doorway, which still lacked a door, and peeked into the rooms on each side of the foyer. With no destination in mind, he turned into the same hallway Ellen had showed him on their last visit. Hunter wandered down the hall, brushing his fingertips along the walls and marveling at how much progress the crew had made in what seemed like a short amount of time.

He stopped halfway and stared at the nook at the end of the hall. Though it lacked a door and shelving, with its walls in place, it looked like a linen closet now, as Ellen had said.

Hunter sauntered toward the closet and tiptoed inside. Its two-foot width felt cramped, but in this moment, the close quarters brought an odd sense of comfort. Hunter turned to face the hallway, as Ellen had done. With his back against the closet wall, he slid to the floor and wrapped his arms around his legs, planting his head between his knees. Hunter closed his eyes.

Once, as a teenager, he had tried to confide in Randy, the friend with whom he had run cross-country, the one he had known since childhood. To be more precise, Hunter hadn't tried to confide; rather, he had tried to determine if it was *safe* to confide—to see if Randy was someone he could trust.

"Do you know anyone who's gay?" Hunter had asked, trying to sound blasé.

"Don't make me puke," Randy had replied. "Can you imagine how disgusting that would be? They should round 'em up and keep 'em together in a colony or something, like they used to do with the fucking lepers."

Hunter winced. Randy's voice echoed in the corridors of his memory. Hunter lifted his head from between his knees, ran his hands up and down along the smooth, white surfaces of the walls. He peered up and tried to determine the height of the ceiling, but without enough natural light, the closet was too dark for him to calculate anything.

Hunter recalled himself at twelve years old, when he first sensed something was amiss. By that point, he had discerned that his attraction to the opposite sex, although present, hadn't felt as strong in him as it seemed to reside in others. And he'd noticed it didn't resonate in him to the same degree same-sex attraction did. But Hunter hadn't known at the time whether to concern himself with it or brush it off as a passing phase.

He had decided to ask his father about it. When you're a boy that age, your father is your most accessible resource for learning how to operate as a man. Due to the sensitivity of the subject, though—not to mention its awkward nature—he hadn't wanted to ask his father about it outright. So Hunter had decided it best to wade into the topic by feigning confusion.

Hunter sat in the passenger seat of his father's car, on his way to one of his middle-school baseball games.

"Dad, did you know some guys don't like girls?"

"Some don't." His father had shot him a quick glance before returning his eyes to the road. "What makes you ask that?"

"There's this kid at school," Hunter had said. "He told somebody he's gay."

"His poor parents, having to hear that," his father had said, shaking his head. "Tell you one thing: No son of *mine* will ever turn out gay, not so far as *I* can help it."

That had marked the first day Hunter shut himself down, the day he had lost his innocence. From that day forward, Hunter went into permanent hiding.

All that time he'd spent seeking someone to trust. Hunter marveled at how fast months and years could accumulate.

Hunter drew his knees closer to his chest, wrapped his arms around them again, and cradled himself in a tight embrace.

The darkness of the linen closet brought peace. And though Hunter felt empty, he savored the comfort he found in this moment of solitude.

In this closet, no one would discover him or judge him. No one would find humor at his expense.

Nobody would tell him how filthy they thought his soul was.

CHAPTER 44

"**A**m I going to hell?"

From the other side of the desk, Hunter watched Pastor Chuck's expression morph into grave concern.

"Why would you think that?"

"So I'm *not?*" Hunter lifted his head and met Chuck's kindhearted stare. "That's one of the biggest things that have bothered me all these years—the fear that I'll end up in hell."

"Because you've felt attracted to the same sex?"

"Yeah."

"Hunter, you're not going to hell."

"But what if I go too far one day? What if I act on those attractions? What if I act on it again, then act on it again, and it's in progress the day I die? I mean, Gabe and I haven't done anything, but ..." He trailed off, at a loss for how to complete his thought. "A lot of people seem to think I'm on my way to hell."

Chuck studied him as though trying to pick precise words for his reply. That was one of the qualities Hunter appreciated most about his pastor: his willingness to slow down and prepare a helpful response rather than offer a platitude.

"Do you know anyone who has stolen something?" Chuck asked.

"How often?"

"Doesn't matter."

"Are you talking about a burglar, or just someone who took a towel from a hotel where they stayed?"

"Either."

"Of course. The hotel thing, anyway."

"Do you think they're going to hell?"

"Because they took a towel?" Hunter said. "No, I don't think so."

"But it's still stealing, right?"

"Of course."

"And the Bible calls stealing a sin." Chuck paused for a beat. "Have you known any Christians who drank more than they should on a regular basis?"

"Like going one drink too far? Sure."

"The Bible tells us not to overindulge in alcohol," said Chuck. "Do you think those people are on their way to hell?"

"Of course not. It's just an issue in their lives, one of those areas where they're vulnerable. A lot of them are sorting through something difficult and there's no easy answer. It doesn't mean they love Jesus any less."

"Hunter, your salvation came by faith. You didn't earn its entrance into your life," said Pastor Chuck, "and you can't earn its staying power. Your salvation isn't based on your actions; it's based on your willingness to believe and let God have your heart."

"But what about in the Bible, that verse in Leviticus, where it puts a spotlight on homosexuality? It doesn't just call it a sin—it calls it an *abomination*."

"In God's eyes, one thing is no worse than another. That verse in Leviticus existed under an old covenant between God and man, a covenant filled with requirements—what we call the Law—designed to show that man could never live up to God's perfection," Chuck said. "God designed His Law not to punish us, but to show us our need for a Savior. When Christ died, He took all our shortcomings with Him to the cross. He fulfilled the Law on your behalf. Everything the Law mandated, Christ satisfied on your behalf. So when you gave your heart to Him, you entered a *new* covenant with God, one that isn't based on your performance. It doesn't require you to earn anything. No action that conflicts with God's Law is any worse than another. They're all equal in God's eyes—they prove our equal need for a Savior, regardless of what we've done."

"But if God went so far as to call it an abomination, don't you think He meant to designate it as worse?"

Chuck reached toward one corner of his desk and grabbed a leather-bound Bible. Hunter recognized the Bible as the one Chuck carried with him to the pulpit when he preached. Chuck turned its pages and settled on the book of Proverbs, angling the Bible so Hunter could read the words. Hunter leaned in and noticed Chuck had turned to chapter 16.

"God calls other things abominations, too. Would you like to see some of them?"

Hunter read verses 16 through 19, where he counted seven items: a proud look, a lying tongue, hands that shed innocent blood, a heart that devises wicked schemes, feet that run toward mischief, a false witness that lies, and a person who sows discord.

"Did you see homosexuality listed there?" Chuck asked.

"No."

"And I don't know about you, but I've told a few lies during my Christian life. I've also caught myself looking on with haughty eyes here and there over the years."

Chuck's words brought comfort to Hunter's heart, yet Hunter didn't know how to respond.

"In Romans chapter 3," continued Chuck, "the Bible says we've *all* sinned and fallen short. Each of us fights a fight of faith, and each has different battle fronts. But God's kingdom isn't a physical place on earth, and though physical works are appropriate, His kingdom isn't *based* on our physical works. Jesus said His kingdom exists in human hearts. It's a spiritual kingdom that exists *inside* His people, and His number-one interest is where your *heart* is toward Him."

Hunter fingered the edge of the Bible, focusing his eyes with such intensity on the columns of text, his vision doubled. He breathed deep.

"I didn't choose to feel gay," Hunter said at last.

Warmth emerged in Pastor Chuck's eyes, his crow's-feet more prominent as empathy lifted them.

"I know you didn't," he said.

"You do?"

"You've spent your life trying to deny those feelings exist, trying to find your way out of them, afraid someone will find out," Chuck said. "I don't believe anyone chooses to be gay. I believe, for whatever reason, the conflict emerged in your life. And that isn't your fault, Hunter."

"How can it *not* be my fault?"

"Think about the apostle Paul: In the Bible, he mentioned struggling with a thorn in his flesh. He didn't specify what the thorn was, but it was something that emerged in his life. He didn't choose it and it wasn't his fault, but that didn't remove the struggle from his midst. It doesn't mean you're a phony or a terrible Christian; it's part of your journey, that's all.

"We don't always choose what happens to us," Chuck continued, "but we choose how we respond. We make decisions, we fall short in some areas, we learn from our mistakes and make adjustments. And Jesus is there with us, standing shoulder to shoulder. He smiles on you as you journey because *He's* on the journey with you."

"I've seen myself as a failure because of all this," Hunter said.

Chuck leaned forward against his desk. "Hunter, I promise you, nobody is perfect. Every one of us is *in process* in this life. As we grow in our relationship with Christ and interact with other people, we walk through the process, step by step, and we grow."

He caught Hunter's eye and held his glance.

"You'll find your way through this journey, Hunter. You and God. You'll find it together."

CHAPTER 45

Two weeks later, Hunter swore he could feel himself thaw in the mid April sunshine. Earlier that day, he had finished his third interview with the sales department of a small, local software company that specialized in skill-training software.

Hunter's regional experience at a large company impressed them. This local company, on the verge of expansion, wanted Hunter aboard. The team members needed to interview two other candidates and, because of the company's small size, needed to finish a large project before activating the new sales position. But they had expressed a strong interest in Hunter and had implied he was their preferred choice. Hunter wouldn't know their decision for a few more weeks, but his latest interviewer had told him—off the record—that his chances of getting the job were 90 percent. As it turned out, the company that downsized him had provided the experience he needed for an exciting new challenge.

God works in unexpected ways, Hunter mused to himself. He perceived God taking care of him.

To reward himself for a successful interview, Hunter had headed home that afternoon, changed clothes, and decided to shoot hoops on the basketball court at church.

In the months since Hunter's secret had come to light, rumors had spread and people had gossiped. Hunter had removed toilet paper from the tree in his front yard more times than he could count. Cars—driven by high school students, he assumed—had cruised down his street at night, stopped in front of his house, and issued a series of sustained horn blasts before squealing away.

Meanwhile, according to what he'd heard around town, Reverend Harper's words had grown more aggressive as the weeks wore on. The pastor had ended his sermon series and graduated to posting a few soapbox videos on the Internet—Reverend Harper called them "public service announcements" on the video page—for the world to watch. Hunter had visited the video page and found it had received a total of 74 views. He'd watched the short, angry blasts and heard, once again, that Hunter (though not mentioned by name) had corrupted his community and that hell might lurk in his future. After his visit to a church service and looking around at the people in the sanctuary, Hunter wondered who in the man's congregation knew how to *create* a web video.

In the end, however, Hunter had decided to walk in love and avoid seeking vindication. He figured *someone* needed to act like a Christian in this situation.

Nonetheless, despite the insults, he sensed God's arm around his shoulders. At night, he would lie in bed and talk to God in prayer before drifting to sleep.

Hunter had reached a place of peace. As the initial humiliation wore off and he discovered more and more residents in town knew about him, Hunter had grown less fearful of what they thought of him. More and more individuals, in fact, had let him know they cared. God would walk with him through this, just as God had stuck beside him through every past challenge.

The basketball clanged against the rim and hit the backboard before returning to his arms in a freefall. One more try.

These days, Hunter noticed a sense of freedom he hadn't expected when the humiliation had first occurred. True freedom like he'd never felt. The freedom of holding *no secret whatsoever*. Nothing to fear. Nothing to guard. After all those years clenching it within dark, iron chambers of his heart, those bars had disintegrated. The issue itself hadn't disappeared, but dread no longer bound him in its emotional cage.

In a way, Hunter felt *happier* than he'd ever felt. He'd had no idea how much pressure had built up since adolescence. He likened it to the molecular bombardment about which he'd learned in chemistry class. The molecules in his life had bounced and collided with increasing force inside a contained space until the beaker exploded and they broke loose. Despite the negative fallout and the unknowns that lay ahead, Hunter felt joyful. Relieved. Free.

Perhaps he'd *wanted* to be exposed. Maybe, on some deep, psychological level, he'd relented, putting himself in a risky situation with Gabe to *dare* others to find out about him so he wouldn't need to verbalize it to anyone. Good-bye, terror. Hello, daylight.

Hunter readied another free throw. This time, the ball slipped through the net, but Hunter didn't get to hear the swish he so enjoyed.

A screech of tires in the parking lot startled him. He fumbled with the basketball before securing it in his arms. The screech sounded like a car slamming on its brakes, a driver trying not to hit a kid who had darted into a street.

Hunter turned and saw Gabe slamming the car door shut. Gabe ran toward him.

"You haven't answered your phone!"

"It's with my car keys over there." Hunter nodded toward a bench thirty feet away.

"I've looked all over for you! Ellen didn't know where you were. I checked your house. I tried coming here by chance because I knew this is where you shoot hoops."

Out of breath, Gabe panted. He looked worried.

"What's wrong?" Hunter asked.

"Remember that minister you talked to? The one who's been railing against—"

"What about him?"

"A kid at his church just killed himself."

"What! When?"

"A few hours ago."

"How? The kids aren't even out of school for the day."

"That's where he did it: at the high school, underneath the stadium bleachers. He must've sneaked out of class." Gabe retrieved his cell phone from his front pocket, opened the Internet browser, and navigated to the *News* page at a local television station's website. He handed the phone to Hunter. "A client told me about it at work."

Sure enough, Hunter found a *BREAKING NEWS* header at the top of the page. The story provided minimal detail beyond the approximate time of death, the location, and the cause of death: a self-inflicted gunshot in the mouth. Because the victim had turned eighteen years old a few weeks prior, he was no longer a minor, so the news station released his identity. His most recent yearbook photo, from the previous school year, accompanied the story. Even a year earlier, he appeared small for his age and looked closer to fifteen years old.

A lanky kid, judging from his photo, a standard head shot. Blond hair, which looked as though his habit was to push it to the side. An aquiline nose. The kid had a small patch of acne near his chin.

Hunter studied the student's photo closer.

And realized he had seen him before.

It was the teenager Hunter had noticed at Reverend Harper's church. The one about whom Hunter had sensed profound isolation.

The recognition sent a sucker punch to Hunter's belly. A taste of bile emerged in his mouth. He felt lightheaded, on the verge of vomiting.

According to the reporter, the student's name was Lucas Hampton and he had left a suicide note. While the reporter provided an extract of the note, not its full text, she quoted enough to reveal Lucas's motivation for ending his life: Lucas was gay.

As it turned out, in the course of vilifying Hunter and Gabe from the pulpit, Reverend Harper had hurt *another* individual. Someone who sat in the pews.

As his pastor's rhetoric grew more and more condemning, the teen felt he could no longer go on. In Lucas's own words, as an extract from his suicide note read, "I realized there's no more hope for me. My family, my church, and my friends will be better off without me. I don't want to face what those two guys are facing today."

Hunter could only assume "those two guys" referred to Hunter and Gabe.

Lucas's note continued, "I love you, Mom and Dad and Kelsey …"—according to the story, Lucas had one little sister—"… so don't blame yourselves for what I did or who I was. It's not your fault. It's mine."

Lucas's words were enough to make Hunter question every cruel, offhand remark he'd ever spoken to anybody, regardless of the subject matter. Hunter knew firsthand how words hurt— and *still* hadn't understood how much they could hurt a person until now.

He tried to swallow but found it difficult.

"I told him …" Hunter murmured to himself.

"Told who?"

When he noticed Gabe had heard him, Hunter met his stare.

"The kid's pastor," Hunter said. "I tried to warn him someone could get hurt."

Hunter chewed his thumbnail. Sorrow enshrouded his heart.

"I tried to tell him people need to know they're loved …"

CHAPTER 46

On Saturday morning, Hunter awoke to the sound of loud, incessant rapping on his front door. Half awake, he turned onto his side. He checked his alarm clock and discovered it was only 7:34.

The knocking stopped. He wondered if it was a dream, the kind that occurs when you're on the verge of sleep, drifting in and out of consciousness. His head fell back onto his pillow and he started to doze.

The doorbell. More raps on the door, louder this time.

Hunter grunted. He threw off the covers. If this was a prank, he couldn't guarantee he wouldn't explode in anger at whoever was on his front porch.

He padded barefoot into his living room and threw open the door. Ellen stood on the other side, her face solemn. Something was off-kilter.

She examined him in his T-shirt and boxer shorts, then said, "Come on."

"Where?" Even to himself, his voice sounded groggy. He rubbed the heaviness from his eyes.

"I need you with me."

"Why?" Confused, Hunter shook himself out of his sleepy haze.

"Just come."

Hunter sighed. Heading back into his house, he brushed his teeth, then threw on a pair of jeans and a baseball cap.

In the early morning, with the temperature in the upper 30s, a fog crept across the windshield as their body heat filled the interior of the car. Ellen turned on the defroster, then returned to her hand to the steering wheel, gripping it with both hands. A relaxed driver, Ellen never gripped the wheel with both hands except when navigating a snow-covered road.

Hot air blew through the heating vents beneath the dashboard. Seated on the passenger side, Hunter positioned his legs near the vent and lifted the edges of his jeans a few inches above his shoes, exposing his sock-covered ankles to absorb the heat. He was glad he'd thought twice and grabbed a hoodie on his way out of the house.

Hunter had no idea where Ellen had decided to take him. He'd asked, but she'd refused to tell. In fact, she had said nothing else during their ride, her hands glued to the steering wheel and her eyes glued to the road ahead. The silence thickened, but Hunter didn't want to turn on the radio: He could tell Ellen was preoccupied. Life had drained from her eyes, in such sharp contrast to her normal demeanor, he decided to tread with caution rather than ask her what was wrong.

Once they entered Brecksville, Hunter concluded they were on their way to Brendan and Ellen's new home. Sure enough, after winding her way through the now-familiar twists and turns, they reached the house. From outside, Hunter couldn't point to any changes since his last visit; then again, only a few weeks had passed, and progress could have occurred inside. Wiring, perhaps?

Without a word or gesture, Ellen parked the car in front of the house and turned off the engine. Zombielike, she wandered toward the home in an aimless fashion. Hurrying out of the car, Hunter caught up with her and kept pace at her side. Although the home's doors and windows remained absent, sheets of plastic covered their designated spaces. Still unsure of why Ellen had brought him here, Hunter pushed aside the heavy plastic and followed her through the front doorway.

Inside the home, ounces of daylight slithered through the window plastic into the rooms, but at the far end of the foyer, dimness permeated the interior hallway. When Ellen reached the intersection, she looked to her left and right, then turned to her right. With cautious, measured steps, she stretched her arms, sweeping her hands up and down the walls as she crept deeper into the murkiness. As she moved her palms along the walls, the friction sounded like a tropical breeze. Hunter followed behind. Outside one unseen window, a bird chirped, followed by the sound of wings as it fluttered into flight.

She stopped at the linen closet. She ran her fingertips along its narrow threshold. A dark void lurked inside.

"It's the walls," Ellen murmured.

The broken silence took Hunter aback.

He felt his eyebrows furrow. He angled himself so he could catch a discreet glimpse of Ellen's face. Her zombie eyes remained rigid, lifeless, as she stared into the claustrophobic closet.

"The walls?" he said, unsure of whether she expected him to take notice of the walls that surrounded them. They remained bare and white, same as before.

Emotionless, Ellen stared ahead, fixing her attention on the void before her.

"It's the walls," Ellen murmured again. "They scare the hell out of me more than anything else."

A chill ripped up Hunter's spine. He started to reach toward her from behind, but hesitated. He cocked his head, unable to take his eyes off of her.

"Ellen?"

She looked to the guest bedroom on her right. Morning sunlight filled the room, which faced east, where workers had left various tools and supplies. Ellen poked her head through the bedroom doorway, then wandered into the room and out of Hunter's sight. Confused, Hunter remained frozen in the hallway and wondered whether he should call Brendan.

Hunter heard a rattling inside the bedroom, a sifting through items of plastic and metal. He wondered why humans felt the urge to snicker when caught in edgy moments. Ellen's behavior seemed so out of character, he could have convinced himself this was a joke, had he not sensed otherwise. But within a few seconds, his nervous snicker departed and, once again, wariness resumed control.

"Ellen? You okay in there?"

No answer. A shadow shifted inside the bedroom doorway.

Ellen emerged with a sledgehammer in her grip. Its wooden handle was two feet long. Its battered head, the color of steel, glinted in the daylight that escaped through the doorway of the bedroom. Hunter felt his jaw slacken. Ellen didn't look at him; if she still noticed him standing there, she gave no indication of it.

"Ellen?"

"These damn walls," she murmured. "These damn walls went up so fast."

"Ellen, maybe it's better if we—"

Hunter scrambled to get out of the way as she drew back the sledgehammer in a long arc and readied her first strike. When she brought the hammer forward and made contact, the *thud* made Hunter sick to his stomach, the way the muted *thud* had sickened him once when his car hit an icy patch and slid into an oncoming vehicle.

The metal head of the hammer tore a deep gash into the wall beside the doorframe of the linen closet.

Hunter was paralyzed with shock for a second but forced himself to recover.

"Ellen, what are you doing?!"

He took a step forward to stop her, but scurried backward again as the sledgehammer returned toward him in another long arc. He stumbled backward, lost his footing, and landed on the hallway floor as Ellen took another swing forward. Another gash appeared above the first, close enough for the tears to merge into one larger hole.

Ellen raised her voice to a shout.

"These damn walls ..."

Another swing. Another gash.

"… walls …"

Another swing. Another gash.

"… walls in my life …"

Another swing. Another gash.

"… closing me in …"

Another swing. Another gash.

"… suffocating the life out of me …"

Hunter scrambled to his feet, waited until Ellen began her next arc forward, then lunged toward her. He wrapped his arms around her arms and chest and locked them tight. The sledgehammer remained in Ellen's grip, but its heavy head hit the floor with a *clunk* that boomed through the hallway.

"Let me go, Hunter!"

Hunter didn't respond. He focused on keeping Ellen locked in his arms.

"I said, let me go!"

Ellen wriggled to break free. The force of her thrashing didn't surprise Hunter, given Ellen's tenacity and the strength of her personality. He tightened his hold but his biceps started to quiver from sustained flexing. He slid his hand toward hers and fought to pry her fingers from the sledgehammer handle, one at a time. She resisted at first. As soon as he pried a second finger loose, she would coil her first finger around the handle again. She dug her fingernails into the tops of his fingers. But Hunter remained tenacious, and after what felt like a full minute of effort, Ellen relented and dropped the hammer. With his chest pressed against her back, Hunter felt Ellen's shoulders grow limp and her muscles relax.

She began to sob. Hunter loosened his arms into a tender embrace and continued to hold her. He placed his head against hers, rested his cheek against her hair, where he picked up traces of violet shampoo.

Hunter had never seen Ellen in such a vulnerable state. At a loss for what his friend needed from him in this moment, he embraced her for several more minutes. He didn't try to stop her tears.

Closed in by life's walls. In his own way, Hunter understood how she felt.

Peering up, Hunter examined the series of gashes that now dotted the perimeter of the linen closet. He shook his head, awestruck at the extent to which Ellen had hidden her emotions all this time and the manifestation of pressure that had come to a boil.

Then he returned his attention to his friend. Sliding his hands toward her shoulders, he rubbed her upper arms with a note of affection. He turned her around to face him. When their eyes met, Hunter found the expression of a helpless child. He brushed his fingers along her cheeks to wipe away her tears and, once again, drew her into his embrace. This time, Ellen pressed herself against his chest as he held her close, wrapping his arms around her as tight as he could. She rested her head against his shoulder, and if Hunter hadn't known better, he could have sworn she fell asleep with the peace of an infant.

PART FOUR

FREEDOM

HOPE

CHAPTER 47

After church the next day, Hunter grabbed a quick bite to eat, then sent Ellen a text message to see whether she was home early that afternoon. When she replied to let him know she was home, he headed to her apartment. She answered the door dressed in a sweatshirt and jeans, her curly hair wrapped in a ponytail. Hunter followed her into the living room, where she plopped onto the sofa.

One look at the circles under her eyes and Hunter knew Ellen had been up all night. She'd worn no makeup today, a state in which Hunter had seen her before, albeit on rare occasion. She gave her hair a quick run-through with her fingers as Hunter eased beside her.

"How do you feel?" he asked with a tentative pat to her knee.

"I didn't get much sleep, but otherwise, I'm okay," Ellen said as she settled into a cozier position on the sofa cushion. "That's a pleasant surprise, to feel okay. You don't know what to expect after you go half-assed crazy the day before."

"Why didn't you say anything to me long ago?" Hunter caught her gaze and offered his warmest expression so she wouldn't doubt his sincerity.

"I'm used to doing things on my own, I guess. You wouldn't have understood."

"I understand how it feels to be alone."

A knowing smirk hinted that Ellen had indeed returned to her normal self. She squinted at him as though studying a specimen under a microscope.

"I never realized this before," she said, "but you and I are more alike than I thought."

"Oh yeah?" He returned her stare in a playful dare. "How so?"

"We hold a lot inside. Deep waters, or whatever they call it," she said. "We prefer to carry our secrets to the grave, keep them harbored in the depths of our hearts till they sink into oblivion. And at that point, no one knows what happened. All they can do is speculate about us. We're two mysterious people who take our treasures with us to the ocean floor, like Mama Cass when she went down with the Titanic."

"Mama Cass didn't sink with the Titanic."

"Then who was Mama Cass?"

"The ham sandwich woman."

"Whatever. Don't screw around with details. I'm having a moment of enlightenment here."

They snickered together. Hunter listened as a car started outside and left the parking lot. Ellen rested her hands in her lap. She studied the smooth, unpolished surfaces of her fingernails before gazing at him again.

"I broke off the engagement," she said.

"With Brendan?" Hunter reacted before he had a chance to stifle his surprise. He looked at her hand, and sure enough, her ring was absent. "When?"

"Last night." She returned her gaze to her folded hands. "I can't do it, Hunter. Not right now, at least. The pressure of everything going on—I bit off more than I can chew in one season." She winked at him. "As you might have noticed, I ran out of storage space and tried to expand a linen closet yesterday."

"I noticed."

"I'm not sure I'm cut out for marriage."

Hunter grimaced. "How'd Brendan respond when you told him all this?"

"Once he was able to bring himself to speak, he wanted to know why I'd done something so stupid to the house. We argued at first, but he came around in the end. Said he'd take a look at it, but it didn't sound to him like the damage was major. Nothing he couldn't get fixed. Sweet guy that he is, he was more concerned about me. We spent the rest of the afternoon getting honest." She met Hunter's stare again, this time with a mischievous glint in her eyes. "I probably freaked *you* out yesterday, huh?"

"It was a first."

Ellen chuckled in response, but grew sober again, furrowing her eyebrows in concentration.

"I don't know what happened yesterday. Everything boiled over," she said. "It's like I lost control of my own life somewhere along the way, and things started to close in."

"If it's any consolation, I know what it's like for walls to close in on you."

She regarded him a moment. "I guess you do, don't you?" She paused, then asked, "How are you and Gabe doing?"

"We're fine."

"I'm sorry some people have treated you shitty," Ellen said. "Like it wasn't hard enough for you, trying to be someone you're not."

"Don't worry about me." Hunter gave her a paternal smile and wrapped his arm around her in a side hug. "So you're gonna be okay?

"I'll be fine. It'll all come together somehow." Ellen shrugged her shoulders and shot him a look of resignation. "It always does, right?"

"I'm your friend. I'm here for you." Hunter gave her a final pat on the knee. "You can always talk to me."

Ellen nodded. She bit her lower lip.

"And don't go demolishing any more houses without warning me first," Hunter added with a wink.

Ellen drew her hand to her mouth, too late to stifle a laugh.

CHAPTER 48

At home that evening, Hunter felt restless. With a touch to his arm, Gabe suggested they take a walk and allow fresh air to invigorate him.

Though brisk, Hunter found the crisp air bearable. An occasional passing car brought life to the night. The sun had disappeared two hours before, but streetlights dotted the road and the moon brought a sheen to the otherwise navy-blue sky as Hunter and Gabe sauntered along the sidewalk.

Gabe reached for Hunter's hand, and Hunter allowed Gabe to wrap it in his. In the darkness, nobody would recognize them. Hunter felt free.

As they walked, the moon cast its glow upon banners affixed to homes and signs planted in front yards. Some carried sentimental messages such as *We Miss You, Lucas*. Others featured nothing more than an enlarged version of Lucas Hampton's recent yearbook picture. One sign included a photo from Lucas's childhood. The community had taken the suicide hard and had come together during its plummet into mourning. Nobody wants to see a teenager lose his life.

Hunter couldn't help but eye each sign as he walked. Another car rolled past, its tires emitting a sound like static on the suburban street.

"You're so quiet," Gabe said. "You must be deep in thought."

Hunter sought words to wrap around how he felt for Lucas Hampton's family.

"I look at these signs and wonder what could've been," Hunter said at last. "Why didn't people celebrate the kid while he was *alive?* That's what he needed. He needed someone to notice him, to care enough to notice something was wrong. Why did it take a kid to kill himself for some people to remember to care?"

Gabe studied him with his compassionate eyes. "I wish I had an answer for that."

They walked past a sign whose artist had used a different color for each letter of Lucas's name.

"This is our fault," Hunter said, watching his breath disperse before him in a little cloud.

"What is?"

"That kid. The one who killed himself." Hunter gestured toward the sign with his thumb. "We caused it."

"What? Why would you say that?"

"We're the ones who brought attention to what he was dealing with. It was difficult enough for him, but to feel like he couldn't find refuge at church—the one place where he *should* have felt like he was loved—must have been the last straw for him. And the whole reason he had to listen to that pastor's words were because of us. The last couple of nights, I've laid in bed and wondered if that kid would still be alive if it weren't for us."

"Hunter, that pastor chose his own reaction. It's not your fault how he chooses to approach things."

"But there must have been a better way to go about all this."

"We didn't get a choice in the matter. Someone else discovered us and decided to talk. You and I didn't go looking for a battle."

"I know we didn't, but regardless, I feel like we've let our churches down. We look like hypocrites—despite the fact we felt we *needed* to hide."

"People would have responded with the same fervor no matter how we handled it."

"But by keeping it to ourselves, sorting through the confusion on our own timetables, and trying not to cause a disruption, we get branded as hypocrites and the community gets divided—until a kid pays the price."

"You can't blame yourself, Hunter."

They grew silent. Hunter shoved his hands into his coat pockets as they reached Hudson's town square. The shops along Main Street, which called to mind Norman Rockwell's pictures of America in its innocence, had closed for the night.

When they reached the clock tower at the corner of the green in the center of town, they strolled to a white gazebo and sat down inside. A nearby streetlamp cast its light upon them. A slight breeze now whirled, which sent Hunter into a slight shiver. Gabe wrapped his arm around him and Hunter allowed himself to settle into the embrace. Hunter felt their shared warmth emanate through him.

"Better?" Gabe asked.

"*Everything's* better." Hunter turned his head to gaze into Gabe's eyes. "You've made everything better."

Gabe rubbed Hunter's arm. "How so?"

"It's hard to explain," Hunter said as a sweet, welcome ache settled within his heart. The ache of vulnerability. "This is the first time in my life I've felt comfortable with myself. *Truly* comfortable. Comfortable enough to let anyone see me deep down. And it's not an attraction thing. It's just ..." Hunter searched for something complex but wound up with simplicity. "It's just ... you."

Gabe rubbed Hunter's arm once more.

"That's not a bad thing, right?" said Gabe with a wink.

"It's not bad," Hunter replied. "That's what makes this so confusing. The contentment is real, and yet it doesn't make sense to anyone else. Here I am, a guy who loves Jesus with everything in me. I'd die inside if I didn't get to talk to Him or spend time with Him. Yet because of *one* area in my life that doesn't make sense to others, I'm told what an abomination I am. Some people tell me I'm going to hell. And you know what? For years, part of me wondered if I *am* going to hell." Hunter paused. "But then, in those moments of fear, I can sense Jesus' touch. I don't know how to explain it, but I can feel His arm wrapped around my shoulder, that sense of love and acceptance I'd always wished I could find with other people. And I can hear Him say to me, 'I love you, Hunter. It's okay. I'm going to work it all out for you.' And just like that"—Hunter snapped his fingers—"I have hope again. Hope that I'll make it through this journey, that I'll be able to help and comfort people along the way. Hope that, decades down the road, at the end of my life, I'll fall asleep one night talking to God, and when I wake up, I'll wake up in heaven. And as I walk on the streets of gold up there, the struggles of this life on earth—these temporary issues—won't matter anymore, because I'll have finally made it home, and I'll climb into those loving, accepting arms of Jesus that I've sensed around me during the hard times here on earth."

Hunter felt Gabe's muscles relax.

Hunter's thoughts started to wander. "One week in summer, back during my college days, I went to the beach with a bunch of friends. We had a blast catching rays during the day, building bonfires at night. But what my friends didn't know is that I'd sneak out of the hotel room after everyone went to sleep. I'd make my way down to the sand and walk the shore after dark. Nights just like tonight, but much warmer. I'd walk half a mile along the empty beach, listen to the waves tumble onto the sand, feel the wind graze my cheeks.

"I'd stop and stare at the expanse of ocean, and it would remind me how big God is. In the dark, I couldn't see the horizon, but I knew it was there. I knew if I got in a boat and sailed due west, I'd end up on the coast of Portugal or Morocco." Hunter felt fervor rise within him as he peered at Gabe. "Then a thought would hit me: God *designed* that ocean. He set the boundaries of that huge expanse and keeps it under control. He knows each person on the opposite shore. He cares for them, and understands their cultures and foreign tongues. And I realized if God can handle that ocean and take an active role in all those people groups with their details, then He can handle any detail in my life." He turned to Gabe. "So why should my own circumstances seem like such a major issue?"

"Maybe because they churn in the depths of your heart and soul," said Gabe. "Language, cultures, people groups—those all come and go. But right now, *this* is your life. *This* is your journey. It affects you *now,* so it's a big deal to you. And if it's important to you, it's important to God—as important as keeping that ocean inside its parameters."

Hunter nodded, grateful to have another individual in his life who understood.

He reached for Gabe's hand, which felt warm inside his own. Hunter rubbed his thumb along the edge of Gabe's palm and stared up at the stars. As had the ocean years ago, tonight those stars reminded him of how big God is.

CHAPTER 49

On Monday afternoon, in deference to the public memorial service for Lucas Hampton, schools and businesses in Hudson closed early. A private funeral for the Hampton family had occurred the prior day. The public memorial service took place on the green at the town square, where Hunter and Gabe had sat the night before. Attendees' vehicles filled nearby parking lots and vacant spots along the streets. Those who lived within walking distance trekked to the center of town. Morning drizzle had cleared; sunshine emerged in time for the service. Although seating accommodated two hundred people, many more attended than organizers had estimated. Those who stood around the chairs outnumbered those seated by a ratio of two to one. Wreaths and flowers adorned the podium area, which paled in comparison to the flood of signs and wooden crosses individuals had placed around the high school in the days since Lucas's death.

A few students at the high school had worked with the city council to arrange this afternoon's event. As it turned out, while few had gotten to know Lucas, many sought a way to honor him. Parents spoke among themselves about how they might feel if this tragedy had befallen one of their own children. Several ministers in the community, including Chuck Barlow, shared words of comfort at the memorial service. Lucas's pastor had received an invitation to speak, but perhaps in a moment of soul-searching, he had respectfully declined.

The high school choir performed a final hymn a cappella to conclude the memorial service. As attendees began to depart, their eyes appeared void to Hunter, their faces reflecting a somber mood. Though the service was intended as informal, some men had dressed in suits and ties; others wore casual shirts and khaki pants. High school sports teams had attended in their uniforms to show solidarity of support for the Hampton family. Hunter marveled at the age range of individuals, from children to parents to retirees, who had gathered for the occasion.

When the choir concluded, he gazed at Gabe and Ellen, with whom he had stood during the service. They considered grabbing coffee in Twinsburg once traffic dissipated.

As the crowd thinned, Hunter looked toward the far end of the green and saw his father, hands in his pants pockets, meandering toward him. His father had worn a shirt and tie. Despite dressing that way in his professional career, Hunter knew his father hated wearing a tie unless he needed to, so he must have taken Lucas's death to heart.

When Ed Carlisle reached the trio, he did so in a manner Hunter would describe as unsure, trying to appear casual as he gazed at the hundreds of people heading toward the perimeter of the town square. Ed nodded to Gabe, and though his father's expression was solemn, Hunter perceived in it neither resentment nor anger toward Gabe. If anything, he detected a sense of peace.

"Hello, Gabe. I believe we've met," said Hunter's father with a handshake, then turned to Hunter. "Can I speak to you alone for a moment?"

Out of respect, Gabe and Ellen took a few steps backward and began a conversation of their own. Hunter couldn't fathom what his father wanted to talk about in this context. He searched for clues in the man's eyes but deciphered nothing. When it came to stifling evidence of what stirred within one's soul, Hunter and his father shared that suit in common. As Ed shifted his weight from one foot to the other, hands still in his pockets, Hunter could tell this wasn't easy for him. He heard car keys jingle in his father's pocket, which meant the man was fidgeting with his hands.

His father gestured toward the now-vacant podium. "Hunter, this whole … situation … has caused me to do some thinking … reevaluating … I'm not sure how to put it. I'm not a words man. But I've thought about what it means to stand with family."

This sounded positive, but Hunter kept his defenses rigid. He remained silent and allowed his father to put words to whatever he believed he needed to say.

With a tentative glance, Ed continued, "The way I responded to you wasn't … right." Ed grimaced and smoothed his eyebrows with his fingers. "I don't know what you're facing in your life. I can't *pretend* to understand. I'd be lying if I tried to act like I've been there. But I … I want you to know I support you as your dad. I'm trying to, at least. The best I know how. I'm not good at talking about … I mean, expressing emotional things, but I want you to know how much I love you, son. I don't say that much … or ever, maybe … but I … do."

Hunter felt tears well up, but he forced them back. Biting his lower lip, he nodded to let his father know he had accepted his sentiments.

Ed shook his head and lowered his gaze to the grass at his feet.

"What happened to that boy, the way he ended his life," said Hunter's father, "I never want that for you. The way things played out with that boy … I can't help but think *you* could've been in that kid's situation if things had unfolded ten years ago. It wouldn't have ended only your life. It would have ended mine, too."

Hunter's father ran his finger and thumb beneath his eye as if to remove a speck from his eye, but Hunter knew the man had wiped away a tear he hadn't anticipated. Hunter couldn't blame him for the disguise. The man never wept. He probably didn't know what to do when a tear came. But Hunter couldn't doubt his father's sincerity.

"Am I making any sense to you, son?"

"Yes, Dad."

"I don't understand why you feel the way you do about… well, you know … but I know there are things you don't understand about me, either. And you're still my son."

With that, perhaps to ease the awkwardness the man felt in this moment of honesty, he gave Hunter a gentle punch to the shoulder, the way he did when Hunter was a child. When Hunter had enjoyed the luxury of life's innocence.

Ed Carlisle scanned the crowd, which had thinned to a fragment of its original size. He took a deep breath and exhaled. The way he squinted let Hunter know his father had more to say.

"How some people have treated you—it's just not right," said Hunter's father almost under his breath. He turned his attention back to his son and looked him in the eyes. "I mean, who is understood one hundred percent by anyone else? Who *doesn't* come a step or two short of people's idea of perfection? When we see them doing something *we* don't like, do we plaster our views about *them* for everyone to see, to humiliate them?"

Absent of a fitting response, Hunter shrugged. Despite all the years he'd wished he could talk to his father, now that it had happened, he couldn't figure out how to react.

"I haven't been a perfect dad to you over the years. I haven't given you all the cheers I should have. I realize that now. But I can say this: I've noticed something about you, Hunter. I've always noticed it. You were never one to cut other people down or humiliate them. You never treated anyone the way you've been treated lately, not from what I ever saw. I've seen a hope or faith about you since you were a teenager. I've seen it come through during this public flogging. And whatever it is about you, I want that for myself. That may sound ridiculous coming from your dad, but nevertheless …" He jingled his keys and coins in his pocket again. "You've been through fire—dealing with this since you were young, and the last few months in particular—and you've stayed strong. So whatever the source of your strength is, it must be genuine. I respect you more than I respect the fearmongers out there. And if it's faith, then one day, maybe I want it for me, too."

Hunter shuddered inside—a *good* shudder. It sounded like his father was proud of him.

His father stammered a moment. "Maybe, uh …"

Hunter couldn't believe what he saw. His father inched forward, then retreated as if to reconsider. He lifted his arms in a cautious way. A hug? If that were the case, the man had reevaluated more than—

Before Hunter knew it, his father had drawn him into his embrace. Hunter fought back tears, tried to swallow the lump in his throat. He felt bad for not responding better, but this display of affection had taken him aback. Though their hug lasted less than three seconds, it felt like dawn in Hunter's heart. Ed Carlisle punctuated the embrace with a quick pat on the shoulder blade before they separated.

"You okay now?" asked Hunter's father.

"I'm okay, Dad."

When they parted ways, Hunter rejoined Gabe several yards away. Hunter took a quick glance over his shoulder as his father treaded across the green.

Gabe didn't ask what the two men had discussed. Instead, with his elbow, he gave Hunter's arm a gentle bump.

Gabe didn't *need* to ask. He already knew.

Hunter now realized Gabe had wound up alone while he'd talked to his dad.

"Where's Ellen?" Hunter asked.

With a shrug, Gabe examined the people around them, then pointed to the gazebo where he and Hunter had sat the night before. "There she is."

Standing beside the gazebo, Ellen conversed with someone, but with passersby blocking Hunter's view, he couldn't determine the other individual's identity. It was a man, but he faced Ellen with his back toward them. Hunter and Gabe meandered toward Ellen, and once they reached the gazebo, they decided to hang back.

She was talking to Brendan. Their conversation didn't appear romantic, but it looked amiable.

Hunter wasn't one to eavesdrop, but in this case, he wound up close enough to where he couldn't help but overhear them. He chalked it up to concern for his friend.

"I'm sorry, Ellen," said Brendan. "I didn't realize how much the pressure had gotten to you."

"It's not your fault, Brendan. I should've said something."

Brendan gazed into her eyes. Creases appeared across his forehead. Even from a short distance, Hunter saw the sincerity in his expression. Brendan paused for a moment, then spoke again.

"Could we give it another try?" Brendan asked. Then, as if fearful she might reject his offer, he added, "We don't need to be engaged if you're not ready for it."

Brendan reached down, took her hands, and enveloped them in his own. Hunter watched Ellen's shoulders ease.

"I don't want to lose the most important person who ever walked into my life," said Brendan, his eyes trained on hers. "And if we can find a way to make this work, keep our communication lines open, I'd like to do that."

"Yes. I want that," Ellen nodded. "I really do."

Brendan continued to hold her gaze. His face beamed as he grinned.

"No more walls between us?" he said.

Ellen shook her head.

"No more walls," she replied.

Hunter felt Gabe's arm wrap around his shoulders.

"No more walls," Hunter whispered to himself.

EPILOGUE

Ten years later, Hunter sat in the den of his home in Phoenix and powered up his laptop computer. When he checked his email, he discovered a message from Gabe Hellman. Though they had parted ways in their relationship under mutual agreement, they had remained good friends and had kept in touch ever since.

Scanning the message, Hunter read that all was well back in Ohio. Gabe remained single, but he had peace. His clinic continued to thrive. In fact, upon adding two more partners to the business, Gabe and his team prepared to move to a larger location.

Hunter couldn't help but smile as he contemplated the season of discovery he and Gabe had shared. Their relationship had lasted more than two years. Looking back, neither Hunter nor Gabe regretted it. To this day, Gabe knew Hunter better than almost anyone else.

Oftentimes, when Hunter thought of Gabe, his mind wandered to their mutual friend, Ellen Krieger—that is, Ellen

Pieper. After slowing down for a year, Ellen and Brendan reinstated their engagement and, after another year, they married. Hunter served as Brendan's best man. Brendan and Ellen finished building their house, where they lived today. On occasion, Hunter still heard from Ellen, but once he moved to Phoenix and time marched forward, she kept in touch less and less. Hunter knew it wasn't intentional on Ellen's part. Ellen Krieger—that is, Ellen Pieper—tended to live in the here and now.

Not long after her wedding, Hunter accepted a sales position in Phoenix. Setting distance between his past and present, spending time in the opposite corner of the country, had helped him come to terms with whatever might lay ahead for him. And he had to admit, he savored the abundance of sunshine and desert heat.

He opened the attachment Gabe had sent with his message—a photo of Gabe standing in front of the new office building, arms folded across his chest. Hunter could see the excitement in Gabe's eyes, as well as the familiar compassion which had drawn Hunter to him the day they had met.

After relocating to Phoenix, Hunter created a blog, which he wrote in the evenings and continued to operate. His number of readers grew by the year. Often he received messages from individuals expressing gratitude for the way he'd voiced how they felt inside.

He kept his identity anonymous on his blog, which allowed him the freedom to express his heart. The journal Gabe had given Hunter on their first Christmas together had proven a pivotal turning point and had given him an emotional outlet. Nowadays, in his blog, he offered encouragement for those walking through homosexuality. Hunter couldn't bring back Lucas Hampton, but he'd determined to prevent another individual from reaching Lucas Hampton's decision to end his life.

Lucas Hampton. To this day, he crossed Hunter's mind on a regular basis. Though he would have been about thirty years old by now, he remained a kid in Hunter's mind. Hunter never forgot the image of the teenager sitting in church, consumed with unspoken sadness.

Hunter closed Gabe's email message and took a moment to ponder the past, his personal growth, and God's grace in the midst of it all. He whispered a quick prayer, thanking God for how He had brought Hunter to a place of peace in his life.

Hunter wasn't perfect. He had struggled to find balance. Yet God had gotten him there somehow.

As Hunter sat at the computer, he felt a pair of arms wrap around him. One hand overlapped the other across his chest.

Hunter located a favorite freckle on the right hand and planted a kiss there. With that, he peered up at the one who gazed down upon him with eyes of love.

"I'm so thankful for you," whispered Hunter.

BETWEEN THESE WALLS

BY JOHN HERRICK

READING GROUP GUIDE

Discussion Questions

1. To which character did you most relate? Why?

2. Hunter experiences growth during the novel. When does his growth begin: before or after his relationship with Gabe begins? Does growth occur after his secret is exposed to the public? Does Gabe experience growth as well?

3. Hunter has kept his sexual attractions a secret for 14 years. Was there a time in your life when you found it easier to build walls around yourself than to face the truth?

4. Much of the story occurs against the backdrop of a cold Ohio winter and the construction of a new home. How does the author use seasons or events to reflect the internal processes of Hunter and Ellen?

5. Jesse Barlow, a supporting character, also appeared in John Herrick's novel From The Dead. How has Jesse grown since then? How might Jesse's battle have changed his outlook or prepared him to support Hunter?

6. Can you identify parallels between Ellen Krieger's silent struggle and that of Hunter?

7. Which chapter do you consider your favorite? Why? Which chapters do you believe reveal the most about Hunter, Gabe and Ellen, respectively?

8. How would you define Hunter's relationship with Kara versus his relationship with Gabe? How does each relationship affect Hunter's personal growth?

9. In the Prologue, we are introduced to a young Hunter Carlisle. Do you think the Prologue's events helped shape who Hunter is today? If so, in what ways?

10. Hunter has solid faith, yet he harbored a secret. Do you consider his actions hypocritical?

11. In Chapter 22, Hunter recalls a classmate, Christopher Patton, and regrets he allowed Christopher to face humiliation alone. Are there events in your life you wish you had handled differently?

12. In Chapter 35, Hunter confides in his pastor. Do you feel his pastor handled the scenario in an appropriate manner? If you were in Hunter's shoes, what would have helped you during that discussion?

13. In Chapter 36, Hunter reveals his secret to his parents. How do you feel his parents reacted to the news? How might sudden, similar news from your child affect you?

14. How has Hunter's relationship with his father impacted Hunter's growth processes during childhood and adulthood?

15. In Chapters 4, 9, 10, 22, 24, 29 and 43, Hunter recalls events from his past. How did those events help shape who he is today?

16. How do religion, emotion and sex drive Hunter? How do these factors seem to drive other characters, or do they?

A CONVERSATION WITH THE AUTHOR

How did you arrive at the idea for this novel?

Early in 2011, a character arose within me: a middle-school kid who was a Christian and harbored an attraction to the same gender. I pondered facets of this character's circumstances. His fears, his feelings of guilt, the hits to his self-esteem—everything about his silent struggle grabbed my heart. At that point, I wouldn't have had the courage to write a book about him. One year later, a news story caught my attention. It revolved around the plight of a high school student on the verge of suicide. This student, about fifteen years old, had endured a continual onslaught of bullying for one reason: He was gay. Although I know nothing about that student, my heart broke for him. My immediate gut response was, Never again. Not on my watch. Not if I can help it. After hearing his story, I decided to chuck my fear and develop *Between These Walls*, featuring a main character whose struggle in adulthood has roots in his childhood. That said, though the news story served as a catalyst for action, my novel is neither based on it nor related to it.

Between These Walls chronicles Hunter Carlisle's journey, step by step, as he processes his feelings in light of his faith. While external events come into play, the crux of the novel's action occurs within Hunter's heart and mind. It's a character study more than a plot-driven story.

How did you go about designing Hunter and Gabe?

A popular stereotype exists for gay men in terms of demeanor, mannerisms and interests. While the stereotype is accurate in some cases, it is inaccurate in many others. A key question I asked myself was, Should I follow the lines of that stereotype, or present Hunter as the opposite? I figured individuals of both types needed their story told, so I decided to capture both ends of the spectrum. I constructed an everyday guy with classic male attributes and interests. In other words, the guy you'd least suspect to be gay. Next, I designed the character Gabe Hellman to align more with the stereotype many people have adopted.

I don't have quantitative data to back up my hunch, but I've long believed more people deal with same-sex attraction than we assume. I believe many hide it well or have a simultaneous attraction to the opposite gender, which enables them to live a "typical" life without raising suspicions. Therefore, I constructed Hunter as, technically, bisexual—but with a stronger, irrepressible draw toward males. This characteristic would allow him to remain in hiding for years yet prevent him from escaping his predicament.

To enhance the story further, I selected character names to reflect who the characters are and how they impact Hunter. I chose the name Hunter to call to mind a hunter-gatherer image, the classic male stereotype—and the last place we might expect to find a gay male. His name symbolizes his attributes and interests, yet belies his deepest secret. Carlisle is a common surname, which I selected at random. It reflects how others view him: an average, ordinary guy beyond suspicion.

For Gabe, I envisioned a character with Scandinavian features, which was simply an author preference. When I perused Scandinavian surnames, however, one proved perfect: Hellman. Hunter is a Christian who fears his homosexual feelings could lead him to hell. In that respect, Gabe represents temptation. So Gabe's last name, Hellman, calls those fears to mind. But Gabe is also a Christian and a good-hearted individual, so his first name reflects that characteristic: Gabe, which is short for Gabriel, the name of an angel mentioned in the Bible. Thus, the full name Gabriel Hellman illustrates the crux of Hunter and Gabe's story: a tug-of-war between faith and feelings.

Why did you incorporate a faith element into *Between These Walls*?

When I began writing novels, I had no interest in writing faith-related fiction. I felt it meant a load of rules and red tape for what I couldn't write or explore. But a difference exists between the Christian fiction genre and weaving faith into a mainstream novel, as John Grisham demonstrated in *The Testament*. When I constructed From The Dead, a prior novel, I had intended to write a mainstream novel with no faith element whatsoever. Its main character, Jesse Barlow—who reemerges in *Between These Walls*—was a preacher's son filled with regret. As I considered that novel's chain of events and who Jesse was, I realized I couldn't give an accurate depiction of him without delving into his faith background. Once I discovered I could weave a faith element into a mainstream novel in a realistic manner, I fell in love with it. I wanted to accomplish it again: to chronicle a character's struggle in a way readers wouldn't find among the Christian fiction genre. And as a mainstream novel, I don't need to censor my characters. They are free to behave and speak the way they truly would, as if we overheard them in a restaurant. The one requirement I place upon myself is that my novels are genuine and plausible—which can't happen if I whitewash the characters or their language.

Did you find any aspects of this novel a particular challenge?

If Hunter feels vulnerable in a chapter, or if the reader feels vulnerable reading a chapter, then it's safe to say I felt vulnerable writing that chapter.

I had never experienced a homosexual relationship as I constructed the novel, so the project stretched my comfort zone and is different from anything I've ever written. It challenged me to view things in a manner I'd never viewed them, and to envision myself in circumstances I had never experienced. To portray Hunter in an honest way, I needed to drop my guard and write about sensitive scenarios unique to males that I wouldn't discuss in everyday conversation. To my surprise, the interaction between Hunter and Gabe proved easy. I handled their dialogue and displays of affection the way I had between male and female characters in my past projects.

Several chapters invade Hunter's privacy, where Hunter is alone or we explore his sensitive thoughts to which we wouldn't otherwise have access. Those chapters proved challenging for me due to the vulnerability of allowing readers into the most sensitive realms of the male psyche. You can find examples of this in Chapters 9, 10 and 16. Hunter would never talk about what went through his mind in those chapters, but I needed to delve into them to tell his story.

Years ago, I watched actress Ellen Barkin in an interview. Her recent film had involved a nude scene, which the interviewer mentioned. Barkin explained her willingness to participate in that scene: She simply didn't want to lose her fear of being nude on camera. That hit home with me. As an author, I never want to be afraid to write or to make myself vulnerable in my novels. Sometimes, in order to tell an honest story or bond with my readers, it means risking what other people will think of me. In other words, I can't be afraid to "do a nude scene" in terms of how I write.

What motivates you to select one project over another?

In general, three elements tug me toward a writing project, including a novel like *Between These Walls*:

1. The story emerges internally rather than externally.
2. Commercial and target-audience appeal.
3. A potential to inspire or encourage the reader — my favorite element.

The third element is fascinating because, when you think about it, the same collection of words can trigger a vastly different response in each reader. It can serve as entertainment for one person. It might inspire another to reach for his or her dreams. And that same novel could provide encouragement to a person enduring pain or contemplating suicide. Impact potential is a privilege, and it's like fuel during the writing process.

How do you perceive the connection between reader and author?

I believe the written word forges a bond between reader and author. When readers choose to buy a book, they've chosen to invest their valuable time in the story. If they decide to continue reading past the early chapters, a bond forms. At this point, I believe the author determines the depth of the bond: In other words, the more I invest myself emotionally in the novel—the more vulnerable I allow myself to become as an author—the deeper the reader will connect with what they read. If readers feel you've been honest with them and they're satisfied with what they read, a degree of trust results. And hopefully, by the end of the book, readers trust the author enough to invest part of their lives reading that author's next novel.

ABOUT FROM THE DEAD

A preacher's son. A father in hiding. A guilty heart filled with secrets.

When Jesse Barlow escaped to Hollywood at age eighteen, he hungered for freedom, fame and fortune. Eleven years later, his track record of failure results in a drug-induced suicide attempt. Revived at death's doorstep, Jesse returns to his Ohio hometown to make amends with his preacher father, a former lover, and Jesse's own secret son. But Jesse's renewed commitment becomes a baptism by fire when his son's advanced illness calls for a sacrifice—one that could cost Jesse the very life he regained.

A story of mercy, hope, and second chances, From The Dead captures the human spirit with tragedy and joy.

"Eloquence with an edge. In a single chapter, John Herrick can break your heart, rouse your soul, and hold you in suspense. Be prepared to stay up late."
— Doug Wead, New York Times bestselling author and advisor to two presidents

"A solid debut novel."
— Akron Beacon Journal

"A well written and engaging story. It moves, and moves quickly. … I don't think I've read anything in popular novel form as good as this in describing a journey of faith."
— Faith, Fiction, Friends

ABOUT THE LANDING

The power of a song: It can ignite a heart, heal a soul … or for Danny Bale, resurrect a destiny.

When songwriter Danny escaped to the Atlantic coast seven years ago, he laid to rest his unrequited affection for childhood friend Meghan Harting. Their communication faded with yesterday and their lives have become deadlocked. Now Danny, haunted by an inner stronghold and determined to win Meghan back, must create a masterpiece and battle for the heart of the only woman who understands his music. As memories resurface, Danny and Meghan embark on parallel journeys of self-discovery—and a collision course to seal their mutual fate. A tale of purpose, hope and redemption, The Landing is a "sweet story" (Publishers Weekly) that captures the joy and heartache of love.

Rediscover *Between These Walls* and other books at John Herrick Online!

Get to know John Herrick

Download reading group guides

Uncover bonus content

Read John's blog

And more!

facebook.com/JohnHerrickBooks
Twitter: @JohnHerrick

CPSIA information can be obtained at www.ICGtesting.com
Printed in the USA
LVOW10s1530150415

434708LV00001B/96/P